WILD CARD

RAKE FORGE UNIVERSITY BOOK 1

ASHLEY MUNOZ

Cover Design: Amanda Simpson from Pixel Mischief Designs

Editing: C.Marie

Proofing: Tiffany Hernandez

❀ Created with Vellum

wild
CARD

ALSO BY ASHLEY MUNOZ

PROLOGUE
ONE YEAR EARLIER

Decker

I COULD FEEL MY NOSTRILS FLARE AS I TRIED TO INHALE ONE OF THOSE calming breaths Marcus was always preaching to me about. Was I supposed to breathe in through my mouth and exhale through my nose, or vice versa? I always forgot. Even after attending sports medicine classes, my mind couldn't seem to keep the order clear, but whatever... shit wasn't working.

My fingers dug into the cool metal separating me from the field. I watched as Marcus slid into third base, a cloud of dust floating into the inky sky. I guess it wasn't exactly dark over the diamond, not with the stark white lights overhead, but it was still annoying. Why the fuck were we out there at seven thirty at night? I had a job to get to by nine...not that any of my teammates would understand. It was technically against the team's rules to have a job while you played. Our focus was to only be split between our studies and our team, but I didn't have that luxury. I had explained this to coach, and even to the owners of the team—yes, the cherished North Carolina Devils had owners and none of us were allowed to talk about it. Shit went to the top fast, but only because we were considered a *family*.

Hilarious if you really broke it down, but the Devils wanted to support the players on and off the field in any way they could...while

1

creating toxic environments and insane play schedules. It was all a little backward, but regardless, they were quick to accommodate me, though only because of my 'situation.'

The evening practice almost felt personal. I understood how childish that seemed, but in the back of my mind, Elias, our team captain, had made this decision after hearing I'd landed the position at Geno's Bar and Grill. I was sure he didn't really give a fuck about the job, but the fact that I had approval to work it. He hated how much distance I kept putting between myself and the team, hated how I'd stopped attending the team parties and helping with the card games. He didn't get it. No one, except maybe Marcus, understood the weight on my shoulders.

I bent down to grab a batting helmet, feeling my stomach tip with anxiety. I already knew the likelihood of getting out of this practice unscathed was next to impossible. There were rumors circulating the locker room and team house. Whispers coasting past my bedroom door, down a muffled hall. Loud jokes made with darting eyes as I walked by. They all knew something I didn't, but it was my instincts that told me something was off about this particular practice.

Elias was planning something. Marcus said I was paranoid, and maybe I was…but I couldn't seem to shake the feeling.

"Duggar, you're up!" Coach yelled from the top of the stairs.

Shuffling up the steps, I walked toward home plate, readying my stance, then I heard my coach yell again.

"Hold up, Duggar!"

I turned for a fraction of a second to see him bent over, speaking to his assistant coach. Fear danced along my insides as I waited to see what he wanted. Caden was crouched behind me in his catcher's gear, waiting with me…eerily quiet. Just the week before, he wouldn't shut up about his girl and meeting her parents. It only confirmed my fear about something being off with this practice.

"Switch it up with Matthews on the hill—he asked to get in a little extra batting practice before we quit. Tell Caden to take a break."

I nodded my understanding even though unease slid through me like sludge. Tossing the bat to the side, I slid my helmet off. My glove was near the fence already since I'd pitched the first half of practice, so

I grabbed it and started toward the dust-covered plate in the middle of the diamond.

Elias kept his gaze down as I passed him, so I did the same. We hadn't been speaking to each other much, not since the funeral—the one he skipped—although I supposed the first sign of our friendship circling the proverbial drain had probably been when he got those devil horns inked into the side of his head. He demanded I get a matching set, said we had to go together, like we were in fourth grade making friendship bracelets. I shoved off the idea with a laugh, reminding him we weren't chicks and the Devils didn't own my fucking body. That was when things began to tilt unfavorably for me.

Adjusting the glove on my hand, I readied myself for the throw. A calmness always overcame me when I stood here, looking down the strike zone. I felt it now, even as nerves rattled me. I cleared my mind, lined up my sight, and tried another one of those soothing breaths before releasing the ball.

It flew from my hand, soaring toward that empty air hanging over home base. My throws usually registered at 96 mph, but we never threw that hard in practices. So, I knew this was closer to mid-seventies or so, nothing crazy. I just wanted to get this over with and head to work. It was the only thing I felt like I could control in my life at the moment, so I wouldn't risk messing it up. I watched the ball soar toward the plate, and right when I thought it would pass it completely—

Crack.

The sound echoed around the field like a strike of lightning. Suddenly I was back in my bedroom, hearing the sounds of thunder rattle our house while we waited for my dad to come home, listening to the constant drip of rain upon the roof as I realized he never would.

A second later, a splintering pain wove through my chest, knocking the air out of my lungs. I pitched forward, slowly trying to play catchup to what had just happened. I'd never in my life been hit by the ball while pitching. I'd done everything right; I was lined up correctly…the pitch was good. How had this happened? My lungs burned and burned as my chest hollowed out. I registered people yelling my name, others yelling something I couldn't make out. I fell face down into the dirt while I tried to process the commotion hovering above me.

3

What the fuck happened?
Hit him in the chest.
It was a freak accident.
That's never happened before.

White jerseys went in and out of focus as my fingers dug into the dirt, my lungs struggling for air.

"Decker, can you hear me?" That was Marcus.

I knew if he was here, I'd be okay. He was the only team member to have my back. I struggled for that fucking inhale…I needed to calm down, needed air. My nostrils flared; my mouth gaped. Nothing came.

Then a body lowered into a crouch next to me, revealing a pair of navy blue eyes and a wicked smile hitching up his face, like he had planned this entire thing. How…how had he done it? Elias had one of his hands on my back, patting me…saying something in my ear.

"You're finished, brother."

I made a sound. It might have been me pleading with him to remember our childhood, our tree forts, or the bond we'd shared in middle school and through all four years of high school. He'd been my best friend; he wouldn't do this to me.

Seconds later, he was standing over me, his spiked cleat leaving the ground. I saw it all in slow motion. My pitching hand was right there within reach, and there was enough commotion that no one would think anything about where he was standing…I still couldn't seem to move, couldn't say anything to anyone. I managed a cough, and a small breath rattled through my lungs as I struggled. It was slowly coming back, but not fast enough.

"No." I tried to speak the word, but it came out garbled and unclear.

I heard someone yell for an ambulance, but I just wanted them to fucking watch their captain.

They didn't.

I saw it in his eyes before he did it: a demon through and through.

His foot came down with a hard thrust.

Everything went dark.

CHAPTER ONE

Mallory

HAPPINESS IS FREE VODKA SERVED IN A PRETTY GLASS. ASK ANYONE.

I tipped my head back, my eyes catching on the soft glow above our table from the twinkle lights. A little jolt of excitement flickered inside my chest like a rogue flame while I ran my finger around the rim of my free drink.

I was finally finished.

Done.

I'd written my final article of the year, and it was going to be featured in the showcase for the coveted Kline Global internship.

"Girl, you have worked so hard for this spot. I am so excited to see the look on Trevor's face when he reads your story." Jules, one of the copy editors in the class, sipped a pomegranate martini. Her silky black hair was tied up into a twist on her head, making her look so much more grown up than me. Even her drink made her look more mature.

"Don't forget us when you get hired on for a paid position at Kline." Lydia smiled over her glass and grabbed for the small basket of fries we'd ordered. My friend, who wore her hair shaved on one side and the rest flipped over in a stylish way, made me feel a little more relaxed. She had demanded we order something greasy, combatting Jules' request for Brussels sprouts.

"Not possible." I laughed into my glass. I could feel my face burn at the mere idea of being hired on at Kline Global. It wasn't even that I might get the internship—hell, anyone at that table could get it—it was just that I had been working on this one story for the last six months. I'd skipped out on other massive story leads, forgoing parties and big senior events…all for this article. I had literally put all my eggs in one basket.

I had to get a spot. Only five articles were chosen from the class, and from those five, only one person would be given the internship. I just wanted the opportunity to be selected. They stopped taking submissions in March, but I didn't have to worry about that. My article was sitting in my editor's inbox, ready for the showcase.

The waiter who'd delivered my free drink passed by again, giving me a flirty wink. He was handsome in that boy-next-door kind of way. He had been making eyes at me all night, which was the most action I'd gotten in months, so I welcomed his advances. Why not? I was riding on a high from finishing my article and could have done with a date or two. I watched as he checked on two more tables then made his way closer to the rear of the restaurant.

Following him with my eyes, I observed him slide the door open to one of the private rooms in the back. I could see a few dozen guys, all wearing dark ball caps flipped backward, and they all seemed to be wearing a red and white practice jersey in some varying state of disarray.

My brows dipped in confusion as I tried to piece together why the Devils baseball team would be meeting in a public restaurant instead of their massive team house. Rumors circulated that they were very private about their meetings. One time Hillary even said she thought they were more of a secret society than an actual team, had this whole theory about how it was the perfect coverup. When I brought up the fact that the entire team had talent and it probably was just a team, she scoffed and told me I was too close-minded.

"Mallory, did you hear us?" Jules asked.

My head spun back toward my friends, all of them on one side of the table, giving me ample space to myself. For a second, I hated that I had issues, hated that I needed the barrier of the table between us or I might hyperventilate. Just once I wanted to go out with people I hadn't known forever and have drinks. I wanted to go to a huge party or a concert and not feel like I might black out any second just because too many people were near me.

My friend's brown eyes narrowed while flitting over my shoulder.

"Yeah, next weekend, right?" I played off my brief inattention and jumped right in. Once her face relaxed and she took a sip of her drink, I did the same. I tried to listen to their stories, but my mind kept drifting toward the room in the back. It must have been the journalist in me, but I wanted to know why they were there. It made no sense; they were all clearly in Devils practice gear, drinking, laughing, and joking. Maybe they were just out for a good time...but then, why be in a private room? Wouldn't they want to try their hand at landing a date or a fuck buddy for the night? These were college guys we were talking about.

Jules talked about her plans to hit up a spa the next weekend and mentioned we all should go. I nodded along, running my finger around the rim of my glass. The rough texture from the sugar rubbed against my finger as I stared blankly at my friends. I wasn't going to look over my shoulder again. I had decided I wouldn't, but then...what if the waiter closed the door again and I missed my chance to get one last look?

I couldn't risk it. Twisting my head, I eyed the open door, grateful it hadn't been shut. We were close enough that I could somewhat hear what they were shouting about, but I couldn't make out everything.

"The games start next week. I hope everyone remembers the rules —three of the bases have been assigned."

Bases? Their season did start in about a week, but how would they divide the bases? Were they fixing the game?

"What about the last card?" someone yelled from the back of the room.

Card...now what the fuck was that about? I needed to get closer so I could hear better.

A second later, the cute waiter from before exited the room, carrying a tray of empty glasses. He twisted around and slid the door shut once again.

I snapped my head around, my face burning like I'd done something wrong. Why was I curious? It wasn't like I had to write any more stories.

7

I was done, completely finished; I didn't need to be curious about the Devils. I smiled, returning my thoughts and mind to the conversation at hand as my friends planned more celebratory activities for us.

"Cheers, bitches. We did it!" We all raised our glasses, clinking them together joyously. I smiled and relished the glowing feeling that burned inside me.

I'd done it.

Tears nearly fell as I considered how proud my mom would have been that I'd achieved this step, small as it was. But steps led places, no matter how big or small they were, and this one felt monumental. I couldn't wait to see that email pop into my inbox, notifying me that I'd been chosen.

Now, it was just a matter of time.

CHAPTER TWO

Mallory

"This is total garbage." The loud thwack echoed through the room.

My editor had just slammed someone's assignment down and was about to cause a scene. Gaping mouths, wide eyes, and a few gasps met my gaze as I searched for the victim. I was a little confused as to why every eyeline I seemed to meet was already aimed toward me. My brain was moving too slow, like walking in mud. I registered that Trevor was standing over me, but I didn't register that his presence had anything to do *with* me.

"I expected more from you, Shaw." The cold words dripped down my spine like tiny beads of acid, burning and destroying one inch at a time.

I finally understood the expressions on my fellow classmates' faces.

Trevor was talking to me.

Oh my god.

"What...?" I blinked.

"Garbage. Complete bullshit," Trevor snapped, adding in a little more flavor for everyone in the room. I winced and felt my throat close. I didn't even know how to respond, because how could he be talking to *me?*

"Surely it's no—"

Trevor interrupted me with a heavy exhale. "When I say something is garbage, I'm not trying to spare your feelings. Trust me."

I watched with wide eyes as he pushed his blue light glasses up with his pointer finger.

I was dreaming.

I had to be dreaming. I focused on the yellow smear on his shirt. That's what dancers do, right, when they're spinning? Pick something to focus on so each spin around the room doesn't make them dizzy. I was feeling really dizzy at the moment, so I focused on the yellow stain with all my strength.

Trevor Gage was our senior editor, but the guy hated my guts. I didn't really know why, but he'd made all four years in this class completely miserable for me. I'd pushed and pushed and pushed through it, but now that we were so close to graduation, I was losing my patience.

"I don't understand…" I slowly stood, wiping my hands on my distressed jeans. There was a worn hole near my inner thigh, where my legs rubbed together. I liked to pretend it didn't exist, because I considered them my lucky pair. Suddenly I was feeling a little betrayed. I tugged my beloved red hoodie around my body, pulling from its comfort while hoping this wasn't what it sounded like. Maybe he was confused and had mixed up my article with someone else's.

The man who was breathing fire down my neck narrowed his watery brown eyes and scoffed. "This"—he swung a stapled stack of pages around, presumably my article—"is. Total. Garbage." He slowed his words, getting closer to my personal bubble.

Most people knew to give me space, because I didn't do well with being touched without giving distinct permission. I had weird reactions to people in my space. My therapist said it had to do with the accident I'd been in with my mother when I was ten. She hadn't made it out, and I was broken for a while from it. I didn't think that had anything to do with hating people in my space, but she was the professional, not me.

"But the deadline for the article…" I pressed on, my tongue feeling too thick for my mouth. I needed him to realize that, garbage or not, my article would make it into the showcase and fill the slot allocated in the school paper.

"The deadline will be met." Trevor stepped closer. I could smell his lunch, and my breathing grew shallow. Heat from his body slammed into me, and while any normal person wouldn't consider it a slam or even pick up on the heat, I did. I felt it, like a furnace burning me up, tiny bugs filled with fire crawling along my skin, daring me to run.

"Please," I whispered, needing him to back up and reconsider featuring my article.

"You're lucky I'm not kicking you off the paper, Shaw. That shit was something I'd find in a middle school paper." He leaned even closer.

I counted to ten in my head. Closed my eyes. Breathed through my nose. Still he lingered, breathing in my space, heating up the inadequate amount of distance between us.

"Please back up," I whispered.

I was twenty-one years old. I had dealt with this little space issue for most my life, but for whatever reason it still flared to life with big fat colors and warning signs for everyone to see.

"Trevor, I think Mal needs some space," Lydia suggested from somewhere to my right. I kept my eyes closed, waiting for this prick to take a step back. The seconds stretched, feeling like hours.

"Of course," he scoffed. "Her little issue. What a fucking nut case."

My eyes watered as his words hit. He always said something like that when I mentioned my need for space. There were four zones of varying distances for personal space when being social. Right then, he should have been at least four feet away from me. He was stepping over that, into the intimate zone, and I was deeply bothered by it.

"Sorry, I'll step back." He raised his hands then let out another laugh.

I lowered my eyes to the floor even as a rush of air filled my lungs from the relief of him moving. I grabbed the file he'd slammed on my desk and slowly followed him to his office. I would sit in front of his desk, providing plenty of space between us while he explained what I'd done wrong. My heart sank as I walked past my classmates. I looked around and found Lydia, Jules, and Ronda all staring at me with grief-laden features. Lydia's eyes even watered.

That hurt. A shard of pain sliced my chest as I realized how stupid we'd been to celebrate the night before.

Bad luck.

Trevor grabbed for a paper covered in bland yellow sticky notes. I quickly noted that if I were editor, I would use a color coordinated sticky-note system, and not a single time would any of them be bland yellow.

"What about the deadline? You said we were short-staffed…you even had Jamie write for sports this week even though she doesn't usually cover it." I tentatively sat, hoping I could talk my way out of being blacklisted. I really needed to be in this week's paper. I had to. I had worked half the year for that article, and if I didn't get into this week's spot, I wouldn't even have enough time to come up with another story.

"I had a feeling you'd let me down, so I had something ready to go," the asshole muttered, not even meeting my eyeline.

Motherfucking asshole.

I clenched my fists at my sides, repeating the same mantra in my head that Dad always told me to say when I wanted to hit someone. *Not worth the jail time. Picture a beach, maybe a whale birth or some other magical shit to get your mind off it.*

"If my article doesn't make it into this edition, there's a chance it won't be seen in time for the showcase…" I hated that I even said it. I didn't want to show any weakness, but I was desperate.

"Not my problem, Shaw. Find me something that is worthy of true journalism, something so good not even I could replicate it. Get me dirt. Get me something that will have people talking for days after it's printed." Trevor leaned forward, bracing his thin hands under his narrow chin. One good pop in the nose and it would make me feel loads better.

Not. Worth. The. Jail. Time.

I didn't even respond because it would be a dishonor to the article I'd already written. It was pure perfection, and everyone knew it. There was no way it shouldn't be included. I could have gone over his head, but by the time we all had our little sit-down and hashed out our issues with our advisors, the paper will have been printed and digitally uploaded, and my name wouldn't be there. So, the point would be moot.

No, I had to figure this out. If not for my internship, then for my mom.

♌

THE GREYING SKY ONLY DARKENED AS RAIN PELTED MY WINDSHIELD. IT boded well for my old Honda, which was in desperate need of a wash. I looked longingly at the white Beemer sitting in the driveway and clenched my back molars together. Taylor was home, which meant she'd probably be entertaining someone...likely some jock who liked eating all my lime-flavored chips and drinking all my flavored water. I wasn't in the mood for someone to be in my space tonight, so hopefully Taylor would be in a good mood and understand my need for privacy.

Fumbling with my car door, I was careful pulling out my laptop bag since the shoulder strap was barely hanging on with just three safety pins. The rain intensified as I made my way toward the door, where I promptly pulled out my keys and made a great show of trying to unlock it. I always tried to make as much noise as I could so Taylor had enough time to move any hookup activity to her bedroom, *where it should always be*...but sometimes I didn't get so lucky.

I pushed the door open, and the soft lighting from the living room wrapped around me like a warm hug. The gas fireplace was on, licking at the glass in jumpy flames. It looked as though someone had cleaned, and...I inhaled the savory scent of bread. Had someone cooked?

"Tay?" I yelled, kicking off my shoes and setting my things on the little entryway bench.

"Mal, you're home," my stepsister yelled from the kitchen.

"Yeah...short day." I padded in my white ankle socks toward the amazing smell.

"Good, I wanted to tell you something!"

I rounded the kitchen doorway, finding my stepsister with an apron tied around her waist and a spoon in her hand.

Her blonde hair was tied back at the nape of her neck, her bangs coiffed perfectly against her forehead. Her eyebrows were threaded or

13

shaded, maybe microbladed. Whatever they were, they were flawless. Same with her lashes. She looked like a filter you'd use to make yourself look prettier—just like her mom, the woman who had married my dad six years earlier, throwing the two of us together.

"Guess what I got in class today?" She propped her elbow up on the counter and perched her chin on her palm, waiting for me to respond.

A marriage proposal? Probably not humiliated in front of all your classmates.

I blinked. "What?"

I needed food for this conversation, and a good long talk with my therapist because I had a feeling my stepsister had really good news. I wanted to be happy for her, but sometimes it was hard.

She was self-centered and condescending, but mostly she was just not self-aware at all. Never conscious that her comments were rude, or that having sex in our shared space would be considered thoughtless, or that using my dad's credit card for everything she wanted was tasteless. Still, I wanted a sister. I'd never had one, so regardless of Taylor's short-comings, I did try to be nice to her and I did want a decent relationship with her…it was just hard to be happy for her.

I hedged closer to the stove to see what she was making and smiled.

"Are you trying that soup recipe?"

I loved when she tried things outside of her comfort zone—anything to humanize her. It wasn't often that I saw this side of her, but when I did, I got really proud.

She blushed, untying the apron. "It's probably horrible. It wanted me to use the grease from the bacon in the soup—that can't be right, can it?" Her nose scrunched up in disgust as we stared down at the potato soup.

"I think it adds flavor." I mimicked her face so she didn't feel stupid for asking her question. Sometimes if my face gave away that I thought she was asking something everyone should know, she wouldn't try whatever she was doing anymore.

"Well, whatever. It's dinner…hopefully we don't both die." She tossed her apron on the counter and let out a heavy sigh.

"You were going to tell me something?" I grabbed for my can of lime-flavored soda water, grateful there were still a few left. After the day I'd had, it was the little things I was living for.

14

"Oh yeah! Oh my gosh, Mal—this is crazy." Taylor reached into her back pocket and pulled out a simple playing card from a regular deck.

"Are you playing poker or something?" I moved around her to grab a spoon.

She turned with me. "No, silly…this is from the *team*."

She said team like it was holy or revered, holding the card between her fingers like it was made of gold.

"Okay…" I didn't exactly know how to respond even though my mind was racing at the odds of the team gathering at the bar and the cryptic term 'card' being used.

"You're a senior—you must know about the Devils and their card games…" Her blue eyes narrowed on me as her head tipped to the side.

This was when things with Taylor got difficult. She should have already known the answer to this question. No, I didn't know about the Devils, nor had I ever attended a single game, even for the obligatory sports story. That was always given to someone else. I never volunteered because I hated sports. Sure I'd heard rumors about the team here and there from Hillary, but she'd never mentioned anything about a card game before.

"You know I don't do sports, Tay." I took my spoon to the pot of soup and dipped it in.

"Oh…I forgot."

I kept my back to her so I didn't have to see that look on her face, the one where she realized we were too different to hang out. Taylor was popular, pretty, and had exclusively hooked up with guys from the sports teams at Rake Forge University.

"Well, the baseball team gives out these cards to girls they want to hook up with. There's a base number on the back, and that's how far you'll go with your mystery player." She waggled her eyebrows at me. "Sounds fun, huh?"

I leaned forward, snatching the card away from her. This did not sound fun; it sounded dangerous, and my mind kept reaching for the connection to what I'd overheard the night prior. *Bases have been assigned…*

"Yours says home run…"

She brought her hands together and began jumping up and down.

15

"I know! Someone wants to bang me, which means I'm going to wear his letterman jacket to the game next week."

My eyebrows dipped in confusion. "How do you know when it will happen?"

"Everyone knows that after you get a card, the following Friday night they will host a big party—you take the card to the basement, and there you'll be guided to the appropriate room. The guy who gave you the card will come find you, and once you do the deed, he'll leave his jacket behind."

Gross. This whole thing was just too much.

"Do you have any idea how dangerous this is? You could get raped…no one would know who the guy was…this is such a bad idea." I rubbed the stress out of my temple.

"Every girl who gets a card willingly walks down there. Everyone knows exactly what's being asked of them…" She let out an irritated sigh. "You wouldn't get it. Girls who actually enjoy the attention of the male population love this. It's like a total honor." Her shoulders straightened, and our tentative truce ended just as quickly as usual. I typically ignored her barbs because they were an entire language for my stepsister, but sometimes a few landed.

"Okay…but didn't the guy have to give it to you, and isn't that a dead giveaway?" I tried to push forward even though I was starting to feel lightheaded with all the details around this crazy setup. How long had this been going on? Had anyone actually done this…had anyone been hurt?

"No, silly, they make the freshmen on the team deliver the cards so no one knows who sent them, but it's always a junior or senior who's on the other end. They're the only ones who play the game…it's like a rite of passage."

Okay…

I took a sip of the soup Taylor had made and made sure my face was turned away from her when I winced. How much salt had she added?

"So…if a senior, who can get any girl he wants, gives someone a card with, let's say, a number one on it…that means he's willing to just make out with her?" I wiped my mouth. No way was a college-aged guy in a dark room with a willing female stopping at a base number.

"Yes. Most of these guys have girlfriends, and the fun is in not getting caught or knowing who did it. Unless of course you hit a home run, like me. Then the entire school will know who did you." She shimmied her shoulders with pride.

Had she just admitted to possibly sleeping with someone's boyfriend and being totally okay with it? I wanted to let out a disappointed sigh, but I knew what would happen if I showed even the slightest bit of judgment of her lifestyle. She'd clam up and I wouldn't get any more opportunities to talk to her, and this conversation clearly showed why it was so important to have someone who knew what in the heck was happening in her life.

"Just be careful, Tay. I want you to be okay...you know that." I sipped my soda to get out the taste of her failed attempt at potato soup. She did try, and while I knew she was going to end up calling Door-Dash, I was proud that she'd attempted to make a meal.

"I know, and I will...I'm just excited that they chose me." She smiled brightly at me.

I tried to push down the humiliation surfacing from the newspaper incident and the fact that there was no opening whatsoever to talk about it. That was just Taylor, though; she wouldn't think to ask about my day. That was just who she was: a work in progress and someone I knew needed me even though she didn't say she did. In some ways, I needed her too, even though our relationship was as lopsided as a teenager's stuffed bra, I couldn't give up on her. She'd had a really bad life growing up. It wasn't until her mom married my dad that things changed for her, and because of what she'd gone through, I knew being empathetic didn't come naturally. She'd learn, though; I knew she would. She had tried to make soup—she was on the cusp of a breakthrough. I just knew it.

CHAPTER THREE

Mallory

"WHY DIDN'T YOU TELL HIM TO SHOVE THAT ARTICLE UP HIS ASS?" Hillary, one of my best friends, asked, shoving her plastic spoon in my face. I had just dropped the bomb on her that Trevor had turned down my article. So far, she'd cussed in Mandarin, and now she was pacing the floor like a panther.

"Well, for starters, it's my article, so I don't want it up his ass—I want it printed in the paper." I sat cross-legged in a pair of yoga pants and a loose shirt. I needed to try to breathe. Things were happening so fast my chest continually felt like it was bursting open, one fast thump at a time.

I'd woken up from a nightmare the night prior, where instead of Trevor telling me I didn't get the spot, it was my mom. I'd turned into a little girl, and the people in the room were all Minecraft characters.

"Still, that fucker has a flat tire waiting for him." Hillary tossed her spoon back into her pudding cup and angrily put it in my tiny garbage.

"Hil, he's not even worth your energy." I closed my eyes and envisioned a peaceful lake. Suddenly Hillary was on the lake, in a kayak, waving at me. I opened my eyes.

"Get your dad to whack him," she whispered, sitting inches from my face.

I closed my eyes tight and kicked my legs out from under me. "My dad isn't in the mob."

"He's a millionaire—don't be a baby about this. Just tell him what happened, and I bet all on his own, he'll decide to kill him."

"He's not in the mob!" I yelled at her, standing up. I grabbed my shirt from the hem and tugged it over my head.

"But he's got the money to make him disappear, so just tell him. That's all I'm saying." She winked at me conspiratorially, lifting her hands in mock surrender. Hillary had met my dad a thousand times over the years, and she knew he wouldn't hurt a fly. I had no idea why she kept going on about the mob.

"What I need is an idea. I'm not giving up...I know I don't have six months, but I can wrangle something together. I mean, I have to try." I grabbed for my red hoodie and held it close to my chest, wishing it still held the power to feel lucky. Even if it wasn't real, that feeling I'd once had was everything.

"What you need is a new wardrobe." She carefully tugged the hoodie off my body. I slapped her hand away.

"I'm serious...hey, wait!" I snapped my fingers at her a few times, trying to remember what I'd heard. "What do you know about the Devils and their card game?"

Hillary's pink lips twisted as she pushed her black-rimmed glasses up her nose. "Um...not much. I think I heard they host a party of some kind, hand out these cards, but I don't know what they do with them."

Shit. My shoulders slumped as the last piece of hope drifted out of me like air escaping a leaky balloon. My best friend came and sat next to me, putting her arm around me. She and Juan were the only two friends I didn't have spatial anxiety with. They could touch me any time they wanted, and I wouldn't freak out. That's not to say we hadn't had our issues, but now, we were past it.

"Why are you suddenly asking about the Devils? You don't do sports, babe."

I laughed; as if I needed that reminder, but it also felt good to have someone in my life who knew me in a way that I needed to be known.

"Taylor got this card...it says home run on the back. She was invited to the party...or something." I furrowed my brows, unsure of

19

how to explain all the details she'd provided the day prior. "I also think I saw them meeting in the bar the other night, when I went with my classmates."

"You went without me?" She pinched me.

"Ow!" I pinched her back. "Don't pinch me...we were celebrating my article..." I trailed off, feeling so stupid for jinxing myself with that damn night. I should have just gone home and slept like a good introvert.

"This might be why you didn't get accepted." She crossed her arms.

I scoffed. "Seriously, Hil...you're ridiculous." I stood, moving to my door, knowing she'd follow after me.

"You know I'm right. Don't go places without me anymore," she scolded while we treaded down the hall into the kitchen. On the back porch, we saw Taylor face timing someone, and in her hand was the card she'd gotten from the team.

Hillary seemed to notice it too.

With both our hips pinned to the sink, my best friend said, "You should write your story on the team and have your sister help you. It's too convenient not to." She turned toward me, her intelligent eyes bright with mischief.

I let out a heavy sigh, facing the window and realizing this might be my only shot.

ⅅ

"Taylor!" I elbowed the front door shut as I ambled toward the kitchen with my arms full. I had bought sushi and boba tea for my step-sister in hopes that she would be open to helping me.

"Mal, you're home early." Taylor walked out of her room, hugging her sweater to her chest. I'd blown off my entire afternoon for this conversation, so yes, I was home early; part of me wanted to keep her in suspense just to see if she'd ask me why. I knew it didn't come natural for her, but she needed to start getting past that issue and pretend to care about others.

I didn't have time to wait for her to care, though.

"Taylor, I need you to do me a favor."

I handed her the food and tea I'd purchased for her, hoping to butter her up to do my bidding.

"What's going on...you have that look in your eye that you get when you're brainstorming a new story lead." She sat down on the coffee table, crossed her legs, and took a sip of her drink.

"You're going to the party tomorrow night, right?" I sat across from her, mentally struggling to push past my sensory issues. I lived with Taylor, so I didn't feel the anxiety spike as much, unless we were crowded in a tight space...somewhat like we were now.

"Yeah, of course." She toyed with the blue straw in her cup and eyed the food bag to our left.

"Okay...I need you to try to record some of what you see, or describe it into your recording app, or just call me so I can hear what's going on while you're there."

Her face scrunched in that unfavorable way. "What?"

"Just hear me out," I started cautiously, but I'd already lost her.

She stood and let out some kind of scoffing sound, her blue eyes widened in shock. "I am not spying on the Devils for you."

"I don't want to spy on them...I just want some insider info on the game." I followed her around the living room like a lost puppy.

"Is this game your next story lead?" The incredulous tone in her voice made me slightly flinch.

"No, I just..." Shit, it would have been a good idea to think of something to say prior to this moment so I had an excuse or something other than spying. "I just want to be sure you're safe."

"No way. I'm not that stupid, Mal. I know what you're doing." She wagged her finger at me, and my stomach bottomed out as the window for my potential story began to close.

I licked my lips and tried a different tactic. "Look, Trevor shot down my last story, but he's giving me one last chance to come up with something to be featured so Kline Global might pick me."

She rolled her eyes, and the sight of it hit me in the chest. "Just ask Dad! I don't know why you do this to yourself. We both have the key to any job we want. You know what Dad would say in this situation."

It burned like acid eating away my esophagus to hear her call *my* dad *her* dad. I knew that it was dumb. He was a dad to her and the only one she'd ever known, but I didn't have the same relationship with her mother. Not even close.

"Tay, it's not that simple. He can't put in a good word for me with this one."

"He has stock in Kline Global, like he's a pretty big shareholder— he could easily make this happen for you." She crossed her arms defensively, her boba tea forgotten on the coffee table, sans coaster.

"I don't want that." I swallowed down the thick need to justify my actions. It would just end up in a confusing argument that we both walked away from without hearing the other one out. She never understood why I tried so hard when we essentially held the keys to the kingdom. My father, a self-made millionaire, was the new king of the city and owned so much of the East Coast it was hard not to feel like the princess he was dying to make me. I worked hard to ensure I didn't act like it, at least, but Taylor hated it when I did.

"I know you don't, but spying on the team and writing about them isn't a good idea. I've heard stories about the team, Mal…" She stalked closer so we were eye to eye. She quieted her voice too, like she wanted to be sure I heard her. "I've heard dangerous things about them, and you need to be careful."

"All the more reason for you not to go alone!" I stood, swinging my hand toward her. This was ridiculous.

"I was invited, so I'll be fine, but if you go snooping where you shouldn't…I think that will end poorly for you, and I worry about *you*." Her eyes pleaded with me to drop this, and for some reason, the look there made me wonder what she knew but wasn't telling me.

I held her gaze and slowly nodded my head in understanding.

I'd drop it for the time being, but there had to be a way to get into that party.

CHAPTER FOUR

Decker

"You coming home this weekend?" my little brother Kyle asked, sounding a little too hopeful for my liking.

I knew my sixteen-year-old brother liked when I was home, mostly because it distracted my mom from wherever it was he was sneaking off to.

"I'm planning on it. I have something tonight, but tomorrow I'll be there." I grabbed the tennis ball my boss kept on his desk and squeezed it. He kept it around so he could bounce it off the wall while he made orders and bullshitted vendors about prices, but I always grabbed it when I needed to release some stress. It seemed to work better than the calming breaths Marcus still swore by.

I hated the texture. It wasn't leather, it wasn't the right size or weight...I twisted my hand, seeing the scar that ran down the back from my pinky to my wrist. The surgeon had done a shit job on it, leaving the raised flesh looking more like the threading on a baseball than skin.

Frankenstein. That was the name my teammates called me when they wanted to be dicks. I could still grip a ball, but I couldn't throw like I used to. I'd been going to physical therapy appointments for half the year, working to get the functionality back in it. For the time being, I supported the team, stepped up to bat, played an outfield position…but that was basically it. Elias ruled the team, was now the starting and prized pitcher of the Devils…and I didn't give a fuck. I had plans for the asshole.

I blinked, focusing on the conversation.

"Just…don't do that thing where you talk to her about the house. She hates when you bring it up," Kyle cautioned.

Yeah, I already knew my mom was over me talking about selling the house, but she couldn't afford the mortgage and I worried about her. I was so close to dropping out of school and moving back to help them out. I thought maybe I should…thought maybe it was what my dad would have wanted.

No matter what, stick it out, Dugger. Just stay at it and finish well.

"Yeah, I know," I muttered in response.

"'Kay, well, I gotta go. You still want me to do that thing tonight, right?"

Shit. I was such an idiot for asking this of him, but… "Yeah, be careful. He can't get seriously hurt." My words were tight, careful. Incriminating.

"I know. Not my first job, bro."

I let out a heavy sigh, wishing I was letting out a lungful of smoke. "Don't fucking tell me that, Kyle. Don't do that to Mom."

"Don't pretend you didn't run anything when you were my age. I read the walls in the school locker room—Decker 'Dugger' James is written all over those fucking things." He laughed, and it loosened something in my chest.

I missed him.

I thought of his light green eyes that were like mine, but different. His lighter hair matched our mother's, and he was tall but still gangly. He was good though. Deep down, he was good. Better than me. The thought of him running deals or fixing races made my skin crawl.

"Yeah, well maybe Scotty should just handle it."

My little brother scoffed. "Scotty would kill him."

That was true. I let out a heavy sigh.

"Okay, just be careful."

"Will do, see you tomorrow," he signed off and hung up.

I squeezed the tennis ball a few more times before grabbing my apron and returning to my shift.

CHAPTER FIVE

Mallory

I CLASPED MY SIDE AS I LIMPED HOME, HAIR MATTED TO MY CHEEK, sweat glistening on my reddening face. It wasn't great and I was likely seconds from an early death, but I was out of options.

When I got really stressed out, I ran. It probably wasn't healthy to associate running with the stressful moments of my life, but here we were, me running like a murderer was after me, all so I could work out a way into that party.

I had considered wearing a disguise, acting like a vendor of some kind, but I was fairly certain it wasn't normal for beer vendors to attend team parties. I could have gone as a player, but I'd have needed to up my makeup game quite impressively. I thought maybe I could just try my luck at showing up and stay until I got kicked out...which was the current plan. Taylor refused to hang with me, which was rude, in my opinion, but I also understood it on a strange level.

Opening my front door, I hobbled inside and nearly collapsed. I'd run six miles, and I was not a runner. It had taken me half the day, which was pretty embarrassing, but whatever. I could run the six miles; I didn't think how fast really mattered. Unfortunately, I felt like my heart had caught fire and was about to plop out of my chest any second. I was breathing so hard I didn't realize my stepsister was missing.

Finally recovering, I flipped to my stomach and started crawling down the hall to her room.

"Tay?" She should have been getting ready for the party. "Uh... Taylor, where are you?" I pushed her bedroom door open, but from my vantage point, it looked empty. Then I heard moaning coming from her bed. It wasn't the happy kind of moaning, so I got to my feet and made it to the side of her mattress.

Her room was a mixture of teal and white with a few golds thrown in, all perfectly designed on my father's dime. My bedroom was a mashup of different thrift finds I'd acquired over the years, and the striking differences made me want to laugh. I wasn't very good at spending my father's money, and while I may have resented Taylor for having zero issues with it, at least her things matched and looked nice.

"Tay, you okay?"

A lump in the blankets revealed little except the blonde strands of her hair. I tentatively touched where her shoulder should have been and tried to get her to look at me.

"Taylor?"

She finally lowered the blankets.

"Mal, I feel like death." She sniffed and wiped her reddening nose with a Kleenex.

No...she couldn't look like this. "What happened?"

"I think I must have just caught a bug. I have no idea, but there's no way I can go tonight." She blew her nose and coughed into her shirt.

My heart turned to goo. My little stepsister didn't do well with sickness, mostly because she was so spoiled, but also because her mother wasn't very maternal when it came to things like this. I knew from when we were younger that she just wanted someone to take care of her.

"Want me to call Bev, see if Gareth can come get you? It's Friday, so you can go recover at home where they can take care of you."

Bev and Gareth maintained my father and stepmother's estate while doing whatever else they needed. Bev cooked all the meals and cleaned the mansion, and Gareth drove my father and stepmother wherever they needed or wanted to go. They were really good to us, and I knew they'd come get Taylor in a heartbeat if needed.

Tonight, however, I was channeling someone else entirely. The mystery man in that room tonight would expect Taylor, but he'd get me.

Either he was just handing out cards carefree and didn't really care who ended up in that room, or he had handpicked Taylor and I was fucked. I really was hoping he didn't care as long as it was a willing female, one who would do enough skin-to-skin connection to grab the story before he could hit his home run.

"Damn, girl," someone said to my left. I smiled, remembering what I had on tonight. I was wearing the black dress Taylor had told me to wear. The bodice hugged me tightly, slimming my waist, and the slit opened right at my thigh. It was short, way shorter than anything I had ever worn, but it made my reddish-brown hair look like a dark auburn under these lights and against my natural tan. Loose curls cascaded down my back while little braids lined each side of my head. My makeup was Hillary's best work and completely perfect, with my lashes thick and black, my eyebrows tweezed and shaded, and lastly, my toes were currently wedged into sky-high black heels.

I was thanking my middle school best friend for making me learn how to walk in them, all so we could shine the brightest at our school dance. Then of course Jackie, my stepmother, had ensured I continued my education with every black-tie event my father was invited to.

"Card?" another young man asked from his perch in front of the stairwell leading down to the basement. Checkpoints—they had fucking checkpoints set up in the house, all catered to the game. This was insane.

I flashed my home run card to the fool.

"Lucky asshole," he muttered, but it was hard to make it out completely over the booming bass. His eyes raked over my form, pausing at my chest, where my curls brushed against my breasts. I tried not to wince as a sheen of lust came over his features, tilting his lips in a seductive way. I'd never felt so exposed, like a film of oil was encasing me with every step.

Still, I smiled in response, looking up from beneath my lashes, playing the part, trying to allow this game to be fun instead of terrifying. Other people seemed to be having fun; I could do the same.

Ever so slowly, he moved to the side so I could pass.

I descended the stairs carefully, taking in the pictures on the walls as I went. They were framed photos of the Devils baseball team throughout the years. There was a bronze frame from what looked like the 1970s, and even one from what looked like the 50s. I assumed this house must have been the team house, a fraternity not officially associated with the school, which was probably why they had to be so secretive about this game of theirs. If the school found out, I was positive they would shut it down. *Or would they?*

The basement was layered with a thin blue carpet that was littered with dark stains and old odors. Twin pool tables took up the space to my right, posters of half-naked women adorned the walls, and a low, was-white-at-some-point couch perched off to the left with a coffee table sitting in front of it. Three girls and two guys filled the seats, all nursing cans of beer, and toward the back was a small kitchen, tucked away near an equally small laundry room.

My eyes greedily took in every detail as I made my way toward the back of the house. Every time I was sure I'd reached the place I was supposed to be, there would be someone telling me to keep going. The farther I went, the thicker the smoke was and the more inebriated everyone seemed to be. *Interesting development.*

Tiny hairs on my arms and neck rose as I began to sort through the information I had gathered thus far. This was a dangerously bad idea, and any girl who willingly came down here was definitely not making good life choices. I thought perhaps I should contact the school's guidance counselors after I figured out who all was involved with this.

"The line is this way, baby girl." Drew Seymour leered at me with red-rimmed eyes and a carnal smile. He was devastatingly handsome and someone I hadn't thought knew I even existed. Maybe he still didn't —it wasn't like he'd said my name. He had just called me baby girl and was probably talking to my vagina for all I knew.

I veered to the left, following his directions, itching to scribble down a few notes about everything I was seeing.

"Tell me she's a player tonight." Someone bit their knuckle as I passed.

Player?

This was all kinds of messed up.

31

"Fuck me, whose card is she on?" I heard another yell as I walked through what felt like a maze of leering jocks, all watching to see who was walking in. Finally, I noticed two girls in front of me, both with seemingly more energetic attitudes than me. Their hands were raised above their heads, holding drinks as they gave each boy a free shimmy and shake as they passed.

Should I have been feeling the guys up too? If I didn't, would it make me seem out of place?

Dang it.

I plastered my flirty smile on, lowered my eyes, and batted my lashes. Hopefully that would work. With a few of the guys who moved in closer, I dug deep for the confidence to push past how close they were and dragged my hand down their chests.

Rich Wellington cupped his mouth and yelled over the chaos. "Ladies, we will be splitting you up by bases."

I stopped close to the two girls who'd walked in before me. I wished I knew their names, but I had never seen either of them before. The girl who stopped next to me was vaguely familiar, but I supposed they all would be since we were all from RFU.

"Once you've been accurately placed, you'll then be given a blind-fold. No one here will put this blindfold on you. You must willingly put it on yourself, with the full knowledge that you are going to be led to a room where you will be joined by a specific team member who found your company desirable this evening. This is very important, ladies." Rich stepped closer to our group.

I tried to see how many other girls there were, but it looked like it was just the four of us: first base, second base, third, and home plate. They only allowed one woman per base per party. The conversation I'd overheard at the restaurant played again in my head. As miniscule as the details might have been, they were currently acting as a survival guide, mapping my way through this entire situation.

"You must follow our golden rule. It's of the utmost importance." Rich smiled, bringing my thoughts back to the party. He looked each girl in the eye, but when he got to me, his forehead crinkled like he was confused.

Did he know who had been invited?

My palms began to sweat as he paused, and it felt like an eternity as I waited for him to turn his gaze elsewhere.

Finally, with two furrowed blond eyebrows, he looked away to continue. "You must only go as far as your base allows. The men will be following this rule as well, and there are assurances in place to help enforce this. I don't care if you think you have a connection with the guy or you love him—whatever the fuck it is, I don't care. If you're base number one, you only go as far as your base allows. You will not push for more, or you will be blacklisted, and a formal lawsuit will be filed against you."

What. The. Fuck...

A lawsuit?

I withheld the loud scoff itching its way up my throat. They couldn't... Nothing was in writing. Was it?

Wait...shit.

"This way, ladies."

I was gently shoved forward, and before I could even process what was happening or deliver the barb to not fucking touch me, someone had my wrist pulled up and my card in their hand.

"Home run over here." Someone laughed then handed me off to another guy who led me toward the back of the line. A black silk blindfold was handed to me by a tall guy wearing way too much cologne. I wanted to puke. They were all too close, and I was going to hyperventilate if I didn't get out of the crowd.

Suddenly my heart rate spiked. I wasn't cool with the blindfold. I didn't like not knowing where I was headed...what if this was a human trafficking ring? What if they were serial killers...or rapists?

But Taylor had mentioned that girls came out of this. They lived to tell the tale, to incite jealousy, right?

With shaky hands, I fastened the fabric around my head. My breathing seemed more strenuous, my limbs suddenly unstable as the sounds from the room seemed to amplify and careen through my head. Everyone was laughing or making bets and jokes about each girl. They didn't use our names, just our base numbers, which made me think they had a roster of some kind, or they'd put something on our backs to indicate which base we were.

"Home run, this way." Someone gently pulled my arm then wrapped their hand around mine.

Holding hands I could do because it put space between us. I just didn't want his arm around me. I needed the distance.

"I gotta say, I'm shocked. You weren't the girl I thought would be showing up tonight. As far as I knew, my boy had been eyeing someone else all semester."

Shit. Did one of these idiots actually like my stepsister?

"Hmmm, not sure what happened then," I replied demurely, still trying to keep my wits and gather information about what I could hear and smell.

"No worries. My boy has been known to be a little back and forth. Either way, he'll treat you right tonight. You signed the NDA and all that, about your STD checkup and the use of the condom?"

Wow, they were really thorough. I was momentarily impressed.

"Yeah, left it with…" I paused, hoping he'd fill in the blank for me.

"Paul?" the guy offered, opening a door in front of us. I could feel the air change, and the room he led me into smelled much better than the hall we had just been in.

"Yeah, I guess…can't remember his name," I lied.

The guy laughed, easing my discomfort. "No one ever remembers Paul."

Relief swept through me.

"Okay, I'm going to let you take off the blindfold once I step out of the room. E should be here any minute, okay? If there's any issue what-soever, there's a panic button on the wall." He turned my body and stretched out my hand until it was covering a dime-sized button.

So fucking strange.

"Thanks," I whispered.

"Have fun tonight," he said teasingly before opening and shutting the door.

I pulled the blindfold free and began gathering as much information as I could. I stood in what looked like a bedroom. There was a queen-sized bed covered by a dark blue comforter, and the shade over the window matched. There was a side table with a lamp, textbooks, and what looked like a phone charger base.

I spun, taking in the posters, the chair with a few stains on it, and the small mini fridge. Definitely a team member's bedroom.

I fidgeted with the blindfold, unsure what to do. I wasn't planning on actually sleeping with this guy tonight, but I hadn't considered how exactly I was going to get out of here without doing the deed.

I didn't have time to contemplate any further as the silver handle turned and the door began to swing open.

CHAPTER SIX

Mallory

My eyes were glued to the door as light from the hall leaked into the room. My heart thumped painfully in my chest as my rash decisions began to catch up with me in one rapid motion.

What in the fuck am I doing?

A broad shoulder shuffled through the entrance, followed by a head of dark hair. He was tall, lean muscle that was trim and corded, easily seen under his tee. Narrow hips flared into long, strong legs covered in dark denim that was stuffed into dark brown boots. They gaped like he hadn't had time to tie them—that or he just hadn't taken the time to.

A pair of mossy eyes landed on me. They froze, forcing his entire frame to go rigid, as if the sight of me had literally stopped him in his tracks. My stomach swirled with butterflies as I watched him shut and lock the door. His gaze heated as it moved down my frame, slowly taking in the sight of me. I tried to calm my breathing, but whoever I had assumed would show up tonight, it wasn't anything compared to the man who stood in front of me. There was a rawness about him, a piece of stone that was probably perfect and wonderful on the inside, but his outside was rough and unwelcoming. An invisible piece of corded rope strung taut between us, growing tighter with every second he stood and watched me in silence.

Suddenly, he blinked, which seemed to snap the bond between us. He moved with prowess and a fierceness that made me want to back up a step, but the way his eyes devoured my curves and cleavage told me if I hit the bed, this was all over. He'd fuck me, and I'd be that girl who literally gave her body up for a story.

I stood my ground as he edged closer, my breaths moving in and out of me in tiny bursts.

Oh my god. I was going to hyperventilate. *Are my armpits sweating more than normal? God, this whole thing was a horrible idea.*

His heavy-lidded eyes dropped to the silk bandana I still stupidly held between my fingers while a tic feathered his jaw. It felt like he was imagining what he'd do with it if he had enough time.

I gulped air, my throat as brittle and dry as a scouring pad.

"Taylor, right?" he asked in a silky, smooth tone.

My brain froze. *Shit.* Of course, right. Yes. I was Taylor tonight.

"Yep, that's me, but I'm not sure who you are..." My voice came out breathy and flirty, which was good. Definitely good, but my tongue darting out to wet my lips was absolutely unintentional.

His eyes tracked the movement, those mossy green orbs glossing over.

He cleared his throat, nearly shaking his head as he replied. "I'm Elias. You can call me E if you want."

There was something about him...he didn't feel like an Elias, but what did I know? I hadn't watched a single baseball game my entire college career. I was so far removed from the sports scene that I honestly didn't even know the team had an official name. I had just assumed it was called RFU Baseball, but I was here for this exact reason: to gather information.

Leaning forward just a bit, I lightly said, "Okay...um, so what position do you play on the team?"

This would help. If I knew what position he played, I could start tugging away, question by question until I had more info on these games.

He clicked his tongue, stalking closer. "Isn't that something you should already know? I mean, you were chosen to be here, and you don't even know what positions we play?"

Shit.

Yes, a girl who was likely to be a superfan would absolutely know those things. I felt my face heat as the feeling of failure crawled up my neck.

He didn't seem mad or upset—more amused than anything else. His large hand came up to cup my elbow, and flicking my eyes there, I noticed a long, slightly raised scar that ran along the back of his left hand, all the way to his wrist. On instinct I wanted to know what it was, ask him about it...but that would have been rude and was not the point of tonight's adventure.

"Um...so this whole game...this is kind of crazy, right?" I laughed nervously, folding the blindfold over my fingers. I couldn't meet his eyeline.

He seemed to watch me with varying interest, like I was a puzzle he was trying to piece together, only realizing too late that he didn't do puzzles and wasn't sure why he was here.

"Right." He laughed, stepping toward me.

Coming toe to toe with me, he slowly slipped the silk fabric from my grip. My chest began rising more intensely as his hand went to my waist, running his finger along my skin. Strangely enough, I didn't experience any anxiety when I felt his touch.

I tipped my head back to take him in more fully. He had a strong, square jaw that narrowed at his chin, complete with a small dimple. His bottom lip was pouty while his top was more resolute, and his nose was straight and flared in perfection proportion to his face. His eyes looked dark green, almost muddy under the lights, but they seemed to glow in a way that had me captivated.

He inhaled sharply as his grip moved down and intensified at my hip. Those dark brows caved as though he was thinking of something to say. It went away just as he smiled darkly down at me.

"You're my home run, tonight...better get to batting." He playfully smiled, pulling me closer.

Right—the sex. *Fuck.*

"Okay...but um, I thought we could talk for a bit first." I tucked a few pieces of hair behind my ear. Truth be told? I totally wouldn't have minded this guy pinning me down and trailing kisses down my body while he made me come. If I met him in a bar, there was no way I wouldn't be dying for a night in his bed. Even so, I had principles, and as shitty as it felt, I had to stand on them.

I had told Taylor I would not be claiming this ridiculous home run. Besides, he wanted her.

God, the realization slowly hit me. He thought I *was* her. Did he not know what she looked like? Did they just draw names out of a fucking hat?

His eyes narrowed on me, like he couldn't quite figure me out.

"Not really in the mood to talk tonight, babe. You good with this?" he asked, raising an eyebrow in question.

Shit. Well, I mean…this was for the sake of the article. I could have a little fun for the story. I had to at this point—but I wouldn't have sex with him.

I wouldn't.

I swallowed, putting my hands on his chest. "Yeah, of course."

A quick inhale filled his chest, making it feel…more emotional than it should have, like this affected him somehow.

Before I could unpack the idea, he leaned forward and slanted his head to the side. His eyes held conflict, like maybe he was trying to safeguard his decisions and not kiss me. I understood. This was just a hookup, and there was no need to be personally connected. Internally I agreed, but externally I arched my back, pressing into him, gripping his wrists. My fingers grazed that raised scar and the warm metal of the watch on his left. I felt powerful, holding him by the wrists. They were strong, and the position allowed him to tip my head.

Stupidly—so, so stupidly—I closed my eyes.

Heat flared between us as he pressed his body into mine. Then with my next breath, he was there, his silky lips closing in, caressing mine… coaxing them open with the slightest touch.

A sound came from my throat as my tongue darted out, unable to resist licking the seam of his mouth. He slanted his head to the side as my hands snaked up his chest, wrapping around his neck.

His hands moved down my neck, then to my curves, until he landed on my hip, where he pulled me closer, until I could feel his hardness against my stomach. He shoved his tongue into my mouth, tasting me…

looked between my legs, that silky chestnut hair right at my knees where I could grab the strands and pull while he fucked me with his fingers.

"Do you want more?" The low lights of the room bounced off my skin, my bare breasts glowing. I liked how he looked at me with that same hunger and desperation I had for him. He continued to slide his fingers in and out of me, soaking me as need unfurled inside my lower belly.

"I *need* more," I gasped, sounding like I was in pain.

God, I was though. My hips bucked as my chest heaved.

He watched me, nearly daring me, his eyes hooded with lust. A low hiss left his throat as he pushed three fingers into me.

"You're so hot and wet, so ready to take me," he murmured, kissing my thigh.

"Oh fuck." I exhaled, tossing my head back. I brought my left hand to my breast and began kneading it. My dress was bunched at my hips, my breasts and thighs bare, and my hair was half over my shoulder, trailing down to my stomach.

He kept moving his fingers in and out of me, applying pressure on my clit while I rocked my hips into his hand.

"Yes, oh god, yes…" I breathed. I hadn't ever felt like this, like I was about to catch fire if he didn't finish me, if he didn't fill me.

Suddenly it wasn't enough.

"More," I gasped as he let out a gratified sound from his throat.

Pulling me by the waist, he didn't stop until I was at the edge of the bed and fitted perfectly to his mouth; then his tongue roughly licked up my slit. It was a desperate swipe, his eyes targeting mine while his thumb rubbed up and down the edges of my pussy lips. He pushed my thighs back toward my head so he had access to everything below, and his tongue devoured me like I was the most delicious thing he'd ever tasted. I was bare down there and wasn't nervous about him being there, but still…I was feeling so much. No other man had licked up my ass, but suddenly he was, and it was a sensation I knew I'd die to feel again and again. Every swipe of his tongue and press of his lips was like kerosene on the fire he'd lit.

Panting and writhing, I moved my hips until I was fucking his tongue. He flicked his eyes up, unable to keep from watching. He moved his chin down, sucking my clit into his mouth. He added two fingers while he sucked.

"Yes, more…please," I begged.

"You're so fucking soaked…this isn't enough, is it? You're going to need me to fill you up. You're going to need my cock completely inside you." He lifted his eyes up to mine again. He looked like he owned me. His shirt was still on, the dark tee bunched at his biceps, his hair a mess from my fingers, and those lips glistening under the low lights. God, I wanted this to last forever. To always remember him this way. Whoever he was. Elias something.

My mouth went dry as he bent toward me once more. This time he pushed my hips up and moved his finger down my slit all the way, toward the tight bundle of nerves in my ass, and then, sucking my clit into his mouth, he pushed his finger into that tight space.

I moaned so loud I thought someone might come break down the fucking door.

"I'm coming, oh my god, I'm coming." I closed my thighs around his face as I rode out the best climax of my life.

If he was this good with just his fingers and his tongue, what would it feel like when he…

He sucked me into his mouth with a ferocious intensity, wrapping his arm around my hips so I couldn't move. I bucked against him until my toes stopped curling and the white lights stopped sparking behind my eyes.

"Holy shit, that was…" I finally sagged back to the bed, bringing my forearm to my forehead. He stood, unbuttoning his jeans, and suddenly reality barreled back into me like a freight train.

Holy. Shit.

I almost had sex with him…I can't believe…

"Wait…I just…I have just a few more questions." I rose to my elbows, placing my hands on his chest. I belatedly realized mine fell in heavy gasps. I wasn't against repaying the favor as far as orgasms went, but I would not be crossing into coitus territory.

He froze, his hands on his zipper, his eyes the color of moss on a sunny day, staring down at me.

When I didn't say anything more, he took a step back. His eyes narrowed like he'd returned to the puzzle table, giving it one last go.

"What kind of car do you drive?"

It came out as a whisper, just barely audible to my own ears.

I crinkled my eyebrows while that green flecked gaze studied me. "That's sort of an odd question." I tucked a piece of hair behind my ear then licked my lips.

"Just humor me." He gripped his erection through his jeans. My eyes darted there and my core heated, ready to push past all the reasons I had not to get into bed with him.

What had he asked me again? My mind tried to grasp it, but it felt like oil. Had that orgasm left me braindead? For a stupid moment, I considered this little romp lasting past this night, like he was trying to get to know me—as Mallory, not Taylor. Worrying my lip, dragging the bottom one between my teeth, thinking it over…I finally let out a small laugh and fessed up. "A shitty Honda."

He seemed to stop breathing. He literally stared at me like he'd seen a ghost. His face paled, and his body went totally rigid. *What in the hell?*

"Shit." He finally moved, covering his face with his hands. "Why are you here? Where is Taylor Beck?" he briskly asked, putting as much space between us as he could.

"Wha…what do you mean?" I hesitated, sitting up and covering myself. My nerves rattled and jangled like a billion of Hillary's loose bracelets. I was so confused. How did my car have anything to do with this?

"Taylor Beck was supposed to be here tonight…you're not her."

He knew that by the type of car she drove?

"Nice to see that you know who you're fucking before you get your dick wet," I grumbled, getting to my feet. Why was he being such an ass about this?

"Fuck, this can't be happening. You've ruined everything." He tilted his head back and let out a frustrated sigh.

He gave me one last look before heading to the door.

"Are you fucking serious right now?" My voice went up an octave, like I might be on the verge of tears. I probably was, but this asshole…

Dammit. Why did I care? Why was I suddenly that girl who felt jilted by the guy who was only here for sex?

"Go out and stay to the right, you'll see a door in the back where you can sneak out. You won't have to see anyone, and you can just head home. We're done here."

My mouth opened to say something, but he'd already opened the door and walked away.

CHAPTER SEVEN

Decker

"WHAT THE FUCK HAPPENED?" KYLE YELLED AT ME THE SECOND MY truck pulled into my mom's driveway. Three hours on the road and still it had done nothing to calm the storm raging inside my chest.

I had fucked up spectacularly.

"What do you mean?" I slammed the door of my truck harder than I needed to.

"Elias wasn't supposed to come back, but he did. He showed up and…" My little brother faltered back a step, his face hidden under his hood.

I was on the bottom step when I noticed the shiner on his face.

"Fuck." I stepped up and tilted his head back, letting the porch light reveal more of his face. Kyle tried to brush me off, but I held him firm. "What happened?"

"Elias tried to fucking kill me when he found out I was responsible for what happened to his precious little brother. Pathetic attempt if you ask me—he didn't even manage to put me in the hospital, stupid fucking pussy, but…"

Stalking past him, I trudged up the steps toward the house. I didn't want to hear my little brother trying to act tough in front of me. I had heard how his voice shuddered when he explained himself, and the fact that this was on me…it just dug at me in all the wrong ways. I'd known it was a dangerous idea to ask him to cause the car accident, knowing Elias' little brother would be driving the other car. I hated myself for doing it, but I hadn't been able to think of any other way to get Elias away from his room tonight. Kyle and Jason had grown up together, just like Elias and I had, and their relationship was just as tenuous.

"Mom!" I called, stopping briefly at the small entryway table where our bills usually gathered. There was a bundle of white envelopes that hadn't been touched. I started shuffling them, knowing already they would each be at least a month past due. I tried to grab the bills whenever I dropped in to visit, but occasionally they'd slip through the cracks.

"Duggar, sweetie," my mom responded from the living room.

I heaved a steadying breath, trying not to inhale the scent of my childhood—of my dad. Every single time I walked through the door, I still smelled that baseball glove he'd shoved on my tiny hand for the first time. That white and red striped leather he'd tossed in the air, smiling brightly as he ushered me outside to play catch. It still shredded me when I walked in this house, still ripped me open as raw as it had that first time after the funeral.

"Hey Mom." I leaned against the wall, crossing my arms.

My mother sat on the fading blue couch, a photo album in her lap, an old comedy show playing on the small flat screen in front of her. She still had her scrubs on, her hair tied in a low bun at her neck, concealing her frizzy chestnut hair.

"Come sit with me." She patted the space next to her.

She still didn't understand that I couldn't sit on that couch, or why I couldn't stay in my old bedroom, or why, if I had to stay the night, I preferred to stay in my truck or on the other side of town under the stars.

"I'm good over here…can't stay long."

I never could. She was probably thinking the same thing. I never missed the way her smile fell, or how she cleared her throat and her voice came out strained after I informed her how short my visit would be.

"Kyle was hurt?" I asked, trying to gauge how much she knew. Or if she even cared.

My mother hummed in response, flipping the page in her photo album, retreating to that space in her mind that was surviving her grief by reliving memories as often as she could. She used to come home from a shift at the hospital and take a long bath. Dad would finish dinner and tell us baseball stories while she finished up. She'd come out in her fluffy robe, her hair in a tight braid, and then she'd spend the whole evening with us laughing and playing.

Now, she came home and just sat. No dinner, no bath…dark house, no life.

When Dad died, it was like she did too. Now it was just a phantom…a wraith who roamed these halls and sat on that old faded couch. No one to check my little brother for skipping classes, no one to ask how his day was or how his baseball game went. Had she even cared that Kyle dropped out of sports the year before? Did she even know he was currently failing two of his classes?

"Boys will be boys," she said softly, flipping another page. "Remember when you two slid down that big hill over off Orchard Lane?" Her eyes lit up as she watched me.

I wanted to scream. I didn't like remembering my life when my dad was alive. I didn't want to think back on how happy my childhood was because it was fucking happy and good and full of smiles and laughter. So much so that now…now it was unbearable to go back, to remember it all.

"Have you been paying the bills online, like I showed you?" I rubbed the back of my neck. I needed her to start taking this over; I couldn't keep doing it forever.

"Decker, you know what…" She clicked her tongue in that way she did when she tried to start a story. "I went to log in, and I did that thing you told me to do with my fingerprint." She pointed at me as if I didn't know what a fingerprint was. "But for the life of me I couldn't get it to work." She shrugged, snickering at her failed attempts.

"Did you ask Kyle for help?" I looked over my shoulder to see my younger brother trudge in, heading for the freezer. He pulled out a bag of frozen peas as his eyes slid toward me in that knowing way. It spoke volumes. No, she hadn't asked for help.

I noticed when he opened the freezer that there were at least twenty frozen dinners piled inside. My gut twisted, that familiar wound of grief flaring to life, gaping open.

The walls were too close, the smells too intense. Suddenly I was seeing my dad on that couch with my mom, his arm wrapped around her, laughing at the television…his hands playing with her hair in that way he'd done my entire life.

I knew deep down that my mother was just heartbroken. She was hurt in a way I didn't understand. She couldn't function, and I needed to let her go through it, but I missed her. Kyle missed her. I needed her to come out of this pit of grief and be my mom again. I needed her to sell this house and let us start over. Together.

"Well, maybe we can go over it some other time," I muttered, looking down at the worn carpet at my feet. Wrestling matches with my dad had taken place right where I was standing.

"You headed out?" Kyle asked.

I knew he needed me to stay, if not for mom…for him. But…I couldn't.

"I'm headed over to Westfield, if you wanna come with?" I turned my neck toward the door. Kyle gave me a knowing look and dropped his head, letting the peas drop on the counter.

"Yeah, I'll come."

We both kissed our mom on the cheek then loaded up some blankets in the back of my truck. After stopping for a six-pack of beer and food from 7-11, we drove over to the opposite side of town.

Kyle carried the food and drinks while I carried the blankets. Then we set our things down around the moon-white headstone under the weeping willow.

"You seemed off tonight." My younger brother looked over at me from his place beside Dad's grave.

I put my arms behind my head and watched the stars, thinking of the incident…what I had said to that girl, what I had felt. I was more pissed about that than losing Taylor Beck. My entire plan had hinged on the information my little brother had delivered to me last week, after learning of the meeting Elias had called at that fucking restaurant. The Devils never met outside of our team house for upcoming games, yet the night I was actually free and available to attend, he'd changed the location, so I missed it. *Fucker.*

Regardless, I still learned that he had made plans to break his one rule by joining the game himself.

The Devils played this stupid-as-fuck game where four team members chose four women to hand out a card to. Your game stats and rankings allowed you to choose which base and which girl you picked. It was stupid, but it was also tradition. It was supposed to act as a carrot on a string, making each player do their best so they'd get the high card. Elias Matthews, team captain and motherfucker extraordinaire, had never played a card.

He helped keep track of the games, the players, the roster, and the ranks. He'd never played. Not even for a first or second base card.

Before the incident the previous year, he would joke about how he wouldn't be risking a night of fun for a girl who'd poke a hole in the condom. So, when I learned that he'd not only chosen a girl but was playing the high card on her—I couldn't help myself.

I wanted her, and I wanted him to walk in on me burying my dick inside her.

The only details I could gather before the game were that her name was Taylor Beck, she was shallow as fuck, and she drove a white Beemer.

I figured it would be fine, seeing as she had her card and would arrive in the room before me, but no. I had to fuck that up too.

I didn't usually share things like that with my brother, but something had me spilling the entire story to him—about my pathetic attempt at revenge then seduction.

"What a shitshow." Kyle laughed, popping a taquito in his mouth.

"Yeah…" The chill in the air was a stark reminder of how much time had gone by since our dad had passed. Time just kept going, regardless of how much we wanted it to stop or slow down, to just let us get used to life without him…but time just kept flipping us the bird.

"So, why are you just trying to bang her?" Kyle turned on his side, watching me.

Was it morbid that we came out here and spent time on our dad's gravesite? Maybe…but the groundskeeper, Joe, was a good guy and had actually known our dad as he'd coached Joe's son in little league. So, we were allowed to come here whenever we wanted, as long as we weren't doing anything shitty.

"What do you mean?"

"It's just…if Elias is really doing with this girl what we read in the report, you need to do more than just bang her…you need to completely fuck this up for him. Hit him where it counts," he clarified, sounding much more mature than his sixteen years.

I considered it for a second. The report in question explained a plethora of deplorable things our Uncle Scotty had dug up for us. Ever since that night on the field, he'd gotten involved, and I was unsure why Elias wasn't six feet underground right now. Scotty didn't exactly deal in ethics or morals, but we didn't ask or judge. He'd gotten enough dirt on the guy to build a fucking baseball field.

"You know I don't really like her, right?"

Kyle laughed. "Duh, dumbfuck, but you're playing her regardless— might as well play an ace, right?"

I thought it over again, considered what kind of damage that could do to E if I was actually dating Taylor.

"It would fuck with him…" I trailed off, watching the stars.

We both sat in silence, but my mind kept wandering back to the moment I opened that door and saw her standing in that room.

I hadn't ever been in love, not that I knew of, but the punch to my chest when I saw her wasn't something I'd ever forget. My eyes greedily drank in her luscious curves, her round ass, and those fucking breasts… full, real…perfect. She was all woman and entirely perfect.

I remembered, up close, I could see her eyes were forest green with tiny specks of gold from the reflection of the light in the room. She had a cluster of freckles across her nose, splattered along her cheeks, with just one above her left eyebrow. She was beautiful. The kind of beauty that would take years to fully appreciate, and even longer to fully discover. The kind you'd want to wake up to every day, the kind you'd want to see in your kids and their kids. *The forever kind.*

I couldn't seem to forget the way her hands fit against my chest, the way their warmth seemed to spread into the icy cavern that existed under my skin…it was enough to make my breath hitch.

"Barely," I replied, scratching at my head, realizing a little too late that I still wore just my underwear and a black camisole.

A loud appreciative whistle sounded between what I believed was the fridge and where I was standing.

"Ouch, Juan. Holy shit, what's wrong with you!" I covered my ears.

"Open your eyes, Mal, and stop being such a baby. Explain this look. Right the fuck now," he ordered from his spot at the sink. Juan was always flirty, which always lightened the mood in the room. I'd met him during one of my philosophy classes two years earlier, and we'd been sharing coffee every Saturday morning ever since.

I blinked open my bleary eyes, wishing I could just shut them again and go back to bed.

"Why are you here so early?" I reached for a Danish he must have brought with him. No way in hell Taylor had purchased the white box of delicious fluffy bread.

"You first."

He bit into a pastry, giving me a sexy smirk.

His eyes hadn't stopped roving over my form—or its lack of clothes. Juan was one of my best friends, completely platonic, but he liked to give me shit when I actually found a way to look attractive. I could count on one hand the number of times he had given me that look. I really needed to start putting in more effort.

With a sigh, I sank into the stool and took a bite from the Danish.

"I went to a team party last night…it's a bit of a long story, but let's just say Taylor can never know what I'm about to tell you." I paused mid-bite and narrowed my eyes. "Ever."

Juan paused his chewing as well, his eyebrows rising in curiosity.

I moved on, taking another bite. "Anyway, the guy I almost banged ended up walking out on me and telling me I ruined everything."

The truth tasted bitter on my tongue, ruining the cherry taste left behind by the pastry.

"I'm sorry." Juan choked on his food. "You looked like that"—he waved his arm at me, crumbs flying toward my face—"and he walked out, saying you ruined everything?"

I sighed. "Yes. It wasn't great for my ego, in case you were worried."

My best friend bent over the counter, laughing. Some of his food flew from his mouth, making me tilt backward on the stool.

"Juan, seriously?"

"I'm sorry." He cleared his throat, grabbing for water. "Was the dude gay?"

"How am I supposed to know? He essentially went down on me, was about to fuck me, but stopped with his hand on his zipper." I banged my head against the counter a few times.

"He went down on you?" Juan ran the water at the sink for a second before turning. "How was it?"

I lifted my head with a smile I couldn't hold back.

"That good huh?" He whistled again.

"He knew exactly what he was doing, Juan. Oh my god, and...he went, like...lower too." I stood, moving toward the coffee machine.

"Lower?" He raised an eyebrow, following me with an empty mug.

"Lower, you know...like stuff we only see in porn."

Juan choked on his food again. "I think we might be too comfortable in our relationship, but Mallory, my sweet flower, that is not just stuff you see in porn. Men and women eat ass all the time."

Turned away from him, my eyes widened, and I was suddenly super interested in the warning label on my Keurig.

"I can see that *I've* somehow made *you* uncomfortable, so let's move on." He laughed, turning away from me. "Why aren't we telling Taylor about you getting an orgasm?" Juan opened my fridge, knowing I'd want the creamer.

"How do you know I..."

"Because you look like you had the best orgasm of your life last night, and well, with what he did to you, it's hard not to come from that."

I blushed, feeling my face heat. Just thinking about his tongue inside me, his fingers moving, and that thumb he pressed...god. I needed a fan.

Clearing my throat, I shook the creamer. "I told her I wasn't going to do anything with the guy...I just don't want to hear anything about it from her since I gave her such a hard time about it."

"Okay, but can we at least tell Hillary?" My friend sipped a glass of water while watching me fiddle with the coffee maker. I was doing everything backward today, as I realized too late. Juan noticed and thought it was hilarious.

"Of course we can tell Hillary—hell, she'll probably die from laughter then I can have those strappy shoes of hers that I like," I joked, finally getting the top of the machine to engage and shut.

I didn't want it to slip that Hillary was the one who'd made me look so cute to begin with, or that she had been in on this entire thing from the beginning. Juan would feel left out. I explained the entire card situation and game and everything I had planned to do to my second best friend, watching as his face took on different expressions, until finally he let out a heavy sigh and asked, "So, this guy...who was he?"

Juan was a solid six feet tall with whiskey-colored eyes and dark brown skin. His hair was a deliciously soft black, almost like feathers, and it was always falling over his eyebrow or forehead. Hot was an understatement. He was drop-dead gorgeous, and I had wished a million times that we had any kind of chemistry, but we just didn't.

"Elias Matthews?" I wrinkled my nose at the question in my tone, because it was stupid. I had no idea who he was, and he'd had his tongue on my nipples and on my mouth. He had kissed me, and something told me he wasn't the type of guy to kiss on the lips. *So why did he?*

Juan spit his water out.

"Elias Matthews, as in the pitcher for the Devils?"

I shrugged. I still had no idea what position he played, and thanks to Elias's dark and broody answers, I hadn't gotten any real information about the freaking card game.

"Girl...that's..." Dark hair fell into Juan's eyes as he shook his head at me, as if I had done something wrong to make Elias ditch me in his bedroom.

"I know," I muttered, totally irritated all over again. "He was hoping for Taylor...guess he only knew her by name or something because he thought I was her the entire time."

"The entire time?"

"Yeah, until he asked what kind of car I drove...isn't that a weird thing to ask?" I sipped my coffee, looking outside. The sun was bright, nearly zero clouds in the sky. The heat was already setting in, like a preheated oven. My mind raced with all the things I had to do. I needed to hit the gym before my shift at the bookstore, run by the bank, get gas, and go to the library to filter through school newspaper clippings from the last two decades.

Sigh.

It was going to be a long day.

"And you told him...?" My best friend waved his hand forward, waiting for me to answer.

This was the part I wanted to forget, because the reporter in me was disappointed in myself. How could I fuck up so horribly? He'd already assumed I was Taylor; the correct answer was supposed to be 'white Beemer,' but no. I'd messed up, because for two seconds there I had wanted the gorgeous man devouring me to want *me*, not her.

"I slipped" was all I admitted before fixing my coffee with more creamer. Creamer made everything better.

Juan just smiled at me with his straight white teeth and shook his head.

"Maybe he's stalking Taylor, but hasn't gotten a picture of her yet... but that's a weird thing not to get first, ya know? Like, you should stalk someone based off their looks, then get into the other freaky stuff—what if they're butt ugly? What a waste." Juan licked the cherry filling off his fingers while shaking his head back and forth, like Elias not doing his research was a total disappointment to him.

"I don't know...the entire card situation was weird to begin with. None of the girls knew who would be meeting them in the room. It's entirely possible that the guys didn't either, at least not beyond name." I shrugged, still itching to investigate.

"I agree that Taylor probably shouldn't know about it, but do you think she's in trouble, or in any danger?" My best friend's voice softened with concern.

"I didn't get the dangerous vibe from this guy...more like he was planning on something and I had ruined whatever the plan was, but not in a 'kidnap you and bury your body way'...more like a 'I wanted to surprise you with a new car' kind of way."

"Well, just be careful—both of you." He pointed his finger while grabbing his cell phone. "If you guys need a temporary roommate, you know I'm down." He leaned in for a peck on the cheek. Right as he pulled away, he smiled and said, "As long as it comes with the chance to share a room." He headed for the front door with a quick, flirty wink.

I followed him, crossing my arms and feeling like I was wading through sludge. Damn high heels had killed my feet.

"Wait—you didn't mention why you were here so early." I held the door after he'd opened it.

He shrugged his shoulders, a bright smile meeting me as I waited for him to explain, but he didn't. He just watched me, then when he was about to leave, he asked, "If this guy hadn't stopped, if he hadn't been a complete dick and ruined it…do you think you would have wanted to see him again?"

The question caught me off guard, mostly because I hadn't considered the what-ifs. They were always too painful to take into consideration. Ever since Taylor had entered my life, I stopped thinking about 'what if.'

"I don't know…" I shrugged.

Juan's brown eyes narrowed on me with a seriousness I hadn't seen from him in a long time.

"Let's just say he did it, all right. The next day he took you to breakfast and called to set up another date. Would you go?"

"I don't know…I guess, I mean yeah. If he didn't want Taylor and had actually gone through with it, then yeah, I'd let him call me. I'd want to date him." It was as honest of an assessment as I was willing to give. Sure, if I met the right guy then I'd want to date him. I was a senior in college, and I wouldn't mind meeting Mr. Right. I had no issue with settling down as long as I could still pursue writing.

Juan stared at me a beat longer then let out a sigh. "I just want you to be happy. You don't see yourself the way we do…the way most guys do. You think they only want Tay, but it's because you intimidate them."

I let out a sound similar to one a baby elephant would make.

"You do—you're gorgeous, brilliant, have the entire world at your feet. When you look at people, it's like you know their innermost secrets, and you aren't sure if you'll expose them or not. You may have been awkward in your body at one time, but I can assure you"—he lowered his eyes, taking in my stature entirely—"that isn't the case anymore.

Someone is going to come along and be the one to make you finally believe it. Just make sure you remember you're worth it. No one is doing you any favors, baby girl. You're the prize…the pot the players ask favors to win."

My eyes began to water as I processed his words. They were an ointment to some jagged scars I had on my self-confidence…especially after the night before.

"I love you." I walked into his arms, feeling his wrap around me in a tight hug.

"I love you too. Not enough to ever go, you know…*lower* on you, but I love you like my little sister." He kissed the top of my head before pushing me away, and I laughed, swiping at my face. "I'll see you." He winked and walked out the front door.

I locked the door behind him and walked back to the living room, thinking over what I needed to do in order to get ready and get out of the house. Heading back toward my room, I found my phone and texted Taylor to make sure she was okay.

Me: You at the estate, recovering?

I didn't like to call it 'Dad's' or her 'mom's'; either one was associating familiarity in a way I wasn't ready for. A few seconds went by before I saw the little dots bounce around on the screen.

Taylor: Yeah, I needed some of Bev's chicken noodle soup, but I'm feeling better…thinking of going to get my nails done with Mom.

I watched the screen to see if she'd extend an invitation, but I already knew she wouldn't. She never did. It wasn't that they hadn't in the past; it was just that I always turned them down. I didn't feel comfortable around Jackie because she always compared me to Taylor, as if she was threatened by my mere existence. So, if I was vulnerable, showing my ugly nails at a salon, she'd find a way to bring up my diet and talk about something Taylor was doing differently to make her nails look so much better. Taylor always chided her mother for doing it, but after a few outings, it got old.

I looked down at my nails, just thinking how laughable it all was. I was a daddy's girl through and through, but not in the spoiled princess way. No, I had been helping my father work on cars back

59

before he'd made his millions. My mother had died when I was ten, so he was left doing my hair and picking my clothes, telling me it was normal for girls to wear t-shirts and jean shorts to the swimming pool even when all the other girls my age had on colorful, frilly swimming gear.

He was harsh but fair, loving but distant...until he met Jackie.

By then his wealth was plastered across our local news channel and magazines. He and I both knew Jackie and her single mom routine were just a ploy for money and comfort, but my dad wasn't hard on the eyes. I was fairly sure Jackie had shown up for the bank account, but she had stayed because she fell in love with him.

I set my phone down, trying to brush off the feeling that always came when I started comparing my life to my stepsister. Juan's words bounced in the back of my mind, even as I thought back to being in high school and how much prettier everyone said she was when they compared her to me. How much more socially accepted she was, how it was always her who had the dates while I was home working on my computer. How, even now at twenty-one years old, it was Taylor a devastatingly handsome man wanted instead of me.

You ruined everything.

I grabbed my clothes and headed for the shower, hoping I could wash away these feelings that always seemed to drown me.

ᛒ

MY BACK ACHED FROM HOVERING OVER MY LAPTOP AND NOTES. I HAD A kickass outline created and several color-coded sticky notes ready and set up in my study notebook...but each space that should have had bullet points or notes written in was empty. I had practically nothing to go on from my little jaunt to the Devils' party, and to top it off, there was a tiny chance I was in a bit of legal trouble because of it. I was avoiding the baseball field and their local hangouts at all costs, which wasn't great for my desperate need for a source and more information. I needed to interview someone, but every time I even considered getting up the nerve to saunter toward the locker room or practice field, I got physically ill.

Grabbing for my phone, I sorted through a few texts from Hillary and Juan.

Juan: Pizza 2night?

Hillary: Bring salad and I'm game

Juan: Mal?

Hillary: Mallllllorrrrrryyyyyyyyyyy

Juan: She's ignoring us

Hillary: I bet she's at the library. She always has those headphones in...

Juan: And that horrible music blasting

Hillary: I actually dig some of those nature sounds...they mix violins and guitars in there too. Don't shame her for loving some relaxing instrumental.

Juan: Mallory Shaw, answer us. I'll bring a bag of lime-flavored hips

Juan: I mean chips. And my famous guac

I smiled down at my phone, seeing that it had been well over thirty minutes since their last text. Biting my nail, I knew I wouldn't be able to really enjoy myself until I'd cleared my head.

Me: Sorry, I was in the library...I'll be there in thirty

Gathering my things, I left the library and bypassed the parking lot. When I needed to get clarity around a story, I often needed perspective or just inspiration to dig deeper, try harder, and just...do better. I knew I was a decent writer, but every now and then Trevor would get inside my head and ruin any confidence I had regarding my story.

With this specific one, I was already grasping at straws, so I was needing inspiration more than ever.

I checked my phone for the community transportation schedule and grabbed a seat on the downtown commuter bus. I watched my reflection in the window as the dark city flew by, and the empty seats reminded me that most people were home with their loved ones. This was my last year of being free like this, not being pressed down by a job or a family... freedom to just hop on a random bus and head into the city with no one knowing or caring where I went.

The idea of it burned my chest. I knew my father still wanted me to get involved with his businesses—he'd even offered to purchase Kline

Global so I'd get a paid position. The laughable offer had forced me to leave that specific dinner early. I hated when traces of my dad disappeared and the wealthy tycoon took its place. My dad before the billions would have told me to work for the internship, to earn it. Sometimes it felt like he'd died shortly after my mom did, as soon as he'd married Jackie.

Finally, the bus pulled into the snug space reserved for its massive size, and people shuffled off, heading in their own directions. I pulled my backpack on, gripping the black straps, and started downtown toward the one place I hoped to be the following year. Located only two blocks down and one street over was the news giant, Kline Global. Okay, it was a giant in the same way people viewed David who had killed Goliath. David was clearly the badass hero, mightier than the most feared warrior in the land...but dude was tiny. Kline Global sat snugly in the middle of an empire, only taking up space on one measly floor, but still...I stood on the sidewalk with my head tipped back, staring at the enormity of the gleaming glass windows that speared the sky.

I knew it was closed, the hour well after everyone had gone home, but there were still a few lights on inside, likely a few people cleaning. I walked closer to the front door and ran my finger along the engraving for the company whose internship I craved more than anything.

Sweeping my finger over the K always seemed to calm me down, the L was a woosh of air to my chest, the I, N, and E all small flutters in my stomach. I closed my eyes, imagining myself a year from now, walking out of these very doors, bursting into the bustling city...headed home to my own apartment that I didn't have to share with anyone. A smile crested, and my chest felt light.

Kline Global only extended one internship spot a year to graduating students of RFU, and that internship often led to a paid staff writing position. Several of the staff on the school paper wanted the spot, and many only wanted it for its proximity to the famous glamour magazine that had blown up recently, but either way, KG was their foot in the door.

KG worked strictly to bring awareness to injustices happening around us. From local communities to third world countries, it reported on those stories, doing whatever it took to ensure they began trending and got people talking. They'd recently done a story on a young woman just two cities over who'd been raped, but the guilty party had nearly gotten away with it because he was a local football star. Their articles and stories were featured by major celebrities who dedicated their free time to helping in developing countries, sending foreign aid as well as standing up against social injustice in our own backyard.

It was the kind of journalism that made me want to be a writer, the kind where real change could be made. I wanted to do something with my writing, make a change, help someone find justice in something... report on what mattered. Sure, I loved the funny parts of social media like the next person, but there was something burning in me that just aligned with Kline Global and its vision.

I closed my eyes, tracing the lettering and taking a few deep breaths.

"You'll get it, Mal. You'll get it," I whispered to myself then turned on my heel and headed back toward the bus station.

CHAPTER NINE

Mallory

"YOU BETTER HAVE THE LIME-FLAVORED CHIPS," I SAID AFTER unlocking my best friend's door and slamming it shut.

"Who do you think I am?" Juan placed his hands on his chest, acting offended.

"Where have you been?" Hillary jumped up and ran over to me. She wore a cute romper that made her look ten years older.

"Where did you get this?" I thumbed the mustard-colored fabric, peeling my sweater off and setting my things down.

"My sister."

Of course her sister had hooked her up. Hillary had an amazing older sibling who always set her up with trending clothes and makeup, always making sure her little sister had the latest and greatest. I loved their relationship, but sometimes I looked at it in the same way I looked at lions in the zoo: total fascination mixed with a little trepidation. I often wondered what it would be like to have that sort of connection with my stepsister. What would it be like if we acted like real siblings and not just acquaintances?

"Mal, seriously—we actually went to the library in search of you, then your house…where were you?"

"Geez, stalk much?" I joked, grabbing for a slice of pizza before landing on the superb leather couch. Juan's parents owned a chain of restaurants and were insanely wealthy, and he was a hybrid mix of both me and Taylor: never turning down a handout from his mom or dad but working for most of what he had. These couches had definitely been a handout. Both Hillary and I were exceptionally glad he'd decided to take them up on it.

"Where's the roommate?" I looked around, wondering where Juan's recluse roommate was. He usually snuck out of his room if there was pizza around—that and Hillary, although hearing she preferred women had nearly crushed the poor guy.

"Some guy in C block is having a video gaming marathon...or computer game. I don't know."

Hillary and I burst out laughing.

"C block? You aren't in prison, G." Hillary called him G when he pretended his life was much harder than it was, as he liked to do.

"My apartment building has a big-ass A on the front, and there are six units here. Over there"—he pointed out his window—"is a section with a B on the front, and there"—he pointed toward the right—"has a big-ass C. I call them blocks."

I snickered again, swallowing more pizza. He was ridiculous, but I loved him.

"So, any word from *THE* Elias Matthews?" Hillary rolled her eyes, and I knew it took all her strength not to fake putting her finger down her throat. She hated what sports did to normal people. It turned us all into idiots, acting like some people were better than others just because they could throw a ball. Pfft, ridiculous.

I shook my head. "Nope, and good riddance."

"Hmm...if he was after Taylor that hardcore, I figured he might hunt her down at your house," Juan speculated, flipping through our Netflix options.

"Do you think he will?" I felt a frown tugging at my mouth, because I really didn't want to see the asshole again. The embarrassment still sat like a burn mark on my chest. For some reason it burned extra right where my dumb heart sat. I blamed it. I knew my vagina was definitely to blame, but my desire for that story definitely came from the heart. So, it was grounded for the foreseeable future.

"Dunno, I mean…" He shrugged. "If it were me, and I were after you…" He looked up at me, giving me that serious Juan Hernandez look that made every woman swoon right into his king-sized bed. "I'd definitely be back."

I threw a couch pillow at his head and laughed.

"It's not me, it's Taylor…but I guess I see what you're saying."

"Just be careful—I get weirdo vibes from him," Hillary declared, going for a bottle of wine from the kitchen.

"You've never even met him."

"I know, but I can just tell." She didn't joke around about being able to "tell" when it came to her vibes about people, and she usually wasn't wrong.

We laughed, ate chips, and watched three movies before I fell asleep on Juan's heavenly plush couch. I often stayed over at his house so it wasn't a big deal, but waking up at two in the morning and realizing I had an early class at seven was.

I clutched my things and tiptoed out of his apartment.

I'd grabbed my car from the parking lot after my bus ride back to the school. So, with my key in hand, I headed toward the obnoxiously bright parking light I'd parked under. Safety first. Except, did I even have the right key out and ready to go so I didn't fumble when I got to the door? I looked down for a nanosecond and managed to run into something.

"Ow, what the hell!" I rubbed my shin.

"Geez, what the fuck?" Someone growled from the ground.

"Oh shit, I'm so sorry." I wasn't even sure it was my fault, but I was an automatic apologizer in these kinds of situations. Okay, in all situations. I looked down and saw someone crouched by a truck tire, a hand running over their forehead.

"What in the world are you doing on the ground?"

The crouching stranger stood, towering over me by at least several inches, and that familiar burning sensation in my chest returned stronger than ever.

"I was checking my tire—"

"You!" My tone was clipped and cold because that was exactly how I felt about this asshole.

He took a step back, rubbing a hand in his eye socket like he was exhausted. It was two in the morning, so he probably was.

"You...what are you doing here, shitty Honda?" He looked around like he genuinely was confused how I had gotten there. Once his stare settled on me again, his eyes narrowed on my hair, then my shirt...and the bra I held in my hand.

Oh no he did not.

"Are you calling me 'shitty Honda' in your head?" It was late, and my manners were still back in Juan's apartment, sleeping.

His eyes seemed to narrow. It was hard to make out with the shadows covering his face.

"I am not calling you anything in my head." Strong hands flew to his chest in defensiveness.

I scoffed. "Sounds like you are."

"Well I'm not. What in the fuck are you doing here?" He repeated himself then grabbed something out of the back of his truck, a back-pack of some kind.

"You don't live here, do you?" I ignored him, looking back toward Juan's block of apartments.

Please, Lord, don't let this asshole live here. Wait...he lives in the Devils team house...right? So, why is he here? I wanted to ask him, my throat itching with the sensation, but I knew he'd probably tell me it wasn't my business... and he'd be right. I didn't know him; therefore, I didn't need to know anything about him.

He ignored me, still looking me over, a twitch working its way into that handsome jaw of his until those eyes landed on my lips and stayed there. "You dating someone who lives here or something?"

Why did he sound so angry?

I sidestepped him and replied with "Or something."

I didn't give him a second glance, keeping my eyes low as I walked toward my car.

"It's late—you need to be careful out here," he yelled at my back.

I stopped, turned slightly, and tried to discern the look on his face. Maybe the other night had just been an off night for him, but how he'd treated me really did say all that needed to be said about his character. I'd never listen to this guy, not in a billion years. If he said, "Don't step there, it's lava," I'd step there on principle and then die. But it would be worth it.

I turned, ignoring him once more, and continued toward my car.

"I'm serious...I don't want to see you out here again."

I laughed under my breath. I didn't give a single flying fuck what he wanted, but I was cold and tired. So, I unlocked my car and started it up. Driving away, I totally ignored how he stayed there watching me until I made the turn out of the parking lot.

♌

TAYLOR MENTIONED THAT WHEN SHE'D GONE HOME TO RECOVER, MY DAD asked that we come into the city for a meeting. She'd ended up staying at home for two days, and we were finally getting our first chance to talk about the party.

After arguing over whose car to take, Taylor drove us downtown. It was a measly three blocks away from Kline Global, but not once had I ever considered popping in to say hi to my dad during one of my therapeutic excursions.

"So, it totally sucked?" Taylor asked as we veered from the freeway toward the exit that would take us to my dad's building.

"Yeah...the guy never even showed up. Isn't that crazy?" I adjusted my seat and dug in my purse to put my sunglasses away and locate my lip-wear. I liked lipstick for color, but I needed moisture. I was also trying to avoid my stepsister's reactions as I gave her a version of the truth that I hoped wouldn't end up biting me in the ass. I essentially omitted the part where the guy showed up and then kicked me out.

"You didn't know who it actually was though?" She fiddled with the buttons on the dash, turning the air conditioner on. She was dying to know who'd invited her, but if I told her it was Elias...then what? He was a total asshole. I mean, I didn't feel unsafe around him or like I was in danger...but still. What a dick.

"No...they only told me to wait in the room and said he'd be there shortly. Except he never showed up." I shrugged, feeling my face burn at the lie. I would have rather died than admit I gave in to whoever it was that had invited her. It was mortifying enough that he'd kicked me out once he realized I wasn't her. There was no way I was telling her.

"Well, I'm sorry about your article. I was hoping you'd get something juicy out of it."

I shrugged again, feeling like it was my default mode. "It's fine. At least I got to see the process and everything. Which reminds me…" I dug around in my massive purse to see if I'd brought my notebook. "Did you get to keep a copy of the contract you signed?"

She nodded, putting her blinker on. "Yeah, it was really basic, but I still have it."

I could have wept with joy. "If you can get me a copy, I would be so grateful."

"Mal, you aren't going to share it in your article, right? You won't share my name…?" She worried her lip, slowing for the red light ahead of us.

"No way. I'd never do that to you." I looked over at her. "You know I wouldn't, right?"

She glanced at me briefly before the light turned again. Quietly, she replied, "Yeah, I know."

Good. I wanted to be done with this conversation, because I hated lying to her.

"What do you think Dad wants?" I asked as Taylor maneuvered in the parking garage.

Her small sigh told me she'd been talking to him behind my back. Sometimes during family brunch, the two of them would start talking business and I'd usually just check out, but with graduation creeping up on us, I wondered if there was something I had missed.

"What aren't you telling me?" I flipped the mirror down, adjusting my makeup and applying my lipstick. I didn't really need it, but I liked to look professional when we entered my father's building.

"Don't freak out," Taylor softly requested while tugging her mirror down and pulling her lipstick free.

I turned my face to watch her apply the soft coral color to her lips, waiting for her to spill. I should have asked the question on the trip here, and now I was on pins and needles.

"Look, I know you don't want anything to do with the company, but

I do. I'd be stupid not to get involved with it. There's going to be someone who takes over for him when he retires, and since you don't want it…" She trailed off, snapping the lid of her lipstick back on.

I breathed in through my nose and out through my mouth. I knew we'd just get into an argument if I said anything. So, I opened my door and got out.

"You're not mad?" She chased after me, locking the door on our way to the elevator. The loud chirp echoed off the white cement at our feet.

"I'm not mad. I just want you to be happy, Tay. That's all." And free from the disgusting men who would eat my little stepsister and her fat bank account for breakfast. Someone would inherit my father's fortune through her, and she was naïve enough to accept that guy even knowing he might only be there for the money. She'd do all this to fulfill some misplaced desire to please the only father she'd ever known. My dad wanted one of us—actually, both of us—to work for him. I was sure he wanted to play us like chess pieces, corporate moles, or arm candy for the men he wanted to negotiate with. I wouldn't play his games, and I had hoped my stepsister wouldn't either.

We rode the elevator to the lobby, where we disembarked and checked in with security. Once we had our badges on, we ventured toward the gleaming chrome elevator doors that would take us up to his office.

Twelve floors later, we were exiting and padding across marble floors that had recently been waxed. Glass windows stretched along the walls, showing off the city and the gleaming sun, blue skies, and zero clouds. It was a gorgeous day, and I could almost feel the heat as we bypassed my father's secretary and pushed open the glass doors to his office.

My father wanted a completely transparent 'brand.' He didn't hide anything, and in turn, he hoped whoever he did business with wouldn't hide anything either. It had worked wonders for him so far, and my step-mother Jackie liked that he could never be alone with anyone or cheat on her in his office. Maybe she liked to ignore the fact that he did have blinds, and with a push of a button—total privacy. But my dad wasn't a cheater…he just wasn't built that way. Not after losing my mom.

"Girls!" he exclaimed, standing from his chair and walking toward us.

We both leaned into his hug before taking the comfortable chairs in front of his desk. Once upon a time, there had been only one chair and a much smaller desk...but once Taylor came along, he always made sure there was a chair for each of us when we came to visit him. Memories of being sixteen and stuck in his office for the day came barreling back. His money was new to me, just like his new wife and daughter, and while they all seemed to get along swimmingly, I was left in the deep end, treading water.

"I wanted to talk to you about an upcoming dinner event." He perched on his desk, his Tom Ford suit barely shifting as he tucked his hands into his pockets. I liked that he always got right to the point. No mincing words or fluffy pleasantries. "This dinner will be an important one, and I'd like you both to attend. I plan on having a few investors and shareholders at this event. As you know, they're weighing in on the future of Shaw Corp..." He trailed off, bringing his hand up to his chin. My father's hair was still mostly dark, just a single streak of grey running along each side. His tan skin looked darker than normal, evidence of his recent trip to the Caribbean. He liked to take Jackie every chance he got.

"We always attend your events, Dad—what's so different about this one?" I asked, curious about his behavior. He never felt the need to warn us or have a special conversation prior to other events.

He hesitated, looking at Taylor for just a brief second. "You both graduate this year, and you're going to be more involved with business meetings and events...I just want you to be prepared. Don't wear those ratty tennis shoes you like to wear." He leaned forward to grab my shoe in jest.

I relished the soft smile he gave me because, for a second, he looked like the Charlie I grew up with. Ratty shirts, flannel, denim, and coupons...we had practically been poor once upon a time, back after Mom's accident. For five years, I had him all to myself, and those years I'd cherish for all eternity.

"I'll dress appropriately, Dad." I laughed softly, gently kicking him with my shoe.

"You need to bring dates as well, please." His gaze went toward Taylor again, and the smallest wince seemed to spear his features.

I looked over at Taylor, whose head was lowered, her arms tucked in tight.

"Why?" I asked the question, but she was nearly screaming it with her tense jaw and dipped eyebrows.

A muscle jumped in my father's jaw while he looked down at his desk. There was obviously something the two of them weren't telling me. The tension between them could have been cut with a knife, but I didn't understand why he'd wanted to see me along with her if they were just going to keep it a secret.

"I just need you both to have a date. I can't make it seem as though you're available. Even if it's that friend of yours, Juan—he'd be fine to bring. Just don't come alone, okay?" He stood, walking slightly past our chairs, which was his silent request that we leave him alone. It had taken nearly thirty minutes to get here. I'd skipped an important class to come, and he was already dismissing us?

Taylor and I stood, giving each other quizzical looks, but we didn't ask anything more. His terms were easy enough to understand. There would be hunters attending this party, men looking for an easy ticket to my father's fortune, and he wanted us to appear unavailable, which was good. For a second there, I had thought he'd be willing to marry one of us off to secure a lucrative deal, but if he wanted us to look taken, he obviously wasn't interested in trading us like we were the latest commodity to hit the market.

I walked out, feeling the slightest bit of relief rush through me. I kissed my dad on the cheek on the way out and joked, "This definitely could have been texted, old man."

He laughed and pulled me into a hug while tugging Taylor under his other arm. "I know, but how else am I going to see my girls?"

We walked with him as far as the elevators, and for a second, I didn't mind sharing my dad with Taylor. For a second, I felt like I could share anything with her if it felt like we were really sisters. Later I would wish I had known that feeling would come back to slap me in the face.

CHAPTER TEN

Decker

INFORMATION WAS A FORM OF CURRENCY IN THIS SCHOOL. IF YOU WENT off my bank account, I'd be considered practically destitute. Every penny I made, I either used for rent or gas or sent back home to Kyle to help with bills. My mom would never take my money, but she was either going to lose the house my father had built for her, or she was going to take my help in the form of Kyle intervening. But, if you went based off the number of favors people owed me and information I had on people, I was rich as fuck.

I ignored the way the group of players locked their jaws and squared their shoulders as I passed by them. They'd heard one version of what had happened between Elias and me over a year ago and decided to start up shit, spreading rumors about me. I was fine with that; it only added to my credentials as a hardened criminal, so people didn't double-cross me when they fed me information.

"Frankenstein." One of them coughed the name into their hands, and I withheld the urge to trip the fucker.

Once I knew they were gone, I stretched my hand at my side, feeling the familiar ache. It only made me want my revenge all that much more. Walking down the east hallway toward my philosophy class, I threw my backpack down and slouched in the back row. A few girls passed, flirting with their eyes and batting their lashes. It wasn't uncommon for one of them to drop into the seats around me so when class was over, they'd be the first to walk out with me. It was a boring routine, and honestly it didn't hold much appeal. It wasn't like I dated a ton…I didn't have time to date, or to even hook up.

Shit, the last time I had gotten anywhere close to hooking up was when I was in that room with the girl who wasn't Taylor Beck. Thinking of her made me remember her little appearance in the parking lot the other night. I had no idea how or why she'd come to be in my parking lot, but I didn't like it. The idea that someone had put their hands on her, had mussed that hair…it just…well, fuck, it bothered me and I had no idea why. I didn't know the girl, had been a prick to her when I essentially kicked her out of the room. Then with the way I talked to her in the parking lot…

But there was something about her that felt…just different. Something like freshly cut grass, the leather on a baseball, and *home*.

"Finally," my friend Juan said accusingly as he sank into the desk next to mine.

I laughed at his comment and dipped down to open my backpack.

"Finally what? You're the one who's late."

He eyed the front of the room before peeking over his shoulder. "You missed like the last three days of class—what in the heck happened?"

My family happened. Elias changing plans and punching my kid brother happened. Working my ass off so my mom didn't lose her house happened.

"Not much, just picking up a few extra shifts." Not that he'd understand that. I heard his parents owned several restaurant chains and he was rich. I hadn't known Juan for very long, just the length of this course, which had started back in January. He was cool to talk to, he liked sports, and he didn't bullshit. I knew he lived around my apartments too, but we'd yet to hang outside of class.

"Well, Flynn Rider has been in a mood. I'm glad you're back," he joked, lowering his voice to a whisper.

I smirked at the use of our teacher's beloved nickname from some Disney movie, then looked over at him and noticed he was barely dressed. He had on a pair of sweats with a hockey emblem on them, the one for our local team, the Hornets. He wore black Adidas sandals with socks and a large black hoodie, and even his hair was mussed like he'd just woken up.

"Did you just wake up?" I laughed because it was almost noon.

"Dude, my two best friends wrangled me into a TV marathon last night. They wanted to watch this new series on Netflix, and I should have told them no, but they made a seven-layer dip."

My shoulders shook with laughter while I leaned forward, arranging my notebook in front of me. "Sounds like your friends are chicks, and if they're single then you should definitely invite me to the next marathon night."

Mr. Flynn started handing out sheets of paper, talking about the quiz at the end of the week while Juan leaned closer.

"I make it a point not to know if they're dating anyone, although one of them seems to have a pesky habit of getting herself into trouble. Either way, they're both handfuls—I think I'll spare you."

I laughed once more and considered again the red-haired beauty from the night at the Devils' house. I needed to stop thinking about her. Instead I needed to focus my efforts on the girl who'd stood me—Elias —up. I needed to go see Daniel, deal in the only currency I had plenty of, and find Taylor Beck.

ʊ

I OPENED THE FRONT DOOR OF THE TEAM HOUSE, HEARING LAUGHTER echo up from the basement. My freshman and sophomore year had been spent down there, drinking, playing pool, and organizing card games with everyone else. After Dad's accident, everything changed, and it just didn't hold the same appeal—not to mention that some of the team now liked to fuck around by calling me names.

I walked toward the kitchen, looking for Marcus. I needed to know if anyone was talking about the last card game, the fact that Elias hadn't shown up...or if they knew I had. It was no secret that I hadn't gone to one since the incident with Elias.

There, nursing a beer while sliding his thumb along the screen of his phone, was my best friend. Dark ink wrapped around his equally dark skin, a stark reminder of why he was usually the one the ladies hit on when we went out. He stood a few inches taller than me and, regardless of the monikers the sports bloggers gave him, was genuinely a nice person. He'd helped me open more cans of beer, water bottles, and Gatorades after my accident than anyone should have to, worried that I wouldn't stay properly hydrated. He had even made meals for both of us, acting like it was part of one of his courses…but he was full of shit. He just wanted to make sure I was fed.

"Baby D." He smiled.

I rolled my eyes at the nickname he had for me. He had started calling me that our freshman year when we faced off against a team and another player nearly dwarfed me. Marcus thought it was hilarious how tall the dude was, and since my name started with D, he began calling me baby D.

"What are you up to?" I leaned in with my hand for a shake and a quick slap on the back. His classes were sporadic enough that our schedules didn't match up often.

"Just making appearances." He looked around, making sure no one overheard him.

I nodded. "Same here." I looked around, seeing one of the underclassmen walk past with his phone up to his ear. As members of the team, we may have been provided special allowances to live outside of the house, but we were required to show up, to show our solidarity and, for lack of better words, team spirit.

The owners wanted to cultivate a brotherhood on the team. For generations, they had successfully done so, weaving a network of loyalty and unwavering dedication. Once a Devil, always a Devil; they took care of you as long as you followed the rules.

"I need to know something, man." I reached over, grabbing a beer and keeping my gaze on the entrance to the kitchen.

Marcus tipped his head, encouraging me to continue.

"Anyone talking about the card game…or what happened to E?"

Two players walked in and opened the fridge, describing a chick's chest in graphic detail, then grabbed two beers and headed out.

"A few are. Said the wrong girl showed up…once E said it was your

76

little brother who fucked up his little brother, no one really questioned anything, but I don't know if they're curious about the girl who showed up. She wasn't authorized to be down there."

No shit.

I hadn't told Marcus of my plan to be down there that night, taking Elias's spot, setting up the car accident with my little brother so Elias's Mom would call, nagging him to drive over to Pinehurst to check on him. The plan was supposed to be for Elias to get stuck on that call for thirty minutes then explain why he couldn't go. By then he'd walk in on me fucking this girl he'd handpicked, and I'd walk away with a smile on my face.

All of it had gone to hell.

"No one is dropping names?" I asked, popping the lid off my glass bottle.

Marcus took a big swig of his, shaking his head. "Other than the accident between your bro and E's, no."

Relief nearly made my shoulders visibly sag. The longer he didn't start putting things together, the longer I had to make my own plans.

"You running a deal?" My best friend quirked a curious brow.

I smiled at him. "You know I don't run those anymore."

"I do know that. I also know your family history, and the very fact that E is still alive tells me you're saving something for him."

Dude knew me better than I thought. I watched my feet, not answering him.

"Just be careful. Don't get caught. You're already in enough shit with Coach and the team since last year. You don't want any more attention on you. Just finish the season, get your Devils status, and then get the fuck out of here."

I nodded, because he was right. That was the plan: keep my head low, get my secured spot on the team so I'd have it for the rest of my life, and then get out. I just had one last thing to finish up before I did.

"Yeah, I'm good, man. I'm not running anything," I replied easily, tossing the bottle cap in the garbage can.

Marcus smirked, following suit with his cap. "Something tells me you're full of shit, brother."

He wasn't wrong, but I couldn't find it in me to care.

CHAPTER ELEVEN

Mallory

THE DAY WENT BY AS LAZILY AS A FAT CLOUD ON A SUMMER DAY. THE shift at the local bookstore didn't do much to distract me from the article burning a hole in my computer or the fact that I needed more info. There was also the little issue that eventually someone might notice it hadn't been Taylor Beck who'd shown up that night. It was only a matter of time before someone checked up on that.

Eventually it would bite me in the ass, but I was hoping to have my article finished first. The only problem was that I didn't have enough information. I needed more answers in order to form a full opinion piece.

I was pulling into my small driveway, celebrating the fact that I'd beaten Taylor home for once, when I noticed a truck rolling past our house going slower than normal. It was already dark out, and since I hadn't been home all day, there weren't any lights on outside. The thing about my father getting Taylor and me the townhouse was we both knew the units on either side of ours were occupied by his security teams. We weren't idiots; we knew if anyone found out who we were or who we were connected to, we'd have problems. So, this arrangement allowed us some semblance of normalcy while maintaining the image that we were just two regular girls going to college.

Not wanting to deal with whatever was happening with the slow-moving truck, I decided I'd risk the hoarder's nest of a garage. The truck that had gone past had just done a U-turn when I ran under the half-lifted garage door. I dodged two piles of magazines and a treadmill when I finally made it to the wall and slammed my hand down on the button to close the door. It was probably just a DoorDash delivery person looking for the right house, but it still freaked me out, and if anything nefarious were to happen, my dad would get his way and force Taylor and me back home, living with him.

Not many people knew who my dad was, nor did they know about Taylor's connection to him. It helped that I lived like a pauper, not landing on anyone's radar around school. So far, no one had connected me to the millionaire.

Letting out a sigh, I heaved my purse and bookbag into the small laundry space beside the garage door and toed off my shoes. I rarely got the house to myself, so the fact that it was still dark and there was no sign of Taylor had me nearly jumping for joy. How long would this last?

I started listing things I was going to do. Firstly, a bath with music… ooh, and candles. I started stripping. My socks came off first then I undid the button of my jeans, and just as I began jumping out of the left pant leg, the doorbell rang.

Fuck.

Suddenly, I remembered the truck, and the tiny hairs on my arms and neck stood on end. The house was still dark; maybe I didn't have to answer.

Another ring echoed throughout the house. Curiosity would hound me all fucking night if I didn't just see who was on the other side of that door. Suddenly, I knew why all those girls always died so fast in horror flicks. I knew, and still I walked to the door.

I flicked the porch light on and carefully cracked the entrance, hiding my body and the fact that I was currently pants-less. Eyebrows shooting up, eyes widening, I could do nothing at all to keep the shock off my face…because what the actual fuck?

"Hey…uh…" The man who'd kicked me out of his bedroom then scolded me about walking in the parking lot the other night had an expression that seemed to mirror my own.

His sexy smirk died quickly as he sized me up. My eyes hopefully shimmered with hate and not lust as I took in that sharp jawline, those high cheekbones, and those dark mossy eyes hidden under the bill of a dark Devils hat. Why did he have to look so good? How was that even remotely fair? My thoughts quickly sobered as he tipped his head just the slightest bit, and I noticed the way his eyes narrowed on me, as if I had yet again ruined something for him.

"What are you doing here...?" If his voice had been a whip, I'd have been on the floor bleeding. His eyes narrowed further, nearly slits as they moved to the emptiness behind me.

My heart sank into my chest, down, down, down. Why, for even one tiny second, had I thought he was here to see me? I hated that subconsciously I had tethered myself to the idea. He was an asshole, and I wasn't the type to cater to those...but there was something about him. Something about that night, the way he watched me before he touched me, like every place he pressed his fingers to was calculated and measured. The way his lips felt fevered on my skin, the way his tongue lavished me, like I was a delicacy...something sacred...

"Isn't this where Taylor Beck lives?" He stepped back a foot or two to catch the numbers on the side of the house. His words were a bucket of ice water, bringing me back into the moment.

Hurt slithered in between my ribs, stupidly...so, so stupidly.

"I...uh..." I cleared my throat, hating the burn behind my eyes. A whisper of lust brushed against my core, remembering those eyes that night...but it was all fake. All for Taylor.

"Why would I give you that information?" I crossed my arms, deciding we'd go a different route.

My heart thrashed to protect, protect, protect.

Elias looked behind him at the street, where his truck was parked. It was the same one he'd bent down to inspect that night in the parking lot, but I hadn't even noticed it when he drove down my road.

"Maybe I'll come back later."

His boot scuffed against the concrete near our welcome mat. His head dipped, but instead of turning around, he lingered.

"Why are you...what..." His questions died on his tongue as he slowly lifted those eyes. They stared at my pink toenails then slowly moseyed up my body like suddenly they'd grown phantom fingers, raking over my skin and hair like he wanted to touch me. I noticed his hands clench at his sides.

"What do you want with my stepsister?" I was tired of the questions, and I didn't want him to come back to ask them.

"Stepsister?" He choked on the word, running his left hand over the side of his face.

He had a day's worth of scruff on his jaw, more than the night his face had pressed against my skin.

"Yeah, what do you want with her?"

My heart thundered as I waited for him to confirm that he wanted to date her or fuck her.

"It's a business thing," he muttered, taking a step back.

Relief sailed through me. I tried to tamp it down because he still wanted her, not me, but I could still feel it billowing inside.

"Okay…well, I can tell you she doesn't *do* business unless it involves at least six digits. She avoids responsibility like the plague and will avoid you too, so good luck." I smiled and pushed the door, ready to close it in his face.

"Wait." His large palm pressed against the cute teal wood finish, his pinky grazing the obnoxious white wreath I knew had cost Taylor fifty dollars at some uppity home shop.

I paused, watching the bulge in his neck move up and down, his eyes assessing me with what seemed like caution…and maybe curiosity.

"I need a shot with her. I need…" He trailed off, his head dipping once more. "The other night, you seemed like you were looking for answers to something."

I lifted my left eyebrow. Was this Lady Luck finally throwing me a bone? I wasn't in the habit of denying bones, so I sagged back an inch, only to remember I wasn't wearing anything but a tank and a thong.

"I was…" I mumbled, trying to hide myself a bit better. The angle was wreaking havoc on my neck.

"I'm not going to hurt you. You can come out from behind the door," he suggested, softening his tone.

"Uh…no, it's not that. I just…what were you about to say?" I internally begged for him to say he'd be willing to spill all the secrets about the game. My stomach clenched with anticipation. *I'm so close.*

"Tell me why you won't open the door first." His mouth slung to the side in a mischievous smirk.

Red-faced, I lightly shook my head as my answer tumbled out. "I'm not exactly wearing pants."

A light scoffing sound left his chest as he dipped his head, and when his sharp gaze returned to mine, it was with a heated look that I refused to acknowledge. It was the same look he'd given me when he first saw me in his room that night.

"You do realize I had my face buried between your legs the other night, right? My fingers too…so I think it probably wouldn't be too crazy if I saw you without pants."

It was my turn to scoff and internally slap away the lust-soaked images he'd planted.

"That night was…well, let's just pretend it didn't happen, how about that? Now what were you saying about me wanting something and you needing a shot?"

The dip between his eyebrows made it seem an awful lot like I'd hurt his feelings, especially with the way his neck turned red, but maybe he was just ashamed of talking about being in between my thighs when he was here to ask about dating my stepsister.

"What if I offered you a trade?"

He'd hooked me. Locking my gaze with his, I carefully left the safety of the door and allowed it to open enough for him to enter. I walked a few steps away, fully aware that I was now flashing him my ass before dipping to grab a pair of sweats Juan had left in case of emergencies.

The man on my stoop walked in after me, shut the door, and then sat down on the nice lounger chair my dad had purchased. My thrift-store furniture was currently in the garage.

Clicking on a lamp, I sat across from him on the couch. I tucked my legs underneath me and hated how aware I was of my form. I had thighs, I had an ass, I had boobs. All of this anatomy often battled it out when I tried to tuck my body into the couch. More often than not, there was at least something protruding in an undignified way.

"Nice place." His elbows landed on his bent knees as his eyes searched the space, moving across the brick fireplace and settling on my borrowed sweats.

"Nothing less than the best for Taylor," I muttered quietly, immediately wincing at how immature it had sounded coming out. "Anyway, this deal…" I kicked out one of my legs, loathing how awkward this all felt. Plus, I wanted him to leave. A bath was calling my name, and who knew when Taylor might get home.

"My name is Decker James…not Elias Matthews. We should start there. I'll save you the long story, but Elias is really into Taylor, and I need her to be into me. I need a shot with her, a real one."

Well, that was unexpected.

"Wait…what?"

He let out a heavy sigh and dropped his head like it weighed a thousand pounds.

"It's a lon—"

"Yeah, long story—you don't need to tell me all that, but I want to be sure I understand. Are you only after my stepsister to get one up on this guy or something…or do you actually like her?"

He paused too long. The muscle in his jaw jumped while he kept his gaze downcast, toward the floor.

"It's complicated." He finally exhaled, looking up.

"Well, I'm not setting my stepsister up for some weird game or Devils bet situation, but if you like her for real then I'll help you."

He watched me, every second turning more and more intense. It was like I'd just turned him down or said no to something, and that was just strange. How hard was it to confirm that you actually cared about someone and wanted a real shot at having a date with them?

"Okay" was all he replied with. I resisted the urge to walk over and punch him in the arm.

"What's in it for me then?" I needed to stay focused on the idea that he'd serve up this story on a silver platter, regardless of the fact that I wanted to cry because he was here to get a shot with my stepsister, the girl who got every guy. Memories of my junior and senior years of high school came back like a punch to the throat. So many guys had pretended to get close to me, when in the end they either wanted my dad's money or my stepsister. *Never me.*

"Whose sweats are those?"

His right finger lifted just the smallest bit, pointing toward my legs.

I stared at him. He stared back. What in the hell was with this guy? He'd clammed up about Taylor but couldn't stop asking me weird questions.

"Why?"

"Because that emblem on the side…it's familiar."

I ran my finger gently over the stitched hornet that fell at the hip. I wasn't sure what the hornet situation was or what it meant to Juan, but I knew he was a sports guy and he had like five pairs of these sweats. He seemed to leave them everywhere. I knew Hillary had a pair at her house, maybe a pair in her car too.

I waited a few seconds to reply because I wanted to control the situation. This guy had been an ass to me both nights, and now he was here in my home, asking me about sweats when I had asked him point-blank about what was in our deal for me. I felt like he was toying with me, so I decided I'd toy right back.

"They belong to a guy." I leaned forward. "Now, what's in this for me?"

He looked like maybe he'd slammed his back molars down or ground them together. I couldn't figure him out. He seemed to be all over the place.

"I'll give you whatever answers you were trying to dig for that night." His eyes were still on my sweats until he finally flicked them up to my resting bitch face. My knuckles pressed into the side of my head as I relaxed against my fist.

"I want info on the card game…a lot of info."

His silky dark hair was covered by that hat, but I remembered how soft it felt, how good it felt under my fingers.

"I can answer anything about the Devils, whatever you want." He waved off the question, keeping his gaze lowered.

"And in exchange, I talk you up to Taylor…get you a date, or invite you over and see if she warms up to your charming personality?"

He laughed, his white teeth flashing, but he smothered it with his hand.

"Something like that. I want her to give me a real shot."

Painful heat seared my chest, but I ignored it.

"Deal." The sooner we were done with each other, the better. "The only condition I have is that you don't hurt her…physically or emotionally." I held up my finger toward his face like I was telling him off. "And don't fuck where I eat or sit."

He shuddered, his eyebrows drawing in tight. "Who the fuck does that?"

I smiled at him, standing and needing him out of my space so my stupid idiot heart would stop trying to convince all the other parts of my body that we liked him.

"Taylor does. Frequently." I leaned forward to open the door, despite the fact that he was still sitting. "I'll meet you tomorrow at the bookstore on Fifth. There's a small coffee shop inside."

Decker sat, watching me and waiting like he wanted to say something else.

"So, you'll meet with me, I'll give you info, and then we'll figure out a way for me to start hanging around Taylor?" he clarified. He still sat in the chair, his greenish eyes dancing with amusement.

I heaved a sigh.

"Yes. We meet first, let me get some notes on the game. We will probably only need to meet three or four times to get the information I need for my story…and at those meetings, we can schedule playdates for you and Taylor."

His eyes narrowed, those gorgeous lips pressing together in a way that told me he didn't like the term playdate being used. Whatever.

Finally, he stood and moved until he was towering over me. I could smell his spicy, woodsy cologne, and just like that night, I wanted it to wrap around me until I couldn't breathe.

"Guess I should know your name." He stepped out, only to turn and brace himself against the door with his left arm, giving me a sexy smirk.

Damn him.

I blinked, hating the magnetic pull I felt to this man who wanted my stepsister. I took a step back from him, and then another. Why was he being all sexy and charming with me when he wanted to bang Taylor? Maybe it was in my head…stupid fucking hormones.

"Mallory Shaw. Nice to officially meet you, Decker James. Looks like we're both big-ass liars."

I slammed the door in his face.

CHAPTER TWELVE

Decker

THE SUN WAS BOUNCING OFF THE ALUMINUM NAPKIN HOLDERS SET UP along each of the small tables inside the café. I looked around, taking in the shop. There was a glass case that doubled as a counter, and it was full of pastries. On the counter behind it was an espresso machine and a perky-looking high schooler making a latte.

I kicked my leg out in front of me, taking in the other side of the space. The checkered black and white tile started right as the laminate wood of the café stopped. Dark mahogany bookshelves lined the walls, with a myriad of spines and colors spread along the racks.

I was actually itching to go browse the selection and see what new books might be in. I was a closet book nerd, something I didn't share with many people, but the second a new Sanderson or Rothfuss novel was available, I was front and center for a copy. It was something my dad had made me do at a young age. He had started my love for reading by taking me to the library during story time then letting me get lost in stacks too mature for my age, letting me read things that would keep me up far past my bedtime, always sneaking me a flashlight to read by.

The front door of the bakery opened, a soft bell jingling as it swayed shut. Mallory's hair was the first thing I saw, its reddish brown coloring at odds with the golden sun snatching the highlights in her strands and broadcasting them to anyone who was watching. And I was watching. I couldn't stop.

Her unruly hair was braided into a crown on top of her head, taming some of her raw features, making her seem demure...sweet. It didn't fool me; I knew a tiger lay beneath her skin, something with teeth and claws. That beast didn't even compare to the one I had discovered that night in Elias's bedroom. The way she'd tugged at my hair and arched her back...the way she had cared that we stopped... I still didn't know if it was just the rebuff from someone on the Devils or if she'd actually felt anything when I put my hands on her body, but there had been something there when I pulled away and she realized we wouldn't go any further.

It was dangerous that I wanted to know. It was territory I needed to stay away from.

"Decker." Mallory gave me a thin smile while sliding into the spot across from me.

I gave her a genuine grin, unable to hold back. I liked seeing her in the daylight...I liked seeing her *period*.

"I've never been here before. It's a pretty cool place," I said, gesturing toward the bookstore at her back.

She didn't even turn to look, which made me curious about her reading habits. I liked girls who read. A silly, very stupid dream of mine was to wander around a bookstore, hand in the back pocket of the girl I was with, her nose in a book, her thumbs running over the ivory pages while I searched for a classic.

It was stupid.

"The bakery has amazing cinnamon rolls." She flicked those green eyes at me and gave me a real smile. It was reserved, maybe even a regret ...like it was something she hadn't meant to give away.

"Can I order you one, maybe a coffee?" I asked, weirdly hopeful that she'd accept the offer.

"No, I ate before I came." She didn't look up.

"Okay..."

"Let's get started." Her eyes stayed on the notebook in front of her, little strands of reddish-brown hair kissing her neck.

"What do you want to know?" I moved my hands until they were under the table; otherwise I was going to brush those stray strands away, force her to look up, and let me see those eyes.

"So, the games…when did they start? And this is all on the record, by the way." She looked up quickly with another tight smile.

"As far as we know, they've been going on for over fifty years, but there's not really any proof of that. Just old letters and newspaper clippings—gossip and whatnot."

"Okay, so how does it get passed to the next generation?" She pressed her pen to the corner of her mouth, and those green eyes locked on mine with such curiosity that I wanted to drag out my answer just to keep her looking at me like that.

"You saw underclassmen at the party, yes?"

She blinked and leaned forward. "Yes…so?"

"So, yeah. They deliver the cards, getting involved their first year, and then they participate their senior year and have already started the next graduating class on the game…and so it goes." I waved my hand in a forward motion.

The smell of cinnamon rolls permeated the air, and suddenly my stomach was screaming at me to try one. From the way Mallory's nostrils flared and those eyes roamed toward the glass case of goodies, I knew she wanted one too.

"Hang tight." I stood and jogged over to the counter.

I wished I knew how she took her coffee, but she'd have to settle for it black and the cinnamon roll. Once I paid, I took our coffees and the water bottle I had purchased for her and walked back to the table.

A small blush crept into her face as she gently took the water from me.

"You didn't have to do that." It was a tiny mumble quickly followed by her twisting the cap on the water and tossing her head back to take a drink.

I smiled. I didn't want to sit there and argue about me buying shit. She had seemed irritated enough when I was in her living room the night before. Thinking of it had me thinking about when she'd opened the door, that black thong running between her luscious ass cheeks. Then there were those hockey sweats she wore, which had me wondering if she was seeing someone. Or maybe it was casual...though the only reason someone would leave sweats behind was if they took them off pretty regularly, right?

She cut into my thoughts. "Okay, so it's passed down...is it like its own fraternity then? I've heard the baseball team all lives in that house, but I also know there's no official label for them."

I sipped the coffee, moving past the image of her with another guy, and instead thought of this deal we'd struck. I wished she would have considered who was offering the deal before agreeing. Beyond just finding her attractive, I actually liked this girl, and well...she deserved better than the terms I'd omitted from our deal.

"It's an unofficial fraternity that doesn't have to play by any rules, doesn't have to answer to anyone. They operate more as a secret society than anything, but there are members who don't live in that house. You don't know it because they like to make it seem like everyone is there, but not everyone agrees with what they do."

The high school girl walked over with a plate the size of my hand, a massive glazed cinnamon roll in the middle. My mouth watered.

"Here you go." She set it between us then dug in her apron for two forks like I had asked her to.

I grabbed mine and dug in. The first taste melted in a buttery sweetness that made me groan in utter satisfaction.

"Good, right?" Mallory smiled as she watched me. Her teeth dug into her bottom lip while her eyes danced with excitement, as if watching me taste this for the first time was the highlight of her entire day. It made something in my chest twitch.

"Share it with me." I ducked my head before pushing the plate toward her.

She blushed again. "No, it's okay."

"Come on, I know you want some." I took another bite, groaning obnoxiously loud.

"No...I'm trying to eat better, and that is definitely not better." Her eyes stayed pinned to the paper in front of her while her nostrils flared.

"Why? You're perfect...is it a medical thing?" I raised an eyebrow.

She had the most delicious curves I'd ever seen; there was no fucking way she wanted to lose any of that.

"Why are you being so nice to me?"

I paused mid-chew, watching her—unsure of what she was talking about. The expression I wore must have spoken for me, because she let out a small sigh before explaining.

"You were pretty mean the other night, kicking me out, telling me I ruined everything. Then the parking lot…"

Right, shit. I had been a bit of an asshole.

"I'm sorry about that…I guess I should have apologized for that last night." I felt my face heat like I was in middle school again.

"So why did you do it then?"

I tried to ignore how cute she was when her head tilted to the side like she was trying to figure me out.

"I was just mad…at the situation and the reason I was there. It's complicated, but it wasn't about you."

"I thought maybe it was something I did, or…just the way I didn't look like her."

I choked on the sweet, sticky dough in my throat. Was she serious?

"No, definitely not anything you did. I was…uh…" I rubbed the back of my neck. I knew I shouldn't say this, but… "I was definitely enjoying myself, but the questions you were asking tipped me off."

She brought her hands to her face and laughed. "I should have known."

I smiled, loving the shade of pink her face had turned. I briefly considered what it would take to make her do it again so I could sneak a picture. Would that be creepy? Probably.

"So, tell me why you don't want part of this delicious cinnamon roll."

"It's just…a personal thing." She tucked those loose strands behind her ears.

I chewed, watching her closely. I'd been in enough nutrition, sports medicine, and psych classes to know this was probably deeper than I even knew, and it was also her own shit to sort through. Not my business.

"The other night…was that your first time participating?" She meekly transitioned us back to the topic at hand.

I nearly choked again just thinking of her that night, those perfect tits fitting perfectly in the palm of my hand.

Fucking hell.

If I kept thinking about it, I was going to get more than a semi here in this little bookshop café.

"Yeah…it was." I let my eyes roam down her form, not hiding the fact that I liked what I was seeing.

Her green eyes, those freckles sprinkled under those dark lashes, and those full lips that were currently pinned between her white teeth all said she was remembering too.

"Was that your first time participating?" I returned the question, hoping like hell none of my teammates had ever had their hands on her.

She laughed and nodded her head. "Yeah, definitely."

"Why is it so shocking to ask if that was your first time?"

"You don't know me, but I'm not exactly the partying type. I'm usually working on the weekends, or writing for the paper, maybe reading…but parties? Not so much."

I fucking liked her. I liked her a lot. "So, you were only there for the article then?"

"Yep. I wasn't even invited, but…uh…you already knew that part." Her face flushed red again. "There were a few guys who seemed to play specific roles in the game—do you know about any of those?"

I wanted to press her about the topic we should have both been avoiding, but right as I was about to talk, the front door opened, and in walked Elias Matthews.

He was on the phone, that gleaming, brand new device shoved up against his face. His eyes flitted toward me, then to Mallory. They lingered on her, traveling down her form, over her hair and down her shirt while he talked to whoever it was on the other end of the call, then he smirked and walked past our booth.

"Who is that guy?" Mallory leaned forward, dipping her pointer finger into a glop of frosting that had fallen onto the plate. Her face was so much closer now that I almost met her halfway to taste that white sugar on her lips.

"Remember the guy I pretended to be?"

"Elias something?" she whispered, leaning closer.

"Yeah." I peeked over my shoulder, only to return to find her sucking more frosting from her finger.

"Sorry." She laughed, wiping at her face.

My jeans felt too tight as I watched her pink tongue dart out and lick the cream from her fingers. Her eyes closed as she let out a little moan, and two other guys sitting nearby turned to look at her. My hard-on pressed against my zipper, and I wanted to take her right there. But fuck, it was more than that...I also didn't want them looking at her or thinking about her. She was a vision in that green shirt she had on, the gold jewelry...and I just wanted to tell them they couldn't have her. No one could.

"Anyway, he's the head pitcher for the team...kind of a big deal according to anyone in the baseball world." I moved on from the frosting. I had to, or else I was going to lean over and do something I shouldn't.

"The competition," she murmured, writing something down in her journal.

I crinkled my eyebrows together in confusion. "What do you..."

"He wants Taylor, you want her..." She moved her hand, pointing the pen back and forth between E and myself. "He's your competition."

No, he wasn't. I didn't want whoever Taylor was. He could have her; I just wanted him to pay for ruining my career.

"Right...yeah." I cleared my throat and moved to stand.

I suddenly didn't want to be in the same room as Elias, especially not with the way Mallory kept glancing between where he was standing and where we were sitting. Did she think he was attractive? Most chicks did, but for some reason the idea of *her* thinking that way about him soured my stomach.

"We're just getting started...I..." She began to argue with her hands out and eyes wild, but I cut her off.

"We'll get together again soon. In the meantime, text me anything you think of for your article." I grabbed her pen from her hand and jotted down my number in her notebook, unsure why my stomach knotted at the idea of her having it...or if she'd use it.

Shit, this wasn't a good idea. If I knew what was good for me, I'd ditch this deal, come clean, and cut ties. But even as I walked away, there was a part of me that wanted to turn around and see if she was still there. A part of me wondered if she'd use the number I'd given her, and the other part wanted to ghost her. I didn't deserve someone like her. She seemed like someone good and full of dreams, someone happy and still untainted by life. Sometimes I wished I wasn't a devil, because she was the kind of girl who deserved someone who'd never put her through hell. With me it was practically a guarantee.

ｼ

"HOW IS YOUR DEVIOUS PLAN COMING ALONG?" MY KID BROTHER ASKED from his spot behind the lawnmower. I was impressed that he'd actually taken the initiative to cut the grass. Usually, he waited for me to come on the weekends to do it.

"Uh...I think there's some hope for it." I smiled, thinking of my meeting with Mallory. I refused to acknowledge that I was smiling because of her. It was merely her cooperation with my ridiculous plan that had me grinning like an idiot.

"Sweet. You know, we could totally nail him for some of the endorsement shit he's been accepting since he hasn't graduated yet." My brother wiped his face with the shirt he'd taken off an hour earlier and tucked it into his back pocket.

"Nah...not worth it. I don't want him to think we're onto him." Scotty had shared a piece of information with both of us regarding Elias and I was currently in the process of exploiting it, but if he looked in my direction at all, it would all be fucked.

Kyle sidled up to me, abandoning the yard. "I saw Elias driving out of the physical therapy office the other day."

I stopped with my hand on the engine, watching my brother, silently encouraging him to continue even if what he'd seen didn't exactly confirm anything.

"He's supposedly only seeing one here in Pinehurst...that way no one at RFU knows," Kyle continued, his hands tapping out a rhythm on the frame of the car. My little brother worried me just a little bit. He'd grieved our father's passing, but instead of leaning into the things he knew would make Dad proud, Kyle decided to dig into our Uncle Scotty's business dealings. I didn't have the time to go to school full time, work, attend shit for the team, and keep an eye on my little brother.

I shook my head back and forth. "Don't say anything—don't spread any rumors. It could be something completely unrelated."

"I wonder how his father feels about it." Kyle laughed, wiping his forehead with the grease rag I had used for the dipstick. I cringed, grabbing for it.

"Can you at least try to be aware of what you're doing and what's around you?"

His eyes danced with amusement. "I can't promise that, big bro."

I stuck my head under the hood, ignoring the tiny prick of pain in my chest. I knew he was running deals with Scotty. It would have been one thing if Scotty was some idiot, low-level runner, but he wasn't. Scotty worked for some big-shot boss out of New York and was in charge of lower-level deals down the east coast, but my little brother didn't need to be anywhere near that shit.

"So there's another rumor…and it kind of connects to your devious plan." Kyle leaned on his elbows while watching me work. The sun was high, forcing a sweltering kind of heat to swallow us up. I just wanted to be done and head back to school, but I'd promised Kyle I'd hang with him and my mom I'd fix her car for her.

"What's this one about?" I humored my baby brother.

"Elias Matthews is broke. His family is banking on him going big to get them out of some big financial trouble."

I looked up, trying to understand what my brother was putting together. "That's a problem."

"Indeed. I think we finally figured out why he made that deal…" Kyle gave me a knowing look before returning to his lawnmower. It left me considering a few different options. If money was the driving factor, it would make him more desperate.

Which would make it all the more imperative that I start dating Taylor Beck.

CHAPTER THIRTEEN

Mallory

THE SUN KEPT PEEKING THROUGH THE TREES AS I WALKED WITH JUAN and Hillary through campus. We were laughing about something Hillary had said—as per usual because she had no filter—so I didn't even realize we'd ventured toward the massive baseball field on the opposite side of the school. We never came this way, and since I had no classes until later that afternoon, I wasn't paying attention to where we wandered.

"Why are we here?" I felt like everyone on the team knew what I had done, especially seeing that little group meeting I witnessed at the bar and knowing it was Elias who'd been leading it. I was finally able to connect a few dots after my little café date with Decker. Not a date—it wasn't a date. I had to keep those thoughts categorized correctly, or else I'd get confused by his easy smiles and flirty behavior.

"Figured Hil and I could scope out this man who had his tongue down your throat the other night." Juan smiled brightly, his dark shades covering those whiskey eyes. I wanted to punch him, but I was also curious about the players on the team. It was about time I checked out their roster, see who played what…even though I had no idea what 'what' was.

I watched as a few players tossed the white ball from glove to glove.

"So turns out Elias wasn't who he said he was…that was just the name he gave me." We walked closer to the fence, still keeping close to the tree line so we had some coverage.

"Shit…then who was the one in the room with you?" Hillary asked, sipping her iced coffee. Her face pressed against the metal fence while we watched the players run and slide impressively fast to get to their next base.

"Decker James." I searched the names on the back of the jerseys within my scope of vision to see if I could find him. I should have known by how quiet my two best friends were that something was wrong. Sure enough, as I pulled away from the fence and took in their concerned faces, I saw they were looking at each other with reserved expressions.

"What?" My eyes bounced from my best friend's black-rimmed glasses and downcast brown eyes to Juan's colored lenses.

"You're positive it's Decker James? As in, a student here at RFU?" Juan clarified with an intensity that threw me for a loop.

Hillary looked up at Juan right as he looked down at her, and I knew, I just knew.

"He's not on the team, is he?"

"Well…he is, but I guess he's in more of a supportive role now," Hillary answered, her hands shifting nervously.

Juan shook his head back and forth like this conversation bothered him.

Hillary spoke up again, getting my attention. "I dated this guy last year who was on the team with him, and rumor is that Decker tried to nail Elias with one of his insane fastballs. I guess Elias was able to move in time, but they basically demoted him, took him off as starting pitcher, and removed him from the team house."

Juan's gaze stayed at our feet, that muscle in his jaw jumping every few seconds. I wondered why he was being so quiet, but Hillary sipped from her pink straw and spoke up again.

"I think he's dangerous, Mal…" She trailed off, casting her gaze out to the field.

My heartbeat sped, like a rally car that had gone off course then got a flat, and then the brakes went out. A shitshow—that was what was happening inside my chest.

Dangerous?

He didn't like Elias; that much I could tell from the conversations we'd had and the way he'd looked at the guy.

"Nah, he's not all that. He's in a class of mine…he's cool," Juan finally added softly. He barely looked up while his fingers dug into the metal near our faces. The journalist in me wanted to interrogate my best friend. There were things he wasn't saying, and he was acting weird.

"Juan, this is serious…you can't assess whether the man is safe or not based on if he shares his notes or not." Hillary shook her head back and forth. Leaning closer to me, she said, "Get this: I guess Elias wasn't the only one who got fucked up. They say the team started calling Decker 'Frankenstein' instead of his beloved nickname, 'Dugger.' I guess his hand got all jacked during a fight. Anyway, he has this grotesque scar running down the length of his hand and up his wrist." My friend's eyebrows waggled as she dished about this guy I had more than a little crush on.

I watched the field, trying to push away this feeling. They couldn't be right, the rumors. I'd seen the scar, but something told me it hadn't been from a fight. Just thinking about those hands made me feel an ache low in my belly. She had to be wrong, but then again…he did hate Elias with a crazy passion that didn't exactly seem healthy and was going after my stepsister, for something *complicated*…

"Girl, you dodged a bullet." Hillary sighed, and we started walking again.

I silently nodded my agreement, not sure how to break the news to my best friends that I had Frankenstein's number in my phone and it was burning a hole in my pocket.

⅁

"SHAW!" MY LAST NAME WAS BELLOWED THROUGH THE NEWSROOM, AND every head turned my way.

I clenched my fists, hating that my legs straightened even though my

98

mind was screaming at them to stay exactly where they were. Fuck this guy and his rude-ass way of communicating. We weren't dogs, coming when he commanded.

Still, I went, and I hated myself for it, but he held my future in those clammy, petite hands of his.

"Trevor." I took the seat in front of his desk, sliding my hands under my legs so I didn't wrap them around his neck.

"Where is your article?" His face was already two inches from his monitor, typing away.

"It's not due for another two weeks."

He made some sound in the back of his throat. "Your notes *are* due, so…" He turned toward me and crossed his arms like he was confident in my utter demise. "Where are they?"

Inhaling a shallow breath, I steadied my voice as I explained. "I'm not turning them in this week."

"Not acceptable, Shaw…you know that." He rolled his eyes, turning back toward his computer. "Even freshmen understand the logistics of being in this journalism course. Notes are always due at the end of the week, regardless of the deadline."

I loved how he constantly condescended to me regarding my position on the paper.

"I understand this, but I'm still not turning them in. I'm a senior reporter—I've earned a little bit of leeway. I have a really good story, Trevor. Trust me on this."

He scoffed. "Trust you?"

His chair swiveled in my direction. His greasy hair was tied back at his neck, and his eyes had dark circles under them. I already knew it was from a Dungeons and Dragons game that had gone too long the night prior.

"You totally bailed on the last story!"

I stood and hovered near his desk, wishing I didn't have this stupid proximity issue so I could get in his face. "You took that story from me! It was well written, informative, and delivered a fantastic punch, but you didn't run it. That was your choice. I'm not budging on this. If you don't want the story then I'll sell it. Either way"—I stood to my full height and turned on my heel—"I'm not turning in my fucking notes."

I walked away, ignoring him calling my name from his little office. People flicked their curious gazes my way before dropping them back to their desks. Trevor got off on causing drama in this stupid class, and he especially loved messing with me; I wouldn't give him the satisfaction today.

I held my chin high while I grabbed my things and left the room, heading straight for the student parking lot. I may have seemed confident in my departure and my defiance, but truthfully, I was just fucked.

I had no notes, not enough to write something worthy of being featured in the showcase. I'd only met with Decker that one time in the café, then I'd ignored the number he'd given me and hadn't called or texted him since hearing about his little rage problem.

I knew it sucked to judge someone based on a rumor, but could I really risk my or Taylor's safety on something like that? No, I couldn't.

Then again...Juan had said he was cool, and I had no story and really needed one. When I considered how many random guys Taylor let into our house, were we ever really safe? I mean, any of those guys could and probably did have hang-ups or issues...who was to say Decker would ever let those issues manifest around me or Taylor? If she wasn't even worried about her safety, I didn't need to make such a big deal about him coming over...right?

Right.

CHAPTER FOURTEEN

Mallory

I STUDIED THE BLUE INK FOR SIGNS OF DECEPTION. IT GAVE ME NO indication whatsoever on the true intent behind being given to me. Decker had said to use it if I had questions about the article, but I'd have been lying if I said I hadn't considered texting to ask about the rumors I'd heard. In fact, that first night after I heard about his nickname, I'd wanted to text and ask him about the whole thing. Surely there was another side to the story that I wasn't getting.

Then I realized how weird that would have come across and decided it was better if I just ignored him and let this crazy idea of the story and of him and Taylor go, especially if he wanted more revenge on poor Elias. Hadn't that guy gone through enough?

Then again...that was a rumor, and I didn't even know Decker.

The more I thought about it, the more I considered Decker's face when he realized I wasn't Taylor that first night. He had an axe to grind with Elias, and that had to come from somewhere...unless Decker was truly mentally unhinged. But, I'd been around him, and I hadn't caught any signs that he was on medication or struggling with his mental health. I wanted to give him a chance; he deserved to explain himself, and if he was telling the truth then I'd just feel like a bitch if I didn't at least give him that.

Letting out a heavy sigh, I turned over and pulled the pillow over my face. I'd been running through the little meeting I'd had with Decker all morning and was no closer to gleaning anything new whatsoever about the man. Sure, he had made it clear that he wanted a shot with Taylor, but he just didn't seem like her type. No, in fact, the other guy who'd walked in, Elias—he looked like the kind of guy she'd go for: tousled blond hair, creamy and freckled complexion, and well over the average height. That and the expensive-as-hell brands he was wearing— yeah, Taylor would definitely go for him.

With that on my mind, I crawled out of bed and headed for the living room. Taylor was thankfully already out there, and was she doing homework? I'd never seen her actually work on homework before, and I was tempted to pull out my phone and snap a picture.

"Hey." I walked to the sofa and sat down. The television pinged on after I grabbed for the remote. I flicked through channels as I waited for Taylor to reply. She never did, so I just kept going. "Are you going to be around for a little bit?" I asked, biting down on my nail. I was about as subtle as an elephant.

Taylor's head finally rose, her gaze finding mine. "I guess. Why?"

"No reason. I have this friend who was going to come over, but I wanted to be sure it was okay with you first." I clicked up a few more channels despite the fact that we only actually got about five.

I needed to turn on Netflix before she noticed I was acting weird.

"I can leave if you want," she offered in a cautious tone. She was always worried that I wouldn't want her there when my friends came over. The other day when Juan and Hillary had come over, it was only Juan who'd been able to convince her to watch a few episodes with us before she finally went to her room. It was progress.

"No, actually he asked if you'd be here. I think he might hate you or something." If I said he was into her, she'd run for the hills, but saying someone hated her always piqued her interest.

"Seriously?" Her laugh came out more like a snort, and I knew I'd won.

The first official playdate was on.

"Yeah, no idea why," I said, not looking her direction.

"Tell him to come over." She propped her elbows on either side of the chair, lifting her chin.

I pulled out my phone and ignored the tremble in my fingers as I pulled up his number.

Me: Hey, this is Mallory. Want to come over for your first official playdate?

I set the phone down, waiting, and thankfully only a few seconds went by before he responded.

Decker: Thought you were done talking to me.

Me: Why would you think that?

I felt guilty, and I hated feeling guilty. I owed him the chance to explain his side of the story…about a rumor I'd heard that might not even be close to true.

Decker: I never heard from you…I drove by your place a few times just to make sure you didn't move away.

Me, not Taylor. My heart did this little fluttery thing.

Me: I'm sorry about that, it was just a crazy week. But if you're available right now, I have her tame and in a good mood. By the way, she thinks you hate her, just roll with that.

My stomach was all nerves and knots waiting for him to finally text back.

But he didn't, and I made it through almost two episodes of *Schitt's Creek* before a knock sounded at the door.

I crawled out of the little nest of blankets I'd gathered and headed for the entrance. Taylor glanced at me cautiously, like a nervous animal.

Swinging open the door, I smiled at my guest and shoved down the part of me that appreciated how good Decker looked in a tight, navy blue tee, or how he looked with that matching Devils baseball hat on his dark, mussed hair. I definitely pushed down how badly I wanted him to show me his hand so I could run my finger down the length of his scar…or explain the rumors he didn't know I'd learned.

His eyes roamed, taking a slow route from my hair down to my toes. I hated when he looked at me like that because it made me feel like an electric current was running between us, like he was ready to eat me alive, all while his desired conquest was just feet from us.

"Hey, you made it," I chirped, shutting us in.

"Yeah…figured I would bring some chips." He stepped closer, handing me a bag of my favorite lime-flavored chips, and I almost launched myself at him. Taylor, however, scrunched her nose. *How did he know they're my favorite?*

"Boo. No alcohol?" Her pink, recently glossed lips pouted as she moved out of the chair.

"Decker, this is my stepsister, Taylor. Taylor, this is Decker, my friend." I watched him carefully, for some reason hoping he'd refute the friend thing and tell her I had somehow become the love of his life. Yeah, I knew I had a problem, and that thought just totally confirmed that I needed help.

"Nice to meet you, Taylor." Decker's lips quirked to the side like he had a secret. Her eyes lit up like she was already in on it. Was this flirting? It had been so long since anyone had done this with me, it was hard to actually recognize when it was happening.

"You're a pitcher for the Devils, right?" she asked, quirking a brow.

Decker's jaw twitched, his nostrils flaring before he gave her the slightest nod.

Taylor's cold demeanor snapped back into place as her gaze went to her phone, effectively ignoring us.

Decker watched her with his eyebrows caving, like he'd never gotten the brushoff once in his gorgeous life.

I cleared my throat.

"Decker and I were going to watch a movie…do you want to join us, Taylor?"

Her blue eyes flicked once to me, then to Decker. They weighed him, seeming to take in every detail: the corded muscle along his forearms, the dark swirls peeking out from the sleeves of his t-shirt, and probably the way his eyes seemed to glitter under the expensive recessed lighting my dad had put in. Was she seeing how beautiful he was? Did she catch the small wince that clouded his features when he flexed his left hand? My mind raced, panicked at the idea that she'd fall for Decker right here, right now…and then game over. I'd be out of a story source and well…no more Decker.

"I have homework, but I can watch whatever you decide. It won't bother me if you turn it on in here."

Then her gaze was back on her phone. I withheld a sigh. I had internally bet myself money on Taylor declining the movie and going back to her room, which would have totally messed this entire thing up for us.

Grabbing the bag of chips, I headed to the kitchen in search of a bowl. Decker followed on my heels, whispering under his breath as we both crouched down to dig through the lower cabinets.

"Is she always this closed off and cold?"

I nearly laughed. "Yes...unless of course you're famous or have a large bank account—then she's as warm as asphalt on a sunny day." I shouldn't have said that. What was wrong with me?

I looked up in time to see a line form between his eyebrows.

"I'm sorry, that was really rude of me. She does take some getting used to, but Taylor is used to hookups. As long as I have known her, she's never had a relationship. Maybe she wants you to work for it or something?"

"She probably knows about me." Those eyebrows stayed caved in, his lips thin and his jaw locked.

I wanted to prod, ask what she knew...what it was that everyone seemed to know that I didn't.

"Just be yourself. You're a good-looking guy who has a lot to offer. Your story will be so cute once you thaw through her icy exterior."

I stood, slamming the cupboard shut. I hated how weak the idea of him having a story with Taylor made me, how I didn't even know him, but because we'd had one stupid moment together, my damn mind and body had decided we had dibs, regardless of the fact that on the night in question of said dibs, he was busy trying to seduce someone he thought was Taylor. It was stupid—all of this was stupid.

Decker trailed after me, clearing his throat. I dumped the bag of chips in the bowl and headed for the couch. At least I'd get my favorite snack out of this ordeal.

"Uh..." Decker glanced at the spot next to me and at where Taylor sat in the chair.

Right, he'd want to sit next to her because he was trying to seduce her.

With my eyes I told him to just sit down and work his way up to sitting next to her. With his eyes he told me to make it happen. But I'd already made this night happen—he was in my living room, mere feet from my stepsister. This was as good as it was going to get.

I cleared my throat, narrowing my eyes, pressing my point without actually using words.

He finally gave in, letting out a sigh and throwing his back into the seat on the cushion farthest from me.

Fuck you too, buddy.

"What are you guys watching?" Taylor asked, sipping from her plastic tumbler. Lemon water from the looks of it—sometimes that was an entire meal for her.

"I don't know…what are you in the mood for?" I asked Decker.

His knee bounced while I began clicking through options on Netflix.

"How about that new horror movie…the one with the house and those kids?" Taylor asked, taking a loud sip. Suddenly she was invested in a movie that literally sounded like every horror movie I had ever seen.

"Do you know the name?"

"I know what she's talking about. It's…" Decker's body was suddenly next to mine, his hand grabbing for the remote. He smelled so good I wanted to groan.

One time I'd gone to some fancy cologne store with Juan, helping him look for something new. We sprayed all these little cards, trying to find the right scent for him. I ended up inhaling so much my nose hurt, but now, here smelling Decker, it felt like I'd finally found that perfect aroma, and I wanted to plaster my face to his neck and breathe him in.

Instead I pulled away from him, yelling, "No grabbing!"

"It's just easier to find it than to try to tell you…you're going to get irritated." His strong, very defined arm was nearly across my folded legs, his eyes set in a stern manor, like I was being ridiculous.

I held the remote higher because pride is a fickle beast, one that kept me company more often than I cared to admit, but at least it was consistent and loyal.

"Seriously?"

"It's my house—you can't have the remote!" I shrieked as he reached up, but my resistance only made him more determined.

Suddenly he launched himself toward me, covering my legs and half my body with his as his long arm reached up and snagged the prize.

"Ha!" He settled back into the couch, but this time he was in the space right next to me.

My heart was thundering in my chest like an eighth grader who'd just been touched by her crush. His body heat was so close it warmed up my feet, which were basically touching his hip now from how they were curled behind me.

He clicked over a few titles until he found what he was looking for, Taylor confirming the choice and setting her laptop aside as soon as he pressed play. I personally wasn't a fan of horror movies as they usually made me want to pee my pants, but I was here as the awkward chaperone to these two, so...

I tugged my phone out, trying to ignore the music in the movie, the scary images, and the dreary overall vibe in the room. The lights had been dimmed at some point, probably by Taylor, who was sitting next to the switch on the wall. She was huddled under the covers in her chair, but knowing her, she would likely find a way to crawl into Decker's lap at any moment.

Movement by my feet had me looking over my shoulder. Decker's hand was in the bowl of chips, the glow of the television highlighting his corded arm. My eyes wandered up his body, taking in the way his jaw moved as he chewed, his eyes on the movie. A flutter erupted in my stomach as I watched him, taking in how good he looked sitting next to me with the lights out and the television on. I briefly considered what this would feel like if I were turned, my body curled into his, my hand in that bowl with his because lime chips were the best thing ever invented. Suddenly, I realized he was essentially eating them all. I gave my head a brief shake to clear away the images I should never have allowed to take root and went after him.

"Hey! Don't eat them all!" I dove over his lap toward them, not caring at all that I was being awkward, or that it would likely look like we were flirting with each other. Then again, I acted this way with Juan whenever he was over. Taylor probably thought Decker was just another one of my buddies.

"Share!" Decker's mouth was full as he pulled the bowl away from his chest, trying to block me.

"How can you eat that garbage?" Taylor glared from her spot in the recliner, eyeing us like we were deranged.

Decker froze, his face popping up, those eyebrows arched high on his forehead. He seemed like he wanted to say something, but instead he released the bowl and handed it over to me.

For some reason, the victory felt more like defeat. I liked flirting with Decker, having fun with him, fighting over something stupid like chips. I didn't like the rogue emotions he kept stirring in me, and all because we'd had some chemistry when his face was between my legs. It was bullshit, just my desperate need to get laid.

So, I switched things up.

"Tay, can you swap me places? The light from the television is giving me a headache."

"You should just go to bed—I know you hate horror movies. I can see your friend out when it's over," she offered sweetly, adjusting the blanket on her lap.

That was exactly what Decker wanted, so I stood and smiled at her, and when I looked at Decker, the expression on his face was odd. I couldn't decipher it. This would let him get closer to her; this was his plan, and I knew my stepsister would be moving closer to him. Even if she didn't like him, she'd probably try to sleep with him. I didn't judge; she had a healthy and vibrant sex life, so I would just let them get to it. Still, something in me shriveled up and died just thinking about it.

"Night, Decker…I'll see you around."

His jaw tensed, those viridescent eyes locked on mine. He looked angry, like he'd just lost an all-in bet at a poker table or something… whatever. He was probably hoping I would stay and talk him up or try to get the two of them to hang out. He could do all that on his own.

I didn't wait for him to respond as I walked down the hall, and just before I opened my door, I looked over my shoulder to see Taylor move from the chair and claim my spot on the couch.

CHAPTER FIFTEEN

Decker

I WAS RUNNING LATE FOR ONE OF MY CLASSES, WHICH WASN'T EXACTLY new for me, but noticing the dark red-haired journalism student typing away in the newspaper class was. I must have walked past this room a thousand times, but I had never really looked inside...or if I had, I hadn't seen her. I would have remembered. There was something about that wild hair and those green eyes that would have stopped me or made me walk in and ask her out.

The memory of what she had done two nights earlier, leaving me alone with her stepsister, sat with me wrong, like warm milk on a sunny day. I knew why she had done it, but still...there was something wrong about being with Taylor without Mallory present. I understood how messed up that was, especially because this entire situation was my fault and my creation...but that didn't mean I liked it.

I stared at Mallory as she focused on her computer screen, and then I glanced around for any faculty that might be near.

"Psst," I hissed, hanging halfway in through the doorway.

Mallory didn't look up from her computer. A few other students did though, each of them giving me an odd look before looking back toward a small cubicle room. There was a shaggy-haired kid sitting inside, all glass windows, with his door open. He must have been the editor or something.

"Pssst. Mallory Shaw," I whispered again, tossing a pencil at her. The object hit her screen and bounced off, rolling to the ground by her feet.

Her head swung in my direction, her face slack with confusion. I smiled at how unaware she seemed and how surprised she was.

Pinching her eyebrows together, she glanced back at the little cubicle room before glancing my way once more. I waved my hand, indicating I wanted her to follow me out of the classroom. She looked around once more before standing up and following me out.

The hall was mostly empty, most people in class or about to get there. Mallory must have been an overachiever if she was already sitting down at her desk and writing. I stopped a few feet away from the door and slouched against the wall.

"Hey."

She looked down the hall and crossed her arms. "Hey."

I smiled, liking her feistiness. "What are you doing?"

"What did it look like I was doing?" she volleyed back.

Such a smart mouth. If she had been my girl, I'd have grabbed her wrist and tugged her into a secluded alcove or bathroom then shoved my hand up her white shirt and pinched her nipple. Even now, I could see the outline of her blue bra under the two tanks she wore, one slightly bigger than the other. She had this little gold necklace that looked so fucking good against her tanned skin, and I wanted to run my fingers under it.

"It looked like you were entering launch codes to destroy the male population," I joked back, feeling a smile creep up my face. I didn't usually smile. It helped with the rumors circling about me, that I was an angry freak. I slightly wondered if Mallory had heard them yet. The way she snuck glances at my hand told me she had, but she was too nice to me for me to get a clear reading.

She rolled her eyes and let out a heavy sigh. "I was writing up a few notes for my article."

"Ah, right." Now I felt like a moron—of course that was what she was obviously doing in her journalism class.

"What are *you* doing?" With her arms still crossed, she leaned forward, bumping my arm with hers. The action took me by surprise, because my scarred hand was wrapped around my elbow, so when she bumped me, it took me right back to that night in Elias's room when she gripped my wrist, her finger running down the length of my scar. It sent a rush of heat through my chest not having her recoil or act afraid of me.

"Going to class, but I know I owe you a meeting." I ran my hand through my hair, wondering what in the hell I was about to offer and why. These meetings were a waste of time considering she wouldn't be allowed to print a single word. Still, we had a deal, and it wasn't like it was a hardship to be around her. There were a million little warning flags waving in my head, telling me not to do this, but I did anyway. "I usually head to my mom's house once a week to help her out...I know you don't know me very well, but it's a bit of a drive, so it would give us a ton of time to talk."

Her eyes went wide at my offer, so I quickly made sure I fixed it.

"Talk about the game...for your notes." I gestured back toward her class for emphasis she didn't need.

I was an idiot.

She ducked her head, tucking a few strands of unruly hair behind her ears. "Um...okay, yeah. When are you leaving?" Those green irises popped back up, searching my face. God, this would have been so much easier if she didn't look like she did. She had all these little things about her that I wanted to ask her about. Like, why three piercings on her left ear but only one on her right? Did she have a belly button piercing? What did the circular tattoo under her ear mean? It looked cool as hell, but there were all these little pieces to the circle that made me look every time I saw her. I was way too fucking curious about this chick, which wasn't good.

"Uh...after a short shift this afternoon at Geno's, I'll head home, grab a shower, and then head out. I can pick you up." I was officially late for class now; Juan was probably shaking his head, thinking I'd ditched again.

"I can meet you in your apartment complex parking lot...I have to head over there anyway to grab something from my friend's house."

"Okay, then I'll see you later." I smiled at her, withholding the itch to run my fingers across her collarbone. It was so rigid against her necklace, and the way her hair brushed against that indented space was fucking ridiculous. How could something so simple be so hot?

"Okay, see you then." She returned the smile and sauntered toward her class. Did she always swing her hips like that? Her ass looked amazing in those jeans, and that tank top…it rode up just enough to show off the slightest hint of skin along her back. I nearly groaned once she was inside, but instead I turned on my heel and ran toward my class.

𝔻

WORK TOOK FOREVER TO FINISH. MAYBE IT WAS BECAUSE I'D OPTED TO help Geno with his new remodel of the back-bar area, but I couldn't seem to get out of there fast enough. Sweaty and covered in drywall, I drove straight home to shower, rushing through every swipe of soap and scrub of my hair.

I kept telling myself to slow the fuck down, it didn't matter…but for whatever reason, my body knew it was going to be seeing Mallory Shaw and didn't want to waste any time in getting to her. Logically, it was the absolute most idiotic thing I could do, especially since I was trying to seduce her stepsister…but I couldn't quite get my mind and my dick to come to terms on that entire situation.

I dressed quickly, grabbed my bag and laptop, and headed down to my truck. Mallory was already resting against the back taillight, her arms crossed over her chest and a pair of sunglasses perched on her face. I glanced around, trying to figure out where she'd come from. She had said she had a friend who lived here, but was it a male or a female? Was it the same friend's house she'd left at two in the morning the week before?

"Hey." I winced. Fuck the sun was bright today. I needed my sunglasses.

"Hey." She gave me a small wave, leaning away from the truck. Her demeanor was more reserved than it had seemed that morning in the hall, like she'd had time to reconsider this whole thing and now might back out. My stomach felt like it was filling with lead at the idea of her telling me she couldn't go.

"You been waiting long?" I gripped the strap of my backpack and opened the back door to my truck.

She angled her body to the side and swung her arm toward the apartments at our backs. "No, my friend lives over there. I took a nap, ate some lunch, and even cleaned his fridge out..." She ducked her head, laughing. "Sorry, when I say it like that, it does sound like I was waiting. I don't often get spaces to myself since I live with Taylor, so when my friend is gone and I can hang by myself, I go a little crazy."

I smiled at her, wishing I knew who this friend was, because my mind had locked on to the term *his* and now it wouldn't let it go. I didn't need to be territorial when it came to her. I didn't need to do anything but let her set up more time between Taylor and me...

Still, I couldn't help myself.

"Since you're here...do you want to see my place, so if you ever have an issue and your friend isn't home, you can knock on my door?" *Real smooth, Duggar. Really fucking smooth.*

I almost couldn't face her from how mortified I felt, but thankfully she took mercy on me with a little smile and held her hand out. "Lead the way."

So I did. I walked with her next to me, not really needing to show this girl my space but still wanting her to know where I lived in case she ever needed me.

We jogged up the stairs and stopped in front of the door.

"You're in C block?" She laughed, the sound warm like a little ray of sunshine at my side. I wrinkled my eyebrows, bringing my key out.

"C block?"

"It's an inside joke with my friend..." She shrugged then followed me inside. It was modest and humble, nothing fancy or very nice. Every dollar I earned, I shoved toward my mom's house. I couldn't even remember the last time I had purchased something for the apartment.

"My roommate Marcus is usually here too...but yeah, this is my place." Why was this so fucking awkward? Why had I assumed she'd want to see where I lived?

She walked ahead of me, looking up and around, her pink lips drawing to the side in a sly smirk as she picked up a framed photo of me and my kid brother. "I like it."

"It works for now." I shrugged, feeling my neck grow hot. Having her eyes on my space was like opening my head and telling her she could stroll through. *Don't mind the secret doors all locked up; I'll open those suckers right up for you.*

"Yeah, I get that. I think about what it will be like when I have my own place, what it will look like…if it will feel different once I'm done with school and out there on my own." Her wistful look made something in my chest ache.

I wanted to engage in this conversation with her, but it was hitting on far too many triggers for me. Once upon a time, I'd dreamt of a life like that, of what my future would hold…the excitement of the unknown. Now, I just worried about my mom and little brother making it.

"We should head out…it's going to take a bit to get there." I held the front door open for her.

She set the framed photo down and followed me out.

CHAPTER SIXTEEN

Decker

"WHERE ARE WE HEADED?" MALLORY ASKED FROM THE PASSENGER SEAT.

She smelled like almonds and cherries. It made me remember her smell from that night, and her taste…she had tasted just as good as she smelled.

Clearing my throat, I pulled away from the curb. "Pinehurst."

I saw her head turned in my peripheral vision. I imagined how gorgeous those red strands of her hair looked glowing in the sunlight pouring through the windshield.

"Your mom lives in Pinehurst?"

I glanced over, one hand on the wheel while I maneuvered us out of the complex.

"Yeah, my little brother lives there with her."

"That's like a three-hour drive or something, right?"

Had I forgotten to mention that it would be three hours there and three back? I had said it was a ways out of town, right? What did it mean that I didn't feel the slightest bit bad about having her to myself for a six-hour period today?

"Yeah…" I cleared my throat, my hand hovering the blinker signal. "You probably don't want to spend the entire day doing this."

My hand pushed down, signaling that I needed to turn just as her soft voice piped up.

"No...it's okay, actually. I don't have anything planned today, just some homework and catching up with my friends, but that all can wait. I really need to get started on this piece, so I'll go."

I slowly let the air out of my chest as some kind of weird sensation filled its place.

Guilt.

Hope.

"Cool." Like hell I'd tell her I was glad for the company, or that she was wasting her time with me. Once she hit submit on that article, it would be flagged, and the team's lawyers would get involved.

"Okay, well I can ask these while we drive then work on my laptop while you help her out, I guess." She sounded contemplative, like she was trying to figure out where she fit into this plan and why I had asked her along.

Of course, I didn't actually know the answer to that. I shouldn't have asked her, but for some reason I wanted to see her, and if this was the only way...well, then this was it.

"So tell me about the involvement of the other players. Walk me through when and how you knew about the card game based on your own experience on the team."

I smiled, turning toward her, then focused on the road. I liked her journalist face, how her dark brows dipped toward the center of her forehead and her eyes narrowed, the side of her lip hitched. It made me want to ask her questions or draw my answers out just so I could keep that expression on her face.

"You know how most fraternities have rush week, where they let new pledges see behind the curtain a bit, then there's the pledging?"

"Yeah." She wrote down a few things in her notebook.

"Well, we basically throw a huge party, a massive rager, but the only people invited are the ones who are current team members, or previously graduated team members. No one from the outside. This is absolute law." I looked over again, finding her furiously writing. "Do you want to record what I'm saying or anything?"

She let out a small laugh and dug for her phone. "I have no idea why I am so off when I'm around you. That was a rookie move." She shook her head while sliding her thumb across the screen of her phone.

"Off? You mean how you ditched me the other night out of nowhere?" I made sure my tone was teasing, but in all honesty, I wanted to know why she'd left. I hated how it'd felt, especially after it seemed so cool between us before that.

"It worked out for you, didn't it? I saw Taylor take my spot as soon as I left. Besides, you got all weird when she called us out for fighting over the chips. I obviously made you uncomfortable."

I laughed. *This fucking chick.*

"Uncomfortable? No...far from it, I was actually about to..." Shit, it wasn't like I could tell her I had been about to put Taylor in her place or trash her for not loving the best kind of tortilla chip ever invented.

"About to what?"

I looked over, caught that verdant gaze, and let out a sigh. *Maybe I should just come clean...*"I was about to make fun of her for not liking lime-flavored chips, that's all."

"Hmmm, right." Mallory turned to look out the window, and the fact that she didn't seem to believe me just rubbed me wrong.

"You don't believe I would have said anything to her?"

A heavy sigh and she was back looking my way. "I saw the way you two looked when I went into my room. Say whatever you want, but I know guys like you. You may say you want her to eat like a dude and be chill, but you'll never complain as long she's rocking that tiny waist."

Wow. Just...fucking wow.

I didn't respond to her comment because I wasn't even sure what to say. She'd judged me so easily, thinking she knew me, but she didn't. I hated the strange feeling it stirred in me...and maybe if I spoke and eased the tension in the truck, it wouldn't feel so personal.

"I don't know what you saw the other night, but Taylor stayed on her phone through the movie. I even tried to talk to her a few times, but she didn't seem interested at all. I have no idea what I did wrong or if she just doesn't like guys like me, but nothing happened."

I looked over toward her side of the truck, but she wasn't watching me. I wished I could have seen her face, seen if her eyes went wide when she heard that, or if she even cared. I hated that I wanted her to.

"As far as your comment regarding her waist size…well, no offense, but fuck that. Not all guys are the same, and not all guys have the same taste in women."

It was silent for a few miles, until her small breath filled the cab and I heard a soft apology. It was sweet, sincere, but I knew it was hard for her just the same. There was more we both wanted to say; I knew that much. I knew if we didn't have to talk shop, we'd fill the silence with why each of us cared about that night and how it ended, but we didn't.

"How does Elias fit into all this?" she suddenly asked.

I waited, unsure I wanted to venture into this territory yet. I fucking hated him, but I didn't want to explain his role in the game, or how I knew so much about him.

"Elias is the captain of the Devils. He is aware of the games, picks the dates for them and helps configure who gets what base based on the bid the player puts in…but it's rare for him to participate. He was scouted early in college, and because of that he's actually pretty careful about hooking up with girls. He's too worried about attracting a jersey chaser, someone looking to poke a hole in the condom."

It was quiet for a few moments while she jotted a few notes down in her notebook. Every now and then she'd pause and scratch her eyebrow with the cap of the pen.

"Have you participated?" she asked, and I caught sight of her reddening face before she added, "I mean besides with me, have you at least gone and partied, maybe not picked a girl but partied with them?"

I lightly pressed my foot to the brake, getting ready to verge off the freeway, considering for a second all the rejection I felt layered on my shoulders from the past year or so.

"I hang at the house when I need to, but I don't go to the parties anymore. I used to though."

"Why don't you go anymore? I thought it was an honor or something for the team." Her curiosity was genuine and showed that she hadn't heard my story or even dug around enough to know what position I had previously played on the Devils. That both intrigued and pained me.

"When I was a freshman and a sophomore, I enjoyed the parties because I helped deliver the cards. I also helped with the names…most of the players don't know who was picked, just as much as the girl doesn't know who's waiting in that room. There's a roster of girls they pick from, then the lowerclassmen decide the rest."

"That's horrible. There are just so many layers to this that would eventually blow up." Mal brought her hands to her face and shook her head.

"Keep in mind, these are girls who have filled out a form saying they'd one day like to be selected. They're asked to select what base number they're comfortable with and if they have any previous negative experiences with anyone on the team."

"Well I guess that's something." She returned to her notebook, bending over it to scribble more notes.

Trees passed by as we made our way toward my home. The closer we got, the more nervous I became. She would meet Kyle…my mom if she was home. She'd see my childhood home.

"So, can I ask what's in it for the team members?"

I turned to catch the expression on her face, feeling my walls go up.

"Why do you follow the rules, live in the house…play the card game? Surely this isn't how normal teams function."

She wasn't wrong, considering the team acted more like a secret society than anything else, but this was something outsiders didn't know about.

I gripped the wheel, locking my jaw.

"Sorry, that was probably a question that is too personal." Mal crossed something out on her notepad.

"No." Fuck, was I really about to say this? "It's just that the team… once you're accepted, there's a certain amount of protection you have as a member. They may treat you like shit or even stab you in the back, but if you need anything, they'll do it, for the rest of your life. A loan on a house, a job—whatever you need, they'll do it. You're essentially getting inducted into a brotherhood."

I wanted to look over, see if she had the pinched look or if she was glaring. Did it make me a coward to be so loyal to a team that likely knew about Elias's plan to kill my chances at going pro? Maybe, but no matter how hard I dug, there was never any proof I could find.

I could tell she wanted to ask more, but she moved on to her next question with the grace and fluidity of a seasoned reporter. I felt relaxed and comfortable talking with her as long as it didn't revolve around my relationship with E, or my major downfall from the team.

♂

WE PASSED THE CITY LIMITS OF MY HOMETOWN, SLOWING TO NEARLY twenty miles per hour. It gave the reporter next to me plenty of time to gather all the details she wanted. Old brick buildings lined either side of the white sidewalks. Flower baskets hung every few feet, providing bursts of color, and tourists were mingling and shuffling in and out of storefronts.

"Cute town."

I nodded then rolled our windows down so we could hear the chatter, feel the cool breeze that came off the nearby river. There was some kind of banjo and guitar medley making its way through the streets, likely coming from one of the nicer restaurants down the way. They often had live music throughout the day as long as it wasn't raining.

"I can't believe I've never been here before." Her face was turned toward the town outside her window.

"Where are you from?" I slowed for a few tourists passing the crosswalk.

"Greensboro, actually...not too far from here. Back when it was just my dad and me, we used to travel to all the local places we could find. He could never afford much time off work or a big trip, so we'd stay close." She straightened, turning toward me. Her eyes were bright as she remembered her younger years. The way her white teeth flashed and that nose crinkled...

Fuck.

"I remember this one trip...I was eleven, I think. He was trying extra hard to lift my spirits because some girls had been making fun of the fact that my mom died. Kids are cruel—don't ever let anyone tell you differently. Anyway..." She waved her hand and pushed some of that unruly hair behind her ears. "He was trying hard to make the weekend something that would take my mind off school. He must have traded work or something because the next day, he drove us hours away

—it was the first time we'd ever gone that far—and we ended up going near some mountains. I wish I remembered where, but there was this cabin...the outside looked like a fairy tale with these lights strung up everywhere. It was small, only two twin-sized beds and a wood stove inside, but the river behind it was magical. We spent the entire weekend fishing and hiking, and at night, he'd act out parts of my favorite Disney movies. We'd eat Pop-Tarts in the morning, and he let me have as many smores as I wanted."

I laughed softly, imagining a smaller version of Mallory smiling up at the night sky, those lights strung up and her dad making her smile. It made my chest ache. My dad had been like that too. He was good to us kids, always making memories that would haunt us for all of time.

"So, are you and your dad still close like that? He sounds pretty cool." I flicked the turn signal and stopped at a red light. We were almost to my mom's, and I wanted just a little more time with this girl who was starting to make me feel things I never thought I'd feel.

Her heavy sigh made my gut sink.

"No. He ended up patenting some technology used in mechanic shops all around the world. I don't fully understand it, but it's like one of those scanners you plug into your car to figure out what's wrong... well, my dad created a different version that takes it further, explaining what parts you'll need and then finding local stores who have the parts in stock. It does other things too, can read machines other than just cars—this thing can read aircraft parts, household appliances, even NASA has started using it. It's revolutionized the industry...or so they say," she added wistfully, turning her head toward the retreating town.

My mind was spinning. I knew what she was talking about...my dad had ranted about the new technology that had come out a few years before he passed, saying it had changed everything for anyone trying to save a dollar or two on fixing their car.

"Your dad is Charles Shaw?"

Holy shit.

I knew her dad was rich, a big deal...but I hadn't connected the dots.

Another sigh left her chest. "Yeah...but he used to be just Charlie, back before he'd made his millions. I guess it's probably billions now, but I try not to check."

"So, the stepsister…" I edged because it was starting to come together for me. Taylor and Mallory were night-and-day different. Mallory had work ethic, she wore non-designer clothes, her car was older…and Taylor seemed completely opposite. It was why I hadn't been eager to fuck her when I read her file about how shallow she was, back when I thought *she* was her sister.

"Dad met Jackie when I was fifteen. She and Taylor were like tornados in our lives, and I often felt like Cinderella, except Taylor wasn't always horrible—she had a really messed up childhood. She did try, and through the years, she's gotten so much better. But…the money changed everything for us. Suddenly Dad and I went from eating McDonald's on our splurge nights to paying a hundred and fifty dollars a plate in restaurants too glitzy and glamorous for my ripped jeans and Converse. I never grew out of that phase we'd started before he made his money, but Taylor grew with it…she was the easier daughter to show off when investors came to town or when people wanted his family at black-tie events. The older I got, the more I hated that world. Taylor fit within it perfectly, and well…Dad does now too."

This was…not what I had expected at all.

"That's really shitty. I'm sorry you lost your pops." And for whatever reason, I reached over and tugged her hand into mine, squeezing it tight because I'd lost my dad too and I knew how painful that was. Even if hers was alive and well, the version she'd grown up with had died when he made his money. It was when she squeezed back that I knew this wasn't going to be easy. I was going to have to walk away from Mallory once I got my revenge on Elias, because there was no way she'd give me a shot after I slept with her stepsister. Maybe it made me a prick for wanting to eat my cake and have it too…but fuck.

CHAPTER SEVENTEEN

Mallory

I slammed the truck door shut, peering up at the two-story farmhouse-style home. It was weathered with its faded white paint and chipped splotches along the window panes. Flower boxes hung in front of the three lower windows, but there was nothing but dirt and a few old weeds inside each one.

Gravel crunched under my shoes as I followed Decker toward the house. The silence around us was heavy and it almost felt...like death. Like something here had died and now it was just a mausoleum.

"D!" a loud voice boomed from one of the top windows.

I looked up, but with the screen in place, I couldn't see anything.

Decker just smiled and kept moving forward, pulling the screen door open and holding it for me.

"I'm glad you agreed to take a break from being Nancy Drew for a bit." Decker smiled at me as I passed by him into the foyer of his childhood home...at least, I was assuming this was his childhood home. The way he looked at it with such reluctance and affection, it seemed there were memories here that were precious to him.

"Yeah, me too. I'd like to help you, if you want, or I could just hang out. I think a mental break would be good for me though."

The small entryway was barely a square of linoleum with a braided rug thrown down. A pair of soft blue shoes were neatly sitting by the door, and that was it. No jackets or other shoes, no coat rack. A foot off to the side looked like the start of a staircase covered in worn, brown carpet.

It smelled like old leather, vanilla, and...hairspray.

"Come on, I want you to meet my—"

"D! I didn't think you'd be here this weekend. Can you give me a ride to the country club?" a tall, younger version of Decker came jogging down the stairs. He was the kid in the framed photo I saw in Decker's apartment. His eyes lit up when he saw me standing there, a smile erupting on his face as he closed the distance between his perch on the stairs and the last step.

"Kyle, this is Mallory. Mallory, this is Kyle, my younger brother."

"Hey." Kyle ran his hand over his head, giving me a sexy smirk.

Oh gosh. This kid was cute.

Sixteen-year-old me was totally screaming inside at how adorable he was being.

"Is this the one...you know, the one you mentioned?" Kyle asked, and I tried not to spin toward Decker to see his expression. The strangled coughing sound from the chest at my back told me enough.

"Why do you need to go to the club?" Decker changed the subject and moved us farther into the house. His hand landed on my hip, pushing me forward.

There was an older blue couch that framed the room and two recliners facing the flat screen along the adjacent wall. It was comfortable; it felt like a home, and all I wanted to do was curl up under one of the throw blankets and take a nap.

"It's this thing...complicated, but there's a lot of money to be made. Just trust me." Kyle pleaded with Decker while the two went into the kitchen. There was a counter separating the space from the dining room, a small island in the middle, and a big bright window that faced the backyard. I instantly loved it.

Walking toward the large glass doors along the back wall, I saw the yard, and my mouth gaped. Directly outside the French doors was a paved patio with hanging lights that draped over a small table and four chairs. Beyond that was rich green grass, running for what seemed like half a mile. It butted up against a stone retaining wall. To the side was a patch of gravel in the shape of a circle with a charcoal pit in the center, low Adirondack chairs littered around the white rocks, a few with throw blankets on them. An old swing set sat forgotten along the back side of the house, along with a few other old toys. I could see a few bats, a few baseballs, and even a few weather-worn gloves.

"Geez," I murmured, my breath fogging up the window.

The boys in the kitchen went silent.

Suddenly there was a throat clearing behind me, a warm presence at my back. "Our dad had a landscaping business...before..." He cleared his throat again like he was trying to force the words out.

A bone-deep awareness skittered down my spine. It was like a third eye blinking open and being able to see what my natural eyes could not: the silent but gaping wound of grief. Decker was bleeding out from it. His dad was gone, like my mom was...like my dad now was.

On instinct, I reached back, grabbed his hand like he'd done with me in the truck, and squeezed. He didn't need to say it out loud. Sometimes confessing that a parent is gone is like admitting that one is alone. It was just easier not to say it out loud, not to give words to that piece of us that was now missing and that we'd never get back.

Decker squeezed back, and then he tugged me until I left the window, the sight of his father's legacy behind and turned back toward the living room. There, a frail woman had materialized. She had light brown hair with a wisp of grey, and her pale face was beautiful, her green eyes even lighter than Decker's, about the same shade as her younger son's.

"Hello." The woman smiled at me, and her eyes bounced over to her son, who was standing next to me...and who was still holding my hand. I let him go and stepped forward.

"Hi, I'm Mallory." I held out my hand for her to shake.

She hadn't stopped looking at her son, and whatever she saw there had her stepping closer, bypassing my hand, and pulling me into a tight hug. I froze for a fraction of a second, my mind a battle zone of anxiety and panic...but then, her warmth settled into me and I melted. Tears burned the backs of my eyes as I inhaled her sweet smell, matching it to what I'd encountered when I first stepped into the house.

"I'm Penny. Welcome to our home."

I hadn't been hugged by a mother-like figure in…

Come here, butternut…come give me a hug.

I pushed the memory of the last time my mother hugged me down as far as I could and cleared my throat, just like Decker had done.

"Thank you." I pulled away. I had to. She was warm and loving, nothing at all like my cold stepmother.

"Mom, I'm going to work on the yard and change the oil in your car. Mallory has a few things to do while I work, but we will stay out of your way if you need to sleep or…"

"No, I'm headed out. My coworker needed to swap shifts, so I'm going to work this evening." Penny smoothed down her light green scrubs then tugged the end of her ponytail around her shoulder. She seemed empty, and the way she kept looking out the back window…it was sad. I could see she was still riding that grief wave pretty hard. I wondered how recently her husband had passed.

"I'll have Kyle do your oil some other time then. Have a good day at work." He went to hug her, but her eyes moved back to me, almost urgently.

"Will you be here when I get back?"

Was she asking me or him?

"Uh…" Decker looked back at me, then his mom. "No, Mom—we have to get back."

His mother swallowed and brought a hand to her throat before saying, "There's going to be a storm, Decker…"

I watched the family in front of me. Decker looked over to his younger brother, who was in the kitchen eating an Otter Pop, but at the mention of a storm, he dropped the frozen treat and stared helplessly at his big brother.

"We'll be fine. We won't stay long…just two hours or so," Decker said, shoving his hand into his pocket.

I felt awkward, like they'd be saying out loud what each of them seemed to be saying with their eyes if I weren't in the room.

"Decker, it's already getting late…please."

"Yeah, D, don't be an idiot," Kyle added, emphasizing their mother's plea.

Decker looked at me. That storm they were talking about was currently in his eyes as he glared, like I should voice an objection…but the concern on his family members' faces—it was too much.

"I can tuck away and sleep anywhere. I don't have another shift at the bookstore until tomorrow night, and my laptop is here, so I can do my homework." I blinked, watching them as I gave my pathetic offer.

"You work at a bookstore?" Kyle asked from the kitchen, a new color of popsicle in his hand.

"I do. It's a little café too, really good cinnamon rolls."

Decker's gaze was deadly as he stared down at me.

"Huh, isn't that interesting, D?" Kyle said playfully from his perch in the kitchen.

"I don't sleep in the house," Decker said grimly, making me do a double take.

Why didn't he sleep in his house?

"We'll be fine," he insisted. "The sooner I get this done, the sooner we can leave."

Decker turned and headed out the French doors without another word. I decided it was as good a time as any to go grab my laptop from the truck.

Ð

I WATCHED FROM MY PLACE ON THE PATIO AS DECKER MOWED THE GRASS. His shirt was gone, showing off his glorious physique. He must have done this mowing thing a lot because his chest was sun-kissed and perfect; his black tattoos wrapped around his biceps and went up to his shoulders, but nothing touched his back, his forearms or chest. Those dark jeans molded to his strong thighs as he walked behind the mower until he'd covered every inch of grass in the backyard. When he started pulling weeds and I realized I was outright drooling over the way his muscles moved and shifted, I knew I was a goner. There was attraction, then there was drooling. It was totally unacceptable.

Every thirty minutes or so, he'd stop for water. During those breaks, I tried to strike up conversation, but he didn't seem like he was in the mood to talk. I assumed it was because he was in such a hurry. Only about an hour and a half had passed when the sky started to turn. It was subtle with a little darkening off in the distance, but then thick clouds were directly above us.

At that point I decided I should probably help him, especially as I caught sight of his head tipping back and that granite jaw looking like he was chewing rocks. *Hot damn.*

I walked over to a patch of weeds off to the side and, bending over, started pulling with my bare hands. The weed put up a fight as I struggled with it, tugging and straining.

"You little bastard. Come the fuck out of the ground!" I tugged again, only to strip the thing of all its little leaves. "Ow."

"What are you doing?" Decker's gravelly voice asked from above me.

"I'm helping." My hands wrapped around another bunch of weeds as I pulled with new vigor. I managed to strip the tops, but nothing pulled up from the root. My hands burned like I'd pushed a thousand tiny slivers into them.

"You need gloves, and to squat. You're going to kill your back doing it like that."

I stood, looking at him, wondering where the happy guy from this afternoon had gone.

The sky turned a shade of navy I was sure I had only seen in that movie *Twister.* I tipped my head back, and before I could even open my mouth to argue about my weeding skills, a crack of thunder rumbled across the sky, making everything below it shudder and shake. I could feel it vibrate through my body in a way I had never experienced before. Had I ever been this close to—

"Shit," Decker snapped, interrupting my thoughts on thunder. He didn't hesitate or wait before grabbing my arm and running like hell toward his house.

I saw why just two seconds later when a blinding flash of lightning ripped through the cerulean sky.

"Oh my god!" I shouted over the hail that started to pour down two seconds after that. Decker deposited me under the covering of the porch before he ran back out to grab the mower. I didn't see the sense in that, especially when another loud blast of thunder rumbled across the sky, shaking the house.

"Holy shit." I breathed out as rain slapped against the stones around my feet.

The wind picked up, howling as Decker pushed the mower under a little covering at the side of the house.

"Why are you still out here? Get inside!" Decker yelled, running toward me.

Right—inside, where it was safe. I grabbed my laptop off the patio table, thankful it was covered, and ducked in through the French doors. Decker's hand landed on my lower back as I made my way in.

We both stood in the safety of the living room while Decker watched the storm unfold outside. Lightning flashed across the sky again, followed by another loud boom that shook the house. I shuddered, retreating toward the couch, where a throw blanket waited for me.

"Well, I guess we're stuck here, huh?" I muttered uselessly.

"Fuck," he snapped, tossing his sopping wet shirt to the floor. His scarred hand tunneled through the soaked strands of his hair, the sight of him wet and angry turning my mouth dry.

"I mean…" I cleared my throat, trying to seem unfazed by his hotness. "I can drive if you're comfortable with that." I didn't want to. I really hoped he wouldn't make me, but I would, because he seemed like he really didn't want to be here.

"No, it's not that."

I curled my legs up underneath me and relaxed into what would probably end up being my bed for the night. I waited, watching him stand there, staring out the back door, totally unsure of what to say or how to help the situation.

Decker finally moved away from the door, bending down to grab his shirt. He threw it across the back of one of the dining room chairs with a loud sigh that was nearly gloomier than the thunder outside.

He disappeared briefly into the laundry room then came back out with a dry shirt and a pair of loose sweats. I busied myself with watching the storm through the large windows. It was peaceful—until the power went out.

"D!" Kyle boomed from upstairs.

"I know, I'll grab the flashlights." He gave me an odd look then ducked back into the laundry room right as Kyle ran downstairs.

"Crazy storm, right?"

I smiled. "Yeah, it's kind of scary. Decker doesn't like driving in them?" I hesitantly asked. I mean, there was a chance Decker wouldn't tell me, and I was the kind of curious that would kill a cat nine times over.

"Nah...I think D would be just fine, especially with that fancy truck of his, but our dad died in a storm like this. He was on his way home and got caught up in a big storm about a year ago. There was a tree that went down, and the car in front of him stopped too fast." Kyle ducked his head, and I noticed his voice started to strain. "It was a six-car pileup, and my dad's car was the second one in the mix. A semi-truck was the sixth."

My throat dried up. I remembered that storm. Trevor had wanted to run a big story on it, showcasing and interviewing the student who was affected by it. Supposedly it was because the student was a big base-ball player who was being scouted by some of the pro teams. It was a big deal since he was only a junior. According to Trevor, not only was the storm historic, but the spotlight of the player would guarantee us clicks and paper purchases. I was the one who had told him no. I'd almost lost my spot on the paper because of it, and I wondered now if that was the reason the asshole hated me so much, but I couldn't have imagined seeing my mother's death splashed across the front page for the whole school to discuss. I had gone over Trevor's head and made sure the faculty advisors were aware of my concerns. They sided with me and killed the article. It was one of the only times a student had ever gone above the head editor's role, and Trevor had been out for my spot ever since.

"I'm so sorry, Kyle. I lost my mom to an accident too...it was differ-ent, and it's been longer..., but I'm sorry just the same."

Kyle's throat bobbed, but he gave me a sweet smile before nodding and heading toward the laundry room.

The boys were gone for so long that I ended up pulling the blanket higher and letting the sound of rain lull me to sleep.

THE FEEL OF SOMEONE'S WARM FINGERS CURLING INTO MY LEG WOKE ME.

The rain was still pelting against the house, along with a raging wind. The lights seemed to still be out, but I could still make out the figure who was sitting down at the end of the couch.

"Hey." I sat up, trying to figure out why Decker was sitting up, his head bent low, while he watched what looked like a baseball game on his cell phone.

"Hey." His hand tightened around my calf. His fingers had bypassed the blanket and my jeans and had somehow found a way to attach themselves directly to my skin. "Did I wake you?"

I tried to ignore the way his touch made me feel. I tried even harder to erase the burn it made along my skin, but I knew I'd think about it long after his hand left me.

"No, you didn't...but why aren't you sleeping?"

"I can't sleep in here," he grumbled softly, sleepily.

"Oh." I sat up, pulling my legs under me. "Go upstairs to your room. I'm good down here."

He was already shaking his head. "I can't sleep in this house. Not since my dad..." He trailed off, and again, I felt that surge of pain in my chest at why he couldn't say the rest of that sentence.

"Where can you sleep?" I crawled a bit closer to him, hoping he didn't notice.

"My truck, outside...anywhere else."

I kicked my legs out until I was standing, grabbed the blanket, and tugged the one on the recliner free as I held out my hand. "Let's go then."

He accepted my hand, but when I tried to take a step, he stopped me. The flashes of lightning were the only thing illuminating the room every few seconds or so. I paused, trying to decipher what he was doing. I thought maybe he wanted to go to his truck alone, and I suddenly felt so stupid assuming he'd want me to join him.

Tugging me a step closer, he brushed his scarred hand down my face before he pinned his forehead to mine, forcing my breaths to come out in little wisps.

"Tell me what this means." He brushed the pad of his finger along the tattoo inked under my ear.

I reached up, holding on to his wrist, internally batting away the urge to keep this part of me closed off. After my mom's death, things were obviously hard...but once I became a woman, left the house, and realized how much I wanted her with me, things became granite. It may have also been the fact that Taylor and her mother went on a vacation, traveling through Europe after graduation. The invitation that came from Taylor to join was half-hearted and insincere, no matter how hard it was for her to actually extend it. Taylor at eighteen was a nightmare compared to the Taylor who lived with me now. So, of course, I didn't go. I hunkered down into my books, soaking in the library at my father's house, story by story...until things hurt a little less and college began.

Blinking, I watched as the white light strobed across the walls of Decker's childhood home.

"It's originally Nordic. It's called a Vegvisir Futhark, and it means anyone who carries the symbol will be protected from losing their way in a storm or bad weather." I licked my lips, trying to build up the nerve to keep going, "I was going through some turbulent times at eighteen and had been reading a ton of Norse mythology." I dipped my head, releasing my hand, still feeling a little stupid. "The symbol became a rune, making its way into Irish folklore, and since I'm part Irish...I guess I wanted to claim it."

I shrugged, finally daring to tip my head back to catch his gaze.

An entirely different kind of storm brewed there as his jaw ticked and his other hand came up to cup my face. My chest expanded with hope that he'd close the distance between us, kiss me again...let me get lost in him, in the touch of his skin against mine.

"I want to try something," he whispered, slamming his lids closed. Giving my tattoo one last swipe, he turned us and braided his fingers with mine. We headed toward the stairs, where carpet silenced our steps.

Thunder boomed and rattled the house as we ascended into this place he hadn't braved in over a year. I tried to take in as much as I could of different images and pictures of his life, but it was too dark to gather much. Once we crested the last step, Decker walked past two closed doors then paused at the third. He looked at it like it would destroy him any second.

I squeezed his hand, which made him look over at me.

"My little compass," he whispered before grabbing for the handle and pushing the door open.

Lightning bled through the window on the far wall where a set of navy curtains hung open, revealing a view of the sky. A queen-sized bed covered in a dark comforter rested in the middle of the room, and several baseball posters and framed pictures hung along the walls. A nice dresser and small computer perched in the corner. It was cozy but felt forgotten.

"Come here." Decker pulled me to the bed.

He sat down first, kicking off his shoes and swinging his legs up until they stretched in front of him. His hand never left mine as I crawled on after him, ensuring the covers were tugged free as we settled.

A strong arm came around me, bracing me against his firm chest. My head settled into the soft pillow as my chest kept expanding with fear. He was testing this; he hadn't been in this bed in over a year. We might as well have been a pair of hands holding in the pin of a grenade, gasping for air as we tried not to explode.

I felt him breathe in and out unevenly, so I pulled his hand against my heart, breathing in through my nose and out through my mouth, hoping he'd begin to match me. After a minute or so, he did, and we both began to calm.

"Are you okay?" I asked, finally relaxing into him. He felt so good, firm and rigid in the right places.

"I can't open my eyes," he whispered, pain lacing every word.

I gripped his wrist that cradled my stomach, encouraging him to keep going.

"If I see the lightning up here, it'll take me back to that night. I haven't slept in this room since we found out he wasn't coming home. I slept on the front porch for a few nights…after…before making myself a bed in the shed. Nothing since then."

His lips brushed against my ear, and my heart nearly burst. Tears clogged my eyes, but I tamped down the urge to let them fall. He didn't need weakness right now; he needed strength, needed someone to help him through the storm.

"Just keep them closed, Decker...hold on to me and fall asleep. I'm not going anywhere."

Silence stretched as the thunder rumbled, and my eyes fluttered shut. I was sure he was asleep, until I felt his grip on me tighten and heard him mumble near my ear, "Promise me."

I realized as the sounds outside echoed around us that there was a fatal flaw in this night. I couldn't let Taylor have him. I couldn't let anyone have him, because whether he knew it or not, he was mine and I was going to be his. Even if it broke me to let him in, even if it ruined me. There wasn't much left of my heart, but whatever there was I'd shove into his massive palm. Then I'd just let him decide what to do with it. Maybe he'd realize that our tattered pieces matched. He needed someone who matched him, and she didn't. She never would, not with her silicone heart.

Blinking away a tear, I shuddered in response.

"I promise."

CHAPTER EIGHTEEN

Decker

MY PHONE BUZZED WITH ANOTHER INCOMING TEXT, FORCING AN ODD twinge to creep up my neck. I already knew who it was, already knew what it probably said, and just like the other fifteen or so times, I was going to ignore it.

"Duggar! Glad you came. Where were you all weekend?"

All weekend? I had only been gone for a period of twenty-four hours, but fuck if I was about to say that to my manager.

"Just headed home to help my mom out." I set my backpack down on the office table and sorted through it to find my apron.

"Well, we've been busy. There was a girl in here looking for you yesterday, said her name was..." My manager snapped his finger. "Something with a T. Blonde, real pretty."

Taylor? Why would she come looking for me? Unless maybe it had to do with Mallory. Maybe she hadn't texted her stepsister telling her where she was for the night. The alternative reason she might be visiting my place of work wasn't something I could stomach yet. I knew I needed to; the entire goal was to ruin Elias, and in order to do that...I needed to sleep with and potentially date Taylor.

"Thanks Geno, I'll figure it out." I smiled at the old guy and headed toward the back. I knew a few boxes had arrived with fresh inventory, so

I decided I'd start there before the rush started up. Sundays weren't usually too crazy since most of the college kids were at least attempting to get to bed early for a decent night's sleep before Monday's classes.

A few brown boxes were waiting for me against the back wall, just like I knew they would be. I found the box cutter and started opening each one then my phone went off again.

"Fucking hell." I sighed before giving up and grabbing the device. "What do you want, and why do you keep calling?"

"Geez, I texted first, but you weren't answering those," my little brother replied defensively.

I snapped my jaw shut, trying to steer clear of the vindictive comments that swirled in my head.

"Anyway...what the fuck gives, D?" he asked incredulously.

I pictured my little brother with his hair askew, his favorite Raiders shirt wrinkled because the fucking washer had broken, something I'd realized the day before when I was there.

I closed my eyes, completely unprepared for this conversation, and that alone spoke volumes. Kyle and I never talked about girls.

"You slept in your room with her then took off without even saying goodbye!"

I rubbed the stress out of my forehead while I thought of what to say.

"I'm sorry. She had to get back, and I didn't want to wake you," I lied.

I was such a fucking coward. Mallory had wanted nothing more than to head downstairs and make pancakes, talk to Kyle, see if my mom had made it home yet. But I couldn't. Things were already twisted enough as it was, waking up to her against my chest, my eyes darting to the ceiling of my bedroom, looking for relief.

The very fact that I actually slept in my childhood bedroom and woke to inhaling her scent with a fucking smile plastered on my face was reason enough to get some distance. The last thing I needed was to let Mallory charm my family and create an emotional shitstorm.

"I liked Mallory. It's shitty that you guys just left. I want to see her again," Kyle demanded in between yawns.

"Yeah, but I told you about this already—"

136

"You're still trying to go after the sister?" he shrieked, like he couldn't believe I'd even consider something so crazy.

"You already know I am." I stood, heaving the new glasses out of the box then cutting into the next box.

"Yeah, but does Mallory know that? You two...you guys looked like...you looked at each other like you wanted to tear each other's clothes off, so you might want to have a convo about this situation."

"There is no situation. I'm only hanging around her to get to Taylor, and I owe her a story, which is exactly why she came with me yesterday." Napkins—we had a thousand fucking unopened packages of napkins, but Geno kept ordering them. I told him we were good for a while, but the bastard added it every fucking week.

My little brother's scoff made me see red, but he cut me off before I could put him in his place. "Even I know what you're doing is shitty. We both know she can't run that story...you're stringing her along, all for your own purposes. That's jacked up, bro." His tone softened, which fucking enraged me further.

"This isn't even your business, Kyle. If you're concerned about someone, focus on Mom. She needs help around the house, paying the bills, fixing shit. I can't do it all." I spoke with so much venom I actually cringed.

The silence that followed nearly hollowed me out. I loved my brother. He was only sixteen; this shit wasn't his to worry about. He should have been goofing off, being a kid, not worrying about our mother checking out or the shit around the house, but I hated how right he was about Mallory. I hated that there was a chance I cared about her more than I should.

I hated that I was essentially fucking her over where the story was concerned, but what was I supposed to do? Give up my status on the Devils? Fuck...they were all I had left besides Kyle and Mom, although my mom wasn't really there. I was lonely, but I had the team, and they had my back. Even though some of the players were cocksuckers who called me shitty names, they weren't all bad. I couldn't give that up, especially since I'd be job hunting the day after I moved back home.

"Fuck you, D. You deserve what's coming if this is how you're going to be."

He hung up, which didn't surprise me. What did surprise me was his incoming text. It was a picture he'd taken of me and Mallory. It was the two of us in my bed, her tucked into my chest, my arm around her, my other hand dangling over her hip. Her face was serene, a tiny smile playing along her mouth...and fuck, I looked peaceful. I couldn't believe I had slept in my bed, in my room...during a storm. I ignored the fact that it was creepy as fuck that he'd snuck in to get the picture, although on some level, if the tables were reversed and he hadn't slept in his room in over a year, I'd grab a picture too.

I blinked, rubbing the stress out of my eyes, taking a second to think back over the night and why I'd agreed to try to sleep up there in the first place.

Ripping into another box did nothing at all to distract me from realizing I had totally led Mallory on by taking her upstairs.

Mostly I had just been exhausted. Memories had torn at me for hours while I sat next to Mallory. Seeing her on that couch, cuddled under that throw blanket my grandmother had made...it messed with me. But I kept myself busy, trying to get the power back on and the generator running so the frozen things didn't go bad. Once I finally did, I sat down, my fingers greedily searching for any contact with skin that they could make.

When she stood and suggested we go to the truck, there was just this need to touch her, and I originally planned to kiss her, maybe do more with her...then that fucking tattoo. Curiosity got the better of me. Fuck, what were the odds of it being something that had to do with being safe in a storm? Suddenly I just needed her, wanted to hold her all night like my own Irish rune and see if it would keep the demons at bay. Just for one night.

If I could sleep in that room, just once...

I had...and that fucking messed with my head.

So, I did what I could to feel in control.

I deleted the picture and pocketed my phone.

ȸ

**MALLORY: HEY, I'M CRAVING A CINNAMON ROLL...WANNA GO BROWSE
books and share one?**

I flipped my phone over on my knee and continued watching the
game play out on my flatscreen. I'd known she would text me eventually.
After we woke up early and left my house without a word and me not
explaining jack shit about my mom or brother, of course she was curious. I had been mentally preparing to shoot her down, tell her I was
busy and give her some kind of brushoff, but now that her name was
there flashing on my screen, I couldn't seem to do it.

Instead I ignored her.

I'd only respond if she mentioned me hanging out with Taylor. It
was eating me up inside to do it, but she knew the deal, and I refused to
budge...even if she was doing the very thing I had always envisioned
doing when I one day found someone to actually have a relationship
with. I could picture her there, those green eyes narrowed, a pair of
black glasses (which I was sure she owned) perched on her face, that hair
cascading down in a tangled mess of brown and reddish-gold hues. Her
perfect tits would be straining against whatever shirt she wore, and those
curves would be highlighted in a pair of sinfully tight jeans.

I blinked, the game going in and out of focus as I imagined Mallory
smiling, leading me by the hand to an empty section of the bookstore.
She'd spin against one of the stacks, bite her lip, and toss her head back
on a gasp as I leaned in, capturing those luscious lips in a kiss. We'd
make out for a few minutes, my hands greedily roaming her curves until
I made my way down that body and slowly pulled those jeans down her
thighs. Fuck, she'd be in a dark green thong, and I'd shove my nose in
between her thighs, pressing my thumb against the wet spot over her
clit. I'd tell her I liked how wet she was for me, then I'd throw her leg
over my shoulder and dive in. I'd lick through her glistening folds, up
and down her pussy, tugging her open for me so I didn't miss a single
drop of her arousal. She'd beg me for more, grip my hair, and rub
herself against my face until she came hard, screaming my name.

I let out an audible groan as I fantasized about her. I was alone in
the apartment, but I'd never pull my dick out while in the living room,
so like I had at least ten times since meeting Mallory, I walked back to
the bathroom and shut myself inside.

Unzipping my jeans, I pulled myself free of my boxers and gripped my erection. Shutting my eyes tightly, I pictured her falling to her knees in front of me, eyes on mine the entire time she gripped my dick, her red lips skimming the underside of my shaft, licking away the precum on the tip then taking me fully into her mouth.

Moving my hand up and down my cock, I kept imagining the sound she would make while choking on my length. I'd grab the back of her head and shove my hips forward, fucking that pert little mouth of hers while those big green eyes stayed glued to me.

"Fuck." My voice was raspy as I furiously jerked my dick.

I imagined stripping her bare. She'd hold her breasts together, pinning those lips in between her teeth, and I'd fucking come all over her chest and face.

"Fuuuuckkkk." Ribbons of white landed all over the counter and inside the sink as a spine-tingling shudder ran through me, forcing an audible groan from me. I usually did this in the shower, which further demonstrated that I was losing control of my feelings for her. Jerking off to images of having Mallory was occurring too frequently. I needed to get a grip, get her out of my system. Maybe if I kept enough distance, these feelings and urges would start to dissipate.

They had to.

ᛒ

Five days later

MALLORY HAD TEXTED THE DAY AFTER I BLEW HER OFF, ASKING IF I wanted to study with her, even sending a picture of a fresh bag of lime-flavored chips. The day after that she sounded more professional, asking if I had time to answer a few questions regarding her notes and the story. Still I fucking ignored her because I just couldn't bring myself to text with her or see her or talk to her about how much of a coward I was being. The problem was, I had no self-control around the woman. At this point, I was worried if I saw her, I'd lose all sense and just start kissing her.

We both had to keep our heads on straight and remember that we had a deal.

Taylor for the story—that was it. I couldn't blur, cross, or erase the lines…they were the only thing granting me revenge.

I walked toward class, pulling my cell free to shoot off a text to Daniel. He was my go-to guy for dealing information, and while it might have been more worthwhile to just head home and ask my brother for what he knew since he was obviously working with our Uncle Scotty, I preferred to keep him out of it. I needed to know if there was any update on the situation, or if Elias had made any changes or moves. I wanted to know what was going on with his physical therapy appointments in Pinehurst.

If there was a chance to exploit that or find out how he was getting through every game, I wanted to know. I had a feeling they were juicing him up, especially when scouts were going to be attending. I wanted to ruin his chances at having a backup plan, and that was why it was so imperative I close the deal with Taylor.

Once I sent the text, I pocketed my phone and slumped into my usual desk. Just as class was about to begin, Juan crept in, slinking down into his seat. He'd come in so late the past few days someone had taken his usual spot, so we hadn't had the chance to catch up.

I waited for him to ask what he'd missed or what kind of mood our teacher was in today, but he didn't say anything. In fact, he looked like he was completely ignoring me. My eyebrows caved as I thought through what I could have done to piss him off. Nothing came to mind, so maybe it wasn't me at all…maybe there was just something else going on in his life.

"Hey, everything good?" I asked, eyeing the front of the class. Flynn was still organizing his slides.

Juan continued to ignore me, but his jaw tensed and his nostrils flared.

Shit, he was pissed, but about what?

I leaned over, folding my arms on the desk. "Seriously, man…we good?" I didn't even know Juan outside of class; maybe I'd done something to mess with his grade in the class or something.

Suddenly his cell landed in front of me, the screensaver a photo of

Mallory and him. His arm was around her, her petite frame tucked under him. They wore matching grey sweats...the ones I had seen her wear at her house.

Suddenly pieces fell into place as a dull throbbing filled the space between my ears. I didn't like seeing her tucked under his arm. I didn't like that those were his sweats she was wearing, and it must have been his house she'd been at that one morning at two a.m. Fury burrowed into me like a rabid animal.

I clenched my jaw as I stared at the phone.

"Fuck you, man—get that look off your face. You haven't earned the right to wear that look." Juan glared right back at me, his dark brows a shelf on his face. "Five days ago, you did something to piss off my best friend. I stood up for you when she heard rumors about you, but you ended up being a dick just the same. So no, we aren't good. I don't like when people fuck with my friends."

I let out a sigh and sat back in my chair, unsure how to respond. I liked the dude, even if I was getting territorial over a girl I'd brushed aside. I was fucking tired of taking the coward's way out, but there wasn't really a way to salvage this.

"Look, man...I'm sorry if your friend got the wrong impression about me. We aren't dating or anything, we're just working together on something." I was going to hell. It was official.

He laughed, shaking his head back and forth. "Wow...you don't think she told me about the little party? Or the deal you made with her for Taylor?" He leveled me with a serious look, which made me curious if he'd hit me or not. He looked like he might. I'd deserve it and so much worse.

I didn't know what to say to that. He knew I was playing Taylor... and fuck, I supposed I was also playing Mallory, and that wasn't my intention.

"Okay, fine." I watched the teacher as he flicked his gaze to where we sat in the back row. "I like her, but I'm trying not to...so I had to ignore her for a few days. I didn't want to though. I feel like shit about it."

"Well you should. If we weren't in class, I'd kick your ass right now. Your deal doesn't matter anymore anyway."

I turned to him, feeling a strange panic start to blossom in my chest. "What are you talking about?"

Girls in school watched Juan like he was one of those coffee milk-shakes they all drank. They were always watching him. I could admit he did look half decent, but right now he looked like he wanted to murder me. Legit Mexican cartel shit. I wasn't assuming he had connections just based on his skin tone; I'd heard rumors about him too.

"We went to a party last night." He dipped his head, leaning closer. "That pitcher for the Devils was there, and his sights were set on Mallory the entire fucking time. He wouldn't leave her alone. Dude was pretty obvious about wanting her."

Was this what a heart attack felt like?

"He eventually wore her down, even with me trying to interfere. They talked for a bit, that was it, but after the party, I asked her about it, and she seemed excited. She said,'because you fell off the face of the planet,' this would be her new story source."

Fuck me.

I brought my hands to my face and rubbed my eyes. This couldn't be happening.

"I hope you told her how bad of an idea that is," I replied, likely seconds from being kicked out of class. We weren't being quiet anymore. I didn't even know how to do so or if I could at this point. I was about to throw a chair if I didn't get some of these emotions under control.

Elias had talked to Mallory; he'd gone after her. The memory of his cleat going through my hand came back, making me stretch it.

"I told her...but she said she needs this story, even if that means she is dealing with a bad guy. I'll spare you on what else she said...it wasn't nice, and it was about you," Juan added with a smirk.

I started gathering my stuff, tossing it in my backpack.

"Where are you going?"

I leaned toward him before getting up. "To fucking fix this."

ɒ

THE LIGHTS IN THE TEAM HOUSE WERE LOW AS I WADED THROUGH THE halls and stopped at the massive island. Toby, one of the shortstops, was there eating a bowl of cereal. Since it was getting later, there weren't many players around. Most started their evening festivities around six and didn't roll back in until around one in the morning.

I knew for sure there was one person in the house who didn't live by that schedule. Taking the stairs two at a time, I trotted down into the basement and stalked toward the back where my old room used to be, where Elias's was now.

I knocked politely so maybe he'd assume it was one of his lackeys. A few seconds passed, and I waited…then it swung open and my ex-best friend stood there in a pair of loose shorts and a white t-shirt.

I pushed against the door, forcing him to take a few jumbled steps back.

"Whoa, what the…" His hands went up like he was innocent.

"You laid hands on my brother, and I didn't end you—consider that a kindness. But if you think you'll get away with going after Mallory Shaw, you have another thing coming." I stuck my hands in my pockets, hoping I seemed calm and in control, all while white-hot anger pulsed under my skin at the mere idea of him being close enough to talk to Mallory.

Elias grinned, letting out a small laugh. His thumb came up to stroke his bottom lip before he sank into a chair.

"I know you know about the arrangement I made with Taylor's dad…or stepdad, Charles Shaw. I know you know, because you started hanging out with his daughters out of the blue."

I scoffed. Who even gave a flying fuck?

"What does this have to do with you leaving her alone?"

"You think I'm going to sit here and stand by while you move in and take away the opportunity of a lifetime?" He stood, pointing at his chest like he couldn't believe I'd suggest such a thing.

"I think you're power hungry and you've bitten off more than you can chew. These are real people you're dealing with." I slashed my hand toward him, my voice rising a few octaves.

"And real money, Decker. You of all people should know what it's like to want to care for your family." He got in my face, and it took all my strength not to fight him. Our coach had forced us to go to therapy after my accident on the field. Rumors had circulated that I'd thrown the pitch so the ball would give him a dead arm. Another rumor said I had reached for Elias's ankle, trying to trip him, and he accidently caught my hand while steadying himself.

Fucking noise. All of it.

I went to the sessions mandated by Coach, but Elias had made it seem like I had it out for him, so I had to be careful not to engage with anything with him, or else it would just cause more issues. I had a few months left of the season then I'd be done, and my Devils status would be good for a lifetime.

I took a step back, mentally scolding myself to fucking learn the order in which to breathe properly.

"Just stay away from her." I ducked my head, ready to leave before I did something I would regret, like kill him.

Elias folded his arms, giving me a smirk. "Nah...I think I like this sister better."

"Your deal doesn't work like that. You can't just choose which one to take over half his fortune with." I knew a little bit of the deal, but not all of it. I just knew he'd needed to be in that room with Taylor that first night and he hadn't been. Now it looked like I was going after her, and as far as what Scotty had found...it would be a big fucking problem for Elias if Taylor started dating someone else.

"I think you'd be surprised. I think since you tried to go after Taylor, it only seems fair I give Mallory a good shot."

I was in his face again, and this time there was no way I could keep my fist from flying. I landed one good punch before someone ran into Elias's room and broke us up.

Three other players were there in an instant, pulling me out.

"Stay the fuck away from her, E," I warned one last time before they'd effectively removed me from the property.

CHAPTER NINETEEN

Mallory

"HEY, IT'S PARTY GIRL."

I turned to inspect the face of the guy from the night prior, standing with his back straight and a broad smile on his face. It was Elias Matthews—the real one. He'd cornered me at a random party I'd decided to attend with Hillary and Juan. They could tell I needed some cheering up. I guess I wasn't great at pretending being ghosted didn't bother me, but whatever. Elias brought his A game with the smiling, flirting, and trying to get me to go out with him. I was trying to keep a low profile, just wanted to get out of the house so Taylor didn't pick up on my mood. I wasn't expecting to catch the attention of the captain of the Devils, but here I had it, two days in a row.

"It's you again." I held the loaf of bread between us, hugging it to my chest like it was a life preserver. The aisle was narrow, and people kept trying to cut between us, making my anxiety spike as a few people drew too close.

He must have picked up on my issue. His body twisted to block the entrance entirely.

Elias was tall and thick. He looked like a typical bodybuilder or steroid abuser with veins in places I didn't even know veins could be. Today he wore a black tee, a Devils baseball hat covering his blond hair, and the insignia for the Devils tattooed onto the side of his shaved head.

"You were playing hard to get last night." His shoe touched the tip of mine in a flirtatious way. The lights overhead were obnoxiously bright, and I itched to grab my sunglasses out of my bag to help ward off the impending headache I knew was coming. I'd drunk more than I usually did at the party, and I wanted to punch something when I considered how I was reacting to this entire Decker situation. I wasn't a big drinker, especially when I was up against a deadline. The hangover was punishment enough, but I still felt a little foolish.

I shrugged. "Wasn't playing at all, just not interested."

"Why?" His blue eyes narrowed on me. He probably wasn't used to being told women weren't interested in him.

"I don't know." What was I supposed to say? That Decker didn't like him and obviously wanted to hurt him in some way, which seemed like a good enough reason to avoid him?

"Give me a shot."

The words stung. I didn't even know why they did, but I'd imagined what had happened that night between Decker and Taylor so many times I now had actual words in my head for what he had probably said to her. Who knew, maybe they'd exchanged numbers and had been texting this entire week, and that was why Decker had decided to drop me out of nowhere.

"Why?" I asked.

Another patron wanted the discounted loaves of bread at my back, but one glimpse at the giant next to me had them pushing their cart down the opposite aisle.

"Do I need a reason?" He shrugged.

He did, yes—although, again, it wasn't like I actually trusted this guy. Then again...if Decker was done talking to me about the games and the story, maybe this was my chance to get a different view, a different side of things. Besides, I couldn't go back to watching my cell phone for any sign of life from Decker. I'd seen him around school a few times, but I was way too ashamed to approach him. I had literally come off as the world's most pathetic cling-on. I couldn't believe how many times I had texted to see if he wanted to hang out. My face burned at the mere memory of my attempts to see him after the trip to his mom's. I'd thought we had a moment or something. It had felt real, but the way he'd woken up, turning away from me and quickly snatching up his shoes...I guess I realized it then.

Still, on the way home, he'd been quiet but not silent. I had figured he was just emotional after sleeping in his childhood bedroom after not being able to for so long. I was wrong. He'd dropped me like a bad, annoyingly clingy habit.

With that fresh feeling of embarrassment burning in my chest and a deep desire not to deal with Decker James any longer, I smiled at the man in front of me.

"You want a shot? You have it. What exactly did you have in mind?"

⚓

"IT'S CRISPY OUT HERE." HILLARY RUBBED HER ARMS THROUGH HER jacket. She had on two massive sweaters underneath it, a pair of gloves, and a hat. It was North Carolina in early March—not exactly cold, yet my best friend was layered like she was about to be abducted and taken into the Alaskan wilderness.

"Feels good." I settled into the cold bleacher seat. *Never mind—holy shit that is cold.*

"Told ya." Hillary smirked, laying down a blanket for us to sit on.

So much better.

"So, why are we out here on a random Wednesday, watching the Devils practice?"

I narrowed my gaze, trying to sort out who exactly was on the field. They seemed to be in practice jerseys, so I didn't know who was who. It was just a sea of white with that red D on the front left side of their shirts. Some of the players had hats twisted around, others had padding and face masks, and there were gloves and balls being thrown faster than I could blink.

"Uh...we're researching."

"Researching what?" I didn't have to see Hillary's face to know her nose was scrunched and her chin was dipped into the collar of her coat.

Question of the year.

"Hey…that guy keeps looking toward us."

I followed her line of sight, and sure enough, there he was—Elias Matthews. Tall and broad-shouldered, maybe from throwing all those fastballs, or the steroids. Either way, the guy was stacked like crazy. I internally compared him to Decker. Maybe I shouldn't have, but Decker was a permanent fixture in my head and would forever be the standard I measured all men against.

"He's smiling at you."

Yes he was. What a flirt.

Hillary's face whipped my direction only to return forward, facing the field.

"What's going on?"

"He asked me to come watch today," I explained, like that could answer all her questions. She knew he'd talked to me at that party, but she didn't know about the grocery store. She was team *ditch Decker* though, so I had that going for me at least.

"How does this work into your plan?" my best friend whispered conspiratorially, brushing up against me.

"If you keep doing that, Miranda is going to kick my ass." I leaned away from her.

"She doesn't think there's anything going on between us—she knows you're straight." She waved me off.

Yeah right. Hillary had just started seeing Miranda. My best friend didn't know that her girlfriend had made it very clear that if I made any physical contact with Hillary at any time for any reason, she would cut that part off of my body. Girl had issues.

"So, what…is Elias your new lead?"

"I think so. There's a story there…I just need to dig it up."

"No." Hillary stood and started stomping down the metal bleachers.

"Wait—where are you going?" Hil! Oh my gosh, stop." I nearly fell face first into the dirt toward the bottom of the bleachers. Coordinated I was not.

"You aren't risking your heart or your pussy for this story, not more than you already have. You can't tell, but you're already changing." She stomped ahead, crossing her arms over her chest.

I quickly looked around to ensure no one had overheard her little tirade before running to keep up with her.

"Hil, what are you talking about?"

She spun on her heel, her face set in hard lines, her mouth a firm dash against her softer face.

"You spent last weekend with Decker…in his house. You talk about him more than you realize, you light up when you tell me the details about this little deal—but you also look like you lost your puppy when you explain the Taylor part of the story. And the fact that he totally ghosted you! You're in pain over it, and here you are risking even more."

I watched the grass at our feet as I considered her words.

"Yeah, maybe so…but I know the deal. This will actually help me distance myself from him. He's not the only one who can spin a deal to his advantage." The hairs on my neck rose as if I was being watched. I took a second to twist my neck and look behind me. Elias was watching us, but so was someone close to the dugout. A clipboard was perched in front of him, a dark ball cap covering his dark hair, and from where I stood, it looked like a glacial stare was aimed my way. I didn't care. I couldn't.

He'd ignored me for days, and now that Elias was smiling at me and —fuck—jogging over, he suddenly cared.

"He's coming over here." Hillary gripped my arm.

"Ow, tone down your grip, crazy." I pulled my arm free, rubbing it.

"What are you going to do? Is that the other guy? He's running over here too—my anxiety can't take this."

I reached down, threading my fingers with hers to hopefully help keep her calm. Hillary was a *hit first, ask questions later* kind of person. Decker ran behind Elias as the captain slowed to a light jog in front of us. The fence separated us, but I could see his flirty smile and appreciate the way the sun glistened off his sweaty neck and face. He had a group of freckles along his cheeks and nose, which was cute. They paired nicely with his navy eyes.

"Party girl." He beamed, grabbing the bill of his hat.

I shifted forward, about to ask if that was his intended nickname for me because it wasn't my favorite, but my tongue wouldn't work as I noticed Decker's speed. His face was set in hard lines as he drew closer and closer until he rammed his shoulder into Elias's side, forcing him a few feet away.

"I fucking warned you, E. Don't." Decker's tone cut the distance; his eyes could have killed someone on the spot. His mossy green gaze narrowed, his dark brows forming a shelf, highlighting his dipped expression and severe jaw.

Elias began laughing, righting himself, until his fingers were wrapped through the metal links in front of me.

"Back off, Duggar. She's here because I asked her to be."

Decker's gaze left Elias, landing on me. A shudder overtook him as he adjusted his footing in the dirt, his scarred hand stretching at his side.

"That true?" He tipped his chin toward me.

It was such a simple question, but it burned me like a brand. He was asking if I had shown up for Elias, but I knew my answer would hurt him. Regardless of what Decker had done, I didn't want to hurt him. Still, I wasn't a liar either.

"Yeah, he invited me to come and watch." I could have explained about the story, probably should have…but Decker had ghosted me, so who was to say he'd even care?

Decker's body went rigid, his chest heaving up and down in angry gasps like he couldn't get enough air. Rage radiated from him, and I knew as his fists clenched that some of those rumors about him might be true.

I watched, holding my breath as I waited for him to decide how he'd handle this information. I assumed he would throw a punch at Elias or drag him into the dirt, something violent, but a second later he let out a little scoff and began shaking his head.

Those eyes darted to me one last time before he spun on his heel and walked away.

Heat overwhelmed my face as I watched his retreating form. There was a name stitched into the back with red lettering—'Duggar'—with the number four below it. I'd never seen him in his gear before. He was handsome with the way it fit his chest snugly and the pants wrapped around his strong thighs. It was all in a package, covering the man

151

who'd held me in his childhood bed just days earlier while facing down some of the scariest demons in his life.

The coach yelled something from his spot near the catcher, which made Elias turn before returning to face me again. His pinched features indicated he needed to get back.

"Come out with me tomorrow."

I didn't want to. My eyes sought Decker on instinct, but I had to stop pining over someone who didn't want me.

I nodded, unable to voice what felt like betrayal on my tongue. He smiled before dipping his head and running back to the middle of the diamond.

Hillary waited until he was gone before crossing her arms and turning on me.

"So, you're going after Elias now?"

I shrugged. "Why not? Maybe he'll give up some juicy bit about the game or—even better—about what happened between him and Decker. There's a lot of water under that bridge, and I'm just building myself a little paddle boat, Hil." I continued to watch the players move, my eyes betraying me by wandering over to the dugout and the guy inside bent over the clipboard. What did he do for the team? Did he still play at all? What had really happened?

Hillary seemed to think it over for a second, her brown eyes scanning the ground as though the answers were scattered there. Finally, she looked up and said, "Then we have some work to do."

I waited while she spun on her heel once more, heading toward the car. She knew I'd follow because I was curious as hell about what kind of work she had in mind, and my lime-flavored chips were in her bag.

⬠

I FACED THE MIRROR IN MY BATHROOM, PRESSING IN CLOSER AND CLOSER until the reflection looked familiar. My hair was shorter, but somehow with the layers, it seemed longer. The sleek strands framed my face, adding dimension to my jawline. The makeup she'd had me buy had all been meticulously selected by her older sister, who was an influencer with millions of followers on some social media platform that was trending like wildfire. She knew, because of Hillary's big fat mouth, that I had access to credit cards, black cards with no limits. I had never once touched them for a single thing in my college career, but I was certain Kendra and Hillary had put a hefty dent in them today.

I couldn't find it in my heart to care. Taylor had even applauded me for finally using it for something good. I withheld an eye roll because makeup and makeovers didn't sit on the list of something good in my book, but she had a point—my father obviously wanted something from both of us if his cryptic text reminders about his event were any indication. Why not use the cards every now and again?

I heard the knock on the front door and exited the bathroom, shutting off the light as I treaded toward the foyer. I took in a quiet breath to calm my nerves, shoving down the urge to smile or even preen knowing who might be on the other side.

I knew who would be standing there. I'd texted him, telling him tonight would be a good chance to spend time with Taylor. It felt awkward after our encounter on the field, but even if he didn't want to hold up his end of our bargain, I still would. For the first time in a week, he had finally responded to my text, telling me he'd be here by six.

Go figure.

Of course, it splintered my heart like a piece of brittle wood...but this had been the deal from the very beginning, and I couldn't be angry at him for it.

I swung the door wide, letting him in. My eyes stayed on the floor because I didn't want to see his lack of reaction to my makeover changes, or worse, the obvious surprise that I'd fixed my moppy head of curls and finally applied more than just mascara to my eyes. He was here for Taylor, and that was all there was to our relationship. He'd more than made that clear.

"Come on in. Taylor will be out in just a second."

I moved so he could come in, my eyes trailing over his brown boots, untied and gaping open around the dark denim. It was sexy, and I had to force my eyes shut so I wouldn't notice.

"Mallory." My name on his lips, spoken in that timbre...it conveyed a different story than the one he was telling, a story of a different deal he wanted to broker than the one he'd fixed. We were two sides of the same coin, playing a game neither of us would win.

"Decker." I finally lifted my eyes, shifting everything internal to align with my decision not to care about him. It was no use. My heart leapt within my chest at the sight of him, like the tip of a mountain in the middle of winter, an avalanche of desire cascading through me, ruining me. He wore his practice jersey with the red D for the Devils on the right side and red lines running down the white cotton, split open and gaping over a plain white tee.

My throat dried at how hot he looked. His dark brown hair was lightening from being in the sun, but the longer strands were messy, like he'd run his fingers through them recklessly. I wanted to demand that he explain himself, that he tell me why he'd ignored me. There was even a small part of me that wanted to ask what I had done wrong, but that tiny part needed to die. Which was why I wouldn't give in to him.

He stepped inside, and before I could move or create space, his hand shot toward my hip, gripping me to stay put.

Dangerous. This was nothing but dangerous.

He needed Taylor to want him. For whatever reason he had, he needed her...but the way he looked down at me, pulling me flush against his chest made it seem like he needed me too.

"What have you done to your hair?" He leaned in until his nose ran along the smooth strands that hung near my ear.

His eyes closed as he inhaled and skimmed the sensitive skin there, right over my tattoo. I wanted to sink into his arms, beg him to take me back to my bedroom and close the gap that had widened between us over the past week.

"I cut it." I cleared my throat and grabbed his forearm, desperate for space.

His eyes blazed as they ran a path along each change on my face and slowly worked their way down to my thin fitted tank top, showing tanned, freckled skin. He dipped his head to see my skinny jeans that ended above my bare toes, which were painted white. That confused gaze swiftly worked back up to meet my calculated one. I wanted to understand that look he wore, the pinched eyebrows, the worry lines, and the concern softening his gaze.

"I liked the way your hair was before…your shirts and jeans too."
He finally stepped back, and the air that was suddenly available between
us burned like a heat wave.

I nodded, knowing he probably did like those things.

"Guess I'm not going for someone to like me. I want someone to
want me. You know…the way you want my stepsister."

"Hey." A sultry, soft voice spoke up from behind me. Speak of the
devil.

We both turned to see Taylor walking toward us, drawing closer to
Decker, wearing tiny sleep shorts that showed the bottom of her ass
cheeks. She had a sleep tank on as well, showing her perfect silicone
breasts and those nipples alert and ready for Decker's touch.

I swallowed a lump that had suddenly formed in my throat as I
looked at her shiny blonde hair and tan skin, her legs that had zero
cellulite, and the lack of a single hint of a muffin top at the band of the
shorts hugging her hips.

I was confident in myself. I loved my body. I did…it was just that,
when we were teenagers, as I blossomed into the curvy hips and
awkward bust, I became aware of how different I was from her. I began
to notice how the boys our age would look at her and ignore me, unless
they saw a way to get to her through me. Becoming my friend, hanging
out…all so, in the end, they'd get to her. Subconsciously, I had handed
over a few cards to Taylor that never belonged to her. I was so careful to
ensure no one else was given those things freely, but it was so hard to get
them back once I'd let them slip free.

I looked up and realized Decker's gaze was still on me. He had that
look on his face like he was chewing gravel again. I waited him out, not
giving in to that look or what it might mean, until finally he slid his eyes
toward Taylor. There wasn't appreciation in his gaze, or desire…but
maybe that was just what I wanted to see or didn't want to see. Maybe I
was just creating this entire thing in my head.

I needed clarity, and more than anything, I needed space.

"You kids have fun. I'm headed out." I reached for my red hoodie,
like my own little security blanket.

Decker swung his head back in my direction. "Where?"

"Elias wants to take me out tonight, wants to go dancing." I grabbed for a pair of wedged heels, withholding a wince at how stupid of an idea it would be to dance in them all night. I wanted my Converse tennis shoes.

Decker took a step toward me and gripped my arm in a tight hold. "You fucking joking?" he angrily whispered, leaning toward my ear so Taylor wouldn't hear.

"I'm not." I gave him a tight smile.

"Mallory, he's not——"

"He's here, gotta run."

"Mallory, don't," he warned, but I couldn't let it land because I was doing exactly what he was...at least I hoped he was. There was a chance he did have feelings for Taylor, but a part of me knew he was doing this out of obligation to something. I had games to play too, and I didn't need Decker making me feel things when he couldn't give me what I wanted.

I pulled my arm free, waved at Taylor, and ran out the door, swinging it shut behind me.

Elias was outside his truck waiting for me, leaning against it, watching the house like a cat who'd just cornered the pesky mouse that had gotten away from him one too many times.

"Hey."

"Hey yourself." He smiled, but it flew over my head, did nothing to me. Might as well have been Juan smiling at me.

"You ready to go?" I asked as his gaze fixated on my house. It bounced between the truck in my driveway and the front door.

"Yeah." He pushed off the truck and headed toward my door, opening it for me. He even tried to lean over me to buckle me in, but that shit was weird.

"I got it, thanks." I gave him a tight smile and a warning look to back off. I didn't know him that well, and I sure as hell wouldn't be lowering my defenses around him.

I took one last look at the house and the man who was staring at us from the front door before I closed my eyes and faced forward.

CHAPTER TWENTY

Mallory

ELIAS MATTHEWS WAS AN IDIOT, A JOCK WITH NO SUBSTANCE whatsoever. He was perfectly suited for a jersey chaser or anyone who didn't mind a little bleeding in the ears, and yet I sat at the bar listening to his stories of how he'd been endorsed early on in college for all of his athletic gear, his cell phones and laptops…basically all his fancy shit. Oh, and apparently, he was already being scouted by two different pro teams. I was fairly certain at some point he used the term 'best of the best' in describing himself. His face flushed when he said that, leaning closer to me as he trailed a finger down my arm, but he'd still said the actual words.

"So…what's the story with you and Decker James?" I asked coyly.

Elias's light brows dipped, a line formed right between them.

"Duggar?"

I bit my lower lip, leaning forward. "Yeah, something like that. I've seen him a few times, hung out…but I've heard rumors about you two."

Please work. I wanted more info on why these two hated one another, and I knew Decker would never give it to me.

Elias took a long swig of his beer, the foam left behind a white mustache along his upper lip. It made me smirk at how ridiculous he looked.

He let out a whoosh of air, which made me tense. "He tried to ruin my career, but I think God must have been looking out for me. I managed to hit the ball in a way that protected me. Another time, he attacked me, tried tripping me...ended up getting that scar on his hand. He's bad news."

My stomach hollowed out, tipping with defensiveness.

"So, you know him pretty well then?" I sipped my water. I wasn't getting wasted with this guy near me. I'd bought a water bottle from the vending area near the ATM machine and had been nursing it while he drank his beer.

"Yeah, guess you could say that. We grew up together actually...you know, it's a funny story." He crossed his arms, leaning them on the tall table, his face sliding just inches from mine. "So I've actually been into your stepsister for a while...I invited her to the party that night, and now she's with Decker, I guess."

I wrinkled my brows in frustration and confusion. Did Taylor have a magical vagina or something? What was I missing?

"What makes you say they're together?"

His boyish looks only amplified when he smiled and showed his dimples. He pulled his phone away from where it sat in front of him and slid it toward me. There on the screen was Taylor's Instagram feed, with a picture of her and Decker cuddling on the couch, her face nuzzled into his neck while he smiled at the camera.

My chest seized. It literally felt like someone had just launched a missile at us then asked me to absorb the impact on behalf of civilization.

I grappled with my water bottle lid and begged the tears lining my eyes to stay the fuck inside my tear ducts. I didn't need to show this prick that I cared that Decker had actually followed through with dating Taylor.

"Wow...didn't realize they were so close already," I muttered, tipping my face back to gulp back more water.

Elias watched me carefully then slowly slid his phone back to his side of the table.

"You see, that's just it. I have known this guy for a really long time. I know what he looks like when he likes a girl. That day in the bakery...

he looked at you in that way. He likes you. I wonder if he's maybe playing a game with Taylor or something." He shrugged his massive shoulders like it didn't mean anything.

"Why do you say that?" The prick had me hooked and he knew it.

"He still has it out for me for whatever reason." A palm the size of a dinner plate came up and over his shoulder, rubbing at his neck.

I was curious now; I wanted more details, even though I knew I shouldn't. Decker had Taylor...whatever his reasons, he wanted her, and now he had her. I should have left it alone.

"What happened between you guys to make him want to ruin your career and have it out for you?" I resisted the urge to use air quotes because I wasn't buying this guy's bullshit.

Elias let out a heavy sigh then dipped his head, letting his hair fall along his forehead.

"Let's just forget it...want to dance?" He held out his hand, giving me a sheepish smile.

I held back a glare. I didn't want to dance. I wanted more information, but instead I decided to just go with the flow of the night, see if I could squeeze more from him. Even if Decker had made his choice clear, questions led to answers, and some of them might help with my article. So, I put my hand in his.

"Lead the way."

Elias pressed his body against mine while we moved along the floor, shifting our feet briskly to the fast-paced music. I tossed my head back and laughed a few times when he sang along with the lyrics or exaggerated the moves like he was a contestant on *Dancing with the Stars* or something. It was nice. My lungs filled with artificial air, lifesaving but not fulfilling. I would survive the heartbreak of Decker James choosing Taylor. What I wouldn't survive was if I didn't choose myself.

I needed to start choosing me, no matter what...even if it was the villain in the story, the one guy who wanted to spin me around the floor and make me laugh.

Elias and I stayed out until two in the morning. At one point my defenses lowered with him, especially when he drove off toward the back of the bar, laid a blanket across his hood, and watched the stars with me. He didn't mention Decker again, but he did talk about the game—not the card game, but the sport. Still, tidbits led to some questions I had about what I had seen in that bedroom.

He'd mentioned to me that he had invited Taylor to the game that night. I had finally registered that he might know I had gone in her place. My mind briefly considered if that meant the other team members knew as well.

I shook it off. There was no way Elias would be this nice and open with me if he knew I was writing my article. It had probably just been a slip of the tongue.

⅊

IT WAS NEARLY THREE IN THE MORNING WHEN I FINALLY SLIPPED MY KEY into the lock of my front door. The lights were out, and thankfully Taylor and Decker weren't having sex in the kitchen or living room. I immediately let out a sigh of relief.

My wedged heels were off, already dangling from my fingers as I secured the door and headed for my bedroom. I never liked turning on the overhead light; it was too obnoxious. Instead I opted for smaller lamps and hanging lights. Clicking the switch for the hanging lights, I shut my door and started unbuttoning my jeans.

It wasn't until I was shimmying out of them that I turned back toward my bed.

"Holy fuck!" I threw my hands over my mouth.

"Shhhh," Decker said, moving to sit up.

He was shirtless, in just his jeans...and barefoot. The man was *barefoot*, in my bedroom...*in my bed*.

"What are you doing here?" I pulled the rest of the denim material free of my legs then grabbed the same pair of sweats I'd worn the night Decker first showed up at my house.

His eyes narrowed again, just like they had then.

"Why do you have those?"

I ignored his mussed hair sticking up in all directions and the fact that he was in my freaking bed! I was totally going to smell my pillow as soon as he left.

"Why are you here?" I drew out the words, indicating that I

wouldn't be answering any of his questions without him first answering mine.

Finally, he let out a sigh and threw himself back on the bed.

My. Bed.

"I kind of need to sleep there. You gotta move," I said after a few seconds of silence.

"I need you to come here." His voice dipped, nearly shuddering with something I didn't recognize but that pulled at something deep inside me. It reminded me of the storm we had gotten caught in, the vulnerability of seeing him in his childhood home.

Taking a step forward, I was nearly to the edge of my bed when I crossed my arms, protecting my chest. He was so handsome, so perfectly out of my league that it was painful to even acknowledge his existence.

"You need what?"

Fast as lightning, his hand shot out and grabbed me, pulling me on top of him. We rolled, and he was suddenly hovering over my body.

"I need to hold you tonight, Mallory. Don't fight it, and I'm too fucking exhausted to explain it, but please just give me this."

I swallowed, staring into those murky eyes of his, wondering how they shone with topaz colors in this lighting.

"And take these fucking sweats off." His hand shoved the hem of the sweats down my hips, his fingers brushing against my skin, and suddenly I was fevered and desperate for more of what he'd given me that night in Elias's room.

I hesitated, hating my physical reaction to him. He didn't get to just come back into my life and suddenly demand things, not after he ghosted me for a week and humiliated me by ignoring every single text I'd sent. I knew I was being that girl who was demanding too much and I hated myself for it, but I was worth more than what he was offering. I was worth a text back. A heads-up. Something.

"You need to leave." I kept my arms folded across my chest, looking up at the ceiling.

"No." He let out a heavy sigh, settling into my side.

Frustration and something like relief sailed through me at a frantic pace. This wasn't good for my heart.

"Decker, I'm serious. You've ignored me for an entire week and only came around once I said you could hang with Taylor...this is fucking crazy. You can't be in my bed right now."

His body shifted, curling around mine, pulling me closer to his chest.

"I know, and I need to explain myself. I know I do...but let me do it right. Let me look you in the eye and tell you how I feel without bedsheets between us."

I laughed, rubbing my eye. "Great, then you can sleep on the floor, or go home and see me tomorrow."

Was he shaking? His body seemed to vibrate next to me as he waited to respond. I was tempted to move my face so I could see his eyes. They always told me what his voice wouldn't.

Finally, after a few silent beats, he breathed slowly through his nose. It was on the tip of my tongue to tell him he should breathe in through his nose and out through his mouth.

"I know the right thing would be to do what you're asking me to do. I know you deserve a gentleman who'd respect your space and what you're asking...but I'm not a gentleman. I'm a devil, through and through. I can't be away from you tonight. I need to feel your skin, hear your heart...feel the heat from your fucking breath..." He propped his head up on his elbow, looking down at me. "I'm not leaving you. I won't touch you or do anything at all to you...I just need to be near you tonight."

Well fuck.

Butterflies, pterodactyls, and fucking bats were set loose in my chest at his admission. I'd let the suckers fight it out while I turned away from him to get some sleep. I was past fighting him on this. I just wanted to forget.

"Fine." I made a point to let out an irritated sigh. "But I'm keeping my sweats on."

"I'll literally cut them off your legs."

God, the fire in his tone set me ablaze. I wanted to push him, see if he'd strip me and then challenge whether or not he'd touch me. I was a mess, a fucking too-hot kitchen on a too-hot day with no air. He'd ghosted me, and I needed to cling to my anger over his indifference toward me.

For starters, I would finish removing the damn sweats, but only because if he removed them or touched me in any way, I would beg him to do more than that. I just fucking would, and I hated myself for it. Slowly, I pushed the waistband over my hips and down my thighs until they were off. Then I settled into bed, feeling the warm sheets against my silky legs.

Decker seemed to settle into me. His arm went up under my neck, which allowed him to pull me close until I was twisted toward him. His bare chest was an inferno against me, but it was that place low in my belly that started to flare to life, going even farther down; my core ached for him to touch me. Even knowing he may have touched Taylor, even knowing he may be gone in the morning…I wanted him.

I brought my hand up, covering his firm chest, carefully running my finger down the lines and into the grooves of his impressive stomach. I kept touching him, listening to him breathe, feeling his own finger trail over my skin, back and forth like a lullaby. We were in sync with one another, rubbing, touching…breathing. In and out, up and down. There were words, stories, and songs in the prints we left on each other's bodies. Mine spoke of desire, of how badly I wanted him, how I wished for him, and how I knew I could never have him.

His…well…every swipe of his finger over my arm was a tiny flame dancing on my skin. I wanted him to brave going lower, trace the curve of my hip, the dip in my back. The darkness seemed to settle around us, our breaths silent…and just when I thought we'd fall asleep or ignore everything that had happened—or hadn't happened—between us since that night in his bedroom, he spoke up.

"Thank you for this."

I kept my cheek plastered to his chest after his words rumbled under me. "Why did you need it?"

Seconds passed. More darkness. I was fighting sleep, batting and swatting it away as I waited for him to answer.

Finally, the pad of his finger brushed over the tattoo under my ear, just like it had that night in his house.

"This." He applied pressure to the Nordic symbol under my lobe. "And I needed to know you were okay…" He trailed off, and I knew if I had been looking at his throat, I would have seen it bob.

163

"Why *this*?" I whispered, brushing my fingers over the ones he had fastened to my neck.

More time passed, more swipes of his finger against my skin and more moments for me to contemplate what on earth was going on here.

"You make me feel less lost. I saw you over those five days, that raggedy red hoodie, and suddenly it felt like I'd finally found a compass...a way to get back home." That gruffness in his voice made every word seem like it had been dragged through gravel.

My throat was tight, tears clogging my eyes as I processed the sweetest thing anyone had ever said to me. Then anger swept it all away.

"That doesn't feel fair, Decker. You can't say something like that, be here in my bed, and still try going after my stepsister."

Another long pause met me as I ran my finger along the trail of hair drifting into the elastic band of his boxers.

"I need him to care that I'm with her. It's...shit that's from the past but affected me and still affects me. It's just something I need to do."

I began connecting the dots, seeing the bigger picture it created.

He wants revenge.

"The rumors...they aren't true, are they?"

A shudder ran through him, and the hitch in his breathing was the only answer I needed to know Elias had done something horrible to Decker and the story I had heard about the two of them might not have been true.

"If you heard the same ones circulating the halls, about me hitting Elias on purpose or trying to attack him...no, that's not how it went down at all."

"Will you tell me about it?" I whispered, not wanting to ruin the flow of information coming from him.

"Someday...but for now, I just need you to understand that I want to hurt him in the only way I can." His hand trailed down my body, that finger finally brushing against my hip, splaying along my thigh.

"By sleeping with Taylor?" The words hurt coming out, and I knew the answer would hurt even worse, but I had to face it. So did he.

Another painful pause, almost too long to be comfortable, passed between us. His fingers moving were the only indication that he was still awake.

"Just tell me. I already know the answer, but I need to hear you say it, and I think you need to hear you say it too."

A huge swell of air left his lungs as his chest deflated. "I don't know."

"So, it's not off the table then..." I didn't phrase it as a question, because we both knew it wasn't one.

"You knew, that night we met...that was my intention. Sleep with her, have him see it...ruin him."

Pain pierced my chest, barreling into my stomach like a lightning bolt. I knew. He was completely right, but I just thought...

"I guess I thought you were just trying to date her." I sounded small, almost childlike, unsure of why my voice wouldn't work right.

"Nothing has changed from what I originally planned," he whispered.

I believed him, but his hand was now firmly placed on my hip in a possessive way, sending me a mixed signal.

I whispered the only truth I knew to him and hoped he'd see it for what it was. "Everything has changed, Decker."

Tears begged to be freed, and after the week I'd had where he pushed me away, I just wanted to let them free.

"I think you should go." I was so damn proud there wasn't a single shudder in my voice, nothing betraying that I had somehow fallen for him, regardless of knowing the deal.

"I can't," he replied roughly, like he was suppressing bigger emotions than I might realize.

I couldn't help it. I blinked, and the flood gates opened. I turned away from him, out of his embrace, and let the pain flow from me, wishing and hoping that once I woke up, he'd be gone and so would the remaining feelings I had for him.

CHAPTER TWENTY-ONE

Decker

MALLORY WAS CAREFULLY REMOVING THE SHEETS FROM AROUND OUR waists, going slow and cautious. I knew she was trying not to wake me, but I'd been awake for a while, watching her sleep, trying to get my hard-on under control without touching her. It was an act of God that she didn't wake up while I struggled in silence behind her. She'd fallen asleep hugging the far side of the mattress, as far away from me as possible, which was fine. As soon as she began softly snoring, I had pulled her back against my chest, put my face in the crook of her neck, and fallen asleep too.

Something had shifted between us when I saw her climb into Elias's truck. Seeing that smirk on his face while Mallory climbed in, looking like fucking sin...it did something to me. I knew the irony of the situation was ridiculous, but just the same—he was using her, and it didn't sit well with me. The conversation with Mallory after she came home wasn't sitting well either, but I'd had all morning to think that over too. Taylor was work...she was the job, as Scotty put it. Mallory was home. Every minute she lay curled into my side this morning just re-established that she was mine. I'd finish the job with Taylor, without sleeping with her...I had made the decision this morning while holding Mallory that I could never touch Taylor like that. Not even a kiss.

Which royally fucked my entire plan.

The warmth from Mallory's body shifted as she moved her hips to the side, trying to get free of my hold and the blankets. I wouldn't be assisting with any of that. I wanted her to squirm and realize we'd fallen asleep wrapped up in each other's arms. Her ass moved again, but this time it went in the wrong direction. She backtracked, and suddenly she was plastered to my chest, her ass aligned perfectly with my cock.

I had put so much work into calming down, but now I was already hard again. I considered warning her. The gentlemanly thing would have been to warn her, but I'd already warned her I wasn't one of those...so instead I challenged her.

Moving my hand down and over her hip, I splayed my palm flat against her stomach, over her ribs. Her skin was so soft, and I just wanted to run my fingers over every inch of her then follow the route with my tongue. I could feel her breathing change, growing shallower as I continued to pretend to sleep behind her with soft snores.

We stayed like that for a few minutes until she wiggled her ass against me, and fuck if she didn't do it on purpose, like she was challenging me right back.

I moved my hand up, covering her right breast and pinching the nipple between my forefinger and thumb. I heard a little gasp leave her while her ass continued moving against me in an obvious assault. She knew what she was doing just as much as I did.

My other hand came up and around her hip, and I dipped my finger under the waistband of her cotton underwear. They felt stretchy and comfortable, and for whatever reason there was something about the fact that she wore sensible clothing to sleep in that settled inside me. Like we weren't trying to impress each other or be people we weren't... it was just us. I wanted moments like this with her, moments where I saw her wash her face and brush her teeth, moments where I read a book while she dressed in her pajamas and crawled into bed with me. Something real...lasting.

Her huff of breath pulled me from my thoughts as she pushed against my erection, and my fingers trailed lower, over her smooth entrance.

"Decker."

I didn't respond, just pushed two fingers into her and began to slowly rub them in a circle.

"This pussy...Jesus. You don't even know, do you?" I kissed her shoulder, whispering in her ear, right next to her tattoo, the one I knew wasn't just a coincidence. This girl I was falling for had a fucking way out of the storm inked into her skin. *She is meant for me.*

"I can't do this." Her labored breaths pushed her tits against the soft fabric of her shirt, making me withhold a groan.

"This?" I moved my fingers in and out of her wetness with forceful strokes, letting her know how much I wanted this.

She rocked her hips in rhythm with my touch. "No...we can't do this," she said breathlessly while continuing to rock into my touch.

I couldn't help myself. I pulled my fingers from her core, bringing them to my lips, which were right next to her ear, and sucked the taste of her into my mouth.

"You taste delicious, Mallory. Fucking delightful."

"Decker, we can't..." She pulled away from me, and this time I let her go. I wasn't about to force her into something she didn't want, but the way she'd writhed against me told me something different. Sitting up, she tried to climb over me, but since her bed was shoved against the wall, there was no escape. I grabbed her right as her left knee straddled my hip.

"Decker," she warned, stabilizing herself with her hands on my chest.

She was extended over me, her soft pink cotton panties resting right against my boxer briefs. Thank fuck I'd had the foresight to shed my jeans sometime during the night.

"Taylor could walk in on us any second, then this whole plan of yours goes to shit."

I smiled, not caring at all about her concerns, because sometime in the middle of the night when I was staring at the way her hair brushed against her forehead, it had hit me in the chest, nearly as painful and terrifying as that baseball had the year before. I wouldn't risk losing her. I couldn't. I would fix this, all of it, but first...

I began moving my thumb over the moist spot in her underwear, right over her entrance, thinking back to the fantasy I'd had of her in that bookstore.

"You're wet for me, Mallory Shaw. I plan to tend to that this morning, and I don't care who the fuck comes in and sees."

Her eyes blazed with lust, with need, and probably with hate. I knew she was confused, angry at me, and hurt. I was going to explain it all, everything...but I needed this.

"Close your eyes."

She bit her bottom lip, dragging it between her teeth as indecision warred along the planes of her beautiful face.

"Just trust me...please." I rocked my hips into hers while rubbing my thumb up and down her slit.

She let out a soft moan while her hips rolled forward, and then those gorgeous green eyes closed. Dark lashes splayed against her freckled, tan skin. The way she looked on top of me in a black tank, her legs on display, her hair mussed from sleep...my chest felt like it was opening up, making room for this foreign feeling to invade, fill up, consume. She made somewhere deep inside burn in a way that took away my breath.

"I need to see you. Take your tank top off," I commanded, voice a little raspy. I cleared my throat and pushed the material up from her stomach.

Her fingers brushed against mine as she pulled the rest of the material free, allowing the fullness of her breasts to show.

I groaned, watching her palm the left one, rolling the nub between her fingers.

I drew the material of her panties to the side, tempted just to rip the things right off her hips. Her core rested against my erection, still clothed by my boxer briefs. With her eyes closed, she had no idea that I was staring at her with something akin to worship. Her breasts were full, her stomach trim, flaring into perfectly round hips and thick thighs...she was the most perfect thing I'd ever seen, all woman, and I wanted her. Today, tomorrow, the next day...there was no end to how many times I wanted this view.

I slowly pulled my aching cock out, a small pebble of clear liquid already weeping from the tip as I gripped the root and allowed the heat of her body to pulse against it. I wasn't ashamed in the slightest that I was going to remember this moment and jerk off to it until I was old and in need of Viagra. With her eyes still closed, I made sure to watch her for permission as I said, "I haven't been with anyone in over a year...I'm clean."

Her lashes fluttered against her cheeks, but she didn't open her eyes, just nodded her agreement, meaning she was too. Otherwise she would have put a stop to this a long time ago.

Pulling her hips forward, I gripped my throbbing hard-on and rubbed it up and down the length of her soaked slit. I groaned at how good it felt to have her heat against my dick. I wanted to pull her until she was sinking down onto it, but I knew we weren't ready to go all the way. I had some explaining to do first. This was just meant to make her feel good, let her know how much she affected me.

Up and down, I rubbed her pussy while she rocked against me, slowly getting herself off. Her hands stayed up, cradling her breasts as her core moved against me. Her arousal soaked the base of my cock, teasing me to just flip us and push inside of her.

"More, I need more, Decker..." she muttered breathily.

I did too, but if I kept playing with her, I was going to do something we weren't ready for, so I pulled on her hips, indicating that I wanted her to move.

"Reach forward with your left hand and grab the headboard, then do the same with your right, and move your ass until you're straddling my face." I pressed my fingers into the globes of her ass to encourage her.

She paused, her fingers digging into my chest. "I've never...done this specific thing with anyone."

I smiled, loving that her eyes were still closed but her eyebrows had caved and those white teeth pinned her lips in place.

"Good." I laughed, pressing my fingers deeper into her skin, hoping it would leave a mark. I wanted to look tomorrow and see how desperate I had been to have her sit on my face.

Licking her lips, she did as I instructed, gripping the headboard and moving up my chest.

"Come here." I breathed out as the feel of her singed every nerve ending in my head. With my hands around her ass, I drew the material of her underwear that covered her cheeks toward the center of her crack, using it as a way to move her closer.

A gasp left her as I tugged her by the bundled material, forcing her reluctant posture to falter until she was directly over my face. I used my hold to apply more pressure, pulling up on the panties until they were tight against her entrance, then I gently ran my tongue along the constricted cotton.

She hissed while rocking into it.

"You like that pressure, baby?" I asked, repeating what I'd done, carefully licking her only along the wet material of her underwear, just barely tasting her wet cunt. I knew it would drive her crazy.

"Pull it tighter," she demanded from above me.

Fuck. My dick was still weeping with precum, begging me to just hurry this along as I did as she asked. I pulled the material even tighter against her pussy, bunching it in the back, then leaned up, licking and biting against that wet spot. My free hand flew, smacking her ass, and fuck, I wished there were a mirror in here so I could see my handprint there.

I had never been rough with a woman before, because I was still young and, well, if it went wrong or she freaked out, it could go all sorts of backwards real fast. I had never found anyone I trusted enough to let myself go with like that, but with Mallory...I didn't even have to think twice. Her luscious ass begged and begged for that sort of attention.

I wanted so many more moments with her, moments where I rocked into her from behind, getting a view of that backside. Me on top of her, fucking her with abandon, sinking my dick so far into her that we didn't know where she ended and I began. Her riding me while we sat on the couch...the list was endless.

"You've completely soaked these." I loosened my hold on the briefs and snapped them against her skin. "Look at this...you're a mess." Moving the cotton entirely to the side, I ran my finger in and out of her entrance. "Do you hear that?" I moved my fingers in and out of her. "You sound like you want me to fuck you, Mallory."

Fucking her with my fingers, I watched as she rocked and shuddered above me.

"We aren't ready for that though, so what should we do?" I

continued to tease her, bringing my fingers out enough that she could hear the sound of me pushing them back in. "Do you want this, Mal?" I lifted my gaze, seeing her heavy tits move as she ground against my fingers, her arms slightly bent now that the headboard was within reach. She looked down at me, and some of her hair slipped over her shoulder.

"Yes." She moaned, begging with her body.

"You want my tongue inside this pussy?" I massaged her clit with my finger, taking the slickness and rubbing it up along her crack. I knew she liked me to play with her there from that first night. "You want me to suck on this clit and make you scream?"

"Yes...please, Decker." Her voice was still shuddery and quiet, but she didn't have to ask a third time. I pulled her forward until her core was pressed against my mouth and my tongue was licking through her folds. "Oh god." Mallory shuddered, trying to keep her voice down.

"Roll those hips, baby. Hold on to this headboard and fuck my face. Don't hold back." I leaned back to stare up at her, those eyes wide open and full of lust. She nodded, and then those hips rolled, my tongue delving deeper into her and causing us both to nearly lose it.

Her tits bounced as she picked up momentum, treating me like a goddamn horse. If she was like this with my mouth, I could only imagine how fucking good it would be when she bounced on my dick. I groaned into her entrance as I felt her reach back with one of her hands and grip my shaft. Up and down, she rolled the precum on the tip of my erection around and down my length. Hard, swift, and unrelenting. I met the intensity with my tongue, feeling a tightening build at the base of my back.

"Decker...oh my god...holy—" she yelled, tossing her head back and pushing down furiously against my mouth. I was about to blow my entire fucking load as I watched those tits and that hair. When she was finally coming apart against my tongue, I moved.

"There's nothing holy about me, baby. You better remember that." I growled right before I sucked her nipple into my mouth and bit down.

She fell backward on the bed, letting out a cry—whether of pain or ecstasy, I had no clue at this point. She clutched the sheets while she rocked her hips against the air, still chasing her climax. I pushed three fingers into her pussy, milking her orgasm and giving her the pressure she needed as I climbed over her.

Fisting myself, I was about to pump my cock and come all over her tits, but she sat up and pushed at my chest, crawling on her hands and knees until she was grabbing for me and pulling my dick into her mouth.

She licked from the base to the tip twice before those bewitching eyes locked on mine and pulled me out of her mouth. Rubbing her hand up and down my shaft, she kept her gaze tied with mine while she said, "There isn't anything holy about me either." Then she moved forward and choked on my length.

I was sure I'd died. She literally took my breath away with her mouth on me, sucking and savoring every inch of me, all while she watched me with hooded eyes. My release was clawing along my spine, begging to be let free.

I made a pained sound, pulling at her to disconnect, but she gripped my ass, still covered by my boxers, and kept me there, sucking furiously on my cock—begging for me to spill down her throat.

So, I did.

"Fuck. Fuck. Fuckkkkkk, baby." I rolled my hips, gripped her hair, and finished the best goddamn orgasm of my entire life. She moved her left hand to fist my dick, holding it in place while she sucked every last drop of my release down her throat.

I was in so much trouble, because after this, there wouldn't ever be a limit we'd reach where we'd had enough. I saw it in her eyes. Mallory Shaw wanted me, as often, as intensely, and as roughly as I wanted her.

♭

"Something tells me this isn't exactly legal," Mallory said, looking over her shoulder.

I smirked as she brought her hood up to cover her head.

"Are you afraid?" I peered down at her while tugging her closer to my side.

"I'm just surprised you're okay with this...I mean, he's only sixteen."

173

The loud sound of a modified exhaust barreled into us as my Uncle Scotty started the Hellcat my brother would be driving; the bar we were standing behind vibrated from the noise. We stood on a small patch of concrete with a wobbly, rusted bar raised as a handrail, separating us from the crowd. The entire overpass was deserted for the time being as a massive construction project was planned in the coming months, so all four lanes were vacant. It allowed the less law-abiding citizens ample opportunity to take advantage. There were about fifty people on either side of the road, huddled in clumps of fandom as my brother's team fussed over his car. The idiot challenging him hadn't arrived yet.

"He may be sixteen, but he's been driving since he was eleven, and before that he was watching these races his entire life." My hand dipped into the back pocket of Mallory's jeans, and the feeling of her pressed into my side while we watched my little brother get ready for the race just hit me in the fucking chest. This couldn't be real.

"I thought you brought me here to talk and explain yourself." She tilted her head back, smiling. "You know, without the sheets between us."

I laughed at the gleam in her eye. Thinking back to that morning, I remembered how, after we'd both come down from our high, she'd tried to pull those damn sweats on again, and I nearly tackled her. I kissed her until she agreed to get breakfast with me, and I failed to mention we'd be picking it up on our way to Pinehurst. Once she realized, she laughed and mentioned that she'd started packing overnight things in her purse after our night in the storm.

On the drive over, we ate and listened to music, quizzing each other on genres and band names. Mallory also explained her spatial anxiety in case we got ourselves into a situation where there was a big crowd. I was grateful for the information considering we were headed toward a crowd. Still, it seemed neither of us were ready to burst the bubble we were in by talking about everything I had to explain…until now, I guess.

"You'd risk missing this?" I gestured to my brother, who was taking a selfie with some blonde girl. She seemed a little too overly enthusiastic for the girls he usually liked to date. Kyle liked broody girls, the ones nearly impossible to get, but he also liked attention—my little bro was more messed up than even me. That was my observation, at least. He'd never talked about anyone he liked, or anyone he didn't like, for that matter. I looked around, trying to see if his best friend was here since she was usually the reason the other girls didn't brave getting too close to Kyle on race days. She was also the reason my brother had been driving since he was eleven.

"Does he know you're here?" Mallory asked, bringing my eyes back to her.

"Yeah, I texted him earlier that we'd be here."

"We?"

The newer Mustang rolled in next to the Hellcat my brother would be racing on behalf of my Uncle Scotty. The brand-new car was gunmetal grey with a single black stripe down the side, and it was entirely too much car for Kyle.

Fuck.

Scotty was supposed to keep my brother alive. I knew, even beyond what came stock on that car, it was too much power for my sixteen-year-old brother. He was still too eager to make a name for himself in these street races. He was one hell of a driver, but my stomach still tilted as I saw him tip his head back, looking for me. He gave me a single nod, delivered a smirk to Mallory, and then ducked his head, getting into the car.

I swallowed my nerves and remembered what she had asked.

"Yeah, my little brother likes you. Gave me hell for leaving that morning without saying goodbye...he wanted to have breakfast with us, get to know you."

She melted into my side, her left arm darting out around my waist. We watched as the crowd simmered, and music began playing from the small speakers set up on the other side of the road.

"This is quite the setup," Mallory quipped, bringing the cord of her hoodie up to her mouth and beginning to chew on it.

"Getting an itch to write a story about it?" I joked, keeping my eyes on my brother. The man challenging him was clearly in his twenties, possibly even older than me. It wouldn't really matter, but he had more years under him in knowing how to race and handle cars.

"No, this one I'm just going to enjoy for myself."

Kyle buckled the harness in his bucket seat, and I waited to make sure he would grab for the helmet Scotty insisted both racers wear when they did these things. It had been a while since I last attended one, so I wasn't sure if he was keeping up on it or not. Kyle spun his hat backward but didn't reach for a helmet.

Fuck.

I began to move, but Mallory tugged me back.

"He's okay...look at him." The twinkle in her green eyes had some kind of calming effect on me. I knew she understood why I was particular about his safety, so I gave her a nod and watched as my brother warmed his tires and crawled up to the starting line.

"Talk me through what he has to do." Mallory rubbed my back in easy strokes.

Had my breathing become more restricted?

I swallowed thickly. "He has to drive down to those water barrels, drift around it without hitting the flag right there"—I pointed with my finger toward the yellow barrels and orange flags—"then they race back here, and whoever crosses first wins."

"Are there other racers who will challenge the winner?"

I watched as the makeshift board, one of those usually used in gyms, beeped loudly, indicating the startup. With the click of a button, the numbers began to climb right as someone waved a flag. The cars punched into first gear and darted from their starting positions with a roar and squeal of the tires.

I tried to breathe correctly as I trailed after my brother with my eyes. I felt Mallory's hand warm my back with gentle caresses, bringing her question back to mind.

"Yeah, there are a few challengers, I think." I tracked my brother's black car as it sailed down the asphalt, the orange Mustang neck and neck with him.

"Breathe." Mallory kept rubbing soothing strokes along my back, and for the first time in my life, I felt like I wasn't alone. It felt like I finally had someone to help me bear some of the burdens that usually pinned me to the ground, like worrying about my kid brother participating in illegal street races, the fact that he was involved in about a million other illegal activities, or my mom potentially losing her house.

My hand found Mallory's, and I tugged it up, pressing her knuckles to my lips.

Kyle cranked his wheel hard to the left as his car circled the barrels, the tail of his gleaming muscle car gracefully flaring out just enough to clear the flag. It was a perfect drift, and pride inflated my chest as I watched his competitor hit his flag with his taillight.

"Oh my god, he's going to win." Mallory slapped her palm against the bar in front of us.

A grin split my face as I slid her in front of me and brought my hands around her, settling them on her waist. Her head fit under my chin perfectly as she clapped and cheered for my brother. The nose of his car sailed over the finish line with more than a few paces between him and the Mustang trailing him.

His car was surrounded within minutes by girls and a few guys ready to congratulate him. He saw us from where we were, giving us a nod and a massive smile. I noticed his eyes kept darting around like he was looking for someone. The furrow in his brow told me it was the one girl who'd been at all his races but was suddenly missing.

I looked down at the girl in front of me and spun her in my arms.

"I'm glad you're here. I like having you with me." I leaned in, pressing my mouth to hers. The kiss released a tightness in my chest that seemed to build when I didn't touch or have my mouth on her.

"You still need to explain." She breathed the words as she tilted her head, deepening our kiss.

"I know." I brought my hand up her back, sliding my tongue against hers, groaning into her mouth.

"We can't keep doing this every time we need to have a conversation…" She broke away long enough to grab the collar of my t-shirt, drawing me closer. "We need to talk."

I nodded, keeping my hands tucked into her back pockets, pulling her against my growing erection.

"Holy shit, get a room, bro." Kyle stepped up, slapping me on the back.

We broke away, and Mallory ducked her head, laughing.

We stayed, watching every race my younger brother competed in until there wasn't anyone left to race. Our afternoon was spent treating

Kyle to lunch and dessert, and our mom came and joined us once her shift ended. She and Mallory started talking about gardening, which somehow transitioned to their love of some crime show they both seemed to watch obsessively.

That's when Kyle pulled me aside and stuck a wad of cash in my hand. "Today's earnings."

I looked down at the massive roll of green and quickly lifted my eyes to my little brother.

"Since when do these races pay this kind of cash?"

Kyle winced, which told me enough.

"If you're doing anything to skim off the top, Scotty will kill you. Family or not, he won't hesitate," I warned, feeling a fresh wave of panic settle in my stomach.

"I'm not. I swear." He put his hands up. "Look, I may have started working for him a little more than I led you to believe. He's also letting me do work on the cars that rotate in, as a part-time mechanic."

"In addition to the jobs you're pulling and the races?" I asked, my eyes darting around the restaurant to see if anyone was listening.

"Yeah. That's enough to pay for the mortgage for the next three months."

I shook my head. "No."

"Why the fuck do you think I've been doing so much work, D?"

I slammed my molars together, narrowing my eyes. "You failed to mention the part where you were still attending school full time."

Yeah, did he honestly think I wasn't keeping tabs on that shit?

His eye roll nearly made me slap him in the back of the head.

"I have it handled. Right now, this is more important." He waved me off.

"And what about you? What if you get caught?"

"We both know that's not going to happen."

"Just because your best friend's dad is the police chief in Pinehurst doesn't mean he'll keep you safe, Kyle. This shit is big...especially with this much money coming in."

"Just don't stress, okay? Between the two of us, she won't have to sell the house—that's all that matters." He patted my back and walked around me, leaving the cash in my hand.

Mallory and I ended up staying the night in my room again. This time it was a little more domesticated. She'd brought an overnight bag, brushing her teeth and washing her face in my childhood bathroom. She thought she was being funny by bringing along a certain pair of sweats to wear to bed.

"I bet you think you're funny," I said, watching as she swung her hips while wearing a small tank top, one that made her tits look fantastic.

She smirked at me, pulling down the covers. "I get cold at night, and these are so comfortable."

I was in just a pair of black boxers. Even my feet were bare, and this girl was going to try to sleep next to me fully clothed. Hilarious.

"Mallory, I'm not kidding. If you wear those sweats to bed, I will shred them, then I will fuck you for good measure."

Her bright smile melted away my defenses, leaving me with a stupid smile. She wiggled under the covers then tossed the sweats at my face a second later.

I slowly lifted the comforter to see what she was wearing. Her tan legs stretched out on my dark sheets, her white tank top rose to show her midriff, and there across her hips was a dark green color...

My god. My mouth went dry as I threw the covers off her.

She wore a dark green thong, just like in my fucking fantasy.

"Well, you're fucked," I muttered, about to run my hand over the fabric just to make sure it was real, but she stopped me.

Grabbing the covers once again, she chided me. "You owe me a conversation...or two."

I groaned, letting my face fall to the covers.

"I saw a picture last night with you two...it looked real, and I guess I'm just trying not to be that sucker." She plowed past my obvious reluctance to have this discussion.

I rested my head on my elbow so I could watch her while I explained. "Taylor barely talked to me after you left. She mentioned knowing Elias was a bad guy and said you shouldn't be out with him. I sat on the couch, agreeing with her, and all of a sudden she perked up and said she knew something that might get you home sooner." My hand itched to reach over and grab hers. "As soon as she took it, she

179

jumped off the couch and told me I should wait for you in your room. Then she went to bed."

"Wait...what?" Mallory sat up, shaking her head a bit. "That doesn't make any sense. She..."

I knew she was likely coming to the same conclusion I had: Taylor knew Mallory and I were into each other.

"So, that's it...you're not after her anymore, and you magically don't need your revenge?"

I considered it. Knowing what I did, things even Mallory didn't know, I realized in comparison to potentially losing her, messing with Elias's chances at a fat payday...it wasn't worth it. I also knew there wasn't anything I could really say that would explain my change of heart or make her believe I'd changed direction.

I smashed my lips together...then let out a heavy sigh.

"I'm falling for you. When I look at you, you're not just some girl I like. You look like you're already mine. My heart knows it, my dick was on board from the first time we met, I just...I had my reasons for why I wanted revenge, but if it means I might lose you, I can't."

She lifted her hand, cupping my jaw and rubbing her thumb along my lips.

"Don't hurt me, Decker. I may seem tough, but my heart is made of glass, the beautiful kind someone worked hard to create with the sand and memories of the most painful moments of my life. It will shatter if you don't handle it right."

I leaned into her touch, staring into her green gaze. I felt a little pinch in my chest at the things I was still holding back from her, but we had to take all this in stages, one step at a time.

If I told her what I was hiding from her all at once, she wouldn't even give me a shot. No, I needed to convince her I'd keep her safe, her and her heart. I might not have been perfect, but I'd be consistent.

Instead of replying with words, I leaned down and carefully pressed my lips to hers. I wouldn't hurt her, not when doing so would kill me in the process.

CHAPTER TWENTY-TWO

Mallory

"You need to square your shoulders." Decker stared down at me from under the bill of his Devils hat. He stood on the white rectangle in the middle of the dirt mound, gripping a baseball in his left hand.

I eyed the size of the ball and lowered my shoulders.

"Wouldn't it make more sense to start me off on a softball, or maybe a tennis ball?" I winced at the overhanging sun, wishing there were a few trees around the field. Why weren't there trees? How fun would that be to run and play ball through a fun forest? These guys were missing out on an awesome opportunity.

I could see the smirk ghost along Decker's jaw. He wore jeans and one of those baseball shirts like from *The Sandlot*. In fact, this whole look with a pair of high-top Converse looked like one of those cute kids all grown up. It had been two weeks since that night in his bedroom when I asked him to be careful with my heart and he promised me he would.

Well, he hadn't promised, exactly, but he had kissed me. Then he kept kissing me. I told him we weren't having sex, because I honestly wasn't ready to. I needed to know he was serious about me...about us. He did however wake me up with his head between my thighs and his teeth raking over my thong. I surrendered to an early morning orgasm courtesy of his expert tongue, and when he was ready to finish, he mentioned something about a fantasy and asked that I sit on my knees while holding my breasts together so he could come on my chest. Looking up into those eyes blazing with lust and need while he fisted that throbbing erection…it was a sight I'd never forget.

There was something so insatiable about his hunger for me that lit me up. I'd never craved someone like I craved him. I'd never woken up wishing I were still in bed with someone, never nearly burst at the seams when someone showed up at my door or asked if I wanted to learn how to play baseball. This was all new and terrifying, but I loved it and didn't want it to end.

"You'll do fine with the baseball, just remember to keep your eye on it. I'll go really slow." Decker brought my mind out of the gutter and back to the lesson he was trying to give.

I did as he said, thankful Juan and Hillary weren't here to see this. They'd never let me live it down.

I watched as he brought his knee up in that traditional pitcher stance and, true to his word, lightly tossed the ball toward the plate I was hovering over.

I watched it sail toward me, and as it got closer, I became increasingly nervous. Regardless of how slowly it moved, it was still headed straight for me. Nerves rattled my insides as I closed my eyes tight and swung with all my might.

"Babe," Decker droned in irritation.

I opened my eyes. "Did I do it again?"

"Yes, you closed your eyes again. You have to keep them open." He ran over to grab the ball even though it was closer to me.

"Maybe we should switch spots?" I offered, but he only swatted my ass, smirking while he ran back to his perch on the mound.

We repeated this process a few more times over the hour before he finally gave up in need of sustenance. On our way from the field, I grabbed my purse and checked my cell. There was another text lingering on my screen, like there had been a few times in the last week. I'd responded to each of them, but as time went on, it was starting to feel strange that he was still doing it.

Elias: Party girl, when you coming back to watch me practice?

That was one I hadn't responded to yet because it felt flirty.

Elias: We're having a team party this Friday night, want to come and check it out?

I hadn't brought up my article to Elias yet. We hadn't really talked at all since that night we went out. Everything with Decker had felt like such a whirlwind, and I was merely responding to texts but wasn't encouraging any future hangouts or anything. That said, here was this golden opportunity to attend a card game, right as I was on the tail end of finalizing my article. I would be an idiot to pass up the chance to go with a guide.

Biting my nail, I turned to Decker and decided to bring it up. We hadn't officially given each other a label, but we'd made confessions in his bedroom about him falling and me asking him not to break my heart. That had to essentially mean we were dating, right? He called me babe now and always tucked his hand in my back pocket when we walked or looked at books at the bookshop, plus we were physical in some capacity every single day. His mouth was either devouring my pussy or attached to one of my breasts, and I in turn had essentially turned into a Hoover vacuum with how frequently I was going down on him. I mean, that was definitely relationship material...borderline *serious* relationship material.

Right?

"Hey, so I wanted to talk about something with you...but I wasn't sure how," I hedged, keeping my eyes on the ground while we walked. His arm hung over my shoulders, and my arm was around his waist. It was one of my favorite positions.

"Oh yeah?" He tugged on the ends of my hair before shoving that hand in my back pocket.

"Um...yeah, so..." God, what if he ended things because I was still talking to Elias? No, I would not be in that sort of relationship. I'd never done anything romantic with Elias, and I could be friends with him if I wanted to, especially since Decker still had never explained their past to me.

"Here." I handed him my phone with the text still on it.

He used his free hand to shove the bag of equipment higher on his shoulder before accepting my phone.

After a few seconds of him reading, he handed it back.

"So, you want to go to the game, to get notes for the story...that it?"

I looked up, feeling hopeful. "Yes, exactly."

His gaze stayed fixed on the parking lot as we approached it. "Okay."

"Okay?" Surely it wasn't that easy for him to let me go with—

"I'll take you."

He smiled down at me with mischief stamped across his face. Those delicious lips slung to the side in a sexy smile, and all I could do was gape because he was handsome. Sometimes it hurt to look at him and believe he actually liked me, believe he was falling for me.

"You'll take me?"

"Yeah...I mean, I can take you. No need to deal with Elias anymore. Actually...you know..." He cleared his throat, setting the equipment down. "At all."

I slowed my walk, spinning to face him as he settled items in the back of his truck.

"So, I can't be friends with Elias anymore?"

"I just don't see why you need to be. I can answer your questions." He shrugged again, walking toward his door. I walked to mine, opening it and climbing inside. Starting the engine, he began backing up while I waited for him to answer me. "I won't tell you what to do."

Okay...that was vague, but I supposed it was as good as I was going to get. I waited for him to take this opening and explain what had happened or tell me why he didn't like Elias, but he didn't. I tried not to care, but hurt leaked through my chest just the same.

ᴆ

"SO, WHAT'S AFTER GRADUATION?" HE SUDDENLY ASKED WHILE SIPPING on his soda. We'd stopped at one of those make-your-own-pizza places. He'd taken me on several dates over the past two weeks, but I loved that he didn't insist on paying for each one. I knew he didn't have a lot of extra income from bits and pieces of conversations I had picked up on between Kyle and his mom. Being the daughter of a multi-millionaire, it was hard for me not to offer to cover everything. Still, I liked that he seemed okay with our balance.

I sipped my lemonade and began explaining about Kline Global.

"An internship? Gotta be honest, I didn't see that coming." He laughed, jumping up to grab our orders.

Once he returned and we started on our pizzas, I eyed him suspiciously. "Did you assume I'd work for my dad?"

He shrugged. "Yeah. Isn't Taylor getting a New York spot or something?"

I continued to chew, trying to tamp down the confusion swirling in my mind. How did he know that...and how did I not know that? Was Taylor considering a spot in New York? What about... Now that I took a second to think about it, she hadn't shared a desire to pursue anything after graduation except a trip around the Caribbean.

"I don't know," I finally replied, trying to keep the mood light, but it was obvious that I needed to talk to my stepsister. We'd been out of sync since I started dating Decker. I'd barely been home, or I was tucked away in my room working on finals and my article. Some nights I spent over at his apartment, and other nights he'd be in my bed by the time I got home from the library.

"What about you?" I returned the question.

"Me?" He stalled, sipping his drink again. "I don't know...I think I might take over my dad's company. It's been dormant for over a year, but nothing some good marketing can't help."

"What about baseball? Not only going after it...I guess, professionally, but even if that doesn't happen, isn't that the entire point of being a Devil? Playing, having a good word put in for you, etc.?"

I had gathered enough intel about the Devils that I now understood the draw of being part of an organization of its caliber. Their pockets had pockets, and their references were pure gold. Playing for them was literally like having a winning lottery ticket.

Decker chewed, sipped his drink, and wiped his hands before he bracketed his plate with his arms.

"I mean, that used to be my dream." He shrugged like it was nothing. "But then Dad died, and I got hurt. I just...I don't know, I guess I just set those dreams aside while I make sure my mom doesn't lose her house."

My eyebrows caved as I thought over what he'd said, my heart aching to help.

"Is she pretty far behind, or what's going on with it?" I hoped it wasn't rude to pry, but I had to know.

His tense jaw told me maybe I had overstepped with my questioning.

"It just all went to hell after Dad's funeral, and the medical costs… we got hit by bill after bill, and instead of selling, my mom just let them bury her."

I understood that. Grief was too painful all on its own; add in having to give up the last piece of you that felt like the person you lost, and it would be too much at once.

"It's only been a year?" I carefully asked, softening my tone. I'd lost my mother at ten and had years to acclimate to her absence, but it still hurt.

Decker nodded. "A little over."

Suddenly he stood, grabbing his garbage, effectively ending our conversation.

"You done with this?" he asked kindly, like we were just going to push past the topic. I knew he needed to, so I smiled and let him take our things, all while secretly wishing there was a way I could ease some of his burden and he'd trust me enough to let me.

CHAPTER TWENTY-THREE

Decker

"DID YOU GRAB ME ANY DONUTS FROM THAT ONE SPOT?" MARCUS ASKED while wiping his face and neck with a towel. He'd just run eight miles and was curious about donuts. He would be my best friend for that reason alone, aside from being a kickass roommate and all around decent human.

I pulled the small bag out of my bag and tossed it over to him.

"Sweet."

He chewed a few bites while I tried not to shift uncomfortably. The school gym was shitty in comparison to our team workout facility, but sometimes it was just easier to pop in over here versus driving across campus. Marcus and I had both been given special release to live outside of the team house. He'd never told me exactly what provisions he was allowed to leave on, saying it wasn't his story to tell, but I was grateful to have a roommate who understood the pressures of being on that team.

"So, how did the appointment go?"

I resisted the urge to run my hands through my hair and let out an annoyed sigh. My day had been fucking long as ever.

"Good. Really good actually."

"Will they let her refinance?" he asked hesitantly.

I nodded my head. "It almost seemed like they weren't going to at first, but I don't know. Someone made a call and an assessor is going out to the house next week, but they gave her the green light." It felt like a burden had been lifted from my shoulders. I knew it didn't fix all the problems, but it was a step in the right direction. "Either way it will buy her time. I'll be graduated by then, and I can move back home, maybe take up Dad's landscaping business."

I considered again the idea of doing that instead of pursuing something that might make me more money, or even baseball. But I'd been injured for over a year, so there were no scouts looking at me; I'd be lucky to land in Triple-A ball, if anything, but I wasn't sure that was even something I wanted anymore. The more I thought of taking over my dad's business and settling down, the more calm I became. That had to point toward something, right?

Marcus shook his head, snapping his jaw closed. "You don't want to do that, man. I know it. I hate that you're just accepting that you can't play ball. How did your last physical therapy appointment go?"

I let out a heavy sigh, feeling a little too mothered by him. "It went fine." I was on the cusp of being completely finished with therapy appointments. Just a few more months.

"Does he think you can play professionally?" Marcus sounded hopeful, and if I had been a better friend, I'd have felt happy in that hope. I'd have been grateful for a friend who cared about me the way he did. I also wouldn't have lied to him.

I shrugged, hands deep in my pockets. "They said it's too soon to tell."

The way his head lowered and the pensive look on his face told me he didn't believe me.

"What about your other therapist?" He grabbed his water bottle and took a large drink, keeping his calculating gaze on me.

He knew I wasn't telling my therapist shit. Why even bother asking?

"Good...yeah." I nodded. "Real good."

"So, you talked to your therapist about the game then?"

"Yeah. She knows I can't pitch."

"I'm not talking about baseball, man—I'm talking about the card game, and Mallory. There's another game this Friday night."

"I know. I heard about it." I glanced around, curious who else might be listening to our conversation. There was always someone listening.

"The fact that Elias keeps having meetings while you can't attend or moving them so they're not anywhere near the team house is total bullshit. I know Coach doesn't know he's doing that." He scoffed, rubbing his chin.

"You know I don't care. I don't want to go anyway, but Mallory wants to." Marcus had met her a few times, and he liked her, but he was also wary of her because she was technically a reporter.

"Mallory wants to go?" He reared back like he was shocked.

"Why is that so hard to believe?"

"You mean you don't know?" He stood, watching me like I was a zoo exhibit.

"What the fuck are you talking about?"

He let out a sigh and rubbed his neck. "I would have said something, but you keep going over to her house. I haven't seen you in days."

"Just tell me, Marcus." I was getting irritated that he wouldn't just cut to the chase.

"It's been leaked she was the one in that room instead of Taylor Beck. It's also been leaked that she's writing an article about the team."

My stomach dropped out. If that were true...if they knew it was Mallory, then...

"Who else knows?"

Marcus watched me for a second before shaking his head. "Everyone knows, man. They know she's after the story she isn't authorized to write. They're going to shut her down."

My mind raced while I tore through the options available to me. I didn't think they'd hurt her, but they would make it to where she couldn't write her article. *Fuck.* I had to try to fix this.

CHAPTER TWENTY-FOUR

Mallory

"Why do you think they wanted us here so early if they're not even here?" Taylor asked incredulously.

It was early, and my dad and Jackie still hadn't come out to the veranda to start brunch with us. We usually tried to get together every Sunday, but the previous weekend hadn't worked for them because they'd taken a quick trip to the Keys. Now it was Friday and we were here at eight in the morning. Both of us had classes later, although I didn't know if Taylor had been going to hers. Every time I *was* home, she seemed like she was there too...even when she should have been in a class.

It was odd.

"I don't know. His event thing is right around the corner...we could have just postponed," I said, leaning forward to sip my mimosa.

"Exactly!" Taylor jutted her hands out in front of her like I'd just said exactly what was in her head.

"Do you have a date?" It was a topic I'd been trying to avoid since we'd never talked about that photo she had taken with Decker that night, or the fact that I'd made it seem like he was into her then suddenly he wasn't.

Taylor sipped her drink, cautiously eyeing me over the brim of the flute. "I don't know…I mean, I was going to ask Decker, but then you seem to be having lots of orgasms with him, so I don't know." She shrugged like it was no big deal that she heard me having orgasms through the wall. My face burned at the idea that she had heard me.

I must have stayed quiet for too long, because suddenly her eyes were on me.

"You're bringing him, right?"

"I was planning to," I answered sheepishly, like I was ashamed of something. Did she have anyone she could ask? What was I talking about? This was Taylor—of course she had someone she could ask.

Her eyes narrowed as if she was trying to sniff out my lie. "Mal, just promise me you won't go with Elias Matthews." Taylor's lips pursed as she leaned forward. If I wasn't mistaken, she was looking around to ensure no one overheard us.

I shook my head. "Uh…I didn't know you knew him."

"He's dangerous. The rumors…I mean, I've heard rumors about him. I think you should stay away from him." She softly pleaded with me while holding her fork in a viselike grip.

I wasn't sure what to make of that. I didn't get a chance to respond.

"Girls, sorry we're late." Jackie rushed out to the patio in a white wrap dress that ended at her knees and left her shoulders bare. Her blonde hair was tucked back in a neat chignon, her flawless face revealing little as she sat and immediately sipped from her glass. I watched to see if my father was on her heels, but the only person to come out after her was their housekeeper and chef, Bev.

"Where's Dad?" I flashed a quick look from Jackie back to Bev, who was pushing a rolling cart with our food stacked high.

Jackie waved her hand, typing away on her cell. I flicked my gaze over to Taylor and saw she was doing the same thing. I felt empty. I hated when Jackie ignored me. I didn't know why it burned so much, but I knew if Taylor asked where my dad was, she would immediately answer.

"Jackie. Where's my father?" I spoke loudly so there would be no issue with her hearing me.

"He's on a call, Mallory. My goodness, no need to speak so loud." She folded a napkin into her cleavage and reached for her mimosa glass.

The gleaming diamond on her left hand caught the sun, making my eyes burn. I didn't want to hate her, but I hated how she made me feel...especially when I saw that ring. I missed my mother.

I had told my dad a million times that I didn't want to come to brunch unless he would be attending every minute of it. I didn't want to be stuck between Jackie and Taylor, because they always made me feel like an outsider. It wasn't that Taylor didn't try to include me in the conversation, because she often did, but Jackie would just twist it so we ended up talking about Taylor.

Heaving a sigh, I stood from the table and decided to wander until my dad came out. I did love their house, and I loved that despite what Jackie wanted, my father kept it tailored to fit him with rich leathers and dark chestnut wood accents. I ran my finger along one of the bookcases near his library, ready to dig for a book, then I heard him talking softly on the phone.

I knew I shouldn't listen in...but I was curious, and it was just business, so what harm was there?

Pressing closer to the doorway to his office, I tilted my head so I could hear better.

"No...that's not what we discussed," my dad barked.

There was a long pause then a shuffle.

"The stockholders don't have that much sway...no, fuck you, Buckland."

Buckland was one of the lead men on my father's board of advisors. I knew that much from overhearing his business talks over the years.

I pressed further into the door, desperate to catch every word. My father had never raised his voice like this, had never sounded so angry before.

"Mallory isn't up for discussion. She's the oldest, but she doesn't want this, so I won't pressure her. Taylor has been the one..." He trailed off.

My heart raced as I listened. What the hell was he talking about? Taylor had talked to him about taking over or what? What were they discussing?

"No. She'll marry someone her own age. I already have someone lined up...yes, he's already approached me. We're working a deal."

Oh my god. What the hell was he talking about?

"You know they won't ever go for that. No, I told you…I've already spoken with the boy. He's in the city as we speak, meeting with Hamlin. If all they need is for her to be married, fine, she'll fucking be married by the end of the month, with a public wedding by the end of the year."

Feeling my face heat and my heart hammering away in my chest, I rushed down the hall. I bypassed the patio doors, running straight for the foyer and out through the front doors. My chest heaved as I processed his words. I knew my dad was into about a million things that were over my head, but what I had just heard…

There was no way.

He wouldn't do this. He wouldn't. Memories of my father from when I was a little girl came rushing back. Moments in the garage, playing games on the crawler, sliding back and forth along the floor while he worked. Hours on the soft chair he brought out there for me so I could nap. He was such a hard worker, in absolutely every area of his life. He was tender and sweet, and there was no way he'd do something this despicable.

Did Taylor know? My thoughts rushed as I considered how involved she'd become in his affairs lately, asking questions, attending meetings. Decker had known she was taking a position in New York. Did that mean he knew? Was it even the same thing? The end of the month…it was the middle of March, but…before graduation? And who was this guy?

I swung open my car door, nearly laughing at the stark difference of the opulence around the garage and my beater of a vehicle. It was laughable to have me camouflaged in this world, like a checker piece on the chess board, sandwiched between the king and queen. Completely and entirely laughable.

My hands shook as I started the engine and reversed out of the driveway. Maybe I was worried my stepsister would make a horrible decision that could change her life forever, but my entire body shook as I drove the thirty minutes downtown. I parked in a nearby parking garage and walked the rest of the way, relishing the breeze and mixture of sunshine.

My mind kept wrestling with the words I'd heard my father use.

She'll marry someone her own age. I already have someone lined up…he's already approached me. We're working a deal.

What did that mean? Who was he talking about? There was no way it could be…

No.

I tried to prevent my mind from going there, but it wandered just the same. He was with me now, and he'd given up his revenge…but did he know about this? Was there some connection to Elias in this? He wouldn't keep this from me though…there was no way.

My reflection bowed and bobbed as I walked past the shining glass windows of giant skyscrapers. I had walked this specific route so many times I didn't even have to look up to see which building was which or where I was. I just wanted to run my fingers along each of the words that were supposed to paint my future, where I would find a home, a new purpose in life.

I was nearly there when I heard my name being called. It took me a second to register, but once I stopped and looked behind me, I saw him: dark hair slicked to the side with hair product, a gunmetal grey suit perfectly tailored for his body, a crisp white shirt beneath, and a silver tie. He even wore shining black dress shoes. My mouth dropped at the sheer ridiculousness of how good he looked.

"Wow…you look…" I stalled, still taking in every detail of how Decker's clean-shaven face was slightly turning red, his mossy eyes hard set under his dark brows. "Fancy meeting or something?" I tried to ask, but my voice came out raspy.

He smirked, stepping closer. "Or something."

The memory of when I had said that to him in the parking lot came back, making me smile up at him. He took advantage of me lifting my face by pressing his lips to mine. I melted into him, releasing the fears and assumptions I'd been spinning out from. Then a wisp of awareness zipped through me like a live wire upon remembering my dad's words.

He's in the city as we speak, meeting with Hamlin.

I shoved the thought down, even with the obvious clues staring me in the face. He looked like he'd just stepped out of a meeting with investors. My eyes drifted to the ground, as if I could see each of my hopes drift there. It couldn't be him. He wouldn't do this to me, to us.

His eyes seemed to weigh a ton as they bounced along my frame, up my hair and down my figure.

"What are you doing here?" His voice seemed as thick as my heart currently felt. Heavy and thick, rusting over. *Dying.*

I ducked my head, tucking hair behind my ear. The place behind me suddenly felt like it was a life-sized journal, flung open for Decker to read all the pages. It was sacred to me, a most precious spot, and now he was here staring at it with that look like he'd fix whatever was wrong.

"This"—I gestured behind me to the building jutting into the sky—"is the internship I'm hoping to land with my story." I moved toward the wall where the nameplate sat, the words Kline Global imprinted in brass lettering.

"You aren't interviewing, right? You said they only take one person." He moved his focus to where I gestured then it bounced back to me. The fact that he remembered what I had told him felt like a tiny furnace burning in my heart.

"No." I let out a heavy sigh, giving the nameplate a longing look. I just wanted to run my fingers over the letters like the weirdo that I was. I couldn't do that with him here, though. "I just like seeing it…you know, getting perspective. I come here when I need to clear my head."

Understanding lit up his eyes. Before I could say anything else, his hand grabbed mine and we were heading inside the building.

"No, no, no." I struggled in his hold.

"What's it going to hurt to go in and take a look around?" His smile was mischievous and daring. *Devilish.*

"Well, it could mess with my chances of being accepted," I blurted in a harsh whisper. The gleaming white marble under our feet was too glorious to imagine. The building was bright and welcoming, and fifty feet from us was a desk no one was managing. My eyebrows furrowed in concern. Where was the security guard? Anyone could just walk in…and…

"Hurry, come on—we can sneak upstairs." Decker pulled my hand toward his chest and started heading up.

"Decker, no!" I whisper-yelled at him while he tugged me along.

Inside I was coming apart, a cassette tape being unwound, all my hopes and dreams being tugged on and teased. I had never gone inside the building. I'd always just stood outside like a weirdo, running my finger along the letters. The stairs extended up, giving us a view of the lobby below, the desk still unmanned. The first-floor door was wide open, and on the glass doors was something etched in white font that I couldn't understand. Off to the side was a small alcove where gleaming bronze elevator doors waited.

"Come on." Decker pulled me toward the alcove while hugging me to his firm side. I loved the warmth he gave off, and his smell. God, he smelled good.

"Seriously, Decker, this is a bad idea," I muttered as he pressed the up button. Oh my god, what would I do if I saw someone with a Kline Global security badge?

"They don't even know who we are—it's not a big deal."

I swiftly followed in after him at the ding of the elevator. "It won't matter. They're still going to escort us out once they realize we aren't authorized to be here."

"You worry too much, babe. It'll be fine." He laughed, and seeing him smile while in that suit made my stomach flip. I wanted to take him out of those clothes, kiss his mouth, and force him to tell me his secrets.

I looked up, trying not to bring attention to the fact that I loved that he was here with me. I focused on his granite jaw and the fact that a lazy smile tugged his lips to the side. It was *devastating*.

A moment later, the elevator stopped and opened on the fifth floor. Thin, grey carpet silenced our steps as we crept around the corner, and huge potted plants with massive green leaves sat close to the floor-to-ceiling windows. I walked forward, stopping at the glass doors that were currently shut but hid none of the magic happening behind them.

Bustling reporters walking back and forth from copiers to whiteboards. Swivel chairs, bulletin boards, people on cell phones, desk phones ringing off the hook. It was madness and heaven, and I nearly plastered my face to the glass just to get a better view.

"So, this is what you want?" Decker whispered at my side.

I withheld the urge to trace the massive K and G that dominated the doors in sleek lettering. Instead I swallowed a lump in my throat as a man in a white collared shirt walked by with a stack of papers in his hand, not paying any attention to us.

"Yes." I sighed, staring at the cubicles inside.

The chaos. At least twelve flat screens hung on the east wall, all playing different news clips, and on the opposite wall were several clocks, each displaying a different time zone. This, seeing inside this space, was so much better than only having a view of the outside. This was a gift, one I'd desperately needed to keep me grounded.

"And the story will get you here?" Decker asked, turning with me.

I blinked and hoped I wasn't jinxing myself by talking about this in front of Kline Global. "I hope so. My editor hates me, and the last story I wrote, he pulled. If my article and name don't appear, Kline Global won't see them. I need something that will stand out, get people talking."

Decker followed me back to the elevators. "I hope you get it, babe. You deserve it." He squeezed my fingers in his hand, and because I wanted to stick my head in the sand and ignore everything between us, I squeezed his hand back and let him kiss me again.

"So, what are you doing in the city?" I finally braved asking.

"Just sightseein'."

I rolled my eyes. "You are not."

"I could be." He dipped his head until his lips were at my ear, then he tugged the lobe between his teeth.

A rush of heat hit me right between the legs.

"Eat with me," he murmured into the space near my ear.

We exited the building, and as soon as we did, Decker popped on a pair of sunglasses. My heart wasn't ready to see him in a suit paired with Ray-Bans.

I wanted to push aside my fears and go eat with him before we went to the party, but I had to know why he was here. His need for revenge and weird attachment to Taylor in the beginning of all this was too coincidental.

"Decker...I overheard my father talking today, and I am honestly freaking out a little bit." I closed my eyes, focused on my breathing, and tried to take comfort in the way his hand held on to mine.

"What happened?"

I looked up to find his eyes searching mine. "It sounded like Taylor was being set up...in an arranged marriage or something."

I was expecting surprise to blanket his features, a raise of the eyebrow, a grimace, a tic in his jaw…but there was nothing. No surprise whatsoever.

My voice cracked. "Is it you?"

"Me?" He reared back, stepping away from me.

"I just need to know," I begged. Internally I begged him for something else entirely. *Tell me it's not true. Don't tell me anything at all. Don't ruin this.*

He scoffed, rubbing his chin. The sun caught his hair, and I wanted to tangle my fingers there, bring his face back, and kiss him.

"How could you think that?"

I stammered, trying to control my heart rate. "He said he'd made a deal and that person was in the city meeting with his investors. You look so nice, and in the beginning with your revenge plan…I just…I knew it wasn't true, but I had to…"

"I knew about it." He cut me off, his eyes soft and weary.

"What?"

"I knew…it's…" He trailed off, tugging us to the side of the street.

Meanwhile my heart hammered away in my chest, reminding me how fragile it was and how stupid I'd been to hand it over to someone who had such a rough grip.

"My Uncle Scotty…he deals in information. After what happened with Elias, my uncle kept tabs on him. He found out about this deal he'd made with your father…I don't know all the details, but the start of it was that he would invite Taylor to the games, make it official in a way that made sure everyone knew they were dating. I knew there was a key element to making sure a ton of people knew they were together."

I watched him speak, but I felt like my body was disconnected from my head, the two whirling and fighting over what to do with this information.

"I decided to intervene and ruin the start of his arrangement. I figured if I could cast doubt that they were together with enough people, or better yet have sex with Taylor right when he walked in…it would be an efficient form of revenge."

I took in how his face seemed to pale as he finished. Did he notice how much distance I'd subconsciously put between us? I was so angry, so insanely hurt. I just…

"What did Elias do to you?" I crossed my arms over my chest. I needed to know, just to put it behind me.

He hesitated. "I know you're mad, but there's something I need to tell you about the article, about Elias…"

"Just tell me what he did to you."

Decker dipped his head. "He's just dangerous."

My heart cracked, battering my lungs, daring them to gather air. Tears clogged my eyes, because he still wasn't going to tell me…even in the midst of everything. What was he hiding?

"So, you knew my sister was essentially entering into an arranged marriage with someone 'dangerous' and you didn't tell me?" I whispered as wisps of my hair were blown into my face by a rogue wind that cut through the street.

His eyes searched mine, begging me to understand.

"It was something I didn't know all the details about. I didn't feel right saying something about your dad, or even Taylor…it was complicated."

"But you could have explained the revenge aspect…you could have included me." My voice rose as anger spiked through me. "That's my stepsister—how could you think I wouldn't want to know something like that?"

"You were so willing to take her spot in that room, to have someone who wanted her touch you…what was I supposed to think?" he snapped, darting a hand at his chest.

My mouth opened but nothing came out. Hurt slammed into me, along with a healthy dose of self-loathing. He was right, not for the reasons he thought…but I was willing to do what I had to in order to get information on the card game.

"I need some space, I think." I wet my lips, trying to gather the energy to walk to my car. I spun around and headed toward the parking garage. I needed to get home and talk to Taylor.

"Mallory, wait." Decker stormed after me.

"No. I understand…I just—I need some time to…" What was I even saying? Time to…what? Come to terms with the fact that my boyfriend knew my stepsister had signed up for an arranged marriage but assumed I was so self-involved I wouldn't care?

"Mallory, just wait. Just…fuck, just talk to me for a second." He ran in front of me, moving backward while I plowed my way down the sidewalk.

"Decker, give me some space." I stopped, nailing him with a look that I hoped confirmed I wasn't fucking around. I needed to be away from him right then.

He waited, staring at me with an intensity that made me want to crumble into a thousand pieces. Finally, he raised his hands and stepped aside, letting me pass by. I didn't look back as I walked away from him, and I didn't search for him as I pulled away from the city and headed back home.

CHAPTER TWENTY-FIVE

Mallory

"TAYLOR, PLEASE CALL ME BACK. I NEED TO TALK TO YOU." I PRESSED the end button on my cell and tossed it on the bed. That was the sixth or seventh voicemail I'd left for her.

Pacing my bedroom had done nothing to settle my nerves or provide me with answers. The party for the team was in a few hours, but I wouldn't be going. Even if there was a part of me that wanted more details for my story, I couldn't stomach being around Elias or Decker at the moment, and I would be thinking of Taylor the entire time.

Was that why she'd warned me that Elias was a dangerous guy? Did she know what he'd done to Decker? Had he done something to her? My list of questions grew with every passing hour, and as the sun began to dip closer to the horizon, I was no closer to having any answers.

Finally, around four, I received a phone call, but it wasn't from who I needed to hear from.

Still, at least it would help keep my mind off of Taylor. So, I changed my clothes, did my hair, and headed toward the school.

ɒ

"THANK YOU FOR AGREEING TO MEET WITH US, MS. SHAW."

Mr. Geele lifted his hand so I would take a seat at the massive table to his left. There were already four other faculty members sitting at it, one of which was my journalism advisor.

I smiled, taking a seat, feeling nerves jutting under my skin.

"Hello." I nodded, greeting each person.

"Mallory, how are you today?" Ms. Stalkwell smiled at me while tapping away on her cell phone.

"Fine, thanks." I wanted to puke, but that was totally not a big deal, right?

"Well, let's get right to it." Mr. Geele joined the table and steepled his fingers. "It's been brought to our attention that you're writing a fabricated article about the baseball team, with the purpose and intent to slander their team and the legacy. These gentlemen"—he gestured to the two suits sitting across from me—"are legal representation for the Devils."

Oh shit. This was bad. This was very bad.

I swallowed, trying to control my breathing.

"With all due respect to everyone in the room, my story is not, in any way, fabricated."

Mr. Geele waved his hand as if to erase what I'd said. "Did you have authorization to attend that party?"

Authorization? *What the hell...*

"No...I wasn't given a card specifically, but others were allowed in, with a cover charge."

"But you were allowed downstairs with the knowledge that only people who'd signed a waiver were given access. You omitted the fact that you'd swapped the card with someone else. This is a very serious legal situation you've found yourself in."

I looked to each of the teachers in front of me as panic expanded in my chest. How did they know I'd taken Taylor's card and attended the game?

"I wasn't aware..." My voice faltered with nerves, and I cleared my throat. "I wasn't aware of the waivers prior to attending...I mean, that's what good reporting is." I looked to Ms. Stalkwell for help, because she'd get it, right? "That's what we're taught all four years of journalism class."

"While that may be true, Ms. Shaw, you are also taught about journalistic integrity and how your sources need to be obtained in an ethical way. You tricked your way into the game then gathered privileged information that was not legally offered to you. You will abandon this article and turn in every scrap of information you've gathered thus far," Ms. Stalkwell informed me with a bit of a tone.

I burned from the top of my head to the bottom of my feet. Tears prickled at the backs of my eyes, and even my nose felt like it was on fire. What they'd said...it was technically true, but why were they willing to turn a blind eye to something so superficial as a damn card game aimed at sex?

"I understand what you're saying, Ms. Stalkwell, but I had an ethical source...there is a member of the Devils team that has been offering me information. So, the facts are not fabricated or embellished in any way." I tried to explain, but the way the two lawyers were looking at each other didn't feel encouraging.

"Ms. Shaw, that's impossible," one of the lawyers said in a gruff tone.

I kept my mouth shut, my gaze bouncing between the two of them.

"There's a clause in each player's release form." He opened the briefcase that had been on the floor, tugged a piece of paper free, and slid it toward me. "You see, each player joins the team with the knowledge that there can be no divulging of information of any kind to any news source, unless very specific and extreme actions are taken."

"Such as?" I whispered, curious what would be deemed a good enough excuse to spill all the Devils' details.

The men looked at each other again. "We're not at liberty to explain that in this setting, but I assure you the steps were not taken. Therefore, you did not have permission to gather what intel you did, and any player offering you said information was merely playing you, as each person is made abundantly aware of our rules."

"This seems a little backwards, doesn't it?" I held out my hand, hoping someone in the room would aid me. How could they say all the steps hadn't been taken to grant permission for the article, yet they wouldn't say what the steps were?

The two suits turned toward me with grave expressions. "The school has been advised not to discuss the nature of the game with you. There are more things to this game and this team that you don't even know about, girl," the man with jowls explained to me.

"You of all people should know this, given who your father is," the other added, narrowing his beady gaze on me.

I felt small, insignificant...stupid. My face burned with regret, and with assumptions—that I could pull off a story of that caliber. That I could actually be a contender for the internship. That Decker had taken me seriously or had uttered any truth at all to me. Everything had been a lie. Seemed there was yet one more thing Decker knew that he wasn't telling me.

I was so foolish.

I ducked my head, breathing strictly through my nose so a sob wouldn't work its way up my throat. "I understand."

The people around the table smiled and stood, silently dismissing me.

"We will expect your notes by the end of the day."

"One more thing, Ms. Shaw..." One of the lawyers stopped me, sliding a piece of paper toward me. "This is an NDA. You'll agree not to publicly print or post anything about the team in any other paper or on any form of digital publication."

With shaky fingers, I gripped the pen handed to me from someone on my left. Everything was blurry as tears clouded my eyes. I just needed them to stay put until I got to my car.

Signing, I pushed the paper back toward them. Once I was nearly out the door, I was ushered by Mr. Geele, who quietly said into my ear, "This was a kindness. There are other ways they could have handled this."

I turned to look at him, but he was already walking away.

What the hell did he mean by that?

I didn't get a chance to ask as I walked away from the meeting, leaving my hopes for the story to secure my spot in the internship behind.

CHAPTER TWENTY-SIX

Mallory

"HEY HONEY, NICE OF YOU TO COME." MY DAD'S FLAT VOICE MATCHED his flat expression and thin smile.

I didn't extend a smile; even a fake one would have been a betrayal to Taylor. She'd said she had been sick this last week. I hadn't thought too much about it since learning of my father and Decker's role in hiding her arranged marriage and, of course, that horrific meeting at the school. She'd stayed here at the house with Jackie and my dad. I had almost caved and gone to talk to her, but I worried Taylor wouldn't be honest with me if she knew my dad might overhear our conversation. Besides, it was rude to interrogate people when they didn't feel good, even if it was painful to be home alone while my heart shattered and my world imploded.

"It's your big event," I finally muttered in response.

"Where's your date?" He looked behind me at the door, as if a gentleman caller would materialize out of thin air.

I shrugged, eyeing the trays for champagne. "He bailed at the last second."

The long sigh that left my father's chest was like a reaction to learning he'd been abducted by an alien. The man who'd raised me would have never made that sound, or even insisted we have dates to begin with.

"I had a feeling you'd come alone, so I have someone ready for you." My father tugged my arm until we were walking toward the sitting room. *Ouch.* Him assuming I wouldn't bring one actually kind of stung.

"You what?" I tried resisting, but his grip was firm.

"This is Jeff."

A tall, handsome man, older than me but it didn't look like by much, smiled at me, dipping his head.

"Jeff, this is my eldest daughter, Mallory. Would you do us both an honor and keep her company this evening as her date?" my dad asked the guy in the five-piece suit.

His hair was molded so perfectly, I wasn't sure it was even real. It made me miss Decker's silky, loose strands. An ache opened in my chest, like my body had just remembered it'd lost an essential limb or organ and didn't know how to function properly without it. He'd texted and called about a million times over the past week, left me notes and flowers on my windshield, all the while just asking that he get a chance to explain himself. He didn't even know that I knew about the article, or that I had lost it.

My father was about to open his mouth, likely to put his foot there, but just as he was going to explain the need for me to have a date, the crowd moved and Taylor came into view. She wasn't alone.

There on her arm was none other than Decker James.

ƌ

IN SOME STRANGE ALTERNATE UNIVERSE, I WAS TUCKED AWAY IN THE corner with Jeff, actually grateful for his tree-like height and his presence. It allowed me the opportunity to watch the floor and all the guests without being noticed. I eyed Taylor first; she wore a floor-length dress with see-through mesh over the stomach and glistening jewels flowing down her legs like a fountain of wealth. It was beautiful and insanely obnoxious. I nearly looked down to compare myself to her, which was a habit I needed to break. I wore a fashionable dress that cut off at mid-thigh, the capped sleeves making it seem modest even with the plunging neckline.

I inspected the man attached to her arm in a clinical way. Mentally I told myself he was no longer a part of my life, but it was like looking at an amputated limb. I mentally noted that if I had said that out loud to Hillary, she would have slapped me for being gross.

Jeff sipped his drink, droning about shareholders. I nodded, keeping my eyes on the couple. In that same sleek, gunmetal grey tailored suit from the last time I'd seen him and with his hair slicked back, Decker wore a stormy expression, searching the room with interest and a whole lot of rage. Was that a…black eye? What in the heck had happened to him? His lip was cut in the corner, and his upper eyebrow had a stitch in it.

I watched in what felt like slow motion as Taylor spun until she was in front of him. Then, linking her arms around his neck, she gave him a kiss on the cheek, but it was dangerously close to the corner of his mouth. His posture was rigid and cold, like he really didn't want to be there. That was the smallest mercy he could have given me, and I clung to it.

I was curious how long it would take him to notice me, curious if anyone would notice if I were to sneak out of the room entirely and catch a cab home. As soon as they had entered, I had taken the coward's way out and grabbed Jeff's arm, begging him to crowd the corner with me.

Decker's mossy green eyes connected with mine as soon as the thought left my head. Locked like a missile, studying the target, waiting for instructions to detonate, he stared.

"Ah, there she is," Dad said, breaking me out of my staring contest with the man who'd broken my heart. My father was holding my stepmother's hand, and she wore a bright smile, making me slump into the wall as I realized they were going to force me to socialize.

"Mallory, darling." Jackie approached wearing a gold wrap dress that made her blonde hair look luminescent under the lights. She really was very pretty to look at; I just wished her attitude toward me would match how nice she seemed on the outside. My mother had always warned me if someone was pretty to look at but ugly to deal with, then they were just plain ugly. It's the inside that matters.

"Hello, Jackie," I muttered, giving her a tight smile.

"Tell me, dear." She tugged me out of the corner and slid her arm through mine. "Have you heard about this dashing new boy my baby girl has been seeing?"

I looked over my shoulder to see Jeff and my father engaged in a discussion. They were both laughing, so it must have been about something good.

"I hadn't heard." I searched for Taylor on instinct, forgetting for a second that I loathed her entire existence. *How could she bring him as her date?*

"Well, as you know, your father has wanted to see your sister take the family business more seriously, and that includes finding a suitable gentleman she could inherit the dealings with, someone who would look good on the cover a magazine, of course, along with providing deliciously gorgeous children and being a supportive backbone for our little girl."

She'll marry someone her own age... my father's words came back with a hard knock in the heart. That paired with finding out Decker had known...my throat felt like it was swelling shut, and I hated so much of what Jackie had just said. My mind had picked up several words like stones on a beach, ready to toss them back into the bay, hoping they'd hit with a splash. Sister...inherit...little girl... I hated how she always acted like Taylor was my dad's biological kid when she wasn't.

He was *my* dad and her *stepdad*. That was just how it was, plain and simple. Jackie didn't include me in their mother-daughter trips or their conversations or spa weekends, and yet here my stepsister was, on the cusp of inheriting my father's business. I wouldn't have minded if it was Taylor's dream, if she really wanted this, but I knew her, probably better than anyone. She hid behind this thin composure of luxury, but deep down she was a quiet soul looking for purpose. I saw it in the way she tried different recipes and secretly stuck her nose in one of those historical books, and not the fiction kind. She loved reading about the history of America, especially during the early 1900s. She was more than all this.

My father's phone call started to swirl in my head like a bad cocktail.

I had made it more than clear several years ago that I would never help run my father's business in any capacity, not when I was still so hopeful about being a featured writer and landing the Kline internship. That idea tasted like ash in my mouth now. Maybe it was time to step up and help out…maybe it was time to be the dutiful daughter so it stopped falling on Taylor's shoulders.

"Well, I haven't seen anyone around, but I am happy for her. That sounds great." I tried to seem happy, merely because it would make these conversations go smoothly, and ultimately, I loved my dad. But honestly, I had no idea what in the hell she was talking about. I hadn't seen anyone around with Taylor, but we'd been so off since I had started dating Decker, and then with her sickness. I was so caught up with trying to connect what Jackie had said to what I had seen with my step-sister that when the doorbell rang, I honestly didn't think anything of it.

Unless she meant…

She can't mean Decker.

I grabbed a flute of champagne from a floating tray and tossed the entire thing back, all while fastening my eyes on the enemy. Jeff moved in behind me, a little too close for comfort. He was definitely playing the date role like he was up for an Oscar. My eyes tracked with Decker as he moved with Taylor, making introductions around the room. I hated how much I wished it were me standing there with him. My stomach twisted. Why were they doing this, acting like nothing had happened, and wasn't she supposed to be marrying someone?

God, what if that was Decker's ultimate revenge plot? Him marrying Taylor…it would rip my soul out.

I had nearly perfected the art of ignoring the looks Decker kept sending my way and how every time I moved around the room, he'd try to rotate toward me. Seeing him in a suit was just as heart-stopping as it had been the first time, but seeing Taylor on his arm all night was just too painful. She laughed and giggled at everything he said, and each time I found it harder to love my stepsister.

Finally, after nearly an hour of Jeff smiling and flirting with me, I noticed a familiar set of navy eyes that also had inflamed bruising. My feet halted as I took in the rest of his face, the swelling of his nose and the white tape across it, the purple bruising on his jaw. What were the odds of Elias and Decker both showing up bruised? Either they'd had a rough practice, or they had gotten into a fight. Even with the imperfections on his face, he was all swagger and grace with those broad shoulders and stacked muscles. His blond hair was styled neatly in a way that made it look swept back and over, almost like a movie star. After everything had happened the week before, I hadn't even texted him back to tell him I wouldn't be going. He had swung by my house to check on me, bearing flowers and some Chinese food. I'd accepted them, only because I was so confused about the roles everyone was playing. Taylor didn't seem to trust him, yet she'd agreed to marry him. Or had she?

She had received that card, but I thought that was by chance...then Decker had said he'd handpicked the girl he wanted back there, but did that mean she knew about all of it? Decker still hadn't told me about their past and what had happened, so I had no idea what on earth had really gone down. Truthfully, I was just unsure of how I felt about the guy. He had always been nice to me, so what motivation did I have to be angry with him? In fact, I should have just invited him as my date so I wasn't stuck with handsy Jeff.

Elias's eyes found mine, and a seductive smile lit up his face as his gaze seemed to travel the length of me, staying especially focused on my chest. I snickered into my drink; he was being so obtuse, and he knew there was zero chance of anything happening between us.

I smiled back, playing along, and when he got close enough, because the champagne had started hitting, I threw myself at him, clinging to his neck as if we were long-lost lovers. I kept laughing even as his hands went to my hips, gripping me tightly. It was meant to be fun, a joke, but before I could pull away, his lips suddenly landed on mine.

That...I wasn't expecting, but even as the temptation to mess with Decker sat on the fringe of my mind, I couldn't do it. I wouldn't kiss him just to hurt Decker. Instead, I pushed him away, dipping my head so no one would see the devastation I didn't know how to hide. It was there in the middle of my father's house that I realized with absolute certainty that I was in love with Decker James. He had lied to me, screwed me out of a story, and played me like a fucking fiddle, and yet...he still had my heart, and I had no idea how to get it back.

"What in the hell happened to your face?" I asked, jokingly running my thumb over the bridge of his nose.

"Just a rough day at practice." He laughed it off, but I didn't miss how his eyes flashed over my shoulder, where I knew Decker was standing. Something had happened between the two of them.

Elias brought his focus back to me. "Want to introduce me to your famous dad?"

My stomach churned as I considered the likelihood of him now playing me. He obviously already knew my dad, and who had invited him to this party in the first place? Setting the champagne on a traveling tray, I nodded and walked toward my father.

"Hey Dad, I want you to meet someone." Right as we stopped next to him, a circle started to form. Some of Dad's shareholders were there. Taylor came in next, and there on her arm was Decker. A few other friends and associates were there, listening and talking to each other, all vying for my dad's attention.

Dad's eyes narrowed as he watched Elias, which only confirmed that Elias was a big fat manipulator. Why would he want me to bring attention to him? Why pretend?

"Weren't you and that Juan boy dating?" My dad's left eyebrow shot up while his hard gaze landed on me. I nearly choked on my drink.

"Uh...no. Juan is my best friend, Dad." My gaze briefly darted to the man I had been dating, hoping to see something register there, but he was stone cold. His jaw clenched tight, his arm wrapped around my stepsister's waist. My fingers itched for more alcohol.

"Oh, well I just figured since he was always around."

The circle watched us while my face burned.

"Hello, sir, it's nice to meet you. I'm Elias Matthews." He stuck his hand out, covering for me. My father slowly took it with a solid shake, but his eyebrows caved in like he wasn't sure why he was shaking Elias's hand. I didn't know either. I hated politics and pretending. This was all ridiculous.

"You're what to my daughter?" My father glared at Elias.

"Well...I'm not sure yet. We're still discovering that for ourselves." Elias looked over and smiled at me, and I nearly choked on my tongue. Why had he said that? Frozen, my heart thundered in my chest as I waited for Decker's reaction. His mossy gaze caught mine like a jagged piece of glass. The hurt in them nearly robbed me of breath. The bruises on his face added such a brokenness that I wasn't used to seeing. I wanted to reach for him, drag him away, and figure out what was happening there, but he'd hurt me. Lied to me. He'd promised me notes for a story he knew I wouldn't be able to publish.

My dad's jaw ticked, his eyes sweeping between Elias and Decker, and my gaze kept landing on the latter. My dad was like a detective, always knowing these little intricate things about me.

"Okay…well excuse us, we're going to find—" I started.

"Well who do we have here?" Jackie came over, butting in and grabbing my dad's arm.

Her eyes bounced from Elias to me, and the way they went wide and round, even her lips parted as she drank in the sight of my date. I mean, he was good-looking, but she looked as though she'd seen a ghost. I faltered for a second before making the introduction.

"Elias, this is my stepmom, Jackie. Jackie, this is Elias Matthews."

Taylor's eyes hardened on the way her mom was looking at Elias. There were some awkward vibes going on here, and I was starting to piece it all together. Jackie and Taylor were in on the arrangement and were shocked to see him here with me, the oldest daughter. What the fuck was Elias's game plan here?

Taylor glared at me while her hand tightened on Decker's arm. I had no idea why she was suddenly staring with such vehemence, but I was over this entire scene.

"Well, I'm going to give him a tour of the house. I'll see all of you later." I pulled at Elias's arm, and we departed. I took my time, showing him the gardens and the kitchen, which wasn't that amazing, especially because it was full of staff at the moment. Then we wandered to the garage.

"This is bigger than my entire house." Elias laughed, running his hand over one of my father's rare cars.

"We weren't always rich…" I walked around the cars. There were at least twenty-five in this garage, and at least thirty more in the secondary garage. I didn't have the heart to tell Elias this wasn't the only garage.

I watched him move with a calculating gaze, unsure of how to broach the subject of my stepsister, or my father…or Decker. What in the hell was this guy's endgame, and why was my family a part of it?

"So, are you going to try to move on anything with Taylor?" I asked, trying to see if I could get him talking. At the bar that one night, he'd mentioned having a crush on Taylor, which was obviously bullshit, but maybe I could get him to start moving us in the right direction so my questions wouldn't seem so strange. We walked back toward the party, shoulder to shoulder.

"She came with someone else tonight, so maybe I should just let things be what they are."

Not what I wanted to hear. This only made me think he had his sights now set on me instead of her. I would have preferred he take his creepy vibes away from my sister, but I didn't want them set on me either.

He opened the back door for me; it was being guarded by one of my father's security team.

"So, that's it? You're just giving up?"

He laughed, holding my elbow while we started upstairs.

"Come on, there's no way you'd just give up your crush on her." I jabbed him in the side.

"What about you?" He looked over at me as we passed my father's study and wandered toward the library. "What would you do if I went to talk to her?"

I pushed through the large library door, feeling a familiar comfort in the finished wood. "This." I turned in a circle with a smile plastered to my face.

He lightly laughed while watching me with an odd expression on his face. "How about this: I'm starving. Why don't I go hunt down some food for us, and if I happen to see Taylor not talking to someone, I'll talk to her. Then I'll bring some food up."

I slipped off my high heels, finally feeling able to relax. "That sounds amazing."

"Okay, I'll be back." He hesitated for a second before walking out.

I needed something to read while I waited. I veered toward the back, where all the classics were hidden. I knew *Ben-Hur* was buried somewhere on the back wall. I didn't even know why I was in the mood for it, but it was one of my favorites.

"Where is it?" I mumbled to myself, trailing my fingers along leather spines. The low lights in the library created a dreamy vibe with all the dark leather and lush rugs on the wood floors. It was comfy and, on rainy days, my absolute favorite space.

I was thumbing through a rare edition of *Pride and Prejudice* when I heard the door open and shut...then the undeniable click of the older latch falling into place, locking us in.

I swallowed thickly, wiping my hands on my dress. I didn't want to be alone with Elias, especially if he was aiming for some fucked-up marriage ticket. Carefully walking around the corner, still holding the book, I asked, "Did you strike out already? I hope you at least grabbed some of those stuffed mushrooms."

I turned the corner, gripping the book tightly, only to find Decker standing there, hands shoved deep into his pockets and his head lowered.

It was unnerving not being able to see his expression. I could sense he was angry. Down in my bones, I knew he was vibrating with rage that I'd been with Elias all night, but he didn't get to be angry anymore. I hadn't even confronted him yet about losing my story.

"Decker."

His head rose, those tired, mossy eyes getting their fill by searching me from head to toe. The bruises on his face still made my breath catch. I wanted to know what had happened.

"Why?" he asked, voice raspy, and the look of defeat on his face nearly broke me.

I stepped forward, wetting my lips. As much as I wanted to talk to him, I didn't want to hear how much I'd hurt him by being around Elias. I knew it was a small betrayal, but...

"You ended this." I pointed between us. "You lied to me...made a fool of me, offering me intimate details about the Devils knowing I wouldn't be able to publish a single word." The words poured out of me in an angry rush, full of venom and hurt.

"I ended nothing," he snapped. His eyes blazed with such fury that it made me snap my mouth shut.

I opened and then closed my mouth, feeling like the smallest breeze might topple me.

"And your story?" he scoffed, running his hand over his jaw. His eyes were wild as he watched me. He took a few steps back until he was pacing the lavish three-hundred-year-old carpet at our feet. "*He* took that from you."

I flinched. "What are you talking about?"

"Why do you think I look like this, Mallory?" He pointed at his face.

I rolled my eyes, linking my arms over my chest. "Don't even try. The lawyers told me you knew the entire time whatever information you gave me wouldn't be useful because I'd be barred from publishing a single word."

"Why do you think I was in the city that one day you saw me? You assumed it was for that fucking marriage contract, but it was for you! I was there seeing what my options were because I had promised you the story," he yelled, his hair slicing into his eyebrows. I just wanted to walk over and push it out of his eyes.

He was breathing hard as he stepped closer, crowding me. "Elias is the one who demanded you get called down and have the story taken away from you. He's the one who fed them the intel that you were at the party and demanded you sign an NDA."

"Then why are you so angry at me? Did you forget who you showed up with tonight? That door revolved real fast, didn't it, Decker?" I hated that my mind had begun pairing him and Taylor together again, that he'd gone after his revenge. It was all just in my head, but why else was he here tonight with her?

"You're so oblivious." He shook his head, his dark green eyes burning as they narrowed on me.

I faltered back a step at his intensity, my bare feet brushing against some of the cold hardwood.

"I watched you all night. All. Fucking. Night. And guess what, Mallory…so did *he*." He slowly continued toward me.

"What…" I swallowed the lump of confusion down and tried again. "What are you talking about?" Then it hit.

Of course.

I knew exactly why he was upset; how could I be so stupid?

"You're just pissed because his focus isn't on Taylor, aren't you?" I gestured toward the door at his back, raising my voice in hopes that he'd stop paving a path across the floor with his angry strides.

"You think I fucking care about that?" he roared, and I knew if this had been his house, he would have thrown something. My father had gotten that look on his face only one time, after he learned my mother wouldn't make it through her surgery.

When he realized he'd lost her forever.

"Decker—"

"No. You don't get it." He shook his head slowly, defeat hanging around him like a cloud.

"Explain it to me, then, because you're right—I don't understand. You came here with Taylor. You stood on the street just a few days ago admitting that the reason you didn't tell me you knew about Elias and Taylor's arrangement was because I was so desperate you assumed I wouldn't care."

"You fucking kissed him!" Decker roared.

"Why did you come with her?" I yelled back.

Even if I could have argued that I didn't kiss Elias, he'd already made up his mind. He didn't get to set the rules then wipe them clean as soon as he realized he didn't like how others played by them.

I stepped forward, not waiting for his reply. "Why didn't you tell me there was a chance I might not be able to publish my article, especially knowing how dire it was that I write it? How could you not tell me you knew Elias was making that deal with my stepsister?"

"Because I'm fucked up, Mallory, okay?" he yelled in response, getting even closer to me. I could smell his spicy cologne. "I went after the only shot at getting revenge on the guy who'd fucked me over. He was my best friend for half my life, yet when my dad passed, he couldn't even be bothered to show up to his funeral. All he cared about was the team, and those fucking card games."

His chest heaved like he wasn't getting enough air. I found myself oddly trying to match its uneven rhythm.

"You wanted to know what happened between us—fuck it." He tunneled a path through his hair, gripping the ends. "He fixed the hit. I don't know how he did it…I threw slow and easy, but he hit it in a way that made it land in my solar plexus. Knocked the wind out of me, so bad I couldn't breathe. In the commotion, when I was on the ground, he stuck his cleat through my pitching hand."

His eyes were wild as he explained. Mine watered in response.

"I wanted to take from him what he took from me. Before the night we met, I learned that he was injured and wouldn't last long after his first contract if he even landed that. My uncle found out and knew he'd be looking for a different payout. Elias somehow found this opportunity by marrying into the Shaw fortune. I just wanted to mess with it, maybe ruin it, but I'm not a saint. I didn't have good intentions." He brought his hand to his head and began rubbing the stress out of his temple.

I wanted to say something, but my mouth had gone dry. What did I say to that? I finally knew his story, and now I wanted to throw up.

He flicked his eyes to me, his anger simmering lower as he stepped closer to me. "But...then you came along, and from the first time I saw you, I knew you were meant for me. You were stuck on repeat in my head for days. That's why I was so pissed when I saw you in that parking lot, because I assumed you were leaving your boyfriend's house. I couldn't stop, so I pushed harder for the Taylor thing, and there you were again, in my life, and I was already so taken with you, I just couldn't keep doing what I was doing. But...if you're with him, Mallory..." He trailed off, shaking his head. "I can't fucking breathe at the thought of it. Hate me." He slapped at his chest. "Hate me until the day you die if you want, but don't be with him. I can't see you with him."

I felt his desperation, the heat in his words warming me, smothering me.

It was my turn to shake my head, but I felt tears begging to fall free as well. I wanted to shout at him, scream at him so he understood, but I knew he wouldn't. I understood that Decker needed revenge in the only way he knew how to get it, and that was through this fucked-up idea to sleep with Elias's girl. I was just collateral damage...a hiccup in the process.

"Is this just about the guy you hate going after the girl you like? Because he's just playing me, Decker. It's not real."

"Who the fuck said I *like* you? I believe the words I told you were that I was falling for you, which was a joke. I'm gone for you, Mallory—

217

done for. There's no one else for me. You can't tell me you're that desperate for attention." He glared at me, his square jaw ticking.

"Are you fucking serious?!" I cried, ready to throw a book at his dumb, stupid face.

"Just...please." He grabbed my wrist, roughly pressing our bodies together until his forehead kissed mine. His throat bobbed while tears clouded his eyes. "Not him, baby. He's dangerous."

I pushed back the emotions clogging my chest. I needed clarity. He'd confessed so much, but I couldn't get past the idea that this was about Elias diverting his attention to Decker's favorite toy, and I was just collateral damage in their fucked-up dynamic.

"Right now, so are you," I whispered.

I was two seconds from crying. If I cried, I would sob and fucking sob. I wouldn't be able to stop. He was dangerous for my heart; he'd won me, and now he kept tossing me back in the pile like he was willing to bet it again.

Decker merely shook his head back and forth slowly, but I didn't miss how he shuffled closer.

"I need you..."

"Don't." I moved away from him, toward the door, shaking my head. "You say you care, but it was only because Elias started talking to me in the first place that you decided to stop going after Taylor." It was a buried truth that I had to pull out and examine, like a sliver that kept burrowing deeper and deeper. He'd completely ignored me, ghosted me, and while I may have hoped it wasn't about Elias, after everything...I knew now.

"You can't honestly think that," he muttered into the slice of space between us.

I broke free of him, was nearly to the door with my hand on the latch when I felt a jolt in my back. A strong arm was a band of steel around my waist, pulling me flush with a heaving chest. Decker's lips were warm, skimming the sensitive part of my ear, right next to my tattoo.

"You still don't understand all the rules."

My heart paced violently in my chest. I hated that I still wanted him, hated that I had ever since that first night. He had the moon in his chest, and my heart was the tide. We were connected and tied together while existing apart from one another. I felt panic flare as I realized it would always be like this. I'd always respond to him...need him.

"Which rules?" I breathed heavily, keeping my eyes lowered to the carpet.

With his left arm around me and his hand splayed against my stomach, he used his right hand to brush the hair away from my neck. He drew me impossibly closer until I could feel every hard line of his body pressed into mine, and...I bit my lip to hold in my groan when I felt his erection digging into my ass.

Decker didn't answer; instead he skimmed the length of my neck with his nose, inhaling. Suddenly his hands were gripping either side of my hips, roughly holding me against him. My chest rose and fell in desperate bursts while his seemed perfectly steady behind me. I wanted to ask again, demand he answer, but I also wanted to know what he'd do next.

Fevered fingers drew the material of my dress up from my thighs, and I felt him barely ghost over my entrance. I tossed my head into his shoulder as he bunched the material at my waist, leaving me bare save for my lacy thong. I gasped at how quickly his fingers dug into the fabric along my hips, stretching it, and with one hard tug, they ripped.

"Hey!"

Decker spun me and slammed my back against the door. His eyes were still so wild, but there was something else there too, something unhinged...desperate.

"There are rules to the game, rules to what it is we're doing. There are rules to all of this, and you don't get to just walk away from me and decide you aren't going to play anymore."

His fingers came up to grip my jaw, and he angrily pressed his lips against mine in a punishing kiss. I loved the rawness to it. The anger, the rage. I bit down on his lip while he licked inside my mouth like he knew exactly how he'd taste me if he were to go to his knees before me. Once he released me, his lips stayed close to mine, his hands sliding down my hips and along my entrance. Within seconds he was already working me while his mouth devoured mine. I felt like I was shattering from the inside out from the burn of his kiss, the seal of his mouth on mine, the way his tongue delved in, begging me for things I didn't fully understand...the way his fingers were buried inside me, owning me and demanding I come apart at only their bidding.

He leaned back scarcely an inch then roughly pulled the top of my dress down, exposing my bare breasts. His eyes devoured me as passionately as his fingers did when they were inside me.

The moon silently tugged the tide, my chest reacting to the thudding inside his.

I wrapped my arms around his neck while he hoisted me, my back digging into the door, his hand cupping my ass while I rocked against him. I yanked at his tie, ripping buttons and shoving his shirt off while he sucked and kissed along my jaw. His slacks...I needed his slacks gone next.

"Do you want me to fuck you against this door, Mallory?" He breathed the words into my ear, dipping down to capture my nipple in his mouth.

I made a sound of agreement, a hum, or something close to it. Words were a foreign idea at this point. My fingers tugged on the thin belt holding his slacks up, then I was careful with the sewn button of his pants, peeling the buttery material down until I could see the tip of his cock peeking out from his dark boxers. I pushed them down enough to grip his erection.

Yes.

"You want my cock inside you?" He lowered one of his hands and rubbed the tip along my slit. Half hanging against the door, I arched against the wood, needing it to dig into my back while he pinned me there. "Say it." The crown of his erection nudged my entrance, and I considered that this might actually ruin me.

"Fuck me," I demanded, rocking forward against him, needing him to fill me completely.

He pushed inside of me, so hard and so deep I let out some kind of pitiful moan or scream. Whatever it was, it had him grabbing me with both hands again as he pulled out then slammed back into me.

"So fucking tight." He grunted.

He did it again, sliding out, only to slam in until his cock was coated with my arousal and I'd adjusted to his length.

Then we moved like crazed creatures about to combust. I clung to him as he pumped in and out of me, my back hitting the door with loud and obnoxious thuds. His grunts, my moans...if someone were in the hall, they'd know exactly what we were doing. This was madness. I wasn't this girl who got fucked against doors or sat on a guy's face the night after he told me his plans to fuck someone else. I hated that he drove me to this point of obsession, of proving how quickly I was unmade and rebuilt into his plaything.

My chest heaved up and down, my tits bouncing as he pumped ruthlessly in and out of me. It felt like he was punishing me for tonight, like he wanted our disagreement settled this way, and I was saying yes. Figuratively and physically, over and over again.

"Decker!" I gasped as my climax started in my toes, working up to my chest where I was hardly breathing, my head tossed back as undignified moans erupted from my lips. He matched me with groans, my name falling from his lips repeatedly like he was saying a prayer while he claimed his release. I wanted to cling to him, to hold him, have something serene and soft between us, not just wild abandon, but that felt like surrender and forgiveness, which I wasn't sure I was ready to extend.

Decker's chest still heaved heavily while he lowered me, then he adjusted my dress until it was covering me once again. He ducked away, quickly scanning the room. He found a box of tissues near the piano and tossed it my direction while fixing his shirt and tie. The only sound in the room was of shuffling clothes and heavy breathing.

Once I cleaned myself up, I searched for my underwear, only to realize belatedly that he'd ripped them; the remnants were being picked up by the man who'd just fucked me against a door. He shoved them into his pocket, watching me with a guarded expression.

"That isn't how I wanted it to be for us," Decker whispered, buttoning what was left of his shirt. His hand reached around me while he shook his head. The latch lifted while he seemed to contemplate his words. He was taking too long for me, so I ran my fingers through his hair to fix it.

"Then how?"

His thumb ran along my bottom lip. Before I could say anything else, the door opened at our back, forcing us to move to the side. Elias walked in carrying two waters, his face falling as soon as he saw Decker and me still entangled in each other's arms. My confusion swirled and battered against me, making me wonder at his timing. He'd said he was going to come back up...but he didn't carry any food with him.

I didn't understand why my face felt so hot, or why it felt like I couldn't get enough air.

Decker looked surprised, but it somehow didn't settle the feeling I suddenly had in the pit of my stomach.

"So this is why you wanted me to come check on her?" Elias scoffed, shaking his head.

Decker glowered at him, holding my wrist. "Get the fuck out."

"No, you wanted me to see this, right? After we fought tonight about the feelings I confessed having for her, you had to go and fuck her against the door, knowing I was on the other side."

I was going to be sick.

"No!" Decker shouted, likely realizing how fucked up this entire thing was. "Baby, no that's not..." He let me go, trying to face me.

I couldn't meet Decker's eyeline.

"Isn't it?" Elias challenged.

"You came over to the team house, busting down my door telling me to back off your girl, and I explained that I had real feelings for her. Next thing I know, I'm getting this random invite to show up at this party tonight, and now this."

I started for the door.

"Mallory, he's lying. That isn't what happened here. I didn't invite him. I didn't know he was out there." Decker ran after me, but Elias stopped him.

"I think you've done enough," Elias said before I heard the sound of skin hitting skin and someone grunting. I ran down the stairs as I heard someone's body hit the floor, and then a crash sounded. They were fighting, and all I could do was hope the contents of my stomach would stay put until I found a bush or a garbage can.

CHAPTER TWENTY-SEVEN

Mallory

SORROW WAS A CONSTANT COMPANION AS THE DAYS PASSED. EACH ONE was slower than the one before. The sun would rise and fall, and I couldn't seem to give any fucks about any of it. Taylor had been home but was hesitant to break through my frosty exterior. I wasn't exactly mad at her or anything, but the memory of her inviting Decker was still a painful reminder that all of this was because of her.

I'd met Decker and fell for him because of her. He had wanted her first. There was pain associated with her, and I wasn't ready to face it.

Decker had called several times a day. He'd sent messages. He'd sent flowers, the notes all begging me to talk to him.

I wanted to believe him; I had just hit a limit for how much fuckery I was willing to accept within a thirty-day period, and I'd warned him my heart was made of glass. Even so, I'd risked it anyway, and now it lay shattered in unusable pieces.

I didn't know who to believe. Decker had lied in the past...or omitted things. I still had no idea who had invited Elias, and it was odd that he had just shown up. I'd known he was eventually going to head back up to the library, so it wasn't too farfetched to assume he could have just been there waiting without Decker's involvement. Every time I started down this path, excusing Decker...it just led back to that moment when I realized Decker had planned the exact same revenge with Taylor. If it were true that Elias had suddenly confessed to liking me in any way, I would be up next on his list of how to get revenge on Elias.

It was all a mess.

I nibbled on a lime-flavored chip while I stared out the window. I knew I should head to the kitchen and find better sustenance for my body. Hillary and Juan had been by a few times to ensure I was eating and showering, but it was now during the day, so they had class.

It wasn't until the evening after binge-watching a few episodes of some mermaid show likely meant for kids that I saw I had a few unread text messages.

Taylor: I need you to come to Dad's. It's really important!

I skimmed through a few from Hillary about her clingy new girlfriend and found another one from Taylor sent ten minutes after the first.

Taylor: Please Mal, this is really important!

Then there was one from Juan.

Juan: I'm coming to get you. Your sister needs you.

I scrunched my eyebrows at that last one. Since when did Taylor reach out to Juan? That was definitely not normal for their relationship, as far as I knew. I checked the time and saw I only had about five minutes before he would arrive, assuming he was coming from his apartment, though he also could have been coming from the rink.

I jogged back to my room and dressed quickly for either scenario, finishing just as the front door opened.

"Let's go. Vamanos." Juan didn't waste time greeting me or asking if I was doing okay. He moved his hands, waving me out the door. I didn't appreciate being rushed on behalf of my stepsister. We both sped down the walkway until we clambered into his still running car. Juan only took the risk because he knew who inhabited the units next to mine.

"Since when are you buddy-buddy with my stepsister?" I asked, buckling myself into his little sports car.

I caught his eye roll as he shoved his car into first. It reminded me of watching Kyle race for some reason, and that made my heart sputter, like a reminder that the last drops of love were in there but soon enough it would be dry.

"Don't be a snob," he replied, speeding down the road and taking a hard left.

"Seriously, what is the rush?"

He let out an irritated sigh. "You'd know if you paid any attention to your stepsister at all."

"Excuse me." I turned in my seat, glaring at him.

"You've been in your own world for a month, Mal. Did you even know I was offered a spot on the Hornets?" He glanced over at me briefly.

"Shut the fuck up, Juan. Are you serious?" He'd been hoping he'd get scouted for our local hockey team. He was a fantastic player, so I wasn't surprised at all that he'd been offered a contract.

"Yeah, I go in to negotiate terms next week."

"Did I miss anything with Hillary?" I watched the road, now curious how true his statement that I had checked out of my friends' lives was.

"She dumped her high-maintenance girlfriend, swore she was taking a break from dating, and within a week is already dating someone new."

"I hate the girls she dates," I muttered, uneasy that I had missed so much of their lives.

"She hates them too. I think that's the draw...or something. I don't know."

"What else did I miss?"

"There's a rumor going around about you and Taylor, and who your father is. There was a social media post about it, and there are some comments about how you're working the system for that internship." Each word was slow, steady, like he'd rehearsed the entire thing.

I closed my eyes again, feeling all the walls closing in on me.

"You maybe should have led with that." I blinked, watching LED lights peek through overhanging leaves and shrubbery, which meant we were driving up the slope to my father's house. Once he parked, he let out a tight sigh and opened his door. I exited too, legs shaky.

"I love you, Mal. You know that, right?" He walked over to my side of the car and tucked me under his chin. I watched the house behind him, eyeing the lights in the windows, the ivy that crawled along the balconies and windows, the bleak, black door and bronze knocker. I blinked, trying to remember back to the house I grew up in.

It was white with red trim and a tiny brick porch. There were always potted flowers out front because my mom loved fresh flowers. It was a humble one story with three bedrooms and two bathrooms. I remembered the carpets having a few stains here and there and we had a landlord, but Dad had loved the garage that was attached. It was only a block away from my school, and Dad used to walk me there every morning while Mom went to work.

I blinked away tears as my best friend held me tight to his chest, but I couldn't take any more.

"Thank you, I'll be okay. I think I'm going to stay here for a few days." I stepped back and wiped at the rain beginning to fall against my face. He gripped my shoulders before giving me a small nod, then he was watching me walk up the steps to my father's house.

Bev opened the door before I even knocked and tugged me inside.

"Girl, it's raining outside—what on God's earth are you thinking?" Her muddled Russian accent wrapped around me, reminding me of all the times she'd kept me company after Dad married Jackie. She'd play cards with me, gossip about her sisters back home, and even let me tag along with her when she went grocery shopping. She was the closest thing I had to an aunt or a grandmother.

"It literally just started, Bev." I shivered but refused to let her see.

"Well, your stepsister is already here…I'll bring two hot cocoas to the living room." She turned and headed toward the kitchen, and I was left watching her.

I entered the living room, looking around the space. Chaise lounges, small sitting couches, and a lavish sectional all welcomed me, along with a roaring fire.

"Taylor?"

There was no response as I searched the space and came up empty. She wasn't in the living room. Just then I heard yelling near my father's office, so I slowly made my way in that direction.

Before I reached the alcove leading to his door, someone's hand wrapped around me and covered my mouth.

"Shhhh," my stepsister whispered in my ear, then she slowly lowered her hand and turned me around. "Listen."

I blinked rapidly and nodded my understanding then followed her toward the door. We both pressed our ears against the mahogany and listened.

"Bullshit!" my dad bellowed, and something loud hit the wall to our left.

My eyes rounded as Taylor and I turned toward each other in surprise.

"We made the deal for Taylor, not Mallory," Dad yelled angrily at whoever was in his office.

"I don't know what to say, sir...I befriended her and have real feelings for her."

That voice.

I straightened away from the door, staring at the wood. Taylor slowly stretched away from it too, watching me carefully. Did she want me to hear this? Was this why she'd demanded I come? More muttering on the other side of the door had me leaning against it once more.

"Bull. Shit. You expect me to believe you were offered the financial opportunity of a lifetime to set up this little ruse with Taylor, only to have it backfire on you because of that Decker boy, and now you have feelings for Mallory? I'm not an idiot—I know exactly what you're doing, and it won't work. Mallory is not a possibility." My father's curt tone brokered no argument. His angry pitch erected the tiny hairs on my arms.

"I held up my end of the deal. I set up the card game, ensured she was invited, and I had every intention of showing up. By her own account, she got sick. My question is, how did you allow her to pass the card on to her sister, knowing our plan in the first place?" Elias's voice was clipped, and I would have hated to be on the end of what his expression likely revealed.

"The entire thing has gone to shit, which is why I'm cutting ties with you. Taylor may not have shown up, but Mallory isn't a replacement. The shareholders have already discussed a plan B."

I couldn't look at my sister, but I reached over and pulled her hand into mine. Even if she'd hurt me by inviting Decker, this...whatever was happening on the other side of that door...was beyond Decker and Elias. It was beyond everything and shot straight at the heart of our connection as sisters. We'd been thrown together, and she needed me. I should have been more involved with all of this from the start. Taylor squeezed my hand in return as we continued listening.

"*I'm* your plan B. Mallory is the perfect person for the job in New York. I just ensured that her little internship won't happen. She'll need this. Let me be the one who goes with her. We will take it slow so she doesn't suspect anything...but by the time we need to marry, she'll be agreeable. Trust me."

He'd killed my article? He'd been the one behind that meeting? *That* was what Decker had mentioned.

"You sabotaged my daughter's internship?" My father's voice was lethal.

There was a moment of silence before Elias replied.

"I had no choice. Let it be a lesson not to cut me out of deals. Taylor was supposed to show up that night, and instead someone who had no right to be there trespassed into my house—my bedroom—and wrote a fucking article exposing all of it. Do you have any idea what that would have done to me if it had come out?"

"Fuck your team and fuck you. Get out of my house, and don't ever show up here again. We're done. You want money so badly, fine—that's a quarter of what we agreed on, and tell your father he can go fuck himself." A loud thwack sounded somewhere in the room, followed by Elias mumbling something about being screwed over.

"This isn't over. I'm not—"

"Stay away from my daughters, Matthews. This is the only warning you'll receive." My dad's voice was closer to the door, and Taylor and I scrambled back, toward a large potted plant with massive leaves. We both ducked behind it while the office door opened and he walked out.

Storming down the hall, he shot off a quick comment to Gareth before jogging upstairs and out of sight.

We waited as Elias walked out. He held a briefcase in his left hand and toyed with his cell in his right. He was texting or calling someone. My phone buzzed in my pocket just seconds later.

Taylor and I both looked down, then back toward Elias as he walked past us. His steps faltered near the plant we'd ducked behind as the buzzing sound continued. I reached into my pocket to silence it, but his gaze flicked to the plant briefly before his eyebrows creased and he pulled his phone to his ear.

"What?" he asked in a sharp tone.

I kept my breathing to a minimum, just like Taylor. Elias was so close we could smell his cologne.

"He won't be a problem...no, neither will she. I made sure of it, sir."

I looked at Taylor, feeling my eyebrows arch. Who was he talking to? And who was he talking *about*?

"I just got out of the meeting...I can tell you when I get back...I know, but I really don't think Duggar will be an issue anymore." He practically whispered the tail end of that, which made sense since he was still in my father's house...but what a fucking coward.

Elias walked off, still staring at his phone.

I pulled mine out to see why it had buzzed, wondering if he'd sent me something. Taylor crowded my shoulder as we opened my messaging app.

Elias: Hey, I've been thinking about you. Want to come over tonight?

I looked up right as Taylor let out a scoff.

Once we heard Gareth say, "Good evening, sir," and the front door shut, we moved. Taylor grabbed my hand and headed upstairs toward her room but stopped and looked down at my wet clothes then veered toward mine instead.

"You need to change." My stepsister pushed me toward the closet.

It was a massive walk-in with built-in shelving and outfits that were tailored specifically for me but I never wore. My stepmother Jackie liked to ensure that Taylor and I could stay comfortably at a moment's notice. Taylor stayed more often than I did, but I had to admit—the things Jackie picked out were much nicer than what I usually wore.

Opening the drawers, I tugged a pair of sweats free along with a tank top. Peeling off my clothes, I got dressed and, just for fun, hauled a pair of soft slippers off the rack and stepped into them.

"Okay, I'm warm." I walked toward my bed and settled in while she sat down on the window seat, her face toward the glass. Our rooms each had massive, cushioned seats our dad had built in and Jackie had added little decorative touches to. My seat was a cool grey, and Taylor's was mint green, the wood a cream color to match the walls. It was nice, especially with the heavy curtains.

"I failed out of RFU." She paused, kicking her leg out and spinning in my direction.

My stomach dropped out.

She lived with me; how did I not know she'd failed out? I was there with her, nearly every day.

"What? That's not..." I started, but she shook her head, interrupting me.

"I stopped going to classes because I was so stressed." She paused, her eyes tipping up to the ceiling, like she was trying to control her words. "Stressed about trying to prove to Dad that I could take over for him at one of his offices." She swiped under her eyes. "Originally, we were going to wait to start all of this after graduation, so I'd have my business degree and then start the process of job shadowing his current CFO. There was no conversation about Elias, or a deal. It was just me stepping up to help him and give myself a purpose so I could do something other than sit around and spend money...but then he talked to the shareholders."

My dad's phone conversation came back to mind, but I stayed quiet.

My sister sniffed, and a part of my chest broke open.

Her blonde hair looked dull under the soft recessed lighting in the room, and I just now realized she was in sweats and an oversized hoodie. Taylor never wore oversized clothing, which made me wonder if something else was going on.

"You know how it is." She shrugged, finally standing and pacing the room. "They're from old money, old values...old everything..." Using the sleeve of her black hoodie, she wiped her nose, and then she came closer to the bed. "You should know I had no idea the card game was fixed, or that Elias was on the other end of it. I didn't fake any of that. I had filled out an interest form to be a part of the games my sophomore year, and I was genuinely excited about getting that card." She looked off to the side, almost wistfully.

I stayed quiet so she'd keep going.

"After his meeting with the shareholders, Dad approached me." She let out a sigh, gathering her breath. "They agreed to me taking over the New York office, as long as I got married. By this point, the card game had come and gone, and I was oblivious to Dad's involvement."

She crossed her arms over her chest. It looked like she was trying to protect her heart, but I worried it was too late.

"Tonight was the first I heard that Dad had somehow set it up to look as though Elias and I were together. Dad had told me he wasn't going to follow through with it, said he was going to find a way around it, but at that party after you disappeared, one of the shareholders approached me, informing me that they hoped to snag an invite to my wedding." She finally perched on the edge of my bed, her arms still crossed, her cheeks mascara-stained, and her eyes watery.

"So Dad set up the game with Elias to make it look like you were already taken." I was piecing it together, knowing my father was likely trying to buy time, make it seem like she was in a serious relationship— but why would that matter to the shareholders? "Is that why Dad made it so awkward in his office when he said we both needed dates?"

She ducked her head, swiping at her face again. "Yeah, everything kind of blew up once he realized I never showed up to that card game. It was awkward, because I had no idea he even knew about it. What girl wants her dad to know she planned on accepting a hookup card at some college party?"

"But he didn't tell you who was in that room?" I toyed with the comforter, still trying to put it all together.

"Nope, he never said. He saw me come to the house that night because I was sick and asked why I wasn't at the party. When it became obvious he knew more than he should, he let it slip that he'd set something up for me so I wouldn't have to worry about the transition to New York. He left it at that. So, when we met in his office and he mentioned that we needed dates, that was the awkward vibe you picked up on. I screwed up. He tried to set it up for me, but I messed up." She shrugged, her sweater nearly swallowing her whole.

I supposed that made sense, but... "Why Elias?" I asked, still confused by the turn of events.

"My only guess? And this comes from dating players on different sports teams—there's this rule that if they're being scouted or they think they might be recruited then they don't risk anything by fucking."

She looked so solemn. I couldn't help but laugh.

"I'm serious." She stared at me, her blonde brow arching to her hairline.

"Sure, so they get scouted and suddenly they don't have sex anymore? Forgive me, but I have a hard time believing that."

"It's true! At least for most. They won't risk the girl messing with the condom and them getting stuck with a jersey chaser. They may mess around, get off...usually sucked off." She tilted her head, looking up like she was considering something. "But they won't actually go all the way until after they're signed."

"Let's ignore the fact that they can still go pro and be a parent, but go on." I waved my hand toward her.

She rolled her eyes and pulled her knees up to her chest. "Word has it Elias Matthews is the poster child for this rule and hasn't been with a girl since he received an endorsement for all of his fancy electronics last year. He made a big deal of it with his team, talking about how it was going to be a long year until he essentially started next season. There were scouts already asking about him, and one even asked about him starting in Double-A ball this year, but I guess his parents made a big deal about him getting his degree."

My stepsister searched the floor before explaining another thought.

"Elias's father serves on the board with Dad...anyway, my assumption is that somehow he talked to Dad, and Mr. Matthews brought up the game, said if there was a payout available then his son would essentially make it look as though we were dating and serious. I think originally it was to score him as a date, so the shareholders backed off, knowing I was in a serious relationship with someone. That's my guess at least." She rolled her eyes, letting out a heavy sigh.

From what Decker's uncle had gathered, the Matthews had reason to believe it was a more permanent arrangement than that.

I looked away as more and more started to connect in my head. That was why Elias had come sniffing around me. He didn't actually care about me, or the fact that Decker had nailed me against the library door. He was just worried about losing out on being plan B for this New York deal. He'd sabotaged my chances to get accepted into the internship all so he could marry into my family.

My heart sank as I began processing how much I'd been burned.

"That's why Dad said to have a date…in case Mr. Matthews came sniffing around, trying to convince everyone you were still available?" I toyed with the accent pillows Jackie insisted on having on my bed at all times. There had to be at least twenty.

Taylor crawled toward me, getting under the covers. "That's what I was thinking."

My mind circled back to the invites to have Decker hang with her and how foolish this entire thing had been from the start.

"So you decided to invite Decker to the party?" Since we were telling our truths tonight, I wanted this one as well. "Are you guys…?" I tried to seem aloof, like I didn't care what she responded with, but my heart was pounding behind my breastbone.

Taylor rolled her eyes, folding her arms behind her head. "I was trying to call your bluff by saying I wanted to invite him when we were at that brunch. I knew you liked him, but you wouldn't admit it. You just kept inviting him over and leaving, like you were trying to push the two of us together…I knew from that first night that you liked him."

"So why did you end up taking him then?"

She let out a sigh. "We became friends. That day you went with him to his mom's…you never told me. I got worried and freaked out, ended up going to the bar he works at asking around about him. Someone gave me his number. I didn't use it until you guys got into a fight. So, he called a few days ago, saying he needed to talk to you. He said you wouldn't speak to him. He just needed a chance to explain himself, whatever that meant. I told him he could come as my date and then corner you and whatever." She waved her hand.

My entire body vibrated with relief. How could I have been such an idiot?

God, I felt horrible that I'd agreed to the deal with Decker. I was a horrible person. I'd knowingly been with Decker, fully aware that he had intentions to seduce Taylor originally. I owed her for this.

"I thought he liked you. He wanted to try to date you…" I tried to salvage my shitty actions, but I couldn't keep my eyes on her as I spoke. Instead they dipped to my lap.

"But you liked him, and he liked you...and I...was just a pawn." Her voice softened while she finally seemed to connect the dots. "Was it a bet, or what was the deal with him? Don't lie to me," she said softly, tugging at the covers.

My throat felt tight. "He heard about Elias making a deal. He wanted revenge and thought if he got to you first, it would mess with the arrangement. I didn't know *he* knew about the arrangement, nor did I know about the arrangement myself up until about a week ago."

She let out a sound of disbelief. "And let me guess...the original deal was that he offered to feed you info on the card game for the story after you struck out at the party?"

I raised my gaze, and it crashed with hers. Hurt swirled in her blue eyes.

"Tay, you were never a pawn...I didn't know about the revenge until way after we'd made the deal. Initially he just said he needed a shot with you."

"That's exactly what I am—a pawn to Dad, a pawn to you...god, I'm so stupid." She suddenly sat up, and I felt tears burn behind my eyes. "You know what's crazy, Mal?" She paused near the bedroom door. "You're the only person I've ever looked up to. I know you haven't ever seen me as a real sister, and I know it's bugged you that I call Charlie Dad, but from the first day I met you, I considered you my sister. I used to pretend we were blood sisters, and as I grew older, I would change it to us being chosen sisters." Taylor swiped at her face as a few tears streaked down. "One time I sketched this tattoo we'd get, something only the two of us had. I know you've always looked out for me, and when this thing with Decker happened, I just...I kept thinking you'd finally found this guy you looked at like you looked at your newspaper place, and I thought it was special. You kept pushing him toward me, but I knew..." She choked down a sob. "I knew you wouldn't let anyone use me."

I blinked away tears, staring at my sister, and really seeing her as that—my sister. Not step, not obligated, but chosen. I wanted her. I wished she knew how much I wanted her, but I'd never told her.

"I honestly thought he wanted you, Tay." My voice broke as my heart cracked open.

"What about when you fucked in the room right next to mine—did you think he wanted me then too?"

"I didn't mean..." I sobbed, hating myself, hating what I'd done.

"You did, Mal. You knew exactly what you did with him, and what it would do to me. The only reason you didn't feel bad was because I didn't show any interest, and that's because I'm a good sister and I love you. I'd never be with someone you wanted."

"I wouldn't do that either." And I wouldn't, not if it was real with her and Decker.

"I know that, but you didn't listen to me about Elias, and you weren't honest with me. It just hurts because you knew. You knew Decker was doing something where I was concerned, and you didn't warn me. What if I had fallen for him? What if I had slept with him, Mal? Do you honestly think I'd risk losing you over a guy?" She made a choking sound while swiping at her cheeks.

Everything hurt. I hated this. I hated hurting her, and that I'd lied to her.

"I just wish you felt the same about me...wish one day you'd consider me your sister...a real one. Because you've always been my sister, Mallory, and I've always loved you like one." She opened my door and walked out, snapping it closed before I could tell her I did love her like that.

I sobbed into the damn throw pillow, wishing I could turn back time. I would protect her, and myself...I'd do so much better if I could just go back. But I couldn't. All I could do was move forward.

CHAPTER TWENTY-EIGHT

Decker

I ZIPPED UP MY SUITCASE AND TUGGED IT OFF THE BED.

Looking around my bedroom, I checked to make sure I had everything I needed: phone charger, clothes, shoes and shit from the closet. I'd sold my textbooks but kept my laptop; I'd need that for job hunting once I got back home.

Exiting my room, I ambled down the hall with my luggage.

"You're all packed?" Marcus asked, nodding in my direction. He was grabbing a few pictures he'd put out of his family and tossing them into a cardboard box.

"You too?" I nodded and set my things by the door.

We'd both graduated the week before, and now we were moving out of our apartment. I was headed back home to Pinehurst, and Marcus was headed to San Diego with his girl to officially start on their local baseball team.

Marcus set down his box and hesitantly stood. I wouldn't make him be awkward about asking for a hug, not when I was going to miss him as much as I knew I would.

Leaning forward, I opened my arms and swung them around my best friend.

"Don't be a stranger," Marcus muttered, slapping my back.

"You either, and if you need a good landscaper..." We broke apart, me smiling, him glaring.

"I think you're being a pussy about letting your dream go."

What did he know of my dreams? Did he know mine had shifted so significantly that I didn't even recognize myself when I looked in the mirror?

"Yeah, well..." I trailed off, trying to make light of what he was saying. The truth was I didn't deserve baseball; I'd tainted it with what I'd done to Mallory.

"By the way, I heard about Mallory having to drop her story and the rumors the team started. I would have given you a heads-up about that shit if I knew..." He dipped his head to grab his box again.

We hadn't really discussed anything over the past few weeks. Getting to this point had been one stressful exam after another. Add in practices, games, and my shifts at the bar, and we'd barely seen each other.

But talking about it now just took me back to that night when I last had Mallory in my arms, when I had her against that door...when everything between us was perfect.

Then it all went to hell so quickly afterward.

"It's all good, man." I didn't hold any of that against Marcus. I knew what role he had to play on the team, and the role he chose to play. More often than not, he was flipping them the bird, so it didn't hurt my feelings that he'd been on the outskirts of information when I needed it.

"I feel bad for her, though. I heard the team spread a ton of shit about her around school...heard she ended up leaving before she even graduated because of it. I mean, I had no idea her dad was *the* Charles Shaw, but people shouldn't have turned into cunts over it."

She hadn't graduated? Was she okay? What the hell had happened...?

I didn't respond; instead I just dropped my gaze to the floor and toyed with my truck keys.

I had kept my distance from Mallory because, after calling every day for weeks and not getting a single returned phone call, I began to get the hint. She wanted space, time—whatever the fuck it was, it wasn't me.

"So, there's another thing..." my roommate warned, making me lift

237

my head. He watched me carefully for a second or two before clicking his tongue and giving in. "This is the type of shit that's gonna make your blood boil, so calm down before you react." Marcus carefully placed a piece of memorabilia from when he was young in the box before bringing his gaze back up to mine. "E isn't going pro. The team that had been scouting him to sign dropped him after his last game."

I had left that game early because one of the team members had gotten injured, and I'd opted to ride to the hospital with him instead of sitting in that fucking box for the remainder.

"I heard he's headed to New York now, and there are rumors he's getting hitched to none other than Charles Shaw's daughter," Marcus finished with a strenuous tone.

"When did you hear that?" There was no way he was still good for the deal, not after Mallory found out and he'd taken her story away. Mallory knew of my past with him and knew he was dangerous...there was no fucking way either of them would do it.

Right?

I headed toward the kitchen to grab a few things, stuffing them in a small box that'd been lying around. My mind raced, wondering how I could reach her. I could have texted Taylor, but she'd been silent with me recently too.

It couldn't be Mallory. It *wouldn't* be her.

Something deep down told me it was. I wouldn't have felt this panicked if it wasn't.

"I heard it a few days ago. Elias is packing all his shit and heading home to prepare for his new role as CFO, and of course his upcoming nuptials."

My fingers were numb from how tightly I'd been gripping the box in my hand. This news shouldn't have surprised me. I'd walked away...all while he was still going after her. He was still going to get the girl in the end.

"Based on your scowl and your lack of response, I'd say you had no idea what his plans were." Marcus dropped one of his heavy boxes at my feet, letting a sly smile work at his mouth. "I'd also say you might be the dumbest man I've ever met." His soft eyes searched my face...for what, I had no idea, but he wasn't wrong.

I felt like the dumbest man alive. How could I lose her to him?

"You need to go see this girl and fix it. No deals, no lies...nothing but you and the truth."

I ran my hand along the back of my neck, dragging in a ragged breath. My best friend was so much more perceptive than I gave him credit for.

"I told her the truth...she didn't believe me."

"Then make her." He walked closer, lightly punching me in the arm.

"And if she rejects me?"

Marcus watched me, moving his fun jab to a friendly shoulder hug. "At least you gave it your best shot, your hardest swing, tossed in the best card. Don't forget the rules, brother." He winked then turned to grab his things.

I stood there, trying to make sense of it. I knew what he was saying, but my stomach twisted with the knowledge that I'd fucked up. How on earth would she give me another shot? I sure as fuck didn't deserve one.

But maybe...*maybe I should just do it.* What did I have to lose by at least trying?

CHAPTER TWENTY-NINE

Mallory

THE PASTA BOILED WHILE I STIRRED THE MEAT SAUCE. I EYED THE TIMER and wiped my fingers on the apron tied around my waist.

"You testing out a new dish for the hubs?" Taylor asked mockingly.

She was scarce these days, and I didn't know what else to do to get her to talk to me.

I thought back to the conversation I'd had with my father three weeks earlier. After my conversation with Taylor, I had cried my eyes out then woke up the next morning and cornered my father. I'd gone over the details and realized there was something that hadn't added up. Taylor had known about the deal with Elias, but that plan was temporary. He was only supposed to invite her, get her to wear his jacket, and spread the word that he'd finally hooked up—that was it. Then they'd go their separate ways.

The conversation I'd overheard that day at brunch didn't match Taylor's version, so I'd curled up in the leather chair in front of my father's office and asked him an uncomfortable question.

"You said she'd marry someone her own age…" I tucked my knees under me and braced my hands on the arms of the chair.

My father's eyes narrowed, but a few seconds later his greying brows arched toward his forehead. *Dad always looked like that actor Pierce Brosnan, especially now with the silver threading through the sides of his head.*

"What are you…"

"Brunch a few weeks ago—I overheard your conversation."

His brown eyes softened, his body melting into his chair. "You don't know what you heard."

"Then tell me, because from here, it sounds like you were making more of a deal than what my sister understood. How bad is the New York office?" *I jumped right to it because I didn't want to be treated like a child, didn't want him to pretend.*

He shook his head, rubbing his jaw.

I didn't actually expect him to answer, but after a few loud sighs, he leaned forward, meeting my eyeline.

"I need someone there I can trust. I was hoping it would be your sister…but there are complications."

"The board?" *I ran my finger along the leather threading of the chair, trying to calm my nerves.*

"They're pushing back on this. I need someone there, and they aren't budging on the marriage clause. What you overheard was me bullshitting them to buy time. There was no guy, no person talking in the city…I just needed more time to figure out a solution. I had made a deal with that twat Elias for the sake of appearances. I thought if they organically met and made it seem serious through the event I had and past graduation then the board would back off."

That didn't end up happening, though, thanks to Decker and me.

It only took me a few seconds to think it through. My article was dead. Everyone was going to be talking about my last name once I got back to school, and there would be zero chance any of them would root for me to land the internship now that they knew my father owned stock in Kline Global. Maybe this was the best solution all around.

"I'll do it."

His eyes went wide, his mouth gaping.

"I'm serious…I'll do it," *I reassured him, sitting taller in the chair.*

"I can't ask you to do that, Mallory. I'd never ask you to—"

"You aren't asking. It should have been on me to do it instead of Taylor. She's always wanted to please you."

He smirked with the slightest shake of his head. "She's always acted like she owes me something. I've never told you this, but her biological father isn't a good man...he's dangerous."

I raised an eyebrow. "Dangerous as in...?" I waited for him to fill in the blank.

"Think The Godfather, then add in Fight Club and mix it with Dexter."

I blinked. "Oh shit."

"Yeah. He lives in New York, and I knew Taylor even offering to take that office was a big step for her. I never intended for her to go. I wanted to fight the board, get more time, find someone, but I'm out of time, kid. I'm in a corner, and if you wanted to take it...I'd be grateful."

"And the marriage clause?" I could do it. I would do whatever it took to keep Taylor from this.

My dad's silence was answer enough.

"Do you have someone in mind?" I swallowed the thick anxiety eating away at my nerves. My stomach swirled like it had been tossed into the washing machine. I forced my mind not to think of Decker, but the attempt only brought back memories of him holding me in the dark, asking me to promise something I shouldn't have agreed to.

"They do. You actually met him already at the dinner benefit." My dad's face started to look a little green. His lips thinned; his brows became a determined shelf.

"Jeff?" I almost crossed my fingers, hoping I was wrong.

His nod sealed my fate. "He asked about you after that night. You left an impression, so that's a good start." I almost laughed at his attempt at encouragement.

I stood; my dad matched the movement.

"Mallory..."

"I know, Dad. We're family, and this is what family does." I smiled even though my stomach felt like I had shoved a pair of scissors through it. This would mean I couldn't have Decker ever...this would mean the end.

Maybe it was just as well. We'd started off so wrong, and what would Taylor think if I just kept seeing him? She'd think I was rubbing my happiness in her face.

Still, there were things I needed clarity on, so on my way out, I turned and asked, "Just curious—do you know who invited Elias Matthews to your event that night?"

Dad moved papers around his desk before settling them into a pile.

"I did...by accident. He'd wanted a meeting with me, and at the time I was so exhausted I just told him to show up at the dinner and catch a moment of my time there."

Decker had been telling the truth, which meant that the entire dramatic production Elias had put on after he walked into the library had all been total bullshit, and I'd walked away from the man I loved without giving him a second glance for a lie.

How ironic.

Elias won.

♦

I HAD VISITED WITH JEFF LARKIN THE PREVIOUS WEEK, HAVING DINNER at a five-star restaurant where we were sure to be seen by anyone who apparently mattered. He was tall and broad-shouldered with a nice chin. I thought there was a dimple there when he smiled the one time. I'd fought back the urge to laugh when he'd shook my hand. One month earlier, I had assumed I'd be attending an internship then eventually working as a paid staff writer at Kline Global; now I was going to be married to a stranger.

Taylor found out about the news at our family brunch a few days after I had agreed to everything. She abruptly left the patio in a huff of anger.

It'd been ice and silence since.

I had decided on this dinner as a way to officially apologize to her and try to smooth things over. I was leaving for New York in a matter of days, but before I did, I wanted my sister back.

Straining the pasta, I rinsed it then added the sauce and pulled the garlic bread out of the oven.

"Taylor, this dinner is for you," I said meekly, wiping my hands on my apron again. Dad's security team had been briefed about the fact that everyone in school knew who we were, so they were now stationed in a more visible location. I had a driver, at Jeff's request, and a personal security detail named Leo at my beck and call.

My sister subtly inhaled the smell of dinner and tightened her grip on the napkin in her hand.

"Here." I handed her a plate then grabbed mine before sitting across from her.

We ate in silence for a few minutes before Taylor finally broke it.

"I hate that you're doing this."

"What else am I going to do?" I shrugged, swirling the pasta with my fork.

It was pathetic, really. I mean...I had no backup plan. I'd need to finish my degree, but for nearly four years, I'd majored in journalism, and now I wasn't credible thanks to my story on the Devils. The whole school had heard I'd gotten my wrists slapped and shut down; that paired with the truth about my father was a painful pill to swallow. I was leaving. I hadn't even stepped foot in my journalism class since the meeting with the faculty and lawyers.

"You could still apply at other papers. You don't have to give up your dream just because your dream *job* isn't available. What if you intern somewhere else and you end up back here? You can't just give up on it," Taylor argued, moving the food around her plate.

I swallowed and took a sip of my wine. I'd tried to offer some to Taylor, but she'd turned it down for ginger ale, claiming her stomach was upset.

"And what about Dad?" I asked. "Don't pretend you weren't going to do exactly what I'm doing now."

"Yeah, but I don't have any dreams, Mal. I have no plans...I don't mind being the arm candy for some stranger." Her words were strained. Maybe she thought I wouldn't pick up on it or the fact that she kept wearing baggy sweatshirts, but my sister had a secret, one I had a feeling she wouldn't be able to keep to herself for very long.

"I'm older than you. It's my job as the older sister to do this."

Her eyes shot to mine, fast as lightning. "Did you just say sister?"

Here was my opening, to finally explain to my little sister that I loved her.

I spun on my stool until I was facing her. "Tay, I'm so sorry about what I did to you with Decker. Of course I consider you my sister. I love you, and I'll be damned before you go to New York. It's my job—let me do this."

She had tears in her eyes, some already crawling down her cheek. "But I'll miss you."

I laughed, reaching forward to swipe at her tears. "Then come with me, or come visit...but we're not done, and New York isn't even that far. I'm just a few hours away."

She sniffed then threw herself at me. "I love you."

I rocked back, taking her in. My heart swelled a million times the size of a normal organ, I was sure of it. "I love you too."

We ate our pasta, talked about life after our non-graduations, and then stayed up all night watching trashy television while I thought of the one thing that still plagued me, the one thing that, after all these weeks, still wouldn't budge.

A pair of mossy eyes that saw me in ways no one else ever would.

ᴅ

TAYLOR COULDN'T STAY UP FOR LONG. WE'D WATCHED A FEW SHOWS AND she'd passed out on the couch, further convincing me that something wasn't right with her. Once I covered her up, I walked to my bedroom, flipping off lights as I went.

My bedroom was already dark, but once I flipped on the twinkle lights, a dark figure came into focus.

"Decker?" I faltered near the dresser, my heart squeezing in my chest. "How'd you get past security?" I pulled off my sweatshirt, throwing it to the ground. I needed pajamas, but I didn't want to completely strip in front of him. That would take us somewhere we shouldn't go.

He perched against the wall closest to my desk, holding a stack of papers in his hands.

"So, this was your story?"

Oh god. I was going to die. Definitely die.

"Uh…" I stepped closer. I just wanted to grab it out of his hands and hide it. "Yeah." I'd finished the story before it was taken from me, and every now and then I still looked over it, just because I believed it was worth reporting on. It really was a great story idea, and the students of RFU would have loved to see into the Devils' world.

"It's good, Mal. Really good." He flipped a page then gently set it down on the desk.

I cleared my throat, grabbing the papers and tossing them into the wastebasket. That was where they belonged.

245

"What are you doing here, Decker?" I brought my hands to my hips, trying to shove away the itch to wrap them around him.

"I finished the semester and graduated." He shoved his hands into his pockets, and I realized we were too close.

My regular issue with proximity never flared when Decker was around, but now I wished it would kick in, warning me to get away from him. Instead his scent wrapped around me like a warm, familiar hug.

"I heard." Juan had told me. He'd said Decker had graduated and was moving back to Pinehurst.

God, this was awkward.

He took a step toward me, and I wanted to take one back, but he was like an animal—he'd see it as a challenge. So I stood my ground and let him crowd me.

Another step brought him directly in front of me. His hand grazed the back of mine, up my arm and into my hair. I closed my eyes, ignoring how foolish I was being by allowing him to touch me. I should have pushed him away, kicked him out, called Leo…because even if I believed he hadn't known Elias was there that night and he wasn't using me, even if I could overlook the fact that he had known I'd lose my story and about my sister being in an arranged marriage, I was on a different path now, and it wouldn't be fair to lead him on.

His other hand was up, his warm fingers grazing along my collarbone, cupping my jaw. He tilted my head back and stared down at me.

"Tell me it's not true." Eyes the color of moss crawling along stones stared down into me. I had nowhere to retreat, and worse, I didn't want to.

"What?" I wet my lips, tasting the lime flavor on them from the chips I'd devoured earlier. I could barely raise my voice above a whisper.

His eyes moved over my face, like he'd find his answer by merely looking at me. "You moving to New York, getting married…" He swallowed, shuddering as he finished. "Elias."

My eyebrows dipped, confused. "The New York part is true." I lowered my lashes as I confessed that the marriage was true too, but then I splayed my hands on his chest. "Not sure what the Elias thing is." I scrunched my nose, curious as to what in the hell he was talking about.

A gentle tug on my hair had him tilting my head back. "The marriage to him…"

I snorted, trying to push him away, but he wouldn't budge. "No. It's some guy named Jeff. He was at that party, the one talking to me before Elias got there." I shrugged, because talking about my future husband with the guy I loved was surreal.

A low rumble came from Decker's chest, and with his closeness, I felt it in my bones. "Are you fucking kidding me, Mal?" His grip tightened on my face, and that raw possessiveness was making heat slice through my core.

"What do you want from me, Decker? You fucked me and got what you wanted from me. You even made sure my story wouldn't run." My hands turned to fists on his chest, clenching his shirt. I was torn between wanting to pull him closer and push him so far away from me that I had time to run away, all while my mind screamed at my lie. I knew he said he'd tried to talk to someone about it, but that lawyer's words about how steps would have to be taken in order for me to have authority were stuck on repeat in my head. Either way, this was better. I had to push him away. He'd still used me, still lied.

"It wasn't about that and you know it."

I felt my nose burn and my damn chin wobble because I believed him, but now there was no way I'd ever have him, and that would never be fair to either of us.

I ducked my head, pulling free of his hold. "You need to leave."

"You're not marrying someone, Mallory, unless…" He pushed his hand into my hair, gripping the back of my neck, his voice hitching. "Unless it's me."

I lifted my eyes, catching the look in his. Even under the low lights, they gleamed bright and sure, and…I broke.

I blinked and tears slipped down my face. He couldn't keep doing this to me.

"Decker, you used me. You've ghosted me, you've fucked me and lied to me…I'm not marrying you. I'm not anything with you. I'm moving to New York, I'm helping my dad with the branch, and I'm marrying a stranger."

A painful sound emanated from somewhere inside him, and suddenly he let me go.

"You know we're good together. You know we can get past this—why are you doing this?"

"That was my last shot at my dream. What you likely see as a harmless waste of time was my last chance, circling the drain. You knew I couldn't write it, and yet you still toyed with me." I deflected, trying to steer clear of why I was doing this, because I had to...because duty was better than heartbreak.

"I know, and I tried to fix it. I went to the city that day to try to ask for permission for something so you could publish it."

"You said that already, and I still don't know what the hell that means." I tried crossing my arms, but he wouldn't give me room to do it.

We were stuck in this vortex of pain and hurt, neither of us capable of breaking free and just ending it once and for all.

"It doesn't matter. They wouldn't budge anyway unless I..." He shook his head, swallowing hard. "But what I'm feeling for you, Mal...I don't know what to do. I think I'm..." His eyes searched mine with an intensity I wouldn't recover from.

I'd heard enough.

"Go, Decker." I pushed him away as hard as I could. To make sure he left and we didn't end up against my bedroom door; I grabbed my cell and dialed Leo.

I heard Decker make a pained sound behind me, felt his hand grip my hip and tug me back against his chest, but before he could say anything more, Leo opened the door and stalked in.

All muscle and neck, he glared down at Decker, but I was still facing away from him, so I couldn't see his face. I moved, and Leo took my place.

"Mal, don't do this. Let me fix this...just wait, I'm begging you!" Decker raised his voice over Leo grumbling for him to shut up. "I'm sorry. I'm so fucking sorry. I screwed up, and I..."

Leo pulled him out of the room and pushed him toward the door. I knew Decker could fight him, but Leo was a Mack truck. There would definitely be some work involved, and maybe he understood that with me calling Leo, it wouldn't be worth it. I didn't want to talk anymore. It was too painful.

I focused on my breathing while bringing my hand to my chest, belatedly realizing I was standing there in just my bra and yoga pants. My heart was beating so hard I worried it would just burst through my rib cage.

"Mal?" a soft voice asked behind me.

I couldn't breathe. What if that was it? What if that was the last time I saw him, and his last image of me was getting told that I was marrying someone else? I'd never see him again. I had said yes to my father because it was the right thing to do, and I knew Taylor wasn't telling me something. She couldn't get married to a stranger.

"Mallory, you okay?" Taylor came up and rubbed my back.

I finally turned and buried my face into her shoulder. "He's gone, Tay."

She rubbed soothing circles into my back while making soft sounds. "He won't give up, Mal. If it's meant to be, he'll be back. If he loves you then he won't give up."

"It's better if he does. I can't be with him." I wiped at my eyes, needing to put this behind me.

Taylor made a sound in the back of her throat. "Mallory Shaw, stop it right now. That marriage clause is for you to marry someone— anyone. You can marry a homeless guy off the street and they wouldn't care. They just want you to be married, and I know Decker James would—"

"No, I couldn't do that to him. He has his whole life in front of him…" I hiccupped on a sob, even though he had said those words to me. *You're not marrying someone, Mallory, unless it's me.*

Still, I couldn't do that to him. It was too final, and we were only temporary…from the very beginning, he was never going to be mine. It wasn't like I could cheat destiny and steal from a deck that didn't belong to me.

I turned into her arms and hugged her. "I'll be okay, Tay. I know it. This is better."

"You don't have to pretend with me. I know you better than anyone, even if it doesn't seem that way. I'm your sister, Mallory." She continued to rub my back, which only made my tears fall harder.

It wasn't until we'd climbed into my bed and I let her cover me with a blanket that I started to fall asleep, but it was her telling me a story about a girl who was lost, following after a compass she couldn't seem to grab a hold of. She would follow as closely as she could manage, but at the end of each day, she went to bed totally alone and lost. Then along came a handsome prince who promised to take care of her, to wipe away her memories of living in the dark and hand her a new compass, one that would lead her to the people she loved. But he lied. Instead he abandoned her, leaving her with something she knew not how to care for.

I blinked away tears as I felt Taylor spill her own. The story niggled at something in the back of my mind, like she was telling me something, shrouded in fiction. I wanted to ask her about it, but my mind shut down and I slipped into a deep sleep.

CHAPTER THIRTY

Mallory

TIME WAS A RUBBER BULLET, SHOOTING JUST AS FAST AS ANY ammunition, nearly as deadly and effective, but softened by the reality of what lay beneath.

I knew I wasn't in danger. Going to New York wasn't the end of me, or the end of my dreams…but it still felt just as deadly as if I were to stop breathing entirely or walk straight into a prison cell, accepting a life sentence.

I kept a brave face for Taylor, who had finally started wearing her normal clothes around me again. Every now and then she'd begin to say something, only to stop, slam her eyes closed, and shake her head. I didn't want to push her, especially because what I knew she was likely going to tell me was a fairly big, life-altering conversation. Pushing her wouldn't do any good.

"So…" I folded a few t-shirts and set them in a cardboard box. "You're staying, or…what's the plan for next year?" I cautiously asked my stepsister.

We had been tiptoeing around this topic for weeks. It wasn't like she owed me anything, but I worried about her. It didn't slip past me that she suddenly stopped seeing random guys, or that she'd been vomiting in the bathroom every morning.

"I can't stay here by myself...it's too much space, and I'll miss you." She looked up from her container of yogurt, sitting cross-legged on the floor.

"So, you'll go back to Dad's?" I carefully freed two of my jackets and a few more sweaters from hangers. I was almost completely packed, but I'd have been lying if I didn't say I'd been moving like a sloth with these last few items. I didn't want to go.

"For the summer...and maybe I'll come see you in New York for a bit, but otherwise I'm going to talk to the school counselor about returning next year and finishing my degree."

I stopped mid-fold, turning toward where she sat on my bedroom floor.

"Seriously?"

I'd expected her to tell me she was moving back home or taking a year off. I mean, I knew she was keeping a pretty big secret from me, and if I was right about the secret then she would need more than a year off to handle it.

"Yeah, it'll give me time to come up with a plan for a roommate and everything."

"Wow...I didn't expect you to say that." I abandoned my clothing and sat down next to her on the floor. She had a sleeve of saltines next to her and a jug of water.

"Tay...is there something you aren't telling me?" My voice was soft as velvet, hoping to coax the truth out of her, but she just continued eating her yogurt like I wasn't there.

I eyed her stomach, finally not hidden under a massive sweatshirt, and hoped she'd consider telling me what was going on. There wasn't really anything different. The shirt looked a little tight, but there wasn't anything amiss.

She finally looked up from her snack. Her hair was up in a top knot, her face clear of any makeup. It had been a while since I'd seen her this undone.

"I'm not ready." Her bottom lip wobbled.

I sat next to her silently, waiting to see if she'd say anything else.

"You've been ignoring your phone," Taylor suddenly said, pulling herself up from the floor.

"I've just been busy." I shrugged, hoping to avoid this conversation. Again.

Taylor had tried to get me to call Decker, have an official conversation in the daylight, without the chance to have Leo break it up. She'd held me after he'd gone, but the next day I had acted like nothing had happened.

"Don't leave without answering him or talking to him. He's swung by the house every day, but Leo won't let him past."

I moved on to the top shelf of my closet. It held things from my childhood, and I thought maybe I shouldn't take those things with me. I was starting a new life, with a stranger. Jeff had sent a courier to deliver the engagement ring I'd selected online. It was so massive and horrible, and I completely hated it. I'd always imagined if I were to be proposed to, it would be with a ring that was minimal, something the guy I loved had worked hard to afford...not something that was just another purchase for him.

I wanted there to be love put into the decision, I wanted to know he had selected it for me on purpose, for a specific reason.

Instead, I'd received the ring while I was alone. I slid it onto my finger then instantly took it off. Then I cried and cleaned the kitchen. Taylor eventually saw it, and her eyes bugged out at how big it was. She even made jokes about how I wouldn't be able to hold my hand up, and she wasn't wrong. I had no idea how I was going to stomach seeing it on my hand every day.

"You know who else has been calling?" I turned toward her.

My sister scrunched her nose. "That bastard?"

I nodded. "Oh yeah. Begging for me to hear him out, says he fell for me...how sweet, right?" I laughed, and it actually felt good.

Taylor's entire face lit up with humor. "Oh my god...Elias is so pathetic."

I heaved two boxes away from the closet and toward my bedroom door, chuckling under my breath. "I just wish I knew why he thought he could squeeze his arrangement into an actual marriage."

"I am so glad I didn't go that night. I can't imagine what he would have done with holding that over my head." Taylor grabbed one of my suitcases and helped tug it out to the living room. "By the way..." She reached down and grabbed my tablet. "Did you happen to read the latest article from that place you wanted to intern at?" She tapped away at the screen.

My chest pinched at the loss of my dream. I'd decided to be entirely immature about the loss and never read anything done by the group again. It just seemed easier.

"No, I don't think I can."

She made a humming sound. "Well, I'd definitely read this…in fact, I insist that you do."

Why did she care? I was way too selfish to care about social injustice. I'd turned into the worst version of myself as I buried my dream, lost the only man I'd ever loved, and now had to marry a stranger and take over a job I didn't want to do.

She walked over to me and slid the tablet into my hand. "I know a car will be here to get you to take you to New York, but read this… okay? Promise me."

I gently gripped the device and swallowed. Her blue eyes were so sincere, and she hadn't been sincere like this, ever…I had to do it. "Okay, I will."

She leaned in and hugged me tight then swiped under her eyes.

The front door opened a second later, revealing Leo and my driver.

"I gotta go." I cleared my throat, nearly ready to cry. "I'll see you next weekend. Once I'm settled, I'm headed back to Dad's, so…I'll see you then. We're going to see each other all the time." My voice hitched.

Taylor nodded furiously, but more tears streaked down her face. "I know. I just…I'm going to miss you."

I couldn't hold it in. I choked on a sob, pulling my sister to my chest. I hugged her so tightly I didn't think either of us were breathing.

"You did this for me. I was supposed to do it…" Taylor cried into my neck, whispering her confession.

"I'd do anything for you, Tay. Don't ever forget that."

We finally broke apart, our faces soaked, our hearts torn open. I finally had a sister, someone who wanted me in their life, a real relationship, and now I had to let her go.

"Okay, next weekend."

"Yes."

"Mal…read that article."

I nodded one last time before walking out the front door and crawling into the black town car. The soft white leather cradled me while my heart shredded in half. I watched the house, the ritzy wreath I'd given Taylor a hard time for buying, the teal door she'd insisted we get. Tears welled in my eyes as we pulled away from the curb. That house had been my home throughout college, and all the times I had envisioned leaving it behind, it wasn't going to be sitting in the back of a town car with no degree and no internship.

I blinked away a few salty drops that coated my lashes as I thought about my dumb, shitty Honda and the fact that I'd practically donated it to a wreck yard. I had asked if there was anyone who could use it. It ran fine, just had a few rust spots. It was gone now, like Kline Global…like Decker.

Grabbing a tissue, I cleared away my tears and finally pulled up the tab Taylor had mentioned.

The screen displayed Kline Global's website, and there in the trending articles section was something familiar. Was that…?

The Devil's Playground

An expose interview with Decker 'Duggar' James

I sat up straighter in the seat, bringing the tablet closer.

Was this for real?

I started reading, unsure if I could keep my hands from trembling. There was no way…

This is certainly a different type of article for us here at Kline Global, but a special request was emailed to one of our staff writers, and we couldn't resist the opportunity.

This piece will be more informal than our usual ones considering I will be talking with Mr. James and essentially transcribing our entire conversation. For reference, the Devils are a Division I baseball team, ranking number two in the entire country as far as collegiate level, and the names of anyone on the team will either be changed or omitted, along with the name of the writer for the article that's featured below.

What article? I slid my finger up the screen, bringing the rest of the story up.

Aubrey*: Hello Mr. James, thanks for talking with me.*

Decker: *Thanks for giving me this opportunity*

Aubrey: *So, I'm going to try to give you the floor so you can tell us why you agreed to do this article. I feel addressing that upfront might hook our audience a bit more.*

Decker: *The short answer? Love.*

My breath caught in my chest as I read on.

Decker: *I really hope you keep reading, because the article that's included with this conversation was written by the woman I love. It originated from a deal we'd made where she was willing to put her feelings on the back burner so I could pursue...well, we'll get to that.*

This couldn't be...could it? I swiped again, reading further, hating how hope began to inflate my chest. If this wasn't what I thought it was or if it was fake, I'd deflate and probably just die.

Aubrey: *I have to say, this article is one of the best I've read in a long time.*

Decker: *Well, when she reads this, I hope that first, she agrees to be my girlfriend, and second, she understands how talented she is.*

Aubrey: *Below is the article on the team. It's informative and spicy, but there are still a few questions I have. I'll attach them below.*

I scanned the page, and the article I'd written was there. How had he gotten it? I'd grabbed it from him...but then again, he'd somehow snuck into my bedroom without security seeing, so maybe he'd found a way to sneak in again. Still, seeing the words I'd written on the screen—it was so incredible.

Knowing what I'd written, my eyes greedily moved past the article until I saw what other questions Aubrey asked.

Aubrey: *So, Decker, in the article, there's a reference to your past with the captain of the Devils—what's the story there?*

Decker: *I was supposed to start the season last year as head pitcher. I'd been working and practicing more than I'd ever gone at it before. There were scouts asking about me. They wanted to see how I'd do...but then I lost my dad.*

Aubrey: *I'm so sorry to hear that.*

Decker: *Thank you. It was difficult. I was driving three hours back home to help my mom and brother every free chance I had. Meanwhile there were these card games happening, and my captain demanded I attend and help organize them. It got to a point where I just refused to attend them anymore.*

Aubrey: *Based on what I read in that article, I don't blame you.*

Decker: Well the captain did. He started harassing me, bullying me, getting other team members to join in, but I was grieving my dad, and I didn't give in to it. Then, during practice one day, he fixed a hit, nailing me in the chest with the ball. After I fell to the ground to catch my breath, he shoved his cleat through my pitching hand.

I hated being reminded of how much he'd lost by Elias's doing.

Aubrey: After reading the article, I guess there were rumors started about you being the one to do that to him. How did all that start?

Decker: The Devils are like a dysfunctional family—you won't always like everything about it or everyone in it. Regardless of our loyalty to one another, there were several team members who were in on the captain's plans to hurt me. They only helped perpetuate his narrative by spreading rumors.

Aubrey: So did you lose your position then?

Decker: I lost the use of my hand for several months. After physical therapy, I could throw again, but nothing like I had in the past. I kept my position on the team, helping with stats and keeping my batting average up...but I wasn't pitching anymore.

Aubrey: So, this deal you'd started with the writer of the article—it was info you exchanged for what? A chance to get back at the captain?

Decker: Yeah, there was something I needed that she had access to, and I knew she wanted to write the story.

Aubrey: Now, you told me you knew the entire time she wouldn't be able to actually publish it, is that right? But you fell in love along the way?

Decker: I did, and I won't give you excuses as to why I did it, but I lost the girl because of it. That's why I'm doing this, in hopes of getting her back. I just hope she gives me a second chance to prove to her that she's most important to me. More than revenge, more than home...more than anything.

Aubrey: Wow, that's really sweet. I understand the writer was told to drop this article, am I right? That's what piqued our interest in publishing it.

Decker: Yes. The captain intervened and had the team's lawyers threaten her to drop it.

Aubrey: So how is it you were able to share so much info with us?

Decker: There are rules to the game.

His rough words whispered in my ear that night in the library came rushing back. I frantically searched the text for the answers I craved.

Aubrey: Okay, now I'm curious...what rules?

257

Decker: As you read in the article, the Devils are more than just a baseball team. Well, it's all a way to keep the team motivated. So of course, there are rules on how we're supposed to play. They're broken down by card.

Rule number one: the ace—Don't catch any feelings for your base number.

Rule number two: the queen of hearts—Never go past your base number.

Rule number three: the king of spades—Don't talk about the game outside of the Devils' team house.

Rule number four: the joker—Don't ask the same person twice.

Rule number five: a royal flush—Every member on the team, no matter the position, must attend the parties.

Rule number six: the straight—If, at any time, the integrity of the game is challenged or questioned, lawyer up and deny everything.

Rule number seven: the wild card—If you fall in love as a direct result of playing the game, this card trumps all others.

Aubrey: Oh my god, I'm actually getting emotional over this. She's your…

Decker: She's my wild card.

Aubrey: What's to keep other players from selling info and just claiming rule number seven?

Decker: Once you've claimed the rule, claiming someone is your wild card, it's with the understanding that you have to cut all ties with the Devils and any scouts or sponsors who signed you while playing on the team. The article outlines what the benefits are of becoming a Devil, and there are perks that will follow you forever, but if you claim the wild card, that all goes away.

Aubrey: Wow. So that must be hard after being on the team for so long. There must be like a brotherhood that goes with that.

Decker: She's the only thing that matters to me now.

Aubrey: Well I hope she's reading this, because Kline Global will be reaching out to her regarding a writing position. This entire thing has been extremely riveting. Thank you for your time, Mr. James.

I set the tablet down in my lap with shaky hands.

Taylor had known. She'd read it…and she knew. I'd ignored his requests to see me and talk to me since that night, but he'd found a way to give me my dream back while also professing his love.

I leaned forward and told my driver we needed to change our route.

CHAPTER THIRTY-ONE

Decker

I WIPED THE SWEAT FROM MY BROW AND TUCKED THE RAG INTO MY BACK pocket. I mowed and laid new bark chips along the outer edge of the yard, hauled fresh slabs of rock over for the retaining wall, and then applied a fresh coat of white paint over the entire thing.

I was trying to stay busy. I *needed* to stay busy.

I'd moved back home and had even tried sleeping in my childhood bed again. It hadn't seemed like it would be difficult since I'd done it twice with Mallory, except lying there all night proved I was back to not being able to sleep in the house. It was worse now that the bed was tainted with memories of her. So, I slept outside in a newer camper trailer, courtesy of my Uncle Scotty, or so I assumed. I had mentioned to Kyle that I planned on sleeping in my truck until I could save up for one, and the next day the trailer showed up in the driveway.

My mom had finally given in and allowed me to start updating the interior of the house, as long as I didn't mention selling, and actually, the more I was home, the more I realized I didn't want to. My dad had built it for my mother when she was pregnant with Kyle. He'd planned out every detail, maxed out five credit cards, and taken out a small loan to finish it. I didn't want to let it go. At night, when I lay awake, I imagined a life where I had my compass here with me, sleeping next to me

259

every day, guiding me out of that storm that always seemed to swallow me when I entered the house. She'd grow old with me, and I'd never feel lost again.

I blinked, thinking of the previous night's dinner when both my mother and Kyle had asked me about Mallory, whether she'd called or read the article. The first few times were like tearing away surgical tape over a scar. Each time after was like cutting it open. She hadn't reached out. I had done the interview weeks ago, it had finally printed and uploaded to their site eight days ago, and it felt safe to assume she was following through with her plan to marry that fuckin' guy.

I knew Mallory well enough to know she had tried to push me away the last time we were together. Fucking up had been part of our dynamic, and somehow, I'd found the one girl on the planet who seemed to have an infinite amount of patience for how long it took me to get a clue. I knew she realized the truth about Elias, and now with the article, I had truly tried to fix my fuckup regarding our deal...but there had been a look in her eye when I was about to tell her I loved her. It was like she knew she'd hurt me. She knew she couldn't do this, so she pushed.

I still wasn't sure what to make of that, but as far as I was concerned, she was mine, always would be. No ring or fake marriage would change that.

Ducking down, I grabbed a pair of hedge clippers and started toward the shed. There was still a decent amount of daylight left, and I needed to clip all the bushes in front.

Once I rounded the tool shack and walked through the small gap between the house and the garage, I heard the sound of tires crunching gravel. I cleared the gap, seeing a shiny black town car come into view.

Setting the clippers against the shed, I grabbed the rag from my pocket once more, wiping my face and hands. Whoever this was seemed rich as fuck. I didn't want to greet them, sweaty and dirty.

The sun had been out for most of the day, but thankfully it looked as though a swell of clouds might give us a break from the heat. It allowed me to see whoever was exiting that car without having to wince or use my hand as a shield.

The back door of the town car opened a second later, and a head of russet hair popped into view, making my breath hitch.

She bent back down to grab something before standing straight again, then she was explaining something to the driver through the passenger side window. I shifted on my feet, unsure what I was supposed to do while she spoke with him.

A few smiles later, she turned from the car and headed in my direction, wearing a black pencil skirt and matching blazer that seemed more fashionable than functional. Still, it looked cute on her, especially with the loose-fitting white shirt she had underneath.

I wiped my hands again, this time on my jeans, hating how nice she looked in comparison to me. She had on jewelry, her hair was nicely done, and I thought she even had on pearl earrings.

She stepped closer, her high heels wobbling in the gravel, making me skip a step to help keep her balanced. She gripped my forearm right as her ankle twisted to the left.

"Looking every inch the powerful CEO, aren't we?" I joked, even though the honesty of the words made my gut sink. She'd chosen a path I hadn't seen coming, something I hadn't even known was an option for her. It had snuck up and bitten me in the heart. The universe had flipped me the bird and was still laughing.

Mallory dipped her head, tucking glossy strands of hair behind her ear. Having her this close, touching her...it was the worst kind of temptation.

She let me go and hugged a sleek black tablet to her chest.

"Hi." She smiled, her white teeth bright against her tan skin. She'd gotten some sun, and for whatever reason, the realization that time had passed made my stomach clench.

"Hi," I replied, not sure how I was still standing.

"So...uh...this..." She looked down at the tablet. "This is the sweetest thing anyone has ever done for me." Her voice shook as those green eyes slowly met mine.

The article.

"You read it?" I grabbed the rag from my back pocket just so I had something to do with my hands.

I expected if she did end up reading it, she'd just keep ignoring me like she had been for the past few weeks. I had no idea what to expect now. Would she turn me down gently? Go off to New York and marry Jeff?

She dipped her head, keeping her eyes on her feet. Her pink toenails peeked out through the opening of her shoes in a cute way and the heels made her calves look incredible, but it was her eyes I wanted on me. I hated that she kept hiding them from me. She'd come here for a reason; I'd be damned if she backed out of explaining what it was.

I was about to step closer to her, hook that chin with my finger, and force her face up, but her chest heaved and suddenly her head tipped back.

Her eyes were wide and full of…something similar to hope or anticipation.

"I'm in love with you, Decker James. I've loved you longer than I probably even know, and we went about all of this the wrong way, but…" She licked her lips, stepping closer. "If this ends with me in your arms and you in mine, I don't really care about how it started. I just care how it ends."

Her clothes were so clean, and I didn't want to get her dirty, but she'd just admitted to loving me. My heart was racing in my chest, a new sweat breaking out on my skin, purely from need and longing. I could have stood there with her and demanded she explain why the fuck it took her so long to choose me, asked her what she had decided about Jeff. We could talk and talk…but Mallory and I were always better with nonverbal communication.

Fuck it.

I reached for her. Cupping her face with my hands, I tangled my fingers into her hair and pulled her against me. Once her lips were within reach, I slammed my mouth to hers.

She mirrored my movement, forcing her free hand to my chest, slanting her head to the side, and sliding her tongue against mine. Letting out a groan, her left arm ran up my chest and around my neck, holding me closer. I splayed my hand over her ass, and suddenly I needed her somewhere much more private.

Walking backward with her, I managed to move us until we were near the camper trailer. I fumbled for the door, finally finding the latch, and I tugged it, bracing my arms on either side of the door while maneuvering us inside. Once I shut us in, we were all teeth and skin.

"Remove this fucking thing," I commanded, my tongue darting out to suck on the skin along her neck.

She leaned back, forcing us to disconnect, then set the tablet down and began stripping off her tiny black jacket. Her fingers went for my jeans as she began unbuttoning them.

Mine gathered at her back, sliding the zipper of her skirt down until I felt flesh.

I must have growled my approval when I realized she was only wearing a thong, because she began laughing when I snapped it against her ass.

Pushing my jeans down, I ripped my t-shirt over my head then discarded my boots, belatedly realizing I could probably use a shower.

She'd stripped out of her shirt and now her elbow was bent, trying to unclasp her bra from the back. I took a second to appreciate how sexy she looked with her full, gorgeous breasts barely held up by the black cups.

Goddamn, she was a work of art.

My lips descended on their own, my face diving into the cleavage of her chest.

"Keep this on, baby. I want my dick..." I trailed the space with my tongue. "Right fucking here."

"Decker." She sighed my name, and just as she was about to get on her knees, I stopped her.

"I need to clean up." I brushed my thumb over her lips, tugging them down.

She gripped my wrist, shoving my thumb into her mouth, and began to suck. Her skin pressed into the soft, beige carpet at our feet as she finished getting to her knees.

"I want you, Decker, exactly like this—rough, dirty. I want to taste you, fuck you, have you, and I don't want to wait."

"Fucking hell," I muttered, staring down at her.

Thankfully, the shades were all still shut around the camper, so no one could see us. She pulled my erection free from my boxers, it bobbed between us while her eyes rounded, and her lips parted.

I threaded my hands into her silky hair as she brought her mouth forward and licked from the root of my cock all the way to the tip. She let out a satisfied sound that vibrated down my length. She repeated the process a few more times, keeping those forest green eyes on me.

Her mouth finally took me in, deep and fucking perfect.

I hissed while she moved down and over my girth until she was gagging. She'd ease up, suck, and gag. My head tilted, my eyes going to the paneling along the top of the trailer. It felt so good.

"Fuck, baby." I started rocking into her mouth a few times, but I was already ready to come down her throat, and I needed this to last longer.

Pulling free from her mouth, I reached down for her hand and walked her back toward the bed. She sat down, watching me with a hooded gaze, eyes still on my bobbing erection. Sliding back, her hands dragged her closer to the headboard of the queen-sized bed. Resting on her elbows, she watched as I threw my boxers behind me and crawled over her. I didn't stop until I was nearly straddling her chest. I kept my weight off her as I shoved my dick in between her tits and began rocking my hips back and forth.

"So fucking big, baby." I palmed her breast and moved my cock through her cleavage. Back and forth I went, my precum creating the perfect lubricant to move easily.

"I want to hold them for you," she said breathily, leaning up to remove her bra.

Once her tits popped free, she grabbed one in the palm of each hand and pushed them together.

I started moving my thickness through her cleavage with renewed vigor. I had visions of white ribbons shooting out along her face and chest, her rubbing it in and sucking it into her pretty little mouth, but fuck...I still needed more.

Catching my breath, I moved my hand down her body until I was able to test how wet she was.

"Shit. Two fingers in and look how ready your cunt is for me." I added a third and began to rub in slow circles.

She groaned and tipped her hips up until she was matching the rhythm I set with the ministrations along her clit.

"I need you, Decker. I need you inside me." She gasped for air while her center ground against my hand.

I lowered myself over her, pushing her up the bed so there was more room. Her hair fanned out behind her, her nipples pebbled against the chilled air, and her taut stomach heaved up and down as she waited for me to enter her.

"You're so beautiful," I whispered reverently, and I meant it. She was perfect.

She was *mine*.

I kissed her, moving my lips against hers while I carefully and slowly pushed inside her.

She groaned into my mouth, gripping my biceps, pushing against me while I pulled out and back in. I repeated the process three more times until I was fully immersed.

"God, fuck…baby." I pinned my forehead to hers, groaning into her mouth.

Her nails raked down my scalp. "Decker, I need you to move."

I tilted my hips forward so slowly I thought I might combust right there.

"You're tight, Mallory. So fucking tight." I lowered my head, biting her breast then kissing the same spot, knowing she'd have a purple mark there tomorrow. "Do you even know what this feels like?" I moved until my lips were hovering next to her ear. "What it feels like to have your tight pussy milk my cock?"

She shuddered beneath me, her nails scraping up my neck and along my scalp. I was about to come from how good it felt.

To hold off, I kept slowly moving my hips forward, rocking into her. She clambered to fuck me harder than I was fucking her, even took my lip into her mouth and bit down while her heels came up around my waist. Then she was rumbling something sexy while she arched her back, pushing those perfect globes into my chest.

"Decker, fuck me," she begged on a breathy moan.

I was gone. I gripped her waist, holding her for leverage, and then I fucked her in hard, unforgiving strokes. Her breasts bounced as we moved, her eyes closed while her mouth gaped.

"Harder," she begged.

I gripped her chin and pistoned my hips in a way that was going to ruin her. I moved harder, more furiously than I'd ever moved, need completely hollowing out my mind. Mallory's body shifted forward as I grabbed her leg and moved it to the side so I could go deeper. Only then did I slow down and rotate my hips forward, pushing my dick deeper until there was nowhere else for me to go. I hit the same spot over and over…and over…until…

Mallory cried out, moving her hips in cadence with mine. "Oh god. Oh god. Fuck. Fuck. Fuck."

She came apart with a scream right as I grunted into her skin and came inside her.

Our chests heaved up and down, straining for air as we lay tangled together. I rested my head against her stomach, where I pressed a gentle kiss. I imagined for two short seconds what it would be like to see that space swollen with my kid.

I blinked away the image, because Mallory was likely engaged to another man.

I didn't talk while I lay there, stroking her skin, knowing we both needed to clean up, but I just couldn't stop touching her.

"I can't lose you," I softly confessed to her.

My insides felt shaky as I wrapped my arm over her and tugged her closer. All I wanted was to stay here with her, forget about both our futures, and pretend tomorrow didn't exist.

Her fingers ran through my hair, past my ears and down my neck. It felt so good I almost groaned.

"So, you're living at home…but not inside?"

"My compromise." I laughed lightly, knowing the look on her face without seeing it. She'd have that dark brow arched toward her hairline, a light smile playing on her face. "You came here with a driver," I threw back at her.

"I did."

It was my turn to quirk a brow. "What does that mean?"

She smiled, playing with my hair. "Check for yourself."

I inched over the mattress a bit to peek through the blinds.

Two suitcases, a few boxes, and three small bags sat on the porch, but the town car was gone.

I spun my head to look at her. My heart might as well have jumped into my throat. My tongue felt too big for my mouth. Was she staying?

"What does this mean?"

"I asked him to wait until we were out of sight before he emptied the trunk...and I told him I would be staying here for the foreseeable future."

"You're staying?" I asked as though I couldn't quite process what she had just told me.

She blinked and slowly sat up, resting on her elbows.

"I was supposed to meet Jeff tonight for dinner, but..."

"But?" I rested on my elbow, trailing my finger over her thigh. I had to keep touching her. She had to choose me.

"I'm here, and I don't want to leave...but I promised my father I'd help him by taking over the New York office." She winced, pushing some of the hair out of her face with her free hand.

I wanted to push her back into the bed and have her ride me while I explained why here was exactly where she should stay.

"Did you sign a contract to marry him?"

She shook her head. "Not yet. We were going to start signing every-thing tonight. But, Decker...New York is happening. If I don't take it, Taylor will step in...and I won't let her do that."

This couldn't just be chance. This was fucking fate, and it was my shot to keep her.

"If you have to go to New York...then take me with you. If you have to marry someone then...marry me. Be with me. Start your life with me."

I didn't look up for a few seconds. I was obviously still batting down those insecurities that she'd leave me.

She shook her head slowly, rubbing my thumb with hers.

"I'm yours, but we don't have to get married, at least not until you're ready...or you know, we've lived a little. And who knows..." She shrugged, keeping her hand on mine. "Maybe it doesn't even need to be permanent. Maybe we can help my dad find a replacement."

"I just want to be where you are." I smiled.

"On one condition." She suddenly twisted her lips to the side.

I searched her face, waiting for her to say we had to stop having sex or something else equally horrible.

"You let me pay off the mortgage for your mom's house."

I shook my head. "No. It's not your concern—you can't…"

"Yet you'd lay down your whole life to follow me to New York?" She raised that eyebrow again. "Look." She moved until she was straddling me, clasping my hands in hers. "One day, I'd like to move here…settle here with you, watch you mow that back yard while I cook something in that kitchen. I want this to be ours and our future. I know that's probably rushing things a lot, but it's one of my fantasies. So let me do this, please?" She moved against my growing hard-on, her chest heaving as she began to work me up. It didn't take long.

Images of little kids playing in the yard, laughing, filling the space with life…it was beautiful and everything I hoped for one day, and I wanted that with her. I wanted her to be part of it. If that meant she paid it off or bought it then fine, she could, as long as she was at the end of that dream, living it with me, going to sleep at night with me.

"Deal," I said softly, watching as she held me in her palm then slid down onto me.

She waited, adjusting to my length while catching that gleam in my eye. Yeah, I'd made a new deal with her.

"Move your hips, baby," I whispered, placing my hands on hers.

Rolling forward, she let out a tiny moan. "I need to make a quick phone call."

"Yeah, you can get right on that." I pulled her against my cock.

"You're interfering," she murmured, biting her lip.

"Fuck, baby. If this was interfering, we have a lot of interference in our future."

She eyed me, leaning down to kiss my lips. "Promise?"

It was what I'd asked her that night in my bed.

"Yeah, I promise." I jutted my hips up while pulling hers down. She came again, groaning her release while I watched her fall apart. It made my chest swell.

If this was what it meant to play the wild card, it had to be the luckiest card in the deck.

I was done for.

But I'd been finished for a long time. I realized as I watched Mallory crawl off me and move around my space that she was always supposed to be in it, always supposed to be pulling on my t-shirt after sex, always in my head, her lips at my beck and call, her body in my bed at night.

I realized I would follow her anywhere. I'd been trying to make pieces in my life fit ever since my dad passed, but now all of them belonged to her. Wherever she was, as long as she was with me, I'd be okay. I'd fit.

Her smile as she pulled out her phone and talked to her dad, her face as I grabbed her hand and just held it—she completely undid me. I knew then that for the rest of my life, this was all I'd want.

EPILOGUE
TWO MONTHS LATER

Mallory

"TAYLOR!" I SET MY PURSE DOWN ON THE ENTRYWAY TABLE, KNOWING Gareth would likely move it as soon as he realized I'd entered the house. He hated when we didn't use the doorbell.

Dad's house was bright, the summer sun highlighting the lush gardens outside. Taylor had been living here the entire summer so far, although now that I think of it...it had only been about two months since I left our townhouse. I hadn't left Decker's side since that day he helped me carry my luggage into his trailer. We had lived blissfully in a little sex cocoon where all we did was sleep, eat, and fuck. We did occasionally stay in the main house and eat meals with his Mom and Kyle, but otherwise we were like bunnies, without the procreation part. Now we were headed to New York, officially taking things over...and as a married couple.

We didn't have to get married. Dad had convinced the shareholders to back off the marriage clause, but it was Decker who'd swayed me. We'd gone away for the weekend; he wanted to try to replicate that camping trip I'd gone on with my dad when I was a kid. So, Dad had told him the spot, and we found out there was an entire Airbnb setup with tiny cabins along the river.

We rented one, and while out back under the string lights that hung over our little patio, he'd gotten on one knee and said I could either wear an engagement ring for however long I needed to be comfortable, or I could marry him and not stress him out any more about whether or not I might change my mind.

I decided to put him out of his misery.

We married a week later inside a tiny chapel with only ten people present. It was perfect, exactly what I wanted, and I couldn't have been happier—even without officially working for Kline Global yet, although they'd called and offered. I asked if they'd be willing to keep the offer open while I started this new chapter of my life. They agreed, and even offered to allow me to write for them in my free time, if I had any.

Things were good, except for the fact that my younger sister kept dodging my calls.

"She's upstairs, girl," Bev said, walking past me toward the laundry room.

I jogged up the steps, wondering why my sister had texted for me to come after ignoring me for a week. She had almost missed my wedding, although she refused to explain why. I had been too busy then to really focus on it, seeing as Decker had planned a weeklong honeymoon for us, but now—now I wanted answers.

"Taylor!" I stomped up the stairs and threw open her door.

She was sitting on the floor, holding a piece of plastic. Tears streamed down her pink face, as if she'd been at it for a while. My heart pitched, lurching at what could be wrong.

I shut her door and rushed to her side.

"What happened?"

I eyed the plastic object pinned between her fingers and sucked in a sharp breath.

"I've been in denial...because I'm always careful, Mal. Always. I was on the pill too, but I must have done something wrong."

I thought back to when she got sick, sending me in her place for the card game. She'd ended up taking antibiotics, which I knew could mess with birth control...but was that the right timing for all this?

She sniffed, swiping at her tears with her sleeve. She was in another massive sweater, making me realize it didn't matter how, just that it was happening and she was hurting.

I tucked pieces of her hair away from her face, unsticking a few from the dried tears.

"I mean, I had a feeling...then I missed another period. That can't be normal, right?" She tilted her head back, her watery blue eyes meeting mine.

I shook my head, too afraid to use my voice.

"Yeah, I thought so. So I took it...and I guess there's no question." She held up the pregnancy test in front of our faces. "I'm going to have a baby." A loud hiccup left her chest as she crumpled into my side. "My mom is going to kill me. You don't understand...there's—he's going to find out, and...fuck." She cried, her words coming out garbled and confusing.

"Who's going to find out? The father?" Who even was the father? I worried Taylor might not even know. I thought back to a few months ago, when she had entered into a self-destructive phase. There seemed to be a new guy at our house nearly every evening.

One time I had walked in on her riding some quarterback on our couch while wearing only his jersey. It was as if she just stopped caring or giving any fucks at all about me, or even herself.

"No, my dad...my *real* dad. He's going to find out." She grabbed for a Kleenex tucked away in her shirt and blew her nose.

I scrunched my nose in confusion. "What about the father of the baby—does he know?"

"God, Mal. It was so embarrassing...I sent out a text to three potential guys who could be the dad. None of them have texted me back."

Fuck.

"That's okay. You don't need the dad, but it's still so early, Tay. You have to just take this a day at a time." I softly rubbed her shoulder, trying to encourage her.

"I know...maybe after I get my degree, I can calm down and acclimate to the news."

I wanted to be careful with this question...sensitive. "So...you think you'll keep it then?"

She scoffed, her shoulders shaking. "Isn't that the craziest fucking part? I'm already in love with the little thing, and I don't know how that's possible. But yeah, I'm keeping it. I'm scared to death, but I'm going to figure it out."

"You will, and it's going to be amazing whatever you choose."

"Thanks, Mal. Sorry about shutting you out. I panicked."

"It's okay, I get it."

"Do you know anyone who's looking for a roommate next year?" She sniffed once more, swiping at the last of her tears.

"You're seriously going back to school to finish your degree?"

"I said I was." She turned to look at me, now sitting crisscross applesauce.

I tried to copy her, but mine looked less cross and more like applesauce. "I know, it's just...I figured it might not work out if you were going to go through with the pregnancy."

"I'm doing both." Her eyes landed on me, full of determination.

"Okay, I support you. The only person I know who is hanging around in their current apartment is Juan. I can ask if he's going to be looking for a roommate."

"I think I would rather live with my mother and commute than live with him. He's a jerk."

I reared back, totally confused. "Since when do you guys even know each other well enough to know if he's a jerk?"

She let out a tiny sigh, looking off to the side. "He'd come around, oddly when you were in class. Sometimes it felt like he was checking up on me, but I had no idea why. It got worse when I dropped out. It was like he knew. But when you started dating Decker and staying at his place, Juan would bring me breakfast and coffee. He made up this lie saying our coffee machine was broken."

"It totally was." I nodded my head, still reeling from this information.

"Well, whatever. I hate him." She waved her hand like that was the end of it.

"I guess I'm confused. All of those things sound really nice—how was he mean?"

"Because every time he came, he'd give me the food and say something mean like, *Here take this and eat it...maybe try getting some sleep at night so you don't look half dead.* Or he'd say, *I brought you coffee assuming you had another sex fest last night and can't go to class. I hope you used a condom.* Really rude shit like that."

I sat back on my hand, staring at mysister in total shock. Why had Juan been such an asshole to her? That morning he'd randomly shown up at my apartment came back to memory; he never had told me why he was there. Had it been for her?

What in the world…?

"Well maybe one of the daddies will take you in." I tried to joke, but from the way Taylors eyes lit up, I realized maybe she was actually hoping one of them would step up. "Cheers to paternity tests, and for having the best big sister in all the world. We've got this, Tay. Even if no one steps up, that baby will be so loved."

She stood, lending me her hand. "First things first: you have to help me tell Mom and Dad."

I accepted her help, groaning while I stood. "I'll support you with anything but that."

"Too late—you promised. Now get your ass in gear. Also, can you and Decker try to have a baby right now so our kids are best friends?"

"Yeah, Tay…I'll get right on that." I rolled my eyes as she led the way out of her room, the plastic pregnancy test shoved under her bed.

"You're the best."

ठ

THANK YOU FOR READING THIS STORY, PLEASE CONSIDER LEAVING A review— it helps me grow as a writer and encourages me to keep going.

And keep reading for a sneak peek of Taylor's story.

SNEAK PEEK

Enjoy this Sneak Peek from Taylor's Story Coming Later this Year

PROLOGUE

Taylor
Thirteen Years Old

"I KNOW THIS WON'T MAKE SENSE RIGHT NOW." MY FATHER'S CONFIDENT timbre was a shudder down my spine. I had squeezed my eyes shut after I'd stumbled upon the lifeless body on my way to the garden.

"This man tried to steal from me. From us. This was his penance." My father stood, staring down at me, "do you know what that word means?"

Of course, I knew what penance meant. He'd been explaining his murders to me in the same way since I was seven and first witnessed him blowing another man's brains out.

My stomach tilted and my throat grew tight like I might throw up. I was on the verge of tears, but I had learned at young age that my father didn't appreciate them. So, I nodded, slowly cracking my eyes.

"Good. What happens to people who steal from us." He glared at me, wiping the blood that coated his hand. The white rag came away red and ruined.

I swallowed the thick saliva that had coated my mouth. "We remind them."

"Yes, my értékes." *My precious.*

I tried to take comfort in my father's use of the Hungarian pet name for me, but over the years it was getting hard to summon the emotion.

"No matter how much time has passed, even if it is sent to the following generation."

I gave him a firm nod, learning long ago that a wobbly chin, or a waffled stance on why he had to kill people got me in trouble. Usually the kind where I had to be alone, in my room, or worse…shoot something.

So far, I'd been forced to shoot three sheep, and one pig during my father's lessons. The heavy feeling of the gun in my hand and the kick back of the trigger, still crept along my veins sometimes when I closed my eyes at night. So did the look in the helpless animals' eyes. I was never allowed to close mine.

My father had started those lessons with his strong arm around me, holding me in place, then his hand covered mine, his strong finger ghosting over mine so I would feel the power to end a life.

"This is a lesson." He'd always mutter before leaving me alone in the room with the bleeding animal and still loaded gun. I suppose a lesson was better than penance.

"Jakob, take this." My fathers voice pulled me from those darker memories. The silver gun was taken out of my father's hand and holstered into Jack's inner vest. Jack was a good guy, as far as I could tell. His official name was Jakob, but since I was little, he'd smile, hand me a stick of gum and tell me to call him Jack. He was always around when there was blood, or a dead body but never when I was forced to shoot animals.

"Are you ready to spend time with Markos." My father pushed my shoulder, until my feet were moving around the edge of the landscaped yard and cobble stone walkway. I looked back in time to see Jack grab a shovel before I was forced forward.

"I don't like him." I explained, belatedly realizing how foolish I sounded. My father had been forcing what used to be play dates with Markos on me since I was seven, now they were getting closer and closer to real dates and I was still in the dark as to why he kept insisting on them. He didn't care that Markos was mean, or that the angry, spoiled boy had killed a helpless bird that had fallen and broke its wing, or that he pulled my hair when I didn't do what he wanted.

My fathers laugh made me feel small, and helpless.

"You might want to get used to him, értékes. You've two have been matched since birth."

I stopped so fast that my father had to pause and look over his shoulder to track where I'd gone.

"What do you mean?"

"You know what I mean. Don't play stupid. This is a family business. Everything we do, we do for each other." Red dots still splattered the back of his hand as it ran along the strands of my longer hair, and there were even a few spots on his white shirt.

"I'm only thirteen..." I licked my lips, trying to get my tongue to unstick from the roof of my mouth.

His laugh was another shudder, a roll of thunder along my frail bones. "You won't marry until you're older értékes." He tossed his black eyes up to Sloan, one of my father's men, who'd walked close enough to overhear.

"Twenty-one, little one. That's plenty of time to hate little Markos, see if you can drown him before then." Sloan ruffled my hair, letting out a heavy laugh. My father smirked, but it didn't last.

"Markos is imperative to the continuation of this business. You will marry him when the time comes, and you will not fight me on it." His glare was like being trapped in a vault with no way out. It was like being stared down by the devil himself.

I silently accepted this fate, even though a riot of rage and fire burned behind my chest. I slowly trailed after them as the knowledge that I had to get out of this family settled around me like armor. I just needed time to figure a way out of the future my father had doomed me to.

Preorder It Here

ACKNOWLEDGMENTS

This book almost didn't make it. There were so many times I considered pushing back the publication date, or just tossing the entire thing out. It was a sacrifice to get it here, but there's no way in the world I could have done it without these people.

First and foremost, God my creator and giver of words. Without you I wouldn't have this gift, or the support system to publish.

To my husband Jose, thank you for always loving me, cheering me on and asking me what I need. That simple act of love does wonders for my soul. Holding down the household while I ducked away and finished the edits on this book, being fine with me ditching you and the kids for ten days to help my sister. You're what romance is made of.

To my kids, I'm sorry that I wasn't always available to play Catan with you, but I hope you know how much I love you and always will. Maybe one day when you look back through my books, and hopefully well after you're eighteen you'll know that I cherished the time, even if you didn't see it. Kailey, you turning fifteen and getting that necklace from that boy. Kaitlin, you being thirteen and starting that equestrian group, Naomi at almost nine, and obsessed with Marvel and all things dangerous, and my baby boy- Nehemiah, Minecraft professional and enamored with all dinosaur things.

To my sister Rebecca, my brother in law Jonathan, and baby Emma. That little time away from the world, in your house, helping the both of you welcome in your first child was magical to me and essential to this book. Thank you for asking me, and for trusting me with your most precious treasure.

To my beta readers: Amy Elizabeth, Glady's Sollis, Kelly Sirak Drudy and Summer Ford- I can't thank you enough for your help with this book and how fast you rose to the challenge. I was utterly blown away by your willingness to jump in and help me wrangle story points and character flaws into place. I will forever be grateful. Kelly, you especially saved the day as my resident baseball expert, thank you so so much for all of your help on perfecting the sports portion of this story.

To Brittany, you know I love you and I'm so sorry you couldn't read this early. I am just glad you're still here, and still okay. I love you forever.

To my amazing cover designer, Amanda. This was our first time working together, and I couldn't be more grateful to have found you. Your delivery of Decker on the cover was outstanding, now you're stuck with me forever. I hope you're ready for that.

To my editor, C. Marie- as always, I am so insanely grateful for making room for my words. I know you're hot stuff in my industry and could easily turn me away for your famous clients, that I someday hope to be like, but you still take on my projects with enthusiasm and then you completely kill it with your editing skills. I love getting reviews pointing out how flawless my edits are.

To Tiffany, my PA. I adore you and you know that I don't want to do this author thing without you. Ever. Thank you for being in my corner and being an amazing proofer.

And to you, my readers, thank you for taking a chance on me. I care about what you think of my stories and while I know I won't make you all happy, I do strive to give you a story you'll love and to do right by the characters you fall in love with. There's so much more to come from this universe, so hold on to your kindles and keep em charged.

ABOUT THE AUTHOR

Ashley resides in the Pacific Northwest, where she lives with her four children and her husband. She loves coffee, reading fantasy, and writing about people who kiss and cuss.

Sign Up for my Newsletter and Get a Free Book:
www.ashleymunozbooks.com

Join My Reader Group:
Book Beauties

Made in the USA
Monee, IL
25 October 2021